LOSING

DAVID

Acknowledgements

With gratitude to my family, friends, critique partners, and other professionals who worked on this story with me for way too many years.

Thanks go to attorney David Gaffney, who took the time to listen and suggest that a coroner's inquest rather than a grand jury hearing was what the story needed; and to Joan B. Henderson, who took the time to introduce me to him.

A special acknowledgement goes to the memory of Nan D. Arnold, my critique partner who helped me not only with this story but with so many others. She is missed.

Other Fiction
by Cheryl B. Dale

Romantic Suspense

Intimate Portraits
Treacherous Beauties
The Man in the Boat
Set Up

Paranormal Romance

The Warwicks of Slumber Mountain

Light Mystery

Taxed to the Max
Overtaxed and Underappreciated

Copyright Information
Copyright 2014 by Cheryl B. Dale
Published by J&H Press
Cover Art by J&H Press
Edited by L.F. Martin

ISBN: 978-0-9853910-6-5

www.cherylbdale.com
cherylbdale.blogspot.com
cherylbdale@hotmail.com

A playlist of songs in *Losing David* can be found on Spotify.

LOSING

DAVID

by

Cheryl B. Dale

J&H Press

PROLOGUE

"Temptation"
As Performed by Perry Como (1945)
Music by Nacio Herb Brown
Lyrics by Arthur Freed

Harmony Island, Coastal Georgia
June 1946

THERE WASN'T A damn thing personal about it. He didn't hate the boys. Okay, Robby was a sour-faced brat, but David was okay. He liked David.

Didn't matter now. They were in his way, so they had to go.

This isn't real. I can't be doing this.

Not Theodore Rhodes Pack. Factory manager, ex-army lieutenant, Vandy almost-grad. He couldn't be toting a drugged kid.

Not him. No sir.

Theo seemed to float far above, spying on an anonymous man slogging toward the dock. Wreathed in flimsy night clouds, he could see David bob on the other man's shoulders. Watch David's legs dangle, head loll. Hear some man who wasn't Theo grunt under David's weight.

The shells on the path crunched. The two Theos melded. He was back to normal.

Hallucinations, that's all. Tricks of the mind.

No time for stupid imaginings.

Spanish moss streamed from the great live oaks to block all but the most obstinate moonbeam, but no matter. He knew the way by heart.

Not much farther. Getting hard to breathe. Good thing he was fit. Who'd think a skinny sixteen-year-old kid would be so heavy? If the boys had agreed to a moonlight cruise like he'd suggested, he could've slipped them the mickeys on board. Saved himself this nightmare.

No nightmare. James was really dead.

Screw you, James.

James Harmony, richer than the Rockefellers.

His larger-than-life cousin who overshadowed celebrities, bested government auditors, trampled competitors.

Trampled *him.*

He was too winded to laugh. Not like when Sondra's secretary had phoned earlier to tell him James had died. He'd almost sniggered. Lucky the gossip bench caught him when his legs buckled.

When she asked him to break the news to the boys, he'd dredged up the proper gravitas. "Yes. Of course I will."

Good thing he'd chosen his words. David, croquet mallet in hand and curious—the phone seldom rang when James was off the island—materialized as he hung up. "Who was that?"

He'd improvised. "A friend in trouble, but I can't help."

"Gee, that's too bad." David took after his mother. Softhearted. Gullible. Not like James. He held up the mallet. "Feel like a quick game while it's still light out?"

"Sure thing."

Theo, his mind on other things, had lost.

His toe caught a root and he staggered. The kid slipped. "Shit!" He got a better grip.

A rustle in the bushes.

What was that?

Nothing. A rabbit or squirrel maybe. No need to be so jittery. The staff were away or in homes scattered over the island except for the doddery watchman who spent most of the time playing solitaire.

Once David was aboard, Robby'd be a piece of cake. Then the boys would be fishbait.

Bile roiled. *I can't do this.*

He gulped. Yes, he could. And he would.

Waves soughed through pilings. Nearly there.

He stopped, breathing hard, at the woods' edge where croaks of tree frogs and crickets overlaid marshy odors of decayed creatures and moldy reeds. Among glittering pinpoints, the crescent moon flirted with a wispy cloud. Moonlit boats at anchor rocked, silhouetted masts naked and jutting.

No late fishermen or crabbers. Safe to leave the shadows, move to the ramp.

SCREEECH!

"What the hell!"

Just that rusty hinge. *Get a grip.*

On the dock, the cruiser's metal rail glinted. He kicked aside a stack of tarpaulins and threw David over onto the deck. After wiping his sweaty eyes, he rotated cramped shoulders.

Supposing the watchman got up off his ass and made a round, spotted the kid? Better stash him inside the cabin.

A hand on the rail, a quick spring, and he landed on the deck. The cruiser bobbed. "Okay, kid. Moving you one last time."

When he heaved David into the inky cabin, memories flooded. Him teaching David how to shoot a thirty aught six rifle. Him helping David land a seven-foot swordfish. Him and David hanging off the side of the catamaran, laughing like maniacs as the wind whipped them with saltwater and they skimmed across the whitecaps like masters of the sea. David looking to him for approval.

A twinge of regret, then: *I can't think of that.* A live David meant no future for him. No future with Sondra.

Hell's bells, imagining her in James's bed twisted his gut.

Can't think of her either. I'm not half done.

Waves lapped against boats and pilings. A loon's mournful warble added to insect clatter.

Still alone.

Still safe.

Hurrying back, he stumbled over the root again and swore.

In the kitchen, fluorescents glared at the counter where he doctored a glass of milk.

Upstairs, Robby, in shorts but with his scrawny chest bare under the lazy ceiling fan, worked on a model airplane. A cabinet for his 78 records stood beside the desk. Inches below the ceiling, a wall shelf circled the room, holding a track for the Lionel model train.

Little hotshot collected stamps, too.

Theo held up the glass. "Brought you some milk, sport."

Robby didn't look up. "I don't want any."

"It's chocolate milk." With a little something extra.

"I don't care." Brusque, like James.

Christ, his mouth was parched. Everything seemed weird. Was he really doing this? Yes. Too late to back out. "I made it how you like it, with lots of Hershey's syrup."

Robby had this coming. Only twelve but blasé about luxuries most adults couldn't afford. His own bathroom with tub and shower. An RCA radio/phonograph playing in the corner.

"Go away." Robby laid down a glue tube and picked up the plane. "David thinks you're swell. Hang out with him. Daddy may pay you to stay with us while he and Sondra are gone, but you aren't my nanny."

Arrogant little shit. Just like James. Theo's hand clenched the glass. *Relax. Don't lose your head. Too much is riding on this.*

"Aw, come on. You didn't eat much supper."

"I ate plenty."

"I really want you to drink this, Robby."

"Go jump in the ocean. And I told you, stop calling me Robby. It's Robert. Jeez, if you weren't kin, Dad wouldn't put up with your bunk for one minute, much less give you a job."

A red haze. His ears roared. Snotty Robby was all that stood between him and Sondra.

I'll show you.

He calmly set the milk down. Then he jerked Robby up and ripped away the airplane. It sailed through the air.

Robby's eyes widened. "What're y—?"

Theo used a chokehold. "Shut up, you crummy, sniveling brat. You're not going to screw this up for me."

He tried to force the milk down, but Robby twisted. His head bent back.

Theo pressed harder. A bone cracked. Breath whooshed. Robby sagged.

Oh shit oh shit oh shit! I broke his neck.

He let go.

Robby thumped onto the bare waxed floor. The red haze faded, but the room blurred. Theo swayed, rubbed his eyes till they could focus on Robby's crumpled form.

Was the kid still alive? He bent down. Christ. He was dead.

Like James.

He couldn't breathe. *This can't be happening. Not here. I need air.*

That detached person who wasn't Theo took over.

Get a grip. So Robby's dead. He had to die anyway. Does it matter where?

No. Theo inhaled, licked his lips, pushed his hair back.

Stupid brat should've drunk the milk.

He straightened the chair, laid the stupid airplane on the desk and stuck a pin in the cement tube. Then he picked up the needle to silence the stupid Andrews Sisters wailing about rum and Coca Cola, sleeved the record, and put it away.

All stuff finicky Robby would have done before bedtime.

Dead, the kid looked small and defenseless.

Nausea swelled.

No getting sick. Pretend it's that last buck you shot. No difference.

Yes, there was. That waxy flesh creeped him out, made him want to run off howling.

He didn't. He wrapped the kid in a blanket. "Okay, sport. Going for one of the midnight boat rides with your brother your father always fusses about."

Fussed about.

This time, when he trudged through the live oaks, he sidestepped the root.

At the cruiser, a tarp spilling from the pile tripped him, made him drop Robby. The blanket parted. Robby's head, eyes staring, bounced on the dock's weathered boards.

He recoiled, caught himself. No time to be squeamish. Robby couldn't feel anything. He gathered up the boy and blanket.

Get him aboard and out of sight in the cabin.

"Join your brother, sport." He threw Robby into the darkness and closed the door before dragging over the dory.

With the motor and oars tucked inside, it fit nicely between the cruiser seats.

Ready to put out to sea. Soon he would have everything.

As the cruiser cut through dark water, he mapped out his future to take his mind off what he was doing.

What he'd done.

He'd keep the island that his ancestors had settled. But forget that 1942 Buick; he'd buy a new sports car. And the yacht James had scoffed at? His now. Along with hunting lodges, polo ponies, airplanes. And a Girard-Perregaux watch like the one his fraternity brother flaunted.

My great-grandfather's ring! David's still wearing the druid's ring.

The wheel veered. His hand straightened it automatically.

The other Theo—the detached one, the clever one—surfaced.

You can't keep it. It's unique. Someone might see it and guess what you did. Don't be stupid.

But a kid like David had no business with an heirloom like that. The ring should have been his to start with. His grandfather was the oldest son, not James's. So what if he couldn't wear it in public? He'd still own it. Along with everything else. James's money. The island.

Sondra.

Seductive, beautiful, passionate. He was risking everything for her, but Christ, how he loved her. He'd been a goner the first time he saw her, an angel in her nurse's white, all big eyes and sultry smile. He could've killed James for taking her away.

Forget it. James was dead. She'd be his soon enough.

On the open sea, mist rose. Occasional boat lights diffused into hazy glimmerings and faded before he cut the engines. Should he throw out life preservers? Yeah. If they were picked up, the *Harmony Island* logo would confirm the boys' deaths.

Anything else? No. Launch the dory and get in. Then light the fuse.

Mulrennon would never miss a few sticks of dynamite from the farm shed.

By the time the distant boom came and night skies blazed out at sea, he had made it back to the island inlet. He collapsed over the tiller, shaking all over but unable to stop grinning.

He'd done it. The boys were ashes.

The mickeys could have been too weak, the dynamite too old, the fuse bad. But everything had worked. He might have been screwed once by Lady Luck—orphaned, left dependent on James's charity—but no more.

Stay with me, baby!

His hands were steady by the time he moored the dory.

At the house, he bounded upstairs and poured Robby's untouched milk down the bathroom sink. One last check to make sure nothing was out of place, then back down to wash out telltale traces in the boys' glasses before leaving them in the dishwasher.

There. Chores done.

He needed a belt. Bad.

No reason to squander the pitcher of martinis.

The alcohol should have helped him sleep, but it didn't. In bed, he stared at shadows on the ceiling.

This night had been a dream. It was like someone else had carried David, choked Robby, set the dynamite. Not him.

And the strange hush now that it was over. Like the house knew what he'd done. Creepy.

He rearranged his pillow.

Shit, he hated killing the boys. Even runty Robby.

I had no choice. Not when it came down to them or Sondra.

Sondra. Christ, her moist lips. Her breasts ripe for a man's hands. How he loved her. He'd do anything for her.

No. I've done it.

And she was worth it.

Along with the money.

CHAPTER 1

"My Buddy"
As Performed by Henry Burr (1922)
Music by Walter Donaldson
Lyrics by Gus Kahn

Coastal Georgia
May 1962

FOR SIXTEEN YEARS attorney Lawrence Wykerton had dealt with Theodore Pack. For almost that long, he'd absolutely despised the man.

A weakness that went against every principle instilled by his father.

"Give a person the benefit of the doubt," his father had preached. "Everyone has some good inside." "Be fair; consider all viewpoints." "Always, always do what is right."

The younger generation might sneer, but the old platitudes had served Lawrence faithfully for nearly seventy years. He could have gone through life never doubting their worth.

Except for Theo Pack.

That's why, when his secretary buzzed to say Theo was on the line, Lawrence almost instructed her to say he was out. She might bustle in to see if he was ill, but he didn't care.

He knew exactly what Theo wanted.

Confound it.

He shouldn't have let his hopes rise when the Packs' current island sojourn brought no new demands. After all, they were flying out today. Perhaps they wouldn't ask for an advance. Perhaps this time they'd make it till the quarter.

The cursed phone call brought him to his senses. He should have known better. The Packs were always short of money.

Botheration. He did not want to deal with Theo. How tempting to pretend he was busy.

Oh dear, oh dear. What to do, what to do.

As if he had a choice. He squared his shoulders and, ruing his father's training, picked up the phone. "Hello, Theo."

Theo didn't hem or haw. "Lawrence, we need an advance. Will you see to it?"

No apologies, no excuses, no polite "please." Their turbulent history precluded warmth, but that didn't mean common courtesies couldn't be observed.

He picked up the pen from the Harmony Trust folder, open to where he'd been ticking off deceased beneficiaries. The clack of typewriters filtered in from the clerks' room next to him.

"Lawrence? Are you there? Did you hear me?"

He swallowed a sharp retort—Lord knew he'd had enough practice—and managed a neutral tone. "I'm here, Theo. How much?"

Theo told him.

"Goodness gracious." He jotted down the amount. Ridiculous. "I'll send what's available to the usual account."

They'd gone through the drill often enough. If he came up with part of what Theo wanted, Theo would bluster and sulk but manage till next quarter. The boy had finally realized accusations and lawsuits would get him nowhere.

Boy. Humph. Theo was thirty-eight. Long past being a boy, no matter how pigheaded and extravagant he'd turned out.

After hanging up, Lawrence played with his pen and watched dust motes dance in sunshine streaming through a large bow window onto shelves of law books.

The advance posed no real problem; the Packs always overspent their income so he always budgeted a reserve. The problem was protecting the Harmony Trust. He could only do that till next year when the Packs would get control. Then . . .

Hard to think of what would happen without gagging.

The pen stopped twirling.

That was neither here nor there.

He looked at the amount again—outrageous!—and flung the pen down on his blotter. Then he ran a hand through his hair. "Damn Theo."

Unbelievable that a dilettante like Theo Pack could be related to a great man like James.

Ah, James, my friend, my friend. How I miss you still.

At noon Lawrence, somewhat calmed, arrived for his weekly Rotary meeting at the Blue Crab Diner across from the city pier. While he sought his panama, his driver opened the car door.

Pungent odors drifted over from the inland river. An unhurried shrimper, nets raised but followed by gulls hopeful of scavenging thrown-back fish, glided by the pier on its way to the marina. Against a cloudless blue sky, boat and birds stood out in stark relief.

He laboriously swung out his legs. "I must have left my hat, Curtis. Seems like I forget everything nowadays."

"It's right here, Mr. Lawrence. I'll get it."

Part of Curtis's summer intern duties involved chauffeuring The Old Man.

Ah yes. Lawrence knew exactly what his coworkers called him behind his back. His father had once earned the same soubriquet, and his grandfather before that.

Both fine men, but sometimes hard to live up to.

While Curtis retrieved his hat, Lawrence dragged himself out. A speck marred his linen suit sleeve. He flicked it off as the boy, smoothing the panama's brim, reappeared. "Here you go, Mr. Lawrence. Let me help you up on the curb."

Lawrence snatched his hat and shook off the proffered hand. "No, thank you, Curtis. I'm not in my dotage yet."

Mollycoddling him like he was an old man. Sixty-eight was not old, no matter what a rising college senior thought.

"Course not, Mr. Lawrence." Curtis, straight-backed and muscular, the grandson of Lawrence's housekeeper, tilted his head. "Thing is, Mam said she'd whup me if I don't watch out for you. An' if she thinks I'm not, she will, too. I'll pick you up at one sharp."

Blast him. The boy was way too uppity.

Not that he didn't have cause.

One of James Harmony's more controversial endowments provided a college education to any high school graduate in the county who passed entrance exams and maintained passing grades. White or Negro. After his junior year at Morehouse in Atlanta, Curtis held a three point eight average with ambitions centered on Yale Law School.

If necessary, he would call in markers to get the boy enrolled. But fondness for Curtis didn't mean he'd stand for any guff. "I'll tell Mam about your backtalk."

"Yessir." Black coffee eyes in a *café au lait* face feigned meekness even as Curtis called his bluff. "You do that, Mr. Lawrence."

Curtis knew perfectly well he wasn't the only one his grandmother bossed around.

Lawrence gathered his dignity. "Don't bother coming back. I'll walk." He slapped his hat on his head and marched off.

"It's pretty warm, sir. Mam says you shouldn't be—"

"It's not that hot."

"But Mam—"

"Three blocks isn't far. I'll walk. Do not come back."

So there. He strutted away.

Nobody, including Mam through her grandson, would tell him what to do.

Inside the café, she-crab soup, sweet local shrimp, and regular camaraderie swept umbrage aside. By the time the speaker finished tearing apart Kennedy's botched foreign policies and outlandish domestic strategies, Lawrence's stomach was comfortably full and his equanimity restored.

Then while he shook hands with the Baptist preacher, the banker, gray suit snug on his stout frame, tugged at him. "Got a minute, Lawrence?"

Berriman, the youngest brother of a man Lawrence had started first grade with, handled part of the Harmony monies. Lawrence knew at once what he wanted.

The Packs. Always the Packs. Packs meaning Theo. "I do. Needed to talk to you anyway. D'you have a pen?"

After Berriman scribbled notes on a business card about drafting money to Theo's New York account, he launched into why he'd detained Lawrence. His bank had received credit inquiries. Theo was pricing yachts. Expensive yachts.

Careful not to show annoyance, Lawrence listened.

So that's what the rascal was up to. He'd just bought one, hadn't he? Six, seven years ago?

When Berriman asked whether to approve Theo's loan, Lawrence shrugged. "Might help you hang on to the accounts next year."

"You think Theo'll move them when they inherit?"

"A good possibility. He and Sondra aren't down here that much."

Was Berriman always so thick? Of course Theo would move them. Theo would have shifted everything to one of his dubious cronies years ago except for Lawrence.

Berriman, jowly face troubled, chitchatted about whether the Packs' banking business might end up in New York or Palm Beach or, God forbid, Europe.

Lawrence heard him out, ire dwindling. Berriman was worried, not thick. He was like the other locals: unwilling to believe the Packs would destroy the local economy. It would be cruel to disillusion him so Lawrence put on a noncommittal front till he could escape, fuming.

No Town Car or Curtis in sight.

Good. He needed to get hold of himself.

On the horizon, far beyond the outskirts of town, smoke puffed from a Harmony plant. Its steel had helped build Liberty Ships during World War II, and booming automobile sales kept it profitable. Theo, the fool, was already mouthing off about selling it and other lucrative holdings next year when the Trust ended.

Lawrence had pored over every phrase, every word, every comma in James's will, seeking a loophole. But everything came back to that one damning sentence James had insisted on inserting:

"The Trust shall be disbursed on October 2, 1963."

No ifs, ands, or buts to be misconstrued. That was when Robby would have turned thirty, but James didn't specify his son's birthday. Only the date. The courts would do nothing.

Lawrence couldn't complain. That sentence had saved the estate from Theo's depredations so far.

But that same sentence would soon end Lawrence's stewardship, allowing Theo to liquidate companies, leave employees jobless, and squander the proceeds.

Everything James had achieved for the region, for the state, for an entire country at war, would be lost and forgotten.

"I've failed you, James."

There should be something he could do, but he couldn't see what. He'd sounded out Sondra Pack, but she, foolish woman, thought Theo hung the moon.

Heartsick, he strolled the avenue of century-old coastal homes until he came to three small girls in shorts and flip-flops, playing in puddles of sunshine filtered through oaks. His appearance halted their squeals and chalking of squares on the sidewalk.

Then one recognized him. "Hello, Mr. Wykerton. Be careful and don't smudge our hopscotch."

He tipped his panama. "Of course, ladies."

As they watched mistrustfully, he avoided wobbly lines. "There. Missed every one of them."

A chorus of "thank you" followed as he proceeded. Someone had taught them manners.

Beads of sweat on his upper lip made him dig for his handkerchief.

So hot. He envied the girls their indifference to the weather. Curtis would give him that "I told you so" look.

He inhaled deeply. Ah, it wasn't that bad. Not really.

A river breeze, carrying scents of sunshine on water, half-heartedly tempered the sticky Lowland heat. Why, some Junes were scorching, dry enough to wither the resurrection ferns lining the live oak trunks.

No, today wasn't bad at all.

He should have let Curtis come back for him.

Oh, well. Not far now.

He trudged on, the old days filling his mind. How often had James laid an arm across his shoulders to say, "You can handle it, Whitey. You're the only *honest* attorney I know," then squeezed while that unforgettable laugh boomed out. "Personally, that is."

Their private joke.

"No handling it this time. I'm sorry, James."

If only you had gone to the doctor as Sondra begged. If only the boys hadn't taken the boat out that night. If only one of them had survived.

"Stop your whining, old man." Be grateful James had been spared knowing his sons' fate.

Lawrence's childhood home, a Victorian now housing the law firm of Wykerton Perth and Ross, came into view. Pink camellias beloved by his mother still lined the front walk. The azaleas and daffodils were done, but gardenias and plate-sized magnolia blossoms diffused cloying fragrances.

As he plodded down the broad brick walkway, the oval-glassed door sprang open. Clerks in spike heels and summer dresses exited in a flurry of squeals and splash of white petticoats.

He paused. "What's wrong?"

"Rats!" The new receptionist nearly knocked him down. "We have rats!"

"Nonsense." He should have known better than to hire one of these flighty young females.

He reached the veranda steps in time to be shoved aside when his own secretary burst out. Blue shirtwaist dress flapped and sturdy walking heels thudded, but tightly permed hair didn't bounce a lick. "A rat in the office!"

"Come now." Such an uproar. He'd thought better of Ruby.

Inside, he caught several attorneys goggling as Curtis chased a small, furry something across the floor. "Here, here, Curtis!"

Then Megan Mulrennon, navy skirt and white blouse businesslike but copper chignon falling apart, appeared. "Don't hurt it, Curtis. Wait. It's behind the wastebasket."

She grabbed a sweater off his secretary's chair and with two steps threw it over the creature and scooped it up. "Ground squirrel. Must have sneaked through that open window." She brushed by to release the creature outside.

Short in stature, she had a face that would appear youthful even when she had gray hair. Her nose turned up, and her upper lip was slightly longer than the bottom, suggesting a melancholic disposition. The dancing eyes, when she came back inside, dispelled the notion. "I'll have to wash Miss Ruby's sweater for her."

Levelheaded child. Never moody or prone to tears.

He'd watched her grow from a tomboy shadowing the lively David, to a shy teenager working afternoons in his office, to a law school graduate taking on a man's job. She was capable. He'd never doubted her ability else he wouldn't have brought her into the firm no matter how fond he was of her and her mother.

If this new law young Kennedy was pushing got passed, it would mean her salary would have to be adjusted so the firm wouldn't save as much money.

But no matter. She'd soon leave, anyway, with her engagement to that Atlantan. Marriage was inevitable, even for plainer girls than Megan, and her move would sever one more link to the past. He'd miss her.

Though not as much as the attorneys she assisted.

Speaking of which . . . Ah, things were getting back to normal. The male spectators had returned to their offices while the runaway women were sheepishly filing back inside. He held the door for them. "Goodness gracious, ladies. Perhaps I'll start skipping Rotary. Things are much more exciting around here than at our tedious lunches."

In his office, he called Theo's New York banker about the forthcoming draft. Then he opened a law volume, only to slump and push it aside. No use. He couldn't concentrate.

Taking off his glasses, he rubbed his eyes.

Each time Theo had sued for control of the estate, the courts had ruled Lawrence had absolute discretion. An unwanted obligation, but when James remarried and changed his will, he'd asked Lawrence to be sole trustee and guardian for his sons.

How could he refuse? Especially when James confessed that he might have been a wee bit hasty in trying to give the boys a mother figure so soon after being widowed.

Humph. James had glossed over his own appetites, but it would have taken a colder man than James to resist Sondra. Nor had age dimmed her allure, as witness Lawrence's own son who should have long outgrown mooning after Sondra but hadn't, more was the pity.

A bigger pity the Packs would get the bulk of James's estate.

Lawrence massaged a temple. If life were perfect, Theo would break his neck skiing. Or get shot in a hunting accident. Or fall off a yacht and drown. Or crash his plane into a mountain.

Theo and his set drank heavily. Flying while intoxicated might induce a fatal error that . . .

"Tsk, tsk. You should be ashamed of yourself." One did not hope for a man's death just to protect a friend's legacy.

But there had to be some way to save it.

Lawrence had studied James's will for sixteen years; there was nothing there to help. Maybe a closer look at James's other papers would yield something—a word, a phrase, even a comma!—he could use to stop Theo's dismantling everything.

One couldn't hope for Theo to die, but one could dream of fate intervening in other ways. Would that be so terrible?

He sighed. If only the boys had survived.

CHAPTER 2

"I've Got the World on a String"
As Performed by Frank Sinatra (1953)
Music by Harold Arlen
Lyrics by Ted Koehler

South of France
July 1962

SONDRA SELLIN HARMONY Pack, clutching her tennis racket and wearing her favorite Tinling tennis dress with the red embroidered flowers on the skirt lining, sauntered to the hotel elevator and pushed the up button.

Its bell dinged and gleaming doors opened to discharge two men in casual shirts and slacks, one of whom caught Sondra as she straightened her panties.

She flashed a *so-what* smile.

A double take, a quick intake of breath, and his hand shot out to hold the elevator for her.

Oh yeah. Talk about it. A flutter of lashes could still stop them in their tracks.

Inside the elevator, she used her key for the penthouse, then turned to catch him admiring her legs before coming back to her face. She'd got her own eyeful by then.

Uh huh, a stiffie. Those tight stylish pants showed it all.

The doors whispered shut.

Grinning, she took off the headband.

Nice to know she hadn't lost it. She might not be twenty-one anymore, but she could still get men going.

Not that she'd ever follow through. She had Theo.

Peering into the side mirror with a pout worthy of Brigitte, she searched for wrinkles.

Nope. Nary a one, thanks to Dr. Hamm. Only lush lips, smooth forehead, and eyes so blue they seemed purple. Elizabeth Taylor eyes, everyone said. A poet had written verses about them. A shame nobody had ever heard of him.

Only three more days till Theo would be back.

Christ, she missed him. She'd known from the beginning she'd have to share him with his silly sports, but keeping him happy was worth an occasional separation.

A wise woman gave her man plenty of space.

The elevator opened to huge windows hung with burgundy silk draperies that overlooked the blue Mediterranean. Below, the yellow sunshine she adored drenched sunbathers littering a sparkling pebbly beach. Here and there, bright umbrellas protected the sun dodgers.

She never tired of this place. It was tangible proof that she'd pulled herself out of a two-room shack in Mississippi to the world of millionaires and celebrities.

Too bad they didn't have their own house here. Hotels, no matter how plush, got old. But when they first married, Theo had wanted an African hunting lodge, and everyone who was anybody simply had to have a place in New York.

Lawrence Wykerton, stingy thing, had docked their income until those purchases got paid for. That was the first time they'd butted heads, but not the last.

Next year the old fuddy duddy would be history.

Peachie came out yipping happily. She picked up the tiny poodle and crooned, "Is Mama's baby glad to see her? Has her been a good girl?"

The heavy fragrance engulfed her before she saw them.

Scarlet masses, everywhere.

She set Peachie down. Admirers sent flowers all the time, but this!

This was a garden of red roses brought indoors.

One huge vase loomed over the foyer console. In the living room, blooms blanketed a sofa table, a cocktail table, and side tables while the mantel held two smaller vases. Even the dining room across the hall was stuffed.

"Christ, Janie," she said when her maid appeared to take charge of her tennis racket and headband. "There are enough roses here to open a flower stand. Who sent them?"

Janie rounded her eyes. "Aren't they something? Miss Linda took the card."

"I wonder who they're from."

Not Theo. He was in the North Sea on his annual sailing trip with his male clique.

The straitlaced German she played bridge with? Not a chance.

Had to be the British MP who monopolized her every chance he got. He was besotted and yeah, maybe she *had* led him on.

Her secretary appeared. "The card's right here."

"Thanks, Linda." Sondra took the sealed envelope. "How are the invitations coming?"

"Addressed and ready to go."

"You're the best."

Sondra had agreed to co-hostess a charity ball with an Italian contessa of some notoriety. She loved lending her name and Linda's services for these events as long as they were splashy with an abundant attendance of the celebrities in residence.

This affair promised to be both. Yves Montand and that Greek millionaire and some of the Kennedy clan were coming. Not the President or Jackie, but there was always a chance the invitees might later offer access to the glittering couple themselves.

That's how she and Theo had met the luscious Frank Sinatra. And Princess Margaret; the bitch had snubbed them but then she snubbed everyone. And they barely knew the Frenchman who'd introduced them to the Duke and Duchess of Windsor at a garden party.

Theo called the former king a fairy, but she thought he was absolutely charming. And oh, the Duchess's jewelry! Fantabulous.

Like these roses. She held one to her nose. "Mmmm."

"Yummy, aren't they? Thirty dozen. Janie counted. They have to be from the MP." Linda's guess echoed Sondra's.

She put the rose back. "A cliché, so many, but what can you expect from an uptight English politician whose wife keeps him on a short leash?"

Clichéd or not, the batches of flowers were good for her ego. She might have hit forty—not that she'd admit it—but they proved she was still in the game.

As a phone rang, Linda rushed to answer and Sondra ripped into the envelope.

There wasn't a card. Only a folded newspaper section.

What in the world was this?

She spread out a clipped photograph to see a man posed with fists on hips. The article caption read: "Downing's Richard III Wows Hardened London Critics."

She froze, but not because of the headline.

The grainy face of the actor had been circled in red. To the side, heavily underscored, block letters in the same scarlet ink shouted: "DAVID HARMONY'S COMING HOME!"

Her eardrums pounded. "No." No, no, hell no!

Christ. Good thing nobody was around. She pulled herself together as Linda returned.

"A few problems with the wines but now everything's copacetic." Her secretary frowned. "Are you okay? You're white as a ghost."

"Yes." Sondra crumpled the clipping. "I'm fine. Where did the roses come from?"

"I don't know. Janie took the delivery. Aren't they from the MP?"

Sondra went in search of her maid.

Janie, cleaning Sondra's black *peau de soie* heels for a soiree that night, knew exactly where the flowers had originated. "The shop in the hotel. Is something wrong?"

"No." Sondra wet her lips. "I need to change. I want to, uh, to walk in the gardens. Lay out the white capri pants and the pink top with the ruffles."

"Don't forget your massage and hair color appointments."

"I have an hour yet." The words came automatically.

Good thing she'd never been one to panic. As a nurse in Cherbourg during World War II, she'd learned iron self-control. It had come in handy when she watched James die in such agony. She would have broken then if she hadn't been so tough.

No, she wouldn't think of James's suffering. Or the wounded soldiers. Or the dead captain she'd hoped to marry. The terrible parts of her life were over.

Think about how wonderful everything is now. Think about Theo. Think about your homes, your clothes, your jewels, the parties. You're somebody now. You're part of the jet set.

Once changed, she told Janie, "I won't be long. Keep Peachie here, will you?"

Once outside and away from her staff's curiosity, on a secluded path that meandered away from the beach, she pulled out a lighter and lit a cigarette.

The brilliant sun and azure sea held no pleasure anymore.

A private bench nestled within towering shrubbery offered a haven where she could unfold the clipping and soak in every word about stage actor Nick Downing.

The article lauded his performances but mostly gushed about the man himself and his captivating personality. After a second reading, Sondra took one last drag on her cigarette.

What shitass had sent this? And why?

Once she ground the stub into the gravel path, she pulled out her lighter, set fire to the clipping, and held a corner till the last vestige turned black and disintegrated. With steady hands, she lit a new cigarette and inhaled.

Bees buzzed nearby. The midday sun touched flowering shrubs. Her favorite fountain, featuring a large Adonis and Aphrodite—who everyone agreed looked remarkably like her— trickled merrily. A couple holding hands appeared on one of the trails that dotted the precisely laid out gardens.

A perfect spot to relax except for that pissy clipping.

Another crackpot, that's all. Over the years, such notes had appeared constantly. Addressed to her, to Theo, to their attorneys, to the newspapers. Even to Lawrence. Christ, she was tired of the cranks. Why wouldn't these assholes leave it alone?

Someone was jealous. Jealous that the daughter of an illiterate Alabama sharecropper had walked off with the Harmony fortune.

Assholes.

Was it her fault she was smart as well as beautiful? When they'd advertised for nurses during the war, she had jumped at the chance to escape the cotton fields.

They didn't tell her what she was in for. The bullets, the blood, the terror. But she'd kept her bargain, hadn't she?

More than kept it.

And it was worth all the fear and misery. Some dumb clerk had misspelled *Sandra* on her birth certificate, but not till the army changed little Sandra Lynn Sellin to the impressive Second Lieutenant Sondra L. Sellin did she realize how lucky she was.

No more country bumpkin *Sandra*. She was the exotic Sondra, who did her job when the artillery shook buildings they operated in. Who soothed the faceless, armless, legless remnants of men. Who watched a fellow nurse die from shrapnel as they helped evacuate wounded. Who saw the artillery captain she'd planned to marry, laid to the side with his brains splattered.

She shuddered. No, forget that. Forget all the bad memories. Think of the good things.

Like after the war. When she'd heard James Harmony needed a nurse, she'd gone straight to his dying wife because no sensible woman would let her husband hire a beautiful woman.

Her strategy had worked. Kindhearted Livvy had chosen her though James, he'd laughingly admitted after their marriage, had lobbied for the daughter of an old friend.

How clever she'd been to approach Livvy first.

Her self-congratulatory glow faded.

David Harmony's coming home.

By God, she'd earned her position. She deserved every bit of this fabulous life.

And nobody—but nobody!—had any right to send her ugly newspaper clippings.

She didn't know who the hell Nick Downing was, but she did know one thing. David was as dead as his father and brother, and had been for sixteen years. Next year the Trust would wind up—finally— and she and Theo would get it all. Envious assholes could send her a hundred newspaper articles and they would change nothing.

Nothing!

She had a good mind to see who'd sent those frigging roses. Throwing down the unfinished cigarette, she got up and brushed off the seat of her capris. She'd end this now.

The order had come by mail, the haughty Frenchwoman presiding over the flower shop informed her. "With a large banknote to defray the cost, *madame.*"

"Was there a letter or card?"

Appraising eyes frosted. "A typed letter with the order specifics came to us. The missive included a sealed envelope for inclusion with the flowers. *We* do not open such cards, *madame.*"

The envelope bore no return address but may have come from Paris. Or perhaps London. Or Rome or New York. The saleslady shrugged bony shoulders. "*Qui sait?*" Who knows?

Though quick to palm proffered franc notes, the blackclad bitch evinced smug regret that the postmarked envelope with its instructions had been discarded and was irretrievable.

As Sondra left the shop, the sharp aroma of chrysanthemums brought images of James's funeral where monstrous wreaths had sapped the island chapel air and turned her faint. That in turn evoked hazy images of James's sons.

The face in the clipping did resemble David's. The actor wasn't David. Not a chance. But if David had lived, he might have looked like this Nick Downing.

A chill touched her. What if this was some kind of omen? They'd waited so long.

Don't be such a lamebrain.

Theo would be back this weekend. Once he got over his irritation at another anonymous letter, he would mock her premonitions and laugh at her for imagining David could be alive. He would tease her out of her funk and make her scream when she came.

Christ, she missed him.

That night, after the soiree in a luxurious villa where liquor flowed and women glittered with jewels and laughter floated overhead on the high hill looking down on the Mediterranean, Sondra arrived home pleasantly buzzed.

An unwelcome message awaited. Theo's group had decided to extend their Scandinavian sailing trip.

Never would she let Janie see her upset, but after stripping off her Givenchy dress and donning a silk nightgown and climbing into the opulent bed, she cuddled Peachie and lay awake.

She'd counted on Theo. She needed to run her hands over his body, feel him against her, in her.

She needed a good screw, dammit.

Sometimes she wished she didn't love him so much.

But she did. Despite the faint thickening of his body and the sun creases on his face, despite his occasional moods and the niggling signs his drinking might be getting out of hand.

Okay. Intimacy sooner or later led to aggravations, but they were minor. Theo was her life. She hated being weak, but where he was concerned, she was pathetic.

Oh, Theo, what would I do without you?

That hateful newspaper clipping hung in the back of her mind as she cried in the darkness before she fell asleep, the first time she'd cried in a long time.

Peachie, sweet baby, licked at her tears.

CHAPTER 3

"Let's Call the Whole Thing Off"
As Performed by Ella Fitzgerald/
Louis Armstrong (1957)
Music by George Gershwin
Lyrics by Ira Gershwin

Coastal Georgia
September 1962

"GOOD! YOU AREN'T busy."

Megan Mulrennon, dusting off the desk in her tiny office, jumped at George Wykerton's breezy interruption.

He slapped a list of case citations down in front of her and pretended to shield his eyes. "Polishing your headlight?"

Megan glanced at her ring. "Ha ha, George. And good morning to you, too."

"Actually, it isn't a good morning for me. You've got time to help me out with some research, don't you? I have to run over to the bank to cover the checks Mona wrote last week in Savannah. You wouldn't believe the stuff she bought."

So Mona had spent some money. What did George expect, sending his wife shopping with Sondra Pack? Or could his money shortage come from something else? Like the unlucky Friday night poker games the other attorneys ribbed him about?

But George's finances weren't her concern. "Sure, I can help you. I just finished a brief."

After explaining what he needed, George started to leave but paused. "You know, I thought Pop was crazy for hiring a woman. But the Old Man still knows what he's doing. You've worked out okay. Kind of like a legal assistant only better."

"How sweet of you to say so, George."

He, naturally, missed the irony.

She opened his folder with a sigh. The backhanded compliment was all the praise she'd get. George and the other men treated her like a secretary instead of a fellow attorney, but she did what every woman in a man's field did.

She smiled and helped them out.

If she sometimes tired of their patronizing remarks . . . Well, that's just how it was.

Besides, staying busy kept her from worrying about Ron. She stared at her odious engagement ring. Marriage to him meant abandoning her familiar home for crowded Atlanta where people walked fast and talked fast and ran red lights.

Megan hated Atlanta. Rather, she hated Atlanta's sprawl. She loved sitting "under the stars" at the Fox Theatre and shopping at Rich's and watching outdoor musicals at Chastain Park, but the traffic left her white-knuckled. Living there would be a nightmare.

Her stomach cramped.

Think of that later. Get busy on George's work.

Then Sondra Pack poked her teased, artfully bleached head in. "Hi, Megan."

"Sondra. How nice to see you."

Why was she here? The Packs' annual yacht party was over, and they should have left the island early this morning.

Sondra didn't look hurried. Capri pants hid shapely legs while a clinging top bared a tan midriff and tiny waist. Her platinum hair and breathy voice brought to mind movie stars. "Let me see this engagement ring JoBeth's been bragging about," she cooed from a cloud of expensive perfume.

Megan meekly held out her hand.

The 1.872 carat diamond, circled by six small ones for a total weight of 3.456, cost more than the rest of her jewelry combined. Nearly half what she made in a year. She knew because Ron had proudly flourished the receipt.

Gaudy thing. She'd hated it on sight but said yes anyway. If she wanted a family, Ron was her last chance. Like Mom said, he was a real catch.

Her stomach clenched again, but she kept her smile pasted on.

Sondra oohed and aahed. "It's as gorgeous as your mother said. I love that marquis cut. Lucky girl!" She let go Megan's fingers. "JoBeth's so excited."

"She was afraid she'd be stuck with a spinster daughter."

"Bull." Sondra flapped a manicured hand. "You have a *career*. And now a ring, too."

George, smoothing his hair, slipped in. "Yeah, third time's the charm, they say."

His entrance wasn't unexpected; George was crazy about Sondra. But five minutes? This was a record even for him. And, insensitive male, he would have to bring up her other two broken engagements.

So what? She might break this one, too.

The others didn't notice her grimace. Sondra was greeting George with a friendly hug that he enthusiastically returned, saying, "I thought since the regatta was over, y'all would have been gone by now."

"We're flying out as soon as I get back to the island."

His face fell. "I hate to see you go. But can I do anything for you? I'd be glad to."

Oh, brother. Practically drooling.

Sondra patted his arm. "That's so sweet of you, George. But not today."

George, simpering, might be credulous, but Megan knew better. The Packs must be short of money again. And the quarter barely begun. Shrewd of Theo to send Sondra.

Before George's blatant fawning over Sondra became too unbearable, Miss Ruby interrupted to say Lawrence was free.

George scurried to follow Sondra's curvy form out.

Megan went back to her books but heard Lawrence's brittle tones greet Sondra. Then: "Aren't you writing up the Welch interviews, George?"

"Um, yes. I—"

Lawrence's door slammed.

Poor George. Even if he didn't have a wife and family, and even if Sondra wasn't married, he still wasn't in her league. He ought to stop carrying a torch.

Megan found her place and was soon so caught up in research she never heard Sondra leave and even forgot about lunch. Then her phone rang. Miss Millicent India Asbury wanted to revise her will. As she did every six months.

Not that Megan minded.

No, indeedy. The elderly Miss Millicent was a mainstay of her clientele. It was sad that after eight years she couldn't boast as many clients as the firm's newest associate, but that was the breaks.

She'd known from the start a female attorney would have a rough time. Her roommate in law school had to set up her own practice after being rejected by the smallest firms.

Lucky for Megan, she'd known Lawrence all her life. Because of that, he'd taken her on as the first woman attorney in the firm's eighty-nine-year history.

Her profit percentage might not match the men's, but at least she had a job she liked close to home.

So what if she was stuck in the former butler's pantry? Lawrence's office—she still felt funny, downright disrespectful, calling him Lawrence instead of Mr. Wykerton—adjoined hers, and he was generous with his advice.

Like what to do about Miss Millicent's latest inspiration regarding her ten cats.

Her heels clicked on the solid oak floor to his door. She raised her knuckles to knock but heard him talking.

"I most certainly do refuse, Amos. They may bring in any auditors they want next year."

He was on the phone.

A silence, then: "We're too busy figuring distributions to deal with outsiders prowling through years of paperwork. Another audit simply because Theo demands one is an unnecessary burden. Not to mention an insult to our independent auditors."

Megan shook her head. Theo was at it again. Was that why Sondra had come over from the island?

Another silence. "Yes, yes, I know, but he's never been satisfied with my handling of the estate. He can wait one more year to prove I'm embezzling. I'm busy, so if that's all?"

Embezzling?

The receiver was not slammed down, but it did clunk.

She hesitated, then rapped.

"Come in," came the testy response.

Megan edged inside. "I won't interrupt if you're busy."

The harsh face softened. "No, no, my dear. Always time for you."

Barely over five feet tall, Lawrence had pointy ears and a chin like a leprechaun. Benign eyes, weakened by age, peered through horn-rimmed glasses. The starched shirt under suspenders looked fresh as always, but tufts of white hair sprayed out because, when upset, he always combed his fingers through it.

Lately, it stuck out all the time.

"You heard?" he asked abruptly.

She coughed, unwilling to admit eavesdropping.

He harrumphed. "Theo's asking for an outside audit. Again."

"Theo never knows when to quit, does he?"

"He will next year when he gets the money." Lawrence straightened his already neat bowtie. "No matter. I have no intention of caving in to big city lawyers. What do you need?"

Ha. Lawrence didn't require her as champion. Some people called him an old fuddy-duddy, but he was one of the sharpest estate planning and administration attorneys in Georgia. Two attorneys in the office had relocated, one from Loganville and one from Blue Ridge, expressly for a chance to work with him.

Once she got his apposite suggestions about writing up Miss Millicent's stipulation about the cats' bequests, she turned and bumped into George. "Sorry, George. I was just leaving."

"'S okay, doll." He brushed past. "What was that call from Amos Lovett about, Pop?"

"Humph. Theo again. Seems I'm abusing my position in allowing—"

Oh, that Theo.

Lawrence was old school, as honorable as they came.

"Megan." The receptionist, hair teased into a beehive, gave her a message slip. "Miss Millicent just hung up. She forgot something. Urgent, she said. I buzzed but you didn't answer."

Megan hid a sigh. Their last receptionist would have chased her down, but this one wasn't sure whether to treat her like a male attorney or a female secretary. Miss Millicent's "urgent" probably meant she'd adopted another cat she'd forgotten to name in her will but still . . .

A typist reeking of cigarette smoke and Jungle Gardenia perfume stuck a *Photoplay* magazine in front of her. "Look what Sondra brought us, Megan. She met Audrey Hepburn."

Sure enough, a full-page photo showed the actress in a simple navy dress and pearls, smiling at Sondra Pack who glittered in beaded gown and diamonds. The caption read: "Beauties Agree on Helen Rose."

Like she cared.

Before Megan could frame a tactful reply, George trotted out. "Say, Megan, can I get you to write up those Bortens notes for me? I need to finish the Welch case."

"Sure."

"Thanks for checking the citations." He spotted the magazine photo. "What is it? More gossip about Marilyn Monroe killing herself? Oh, no, that's Sondra! Wow."

"You're welcome." Megan moved out of his way.

George snatched the *Photoplay*. "Who's Helen Rose?"

Clerks and receptionist tittered. "A Hollywood clothes designer, Mr. George. She dresses all the movie stars."

"And doubtless anyone else who can afford her." Lawrence materialized and took the magazine from George. "Though not, I daresay, ordinary people like us who work for a living."

People scattered and typewriters resumed their frenetic clacking. Even George thought of things to do.

Reaching her door, back turned so the others couldn't see, Megan grinned broadly.

Lawrence held strong views on Hollywood decadence.

Very strong views.

George ought to have remembered that.

Once at her desk, she opened the Bortens file again.

She'd worked hard to get her law degree. Her mother had been against it, but Dad had backed her. Now, thanks to Lawrence, she was an associate at one of the most reputable law offices in the South without leaving home.

Okay, she did a lot of the men's work without earning near what they did, but like Mom said: *Men have families to support.*

Implying Megan would one day marry and be supported by a man.

Like Ron. Who hollowed her stomach so much she could lose herself in it. Mom was ecstatic over her engagement, but would it be so terrible not to marry?

Don't be crazy.

If she broke this engagement, she'd end up an old maid like Miss Millicent, alone at eighty-one except for ten cats.

Miss Millicent. Okay. Better call her back and stop thinking about marrying Ron and moving to Atlanta.

Ouch. That stomach again. She was going to get ulcers.

Unless she backed out.

She stopped, hand on receiver. She couldn't face her mother if she called off another engagement. Other people's opinions didn't matter, but Mom was a different story.

Then again, facing Mom might be easier than living with Ron for the rest of her life.

CHAPTER 4

"Let's Misbehave"
As Performed by Irving Aaronson (1928)
Music by Cole Porter
Lyrics by Cole Porter

London, England
November 1962

LAWRENCE WYKERTON LOATHED airplanes and long-distance travel. As for actors . . . Well!

His opinion of the acting profession couldn't be voiced in polite society.

Still, he gritted his teeth and flat-out lied; he told his shocked family he was going on a Rhine tour. Then he flew over four thousand uncomfortable miles to London.

All to inspect a British actor on a probably fruitless quest.

He should never have opened that *Life* magazine. Then he would never have seen the slick photograph where the camera zoomed in on a rapt face at eye level with a woman's naked belly.

"British thespian Nick Downing admires bikini," read the tag.

Lawrence had looked once, then again.

If he hadn't seen that face, he wouldn't have been in this position. He wasn't prudish. Heavens no. He enjoyed good whiskey, an occasional cigar, and a ribald joke as much as the next man.

But this plan was, to put it plainly, shaky ethically if not legally.

A huge gamble was what it was. And Lawrence never gambled. Not on cards, dice, or the weather. He never even ran red lights on empty streets at midnight. He had standards.

Or he used to have standards.

Ah well. Sometimes, desperate circumstances called for desperate measures. He'd lived by his father's strictures all his life. Time to explore his own avenues.

Not that meeting with this actor meant he'd follow through.

In London, he enjoyed an unexceptional play in which the lead, the man he'd come to see, proved the high point. As the audience filed out, he sat. Yes? No?

Yes. This might work.

Afterward, backstage in a dingy, crowded dressing room, optimism dwindled. Onstage, Nick Downing seemed muscular and tall. Bigger than life.

In person, the lean actor didn't top six feet.

Not good. James Harmony had towered over most men, as did Theo Pack.

Ignoring Lawrence, the actor grabbed a beer and chugged half the bottle. "You asked to see me?"

An accent, but the voice timbre would pass muster. That was something. Besides, height and build meant little when that face was remarkable for what he needed.

No use to beat around the bush. "Mr. Downing, I'm willing to pay you five hundred thousand dollars." He almost choked, but the sum had to be irresistible. "Ahem. For your services."

Eyebrows shot up. "Five hundred thousand? That's half a million. You're offering me half a million American dollars?"

"Yes. I am."

"That's . . ." Downing's eyes glazed. "Over a hundred fifty thousand pounds."

"Ahem. Closer to a hundred seventy-eight thousand."

"A hundred seventy-eight thousand pounds. Blimey. Really." Downing closed his mouth and swept clothes off a chair. "I'll take your word. Math's never been my strong suit. Sit there."

He waved vaguely toward the rickety chair, plopped down at a dressing table, and tugged at his cravat. "And you're offering this money to me for doing what?"

Something that looked like underwear hung on the chair. Lawrence pushed it aside and sat in time to see the cravat hit the floor.

Messy. "The same thing you're doing now. Acting. The production I have in mind will run about a week."

"A week? I'm a great actor but really. No actor gets paid a hundred seventy-eight thousand quid for a week's work. Come now, tell me the truth. You can trust me." Downing cocked his head expectantly. "Who do you want me to murder?"

Murder? Was the man joking? No signs of humor, but surely he must be joking.

A wagster. Lord help me.

Or was Downing serious? He wasn't smiling.

Nonsense. Lawrence drew on what dignity he had left. His family would be horrified to see him in this shabby backstage dressing room with its scent of talc and mildew. What a pity he wasn't on the Rhine as he'd pretended. These seedy surroundings made his skin crawl.

So did the irreverent man before him.

At his age, he ought to be taking up gardening. Not traipsing round the globe, risking his reputation to hire an actor who was probably conceited, dimwitted, and criminally inclined.

Ah, well. On with it. "You won't have to kill anyone. Quite the contrary. I want you to bring someone back to life."

"Is this about a film?" Downing curled a lip. "Are you from Hollywood?" With studied disinterest, he turned to the mirror, smoothed back a too-long strand of sandy hair. "I don't do Hollywood films. My agent surely apprized you of that."

Hollywood! Did he look like he belonged in so raffish a place as Hollywood?

Lawrence snapped his teeth together. "I'm an attorney. I have nothing to do with acting. Nothing!"

"I see." Disdain vanished. Efficient hands began to open up jars and clean off makeup. "Not from Hollywood." A sigh. "Too much to hope for, I suppose."

Lawrence studied the profile. The nose was a tad off, but the long face and wide forehead were promising. Very promising.

Had James's firstborn lived past thirty, he might have looked like Downing. High cheekbones and dark brows slanting up. A firm chin, though the lips were off. Too stern.

David's mouth had been soft, easy to smile. And David's hair was blonder and shorter.

But the eyes. Uncanny how they resembled James's. Not quite gray, not quite blue. David had inherited Livvy's sky blue eyes, but people wouldn't remember. If they did, well, eyes can change.

Don't get carried away. This man's from a different world. Feel him out.

The sheltered son of James Harmony could never have turned into a cynic with loose morals and few inhibitions, and an ambience that suggested boldness bordering on ruthlessness.

"Ahem. The tabloids call you Satan's Angel," he ventured.

"So it seems." Indifferent hands wiped off makeup.

The tabloids had bestowed the name during Downing's breakout role, after he beat a would-be mugger nearly to death.

The play was successful, according to Lawrence's informant, because of a good script, first-rate sets, and a director known for motivation. But Downing gave the demonic savage lead a naïveté that brought the character to life.

When afterward he undertook an award-winning Richard III for the BBC, jaded critics admitted he was out of the ordinary.

So far, fickle audiences had kept Nick Downing a lesser name in the British theater. Several projects beckoned when his current play closed, but none was particularly lucrative.

Yes, indeed. Lawrence had made it his business to find out everything about Nick Downing.

Everything except whether the man could play the role of a dead boy. That was yet to be discovered, but the resemblance remained the big thing. Without it, there was nothing. If Downing was halfway intelligent, ignorance could be enlightened.

Downing tossed away soiled tissues, took another swig of beer. "If you're not from Hollywood, what precisely do you want me to do for a hundred seventy-eight thousand pounds?"

How best to entice?

Amused eyes in the mirror met his. "Stop staring at me. I'm not a pouf, old man. I've no leanings that way whatsoever."

Dear, dear. He'd thought his scrutiny discreet.

Was that mockery? Not that it mattered. He hadn't traveled this far to bandy words. "If the sum interests you, come back to my hotel."

"Your hotel?" Downing turned, pointed his bottle at him. "Come, now. Didn't you understand me? I prefer young women, not old men."

Old—? He gasped.

Pouf! The man actually thinks I . . .

"I assure you I don't—I have no—I'm not that sort!"

"Really? It's hard to tell, and I know a lot of queers. Though right now, you don't act like a debaucher of younger men. More like a puffed-up hen."

"I'm not! I'm not, I, I, I am not looking for a . . ." He breathed deeply. "What I have to say must be kept private. It's extremely important. A matter of life and death."

Downing sulked. "I told my agent I was busy tonight. He assured me ten minutes would be the most you'd require."

"I'm afraid I misled your agent," said Lawrence without regret, still unnerved. *Pouf!* "Since my letters and calls to you last month went unanswered, I had no choice. It is imperative that we speak privately. I assure you this is a legitimate undertaking."

Legitimate for Downing, at least. No need to dwell on possible consequences for himself.

Downing put down the empty bottle and preened in the mirror. When he spotted a dab of cold cream on his neck, he tackled it.

What did that silence mean?

Lawrence said, "I have credentials. Also references in this country you can contact."

He was accustomed to reading people, but nothing about Downing disclosed anything except indifference. Such self-control would be invaluable for what he needed.

Unless it was vacuity.

He couldn't go through with this. This man would never do. He was out of his mind even to think about hiring an actor.

He breathed in, out. In, out.

No. He'd come this far.

Allowing James's life to be belittled was unconscionable. If Theo carried through with the sale of businesses, he'd throw the entire area into economic chaos.

Downing's face, those eyes. It could work.

Do it!

"Are you interested in earning five hundred thousand American dollars?"

The used tissue narrowly missed the wastebasket. Downing didn't pick it up. "The amount is tempting, yes."

"Then come with me and I'll go into the details."

"Why can't I hear them now?"

"Ten minutes isn't long enough. It's complicated but you'll not regret listening. I'll explain over supper, then a car will take you home or wherever. With, ahem, heavier pockets."

"Oh?" Downing perked up. "How much heavier?"

An impatient rap at the door punctuated the last word. "Nicky, darling, are you ready? We're starving. If you're going with us, come along. We refuse to wait another instant."

A tiny brunette in slacks and sweater erupted into the dressing room, bringing with her a cloud of heavy perfume.

Lawrence recognized her as the maid in the play.

"I thought that bloody Hodgkins would *never* get through reaming me out over that cock-up in the second act and I'm so annoyed I could *spit* so if you know what's good for you'd better not take his side because—"

She saw Lawrence and her animated hands froze. "Oh. Sorry." Her eyes widened. "I didn't know you were with someone, luv. Who's this?"

Lawrence knew perfectly well how a wizened old man looked in the tiny dressing area with its mirrors and bottles and jars and costumes flung every which way. He was every inch the interloper she plainly considered him.

Politeness ruled. He rose stiffly.

Nick Downing hesitated, then hopped up and embraced the girl. "This, my dear Phoebe, is an attorney. About some rather messy litigation." The *sotto voce* words carried as was doubtless intended. "The bobby dunked in the fountain?"

"What!" Her shocked face swiveled. "Nicky, you swore—"

"Don't worry, pet." Downing took her waist. "I'll take all the blame on my strong shoulders. I won't mention you a-tall."

"It was his own fault anyway. If he hadn't—"

"That means I'll be tied up this evening." Downing eased her toward the door. "And much as I absolutely deplore the necessity of begging off, I can't go to supper with you."

"That hateful Gavin's told you *lies*, hasn't he? He fancies you. You *can't* believe—"

"Haven't seen him today, poppet. Explain to the others, would you? There, I knew you'd understand. Maybe I'll ring you later."

Under Lawrence's astonished gaze and despite her complaints, Phoebe was ushered politely but firmly outside.

Downing shut the door, leaned against it, and heaved a dramatic sigh. "Talkative women are so exhausting, don't you know. Especially when all they're after is your tadger."

Tadger? Better not ask.

One thing was certain. For all his languor, Downing could act decisively once he made up his mind.

Lawrence filed away that interesting tidbit.

The mad scheme might work, providing Downing agreed.

And providing he had enough backbone to carry it through.

CHAPTER 5

"I'm in the Market for You"
As Performed by Louis Armstrong and the
New Sebastian Cotton Club Orchestra (1930)
Music by James F. Hanley
Lyrics by Joseph McCarthy

AT HIS DISCREET HOTEL, a refurbished tribute to Queen Victoria, Lawrence ushered Downing into a modest suite of dark antique furnishings and heavy maroon draperies. Really a bed-sitter, the suite nomenclature came from its private bath facility, which to his dismay consisted of a pull-chain toilet and sink with a half-bath surrounded by a shower curtain in a space the size of a broom closet.

At least he didn't have to trek down the hall. At his age, he preferred to keep his toilet habits private.

Without removing his own jacket, he held out a hand. "Let me take your coat."

Downing retrieved a cigarette case and lighter before relinquishing a tweed jacket that would've suited a college professor.

Except no professor would be seen in those indecent narrow trousers. And those ankle boots! Tsk, tsk.

Ah well. The man was an actor. Plenty of time to worry about proper attire later.

He hung Downing's coat, scented with tobacco and cologne, on the coatrack and gestured toward food laid out on a pie-crust table between two armchairs. "Sorry for the plain fare. I felt it best to eat in, hence the sandwiches. But they brought beer. There's whiskey and water, too."

Downing sat down and stretched out his legs. "Beer's fine."

Preliminaries over, Lawrence got down to business. "I must request that you sign this confidentiality contract." He pulled it out from his briefcase. "It states that if you refuse my offer, you will say nothing to anyone of this discussion. Ever."

"And if I break the agreement?"

He slid a stack of banknotes on the table. "Regardless of your decision, these go with you when you leave. If you break the agreement, I'll sue for their return. Plus damages."

"I see. A carrot and a stick." Downing fanned the notes. "Five thousand pounds. Mmm. Nice plump carrot. It so happens I'm fond of carrots." He took the paperwork.

Lawrence closed the curtains against the bone-chilling darkness, set out a mug for beer, and poured himself whiskey. How gloomy this old hotel was, especially at this hour when night overrode glowing lamps scattered around the room.

He sneaked glances at Downing, lost in concentration, lips silently mouthing words.

Was the man literate? Surely he was. Actors had to be able to read. Didn't they?

At last Downing laid the contract on the table. After he pushed back a lock of hair, he exhaled noisily and gazed into space.

Lawrence held his breath. Would he sign or not? What did that vacant stare portend?

Then Downing picked up the waiting pen and, with a flourish, scribbled on the contract.

Lawrence checked the signature.

Good. One hurdle passed. "Help yourself." He waved to the tray and sat down opposite Downing. "Please bear with me. The story is rather complex."

The actor picked up a thick sandwich. "Take all the time you need. I've got the rest of the night." He brooded. "Now that I've canceled a perfectly good carousal." He chomped.

Churlish. As expected, considering the man's profession.

"In 1946, James Harmony, my client and friend, went to Washington, D.C., on a business trip *cum* honeymoon. Earlier, he'd had influenza and never completely recovered. While away, he suffered a relapse that led to heart and kidney failure. Two sons by a deceased wife survived along with the second wife."

How dry his mouth was. He sipped the whiskey.

Chewing muffled Downing's bored "Fascinating."

"No." The astringent whiskey revived him. "Tragic."

"I daresay." Said with total indifference.

No need to take offense. Downing was coarse, the sort to treat death flippantly.

"James's son David was sixteen, Robert twelve. A twenty-two-year-old distant cousin, Theodore Pack, was staying with them at the family home on an island off the Georgia coast. Theo was James's only other kin. James and his first wife took him in when he was orphaned in 1940."

Downing poured beer into his mug until the foam overflowed.

Ugh, slovenly.

"The boys were understandably upset on hearing their father was dead, so Theo gave David a diluted martini and Robby a glass of milk to help them sleep."

Sorrow, unexpected and gut-wrenching, struck. His throat clogged. Wiping his glasses bought a few minutes to recover.

Downing licked his fingers. "This beef is superb. Aren't you eating?"

"Later."

Downing bit off another chunk. "Mmm. Heavenly." He brandished the sandwich remainder. "Did the hotel kitchen cater this for you or did it come from a restaurant?"

Was the man listening? Lawrence perched his glasses back on his nose. "I have no idea. The concierge set it up."

"Oh." Downing picked up on his irritation. "Do go on. Please. Fascinating story. I'm all ears. Truly I am."

Lawrence didn't believe him for a minute.

This is a mistake. The walls pressed in, muted colors and dim lights adding to the melancholy. *I should have chosen a newer hotel.*

"Ahem. Theo was the last person to see the boys alive. The next morning, maids discovered their beds not slept in. And a cabin cruiser was missing. James had forbidden the boys to go boating at night, but David was, er, young. Sometimes he disobeyed. Theo assumed he and Robby had gone out and had engine trouble. He initiated a search."

Sandwich consumed, Downing wiped his mouth and smoothed the napkin before laying it aside. "Unsuccessful, I take it."

"Yes." Livvy's fingers had been long and slim like Downing's. A pianist's fingers. Livvy had loved her music.

"So they drowned." Downing noticed a string dangling from the bottom of his fly. He tugged. It resisted.

Had the man no modesty?

Lawrence averted his gaze from Downing's crotch to his own gleaming wingtips. "No traces . . ." He battled another wave of grief. "No traces were found of them, but search planes did spot debris. It turned out to be charred remains from the cruiser."

He risked a glance. Downing had abandoned his fly, thank heavens, and was eyeing the sandwiches again.

"Sad. Quite sad," Downing said cheerfully. He swept up a ham and cheese on rye. "Blimey, these are outstanding."

Resentment surged, as quickly faded. Downing had never known James or his sons. And wouldn't detachment be necessary to achieve their ends?

Downing had to accept the offer. He simply had to.

"Ahem. Later, an islander reported hearing a huge blast accompanied by a brilliant light at sea that night."

"An explosion then." Downing swallowed. "No bodies were recovered?"

"No, but it had to be their boat. It was ten years old, with twin engines overhauled after being stored during the war. Earlier, James had smelled gas although no leak was found. It was theorized fumes built up in the bilge area and a spark set off an explosion that caused the fire."

"Reasonable." Downing, crust in hand, studied the platter. "Were there no servants?"

"Servants?"

The crust disappeared. Downing snagged another bulky roll.

Goodness gracious. That made three. And they were huge. How could such a wiry body hold so much? Did all actors eat this way? Perhaps acting took more energy than generally supposed.

Downing waved his sandwich. "Surely a wealthy family would have servants. Chauffeur, maids, groundsmen. Someone who saw the boys go out." He bit.

Lawrence blinked as a large portion of the third sandwich vanished. "Er, no. Two secretaries along with James's man and Sondra's maid lived in one wing of the mansion, but all four had accompanied them to Washington. The other employees were . . . It takes, took, over a hundred people back then to run the estate, but none lived near the house. A guard saw nothing but did hear a boat pass. He assumed it was fishermen."

A final bite disappeared. When had the man eaten last?

Downing brushed a crumb from his shirt and pushed his plate aside. He burped.

Disgusting. At least one tray would be sufficient.

"Suspicious," Downing drawled. He lifted his mug in a salute. "Very suspicious. First the father dies, then the sons. If this were a play, I'd suspect murder." He swigged beer.

"Ahem. Yes. At the time, I instigated an investigation because the whole thing—James's death and the boys' deaths right after—seemed too coincidental. But there was nothing to prove otherwise."

Lawrence paused for effect. "Then."

Downing crowed. "Aha! There must be a lot of money at stake for you to offer me half a million dollars to do . . ." He set down his half-empty mug. "Exactly what do you want me for?"

"You're right, there's a great deal of money involved. And I don't want to haggle." Lawrence lifted his glass. "You bear an extraordinary resemblance to David."

Silence.

Downing retrieved a brown cigarette—no, a small cigar—from the gold case and inserted it between compressed lips. The engraved lighter, held with one hand, flared in a quick motion Lawrence had read about in *Theatre World* magazine. Critics and female fans alike swooned over the gesture. Sexy, they called it. Whatever that meant.

And what the devil lay behind that stony face?

Smoke clouds rose, tobacco aroma close behind. Lashes lifted from mocking eyes. "Lawrence, are you trying to tell me you intend to resurrect a boy dead for sixteen years?"

He stiffened. Impudent pup. How dare Downing address him by his first name? How wise was he in hiring the man?

No, he had no choice. Now that he'd met Downing and talked to him, he'd decided.

The plan could work. But only with this man.

He said abruptly, "When James Harmony died, he left the bulk of his estate tied up in trust for his sons. Since their deaths followed his so closely, the estate would normally have gone to the other beneficiaries listed in the will."

"The widow?"

"And the cousin. James left, under certain conditions, both Theo and Sondra substantial bequests. Legatees could draw interest on their shares but if they died before settlement, their shares would revert to the estate and be prorated for the survivors. There were other bequests, but Sondra and Theo received by far the largest shares percentage wise. Which is what mattered once the . . ."

His mouth dried again. "Once the boys died." He set down his drink. He'd had enough. Else why this dizziness? He needed water.

Downing watched. "If I understand you, the boys' parts went to the widow and cousin."

Ah, the man was no fool.

He drank the tepid water.

Not like home. What he wouldn't give for a nice sweaty glass of ice water and one of Mam's buttered biscuits. "Had we been able to distribute it at the time, Sondra and Theo would have received the bulk of the boys' shares, yes."

The dim lights and smoke drifts distorted Downing's features. "But you weren't able to?"

Good. Downing was curious. "No. As it turned out, once we examined the will in detail, a settlement proved impossible."

Slim fingers waggled, inviting more.

He obliged. "My firm did the footwork, but James insisted on writing his will out himself. And"—indignation swelled—"he did so quite against my advice and exhortations. If he had listened to me at the time, we—"

He caught himself, straightened his tie. "Ahem. That's beside the point."

One did not complain about a friend, no matter how justified. Especially a dead friend.

He went on: "In short, there was no provision for the event of both boys dying. Legally, the estate cannot be settled until October second of next year. The date is Robby's, er, what would have been Robby's thirtieth birthday. James specified only the date itself in his will. If he'd designated it as Robby's birthday, we might have been able to disburse funds after the boys were declared legally dead. But he didn't and we couldn't."

Not that Theo hadn't tried, the scoundrel.

Downing stared into the distance.

Smoke plumes tickled Lawrence's nose. Not the time to sneeze. "As it happened, Theo Pack and James's widow fell in love and were married the year after James's death."

"How convenient." Downing's repose continued.

"Yes. Well. They hoped the marriage would allow the courts to end the Trust since they were the two main legatees. Unfortunately, while the boys were declared legally dead, the terms of the will were such that they could not be overturned. James's preciseness as to when and how the Trust should end was definite. Final dissolution continues to be delayed until next year."

"So the widow and cousin are to be congratulated." The actor came out of his reverie. "You spin an interesting yarn, old chap, but I don't see why you need David Harmony. It appears the only way I might fit your scheme would be in a most"—an odd smile turned the regular features disagreeable—"nefarious manner."

Satan's Angel indeed. More like Satan himself.

Oblivious, Downing settled back in his chair with a curling cloud round his head.

A fair-haired Satan. Wicked and hard.

He caught himself. Fancies, pure fancies. Nothing more than fancies. "You will be doing nothing illegal. If you tried to claim the estate, it would be different. But that won't be the case."

Only a flesh and blood man, this Nick Downing. A dubious type but still a man. "As I said, investigations at the time found nothing but a bizarre coincidence. Then some weeks ago, a certain, er, discovery, convinced me Theo had, er, something to do with the boys' deaths."

"Murdered them, eh? Did away with the heirs and scooped up the widow and all the loot with her. What's he up to now? Trying to do away with her, too?"

Insufferable jackass. "No, not at all."

"I would if I were in his shoes. Why share the money? Come to that, exactly what evidence did you find that he's a murderer?" Downing stubbed his cigar in a porcelain saucer.

Too late, Lawrence relocated an ashtray to Downing's elbow. "I'll say only that it's sufficient to convince me to take this drastic step. I've nothing solid to present to the authorities. If Theo is guilty, I must flush him out myself."

Damn and blast. I sound like those pompous old fools I abhor.

"Flush him out?" Downing leaned forward. "Casting me as decoy?" Glinting eyes belied the prim mouth. "That's an outlandish idea. Not to say a dangerous one. If this bloke did murder them, why not let him enjoy the fruits of his labor? Nothing to do with me, is it?"

He laughed.

One moment Lawrence was in the chair, the next he was on his feet, fists bunched. "This is not a joke!"

Downing sprang up, too, clearly taken aback.

"Two innocent boys may have been murdered by a man they loved and trusted. Two boys may have died because—" He caught himself, shot his cuffs, and sat back down.

What was he doing? He understood Downing perfectly. The man was a renegade, a person who cared for nothing or nobody. Even if he had known the boys, he wouldn't give a rip that they were murdered. That callous nature was part of what made him so perfect.

Oh, yes. Lawrence might understand Downing, but he didn't have to like the man. "This is not a joke to anyone who knew the family."

"Sorry." A twitching lip gave the lie to the apology, but Downing did reseat himself. Gingerly, with one eye on Lawrence across the low table. "I'm unused to such high drama off stage."

"Are you interested in earning half a million dollars for a week's work?" Animosity made him blunt. "All taxes paid?"

"Interested enough to risk my life?" Downing toyed with his cigar case, grasped his lighter. "I assume I'll be David."

"Exactly. If Pack did murder the boys, he won't let the money slip away now. He'll expose himself."

Downing had rediscovered the thread at his crotch. He rested one suede boot on the opposite knee and worried the string. "What makes you think he won't kill me?"

Contempt dispelled modesty. What did it matter that Downing fiddled with his fly?

"There might be some danger, yes, but you'll have bodyguards with you always. Trained men who'll keep you safe as possible."

"As possible, eh?" The gold lighter flared. The string at Nick Downing's groin withered in the flame and vanished.

Lawrence's own genitals contracted. He couldn't stifle a tiny gasp.

"Ahem. I've done some research on you. You're tough. You've been put at risk before, in World War II and afterward. I have no doubt you can survive any eventuality Theo Pack might devise."

Downing closed his lighter with one hand and a faint smile. "So you've researched me. What did you find out?"

"That your real name is Nicholas Simeon Dowserman. You were born to an unwed mother in a Liverpool slum and raised by your grandmother, both of whom were killed during the Blitz. When you were seventeen, you and a man argued over a girl. It escalated to knives, and he died. The courts let you choose the army over jail. You fought in France, then Germany. There you formed a, er, connection with an American WAC."

Ah, that caught the man's attention. "After your discharge, you followed her to North Carolina where, in 1946, you and she set off for Richmond."

He was hard pressed not to gloat.

Yes, Mr. Dowserman, I know all about your shady past.

Downing's jaw tightened. "Her name was Rosemarie."

"Pardon?"

"Rosemarie." Downing took out a new cigar and the lighter flared again. He puffed. Hard. "The WAC's name."

Interesting. Had Downing loved the woman?

The lighter clicked shut. A smile taunted. "And we were going to Philadelphia. Richmond was just the end of the line where we had to change trains."

No, he must have imagined some emotion. If Downing had cared about her, he'd recovered. "Why Philadelphia?"

"Rosemarie had a sister there."

"I see. Anyway, in Richmond, you and she were walking across the street to a restaurant when a bus veered out of control. Two pedestrians, your friend and another man, were killed instantly. Another person died later. You yourself landed in the hospital for several weeks. On your release, you went straight to Mexico."

"She'd planned the trip. Philadelphia, then New York to Acapulco. Why shouldn't I go on with it?" Downing gestured with his cigar. "No reason to stay. Her family collected her body while I was laid up. I cashed her ticket in and used mine." A tic in his neck gave him away.

So the WAC's death touched a nerve. A weak point to exploit?

"In Acapulco you participated in several brawls before a short foray to Cuba. Then you returned to Mexico where a souvenir from a jealous husband, that scar on your thigh, expedited an exodus to Australia."

An expressionless Downing feigned a salute with the hand holding the cigar. "Via Argentina and a few other places you omitted."

Good. He *had* found a tender place.

"In 1952, a British theater troupe touring Sydney hired you and brought you back here. In 1958, you stepped into an alcoholic lead's role." Now to cut into the gut. "The critics raved, but that hasn't translated into a decent apartment or a car or—"

A bark of laughter cut him off. "Bugger. You're more thorough than the bloody coppers. But acting on stage is one thing. Pretending to be a real person is far different."

Lawrence exhaled. "It can work. Now I've met you, I have no doubt it will work."

"What makes you so sure?"

"Several things." He ticked them off. "One, you look like David might have looked at thirty-three. You're older, but no one can tell. Second, you're an actor, and this part will be tailor-made. Third, you'll have me to prime you on whatever's necessary to convince everyone you're David Harmony."

"It won't work."

"It will, I tell you." He leaned forward. "I'll fly to London every week if necessary to tutor you." A hideous prospect but necessary. "I was James's closest friend, practically one of the family. I have access to pictures, letters, home movie reels. I can coach you in every detail."

"And when someone recognizes me as Nick Downing?"

"That's the beauty of it. We won't change your identity. What we'll say is that David survived the boat accident—"

Downing started to speak.

Lawrence held up a hand. "Hear me out. Your story will be that a passing freighter picked you up after the boat explosion and took you to Mexico where you met Downing. The boys died before you ever went to Mexico so it's a perfect place to swap identities. We just need to come up with an explanation for how and why you would've agreed to swap places."

"Blimey." Downing studied the ceiling. "You've given this some thought, haven't you? But it'll never work."

"It can. It must." He relaxed hands unwittingly clutching his knees.

"Lawrence, Lawrence. What would you know about David's intimate life? His first girl? His relationships with his stepmother, cousin, friends? Even the servants. You delude yourself if you think I could fool any of them."

"Not at all. You'll be David Harmony for a few days, a week at most. We won't give Theo time to plan. We'll force him to act. Besides"—he lowered his lids to hide satisfaction as Downing nibbled at the bait—"for half a million dollars, one hundred seventy-eight thousand pounds, you can make it work. I'll even advance part of it when this play closes."

"Bloody hell. You know how to persuade a bloke, don't you?" Downing ignored the ashtray Lawrence had carefully placed beside him and ground his cigar into the dish.

Lawrence bit his tongue.

Downing drummed his fingers. "It's tempting," he said. "The whole concept is absurd, but you make it bloody hard to refuse."

"That was the intent."

Downing stood. "I'll think about it."

A grin flickered and spread, as far removed from the sneer as night from day. Slanted brows smoothed. Lips softened. Eyes warmed.

So that's where the nickname Satan's Angel came from.

Almost like an adult David. This man was perfect. "Will you do it?"

"I've other offers to consider. I'll let you know."

At the door, Downing stuffed the banknotes into his coat pocket. "Tell me, Lawrence. What do you get out of this?"

"What do I get? Why, why, I . . ." What penetrating eyes. "The satisfaction of bringing a murderer to justice."

"No eating satisfaction. Not that I care if you pocket the lolly, mind you. None of my business." Downing patted the pocket containing the cash and turned. "I'll think about your proposition. I may even do it. It might be rather challenging."

Lawrence stared at the closed door and snorted. "Challenging, indeed. Your kind would kill his grandmother for that kind of money, fella, and don't think I don't know it. You'll come around. I'll give you a day, two at the most."

What if the man wanted more money before this was over?

He recalled the glimpse of something dangerous and shivered.

No, he could manage Downing. He had the whip hand. Downing would do as he was told.

Of course he would.

Lawrence made sure his door was locked before taking off his jacket and undoing his tie. Then he sat down to a sandwich he hadn't wanted to eat in front of Downing.

Those unnerving gray eyes saw too much.

CHAPTER 6

"California Here I Come"
As Performed by Freddy Cannon (1960)
Music by Al Jolson, Buddy De Sylva,
and Joseph Meyer
Lyrics by Al Jolson, Buddy De Sylva,
and Joseph Meyer

THE GRAY EYES in question were veiled as Nicholas Downing waited for the minuscule hotel lift. When the cage stopped, it was occupied and he had to edge in sideways. Even so, he and the woman passenger were crowded.

The lift creaked before descending.

He started when she leaned into him. Strong perfume filled his nostrils. Sprayed hair brushed his cheek.

"I've got the time, ducks, if you've got a tenner." In a tight red dress with black nylons and plunging neckline, she batted inch-long false eyelashes.

F'gawdsake. Had the interview so unnerved him he could stand facing a tart and not realize it? "Sorry, luv. Sounds like a reasonable offer, but maybe another night."

Sex might help, but not with a whore. He could call Phoebe, do like always. Enjoy the moment, then let it go.

Except he didn't feel like listening to Phoebe prattle. Like others in the business, she was temperamental with an ego to match his. And she bored him. Lately, all she wanted to do was smoke reefers.

Sod it. He was too pernickety about women.

From a pub off to the side, spurts of laughter broke the tinkle of a piano. He could get a pint and chat up the bartender. Enjoy the music, relax. Might be easier to figure out what to do about this unexpected proposal from the disapproving old man.

No matter how schooled a person's features, contempt always showed. He shouldn't let it goad him into another blunder. He ought to refuse, go ahead with his own plans.

One foot turned toward the pub, but he stopped.

Best not. He needed a clear head. He often acted before he thought. Too often. This time he mustn't do something he'd regret.

Work it all out, figure out everything that might happen, how you'd respond.

So he turned his back on the cheerful pub and strolled out into the midnight fog where a chauffeur waited to help him into the back of the hired car provided for his comfort.

Mmm, nice. Plush seats. New motor smell.

The old man was right about one thing. An actor's irregular income didn't support luxuries like private cars.

"Ahhh." He laid his head back on cushiony leather. He could get used to this.

Or maybe not. One part of him wanted to snatch up the offer and another didn't. This play would run six more months at best. Though he'd read scripts for several plays and a mediocre BBC series, none interested him.

He wanted to be a movie star.

He'd worked bloody hard to get this far, but the crown jewel for his career lay in Hollywood, where fame and glory awaited plucking by his hot little hand.

He positively knew it.

Okay, maybe his dream was ridiculous.

Didn't matter. He itched to give it a whirl.

A David Harmony returned from the dead would be great publicity once the papers got hold of it. Enough to jumpstart his Hollywood career.

Could he carry it off?

Faces whirled round his mind, faces of people he had failed.

If only he'd made different choices. Some of them had been made for him, but not all. He could have done things differently.

Couldn't he?

Bugger it. Regrets were useless, part of the past. They had nothing to do with this.

But once he became David Harmony, he would have to be David to the bitter end. Too many times he'd set out with good intentions only to digress or not follow through.

Not this time.

If he agreed, he'd have to finish the charade. While a murderer lay in wait.

So? He'd been in worse spots. The familiar anticipation fluttered his stomach.

I can take care of myself. I've proved that over and over.

The huge sum offered meant the old man wanted him. Badly. But the situation could become intolerable. Was it worth the risk?

Bloody hell, yes. Hollywood stardom was worth any gamble.

He'd planned to go to America anyway. This offered some easy cash to grease the way.

And if he unmasked a murderer, wouldn't that help make up for everything else he'd muffed?

Sod the past. There was nothing there for him except nightmares. He had a good life now doing something he loved. Acting might never make him rich, but it was his calling. He wouldn't abandon it. Not even for the fortune the old man was so concerned about.

The money. Must be a lot for the old man to offer him a hundred seventy quid.

And the old elf himself. He projected honesty, but appearances could be deceptive.

He rubbed a scar on his hand where a woman he'd tried to help had turned on him. The thin raised line reminded him why he should never take a person at face value.

What was the old man in it for? Money? Power? Or simply justice as he claimed?

And this recently found evidence. Was it hard fact or wishful thinking? Or was the entire story fabricated?

Let's analyze this. For once, let's try to be rational and not dive in headfirst.

The old man presented his motives as purest of the pure: retribution for two dead boys. But money could wield a lot of influence. Vast sums could tempt any man, no matter how honest. This might be one of those times. Or there might be misdeeds to cover up, like stealing money one was supposed to safeguard.

Nick shivered. He'd been deceived before because of money. But whether or not an embezzler was hiring him wasn't his concern.

Unless the embezzler got him nicked or killed.

He could accept the risk of gaol. And he was pretty adept at self-preservation; he'd learned early to take care of himself.

Playing David presented the real difficulty.

How would it feel to be David Harmony? Should he give him an innocent boyish charm? Or should he be a sophisticated man of the world? How would they explain his reappearance after so long? When he confronted Theo, should he show outrage or ignorance?

Ignorance.

He would say nothing about a murder. He would meet Theo with his angelic smile, shake Theo's hand, and express utmost delight in returning home. Rub Theo's nose in the news that the rightful heir had shown up to knock him out of the running.

All the while watching his back.

He rotated the shoulder where a piece of metal from the bus accident had left its mark. Once he'd learned he was a survivor, life held few physical terrors. Mentally . . .

I can't dwell on my faults. I can do this. I know I can.

"This could be a challenging role." His composure pleased him. Not a hint of churning emotions underneath. No one could deny he could act. "A most challenging role."

He would have to be on his guard, ready to sidestep and parry and lunge. Otherwise, he would fail in a spectacular way that would leave everyone worse off than before.

Including him.

Did he dare agree?

Stop lying to yourself.

He'd known all the time he'd agree. If he pulled this off, he would prove himself to be the great actor he was.

But let straitlaced Lawrence Wykerton in his conservative suit and ridiculous bowtie stew. The old man was too bloody sure of himself, entirely too disdainful of a lowly actor.

He laughed, low in his throat.

The driver of the hired car glanced in the mirror but kept his mouth shut like someone who'd learned to mind his own business.

Someone as distrustful as him.

But occasionally you had to jump in and hope for the best.

He hummed as they drove on through the foggy London streets.

CHAPTER 7

"Hereupon We're Both Agreed"
From The Yeoman of the Guard
As Performed by the D'Oyly
Carte Opera Company (1950)
Music by Arthur Sullivan
Lyrics by W. S. Gilbert

THREE DAYS AFTER their first meeting and the morning after his proposition was accepted, Lawrence ushered a drooping, weak-eyed Nick Downing into his bed-sitter.

Humph. Hung over. "Looks like you were out on the town last night."

Downing grunted before sitting on the bed and plumping a pillow. *My bed! He's lying on my bed!*

Reprimands were not a good way to start a relationship, but really! A good tongue-lashing might bring the fellow to heel.

No. Not the time. "Watch the shoes. Ahem. I've given your story some thought."

Half-reclining, Downing dragged out his cigar case and lighter.

Lawrence's chest tightened. The fumes would permeate his pillows and sheets like last time, but perhaps the maid would give him fresh linen again.

"The only way we can convincingly turn Nick Downing into David Harmony is to have the two switch identities right after David's death. Your own origins are too easily traceable for any other plan to work."

Nick's lids closed halfway. "Sensible. I'm a believer in sticking to the truth whenever possible. A firm believer."

Confound the man. He wouldn't know the truth if it knocked him down. He was not taking this seriously. "Are you fit enough to do this?"

"I'm fine. Do you have any aspirin?"

"No."

"What about whiskey?"

"It's ten in the morning."

"That's the problem. I don't usually get up till noon. Never mind. I'll be better directly."

Lawrence bit back a tart response. "Ahem. Your story. When you got out of the hospital, you flew to Acapulco. What if you met David there?"

"Acapulco. Ah, such fond memories of Acapulco. I made some less-than-honest money working for a few heavies. I delivered their— but you don't need to know all that, do you?"

Indeed not. He didn't want to hear about any illegal jobs Nick Downing had undertaken.

"Never mind, Lawrence. I won't make you an accomplice in crime. Acapulco is the perfect place for me to change identities with David. I met a lot of people there." Guileless gray eyes opened. "Such a varied lot of people."

He sucked on his cigar.

Lawrence distrusted the guilelessness.

Downing exhaled. "But there's another problem. Say a freighter picked David up and took him to Mexico. Why wouldn't he have come home? Or let someone know where he was?"

"Why? Because . . ." The harsh smoke pricked his throat. He ran a hand through his hair. "That's something we must think about."

On the bed, Downing regarded the ceiling. "Tell me about him. Was he impetuous? Volatile? Unhappy? Unstable?"

"David?"

From lifelong discretion, Lawrence started to deny James's son had been any of those things. Then he sighed. "He was somewhat headstrong. And irresponsible. And impulsive. James enrolled him in St. Paul's School at the beginning of World War II. He ran away once to Texas, and later to New York. He infuriated James when he said he'd rather be a hobo than a robber baron."

He smiled, remembering that scene.

"Not that James took him seriously," he rushed to add. "All boys rebel. David didn't like having his future planned out for him. He may have been a bit mercurial, but I'd hardly call him unstable."

"It would help our case if he was."

"I see." Leaning back, he steepled his fingers. "David was, er, restless. Adventurous."

"Good. That gives us an opening, doesn't it? A restless, mercurial boy, shocked by his father's sudden death, traumatized by a boat disaster that killed his brother, somehow surviving to be picked up by a freighter. I can see it now."

Downing sat up, swinging his feet to the floor. Cigar smoke softened his angular face. "The boat exploded. Fiery bits rained everywhere."

A hand waggled in illustration.

"I was thrown clear. Robert screamed, but I couldn't get to him.

Then his screams stopped. The tide carried me off, and I floated till the freighter picked me up. I begged them to go back for my brother. They didn't."

Were those tears?

Lawrence stared, fascinated by the change from cunning rogue to grieving brother.

Downing swallowed audibly. "I knew Robert had to be dead, but I couldn't cry, couldn't think. On the freighter, I kept seeing the boat explode, hearing his screams. Over and over. The explosion. His screams."

Yes, those were definitely tears.

My heavens, the man was incredible.

"Then"—Downing lowered his voice—"the captain put me to work. It was fate. I'd always longed for adventure and here it had found me. I forgot about getting home."

Plausible. Except . . .

"Why wouldn't the captain communicate your whereabouts to somebody?"

"I didn't want him to. Ah, Lawrence, can't you understand? My father was dead. My brother, too. Nothing would ever again be the same. How could I go back to a place where I'd constantly be reminded of them?"

Downing frowned, abandoned his grief-stricken performance. "Especially when I had a new world to explore. Perhaps I went over the edge. After all, consider what I'd gone through."

He gave a little headshake. "I don't see how I could possibly have been sane. Poor me."

Poor . . . ?

Rationality returned. "So you simply joined the crew? Never to call or write or come home?"

Downing stood. "Too much excitement in learning to cope. Then it was too late. I preferred living in the present, not the past. I think that's how it happened. Don't you?"

"You're certainly convincing. It might work."

"Of course it'll work." Downing sucked on the cigar, looking quite pleased with himself.

Cocky jackass. "And the ship goes to Mexico."

Downing loosed a gray cloud. "Exactly. And Mexico is a wild place where anything can happen. Who knows what went through David's mind once he got there? Would he even think of home? His family was dead. He had a new country to explore." He stretched and yawned. "I had a run-in with some people at the docks not long after I arrived. Maybe I met David then."

Oh my, that smoke. Made Lawrence want to sneeze.

But the plan was promising. "All right. We need to figure out how the exchange took place. Why it took place. Why David would have consented. Why *you* would have consented."

Downing paced and eyed his cigar.

Lawrence smoothed his trouser creases. Why would the two switch places?

"David wouldn't have had a passport," he offered. "He might have noticed the resemblance and got you to sell him yours. No, he wouldn't have money. Maybe he stole your passport. No." He slumped. "That won't work either. You would have reported it stolen."

"Come now, Lawrence. Considering the way I was earning my keep?" The cigar waved. "The last thing I needed was that kind of attention. And it's easy enough to get a replacement if you know the right people. I'm thinking being a crewman wasn't as much fun as David expected. Perhaps he jumped ship and the captain shanghaied me, mistaking me for—Oh, no, even better."

Downing stopped to crow. "Gawd, I am so clever."

Egotist.

"What if the people I worked with found out I was skimming profits?" Downing coughed. "Which, as it so happens, they might very well have had reason to believe."

A criminal. I knew it.

Lawrence shut his mouth and closed his popped eyes. Too late to take back the gasp. This was only what he'd expected. He knew what the man was. No use to get upset now.

Downing, pacing again, didn't notice his distress. "What if I decided a dead boy who resembled me could get them off my back? What if, in the struggle, David killed me and stole my passport?"

"David was not that sort of person!"

"Bollocks. It was a life or death situation. Anyone's that sort of person. Believe you me, I know how easy it is to kill someone. Been there myself several times. "

Several times? The actor had killed more than . . . ?

Dear Lord in heaven.

Downing impatiently flourished the cigar. "And it doesn't matter what kind of person he was. If it happened that way, I'm dead while David's alive and free to live his life. *My* life."

The murder that had put Downing in the British army was practically self-defense. Others could have been, too. Or . . . Of course. The war. He'd fought, killed then. "Oh. Yes. I see."

The story had holes, but Downing told it so plausibly that it was almost believable. Perhaps they could have Downing die other than at David's hands.

He picked up a yellow pad. "All right. Let's tend to details. We'll start with what happened—Theo's version of what happened—the day James died. When Sondra's secretary telephoned about James's death, they were all upset. Theo thought a weak martini wouldn't be out of place for David, but he fixed Robby a glass of milk."

They spent hours shaping their story, manipulating and inventing and weaving it in with Theo's version until, about noon, Lawrence brought out a large manila envelope. "Something for you to study."

"I thought we'd been studying." Nick—by now Lawrence thought of him as Nick—got up and arched his back, kneading one side of it. "Tell me. Do you ever wear anything other than suits and white shirts and bowties, Lawrence?"

"Call me Whitey. David called me Whitey. He couldn't say Mr. Wykerton when he was little." He dumped out the envelope on the sofa table and started arranging photographs.

"I repeat, do you wear starched white shirts to bed, too? Whitey?"

He stopped organizing. "How can you be so frivolous?"

Nick cocked his head. "How can you be so stodgy?"

"Stodg—" He counted to ten. "You need to start memorizing faces. These are pictures of people and places David knew. I've culled them from different collections."

"How efficient you are."

"Someone has to be. There's a lot at stake if you—if we fumble this. My reputation and career, among other minor considerations."

Such as prison, but he wouldn't think of that.

He picked up the phone. "I'll order lunch. We can go through the photos as we eat."

Nick strolled over to the table. "Is it your money paying to bring David Harmony back to life, Lawrence-Whitey, or is it coming from this trust you're so concerned about?"

Confound the actor and his questions. "Room service please," he said into the phone.

Nick thumbed through the stack, pulled out a snapshot.

Lawrence, waiting to be connected, glanced at the photo. "That's the family home on Harmony Island."

The gracious Spanish Revival sprawled out behind a laughing, carefree family on a lawn framed with palms and water oaks. A photo taken before the war and long before Livvy's cancer was diagnosed, when they were still happy.

No time for nostalgia. "Room service? I need lunch sent up."

Nick kept sorting as he ordered.

When he hung up, Nick held up another picture. "What's this? A motorcar in a swimming pool?"

"Yes." He took the snapshot. "A 1931 Model A Roadster. James used it for tooling around the island. When David was eight, he drove himself and a playmate into the saltwater pool."

"I imagine he got a beating for *that*."

"I don't know. I do know James laughed like a hyena when he told me about it."

James had said, 'Little devil boasted to Megan he could drive and he proved it. He just didn't know how to stop!" He'd thrown his head back and roared till tears ran down his cheeks.

Such bittersweet memories. "James said David was as fearless as his old man, and it was a good thing both children could swim like fish. I think he was rather proud of David."

"Proud?" Nick raised his brows. "After he ruined a good motorcar?"

"James was devoted to his family. He might blow up at them occasionally, but he always got over it. He loved them very much." He put the photo down.

Nick touched it. "The people I run around with don't lean toward love or forgiveness."

Oh heavens. He'd forgotten Nick was a bastard with a mother who'd abandoned him. "Yes. Well. Ahem, let's look at the others."

As he picked up the stack, an eight-by-ten glossy slid out. Nick grabbed it before it fell. A woman wearing pearls, her reddish-brown hair braided into a coronet.

Lawrence reached for the portrait. "Don't bother with this one. I didn't mean to put it in."

"Who is she?" Nick held onto the picture.

"Megan Mulrennon, the friend in the car with David. Francis, her father, kept up James's grounds and her mother oversaw the house. He's dead, but JoBeth still manages the house. This is an engagement photo so no need to worry. Megan will soon be living in Atlanta."

Lawrence dropped his hand, then took off his suit coat and draped it over the back of a chair. He adjusted his snowy shirt sleeves and, self-conscious, started to undo his bowtie.

No. He would not let Nick's gibes get to him. He would set an example on how to dress like a gentleman. He defiantly straightened the tie.

Nick still held Megan's photo.

What was so fascinating? What was he thinking?

"Megan was nine days older than David. They were playmates from the cradle."

Nick threw the photo on the table but couldn't drag his eyes away. "You can see by looking at her that she's honest to a fault. If she realizes I'm a fake, she'll raise bloody hell."

How had Nick picked up on that? Lawrence took the photo. Grave, wide-set eyes looked into the camera. "Such perspicacity, Nick. Your reading of her is dead accurate. Very impressive."

Yes, Megan was straightforward and unwaveringly truthful. She'd never condone what he was doing. Good thing she wouldn't know. "As I said, not to worry. Megan'll be gone by then. I'll arrange for JoBeth to be away, too. They're the only ones who might trip you up."

Nick didn't protest when Lawrence put the photo away.

"Good." The angelic air returned. "I really want to know, Lawrence—"

"Whitey."

"Whitey. You keep avoiding the question. Is this interesting scheme your idea? Are you paying my fee yourself?"

Such nerve.

"That is not your concern. Your concern is learning to be David Harmony."

Nick opened his mouth.

"Your only concern." Lawrence hurried to say, "Something was off about your improvisation about the explosion, too. You referred to Robert, but everyone called him Robby."

"Robby, eh?" Nick shrugged one shoulder, a Gallic gesture no American male would use. "All right. But you can't keep me from wondering about your motives, Lawrence-Whitey."

"Wonder whatever you like. But learn your lines first."

Despite the actor's nosiness, the sessions went smoothly, and Lawrence flew home pleased.

This was going to work.

CHAPTER 8

"Pretend"
As Performed by Nat King Cole (1953)
Music by Lew Douglas, Cliff Parman,
and Frank LaVere
Lyrics by Lew Douglas, Cliff Parman,
and Frank LaVere

Coastal Georgia
June 1963

AT FIVE TWENTY, Lawrence, considerate man, stuck his head in to remind Megan she was about to miss the water taxi.

She looked up from papers on her desk. "You're joking. Is it that late?"

"Yes and rain's on its way. You'd better get a move on."

She thanked him and gathered her things. If she missed the taxi, Mom would have to bring over the runabout, and the Packs' spring visit had already run her ragged.

As Megan hurried past residential blocks to the waterfront, an east wind ripped her hair.

Great. The fancy Atlanta hairdresser, prissy man, had spent two hours teasing, pinning, and puffing lacquer over the French half-twist before she and her old law school roommate went to see *Hud*. That night, her ex-roomie advised wrapping her head in toilet tissue, then putting clean panties over it before going to bed.

"Your hair-do'll stay for a week," she'd promised.

It had stayed, all right—today was the fourth day—but it looked like it was plastered-on.

Guess she was back to her braided bun. Ten bucks—eleven with tip—down the drain. She'd use Zelda next time for two dollars total. And she wouldn't have to sleep in toilet paper.

At the city pier, moldy plough mud and marsh overlaid a faint fishy odor. Though the water taxi was moored, its motor hummed. The other regulars clustered around Cap'n Towle, so engrossed in what he was saying, they didn't notice Megan board.

"—then her doggie got loose. Hightailed it off. Pore Miz Sondra carried on something awful, skeered a gator'd eat it."

The Packs must have left the island on schedule. Good riddance. Now life could get back to normal.

Cap'n Towle didn't see her either. "Took Chauncey and Henry 'bout an hour to corner the little booger on the tennis court. Lucky it's fenced."

"Hee hee hee." The attendant for the town's Sinclair gas station, tan coverall smudged, flicked an ebony hand. His cigarette butt hit the river. "Bet Mr. Theo warn't no help."

Cap'n Towle shook his head. "Never said a word to Miz Sondra, you know how he dotes on her. But law, he was chomping at the bit with the rainclouds coming in. He'da been drinking except he was piloting. It was nigh on two o'clock afore—"

He spotted Megan. "Anyways, reckon they was glad to finally get gone." He busied himself casting off lines.

The rest sauntered away, nodding at Megan and shaking their heads at the Packs' peccadilloes.

Conversations always ended when Megan came up.

The divide between blacks and whites on Harmony Island was pronounced. People dependent on the Packs for their livelihood, and that was most of the islanders, took care what they said and did around Megan.

She was JoBeth Mulrennon's daughter, and as manager of the Big House, JoBeth reported directly to the Packs. Not that she'd misuse her authority, but people could get demoted or fired on her say-so.

Megan, who'd grown up among the islanders, respected their withdrawal but grinned at Cap'n Towle to show she didn't mind his gossip. "So the Packs got gone. Their guests, too?"

"Yep." He straightened his captain's hat and fell in behind her. "The last plane left right before Mr. Theo flew out."

"Good." She followed two women into the cabin. "I don't know about y'all, but I'm tired of unplanned fireworks going off at all hours."

The housekeeper for the bank president, clad in white bib apron, support hose, and brogans, guffawed from behind an armload of hand-me-downs she was taking home; what her grandkids couldn't wear, her mother pieced for quilts. "Lord God almighty, ain't that the truth. Wouldn't be so bad, but you can't never tell if they really are fireworks or one of 'em shooting off his gun."

Cap'n Towle went through to the wheel. The others settled on the hard benches to converse or not.

Since school was out for the summer, only a dozen or so adults rode. Like Megan, most of them held mainland jobs.

On the winding inland river, reeds in inky water rushed past. An egret stopped its fish hunt to watch Megan watching it. A couple of cormorants, barely topping the water, floated under a single line of brown pelicans swooping across the gray horizon.

Island scents and sounds of home dissolved all tension during the twenty-minute ride to the island's main pier, where Cap'n Towle's two decades at the helm nudged them against the pilings gentle as a baby's kiss. Megan collected her purse, umbrella, and shoe box containing her heels before following the stragglers onto the deck.

No salty breeze from the beach today. Just a westerly marsh wind plumped with humidity.

Rain was coming, and soon.

Her navy suit modeled after a red one of Jackie Kennedy's was about to get wet, sure as anything, and it not a month old. It was a cotton-linen blend though. Maybe water wouldn't hurt it.

"Miss Megan." Cap'n Towle, tying off ropes, checked to make sure the others had disembarked. "Don't reckon Mr. Lawrence said what's gonna happen to the island."

His anxiety arrested her. "The island?"

"When the Packs get it this fall. When Mr. Lawrence don't have no more say-so over it."

"Have you heard something?"

She knew Lawrence was worried about Theo's plans for the local businesses. But the island, too?

"No, no. We was just wondering. The Packs don't hardly ever come down 'cept for Mr. Theo's doings. They ain't ever gone live here like Mr. James did. Maybe they'll sell out."

"Oh, I doubt that."

Theo was too proud. "My island," he would boast. "My island settled by my ancestors before the Revolutionary War. Been in my family since 1765."

"No." She shook her head. "They'll keep the island."

Cap'n Towle looked skeptical.

"They will. Where would they hold their hunting parties and yacht regattas?"

That brought a laugh.

With Cap'n Towle reassured—she was good at reassuring people; sometimes too good—she checked the skies.

Better hotfoot it. She rushed past the old cow pasture used as a runway, where Theo's red Cessna and other planes had been parked the past week.

The field looked a lot better empty.

Barely six o'clock, but the grim light pretended it was closer to nine. Treetops shivered in strengthening winds. Gulls sought shelter.

That thin gray wall rising up from the river in the southwest might be mist, but it wasn't.

One large drop splattered, then another.

Time to run. She cut through her backyard and barely made the sliding glass doors before the bottom fell out.

Beyond the breakfast bar, Mom lounged in front of the console TV with a glass of iced tea at her elbow. Flickering light bathed her face. Slippered feet rested on an ottoman.

Years ago, Mom had fallen into the habit of listening to the news every night. Now TV replaced the radio: fifteen minutes local from Savannah, followed by the national Huntley-Brinkley Report.

Megan edged round a heavy bar stool. "Hi, Mom."

"Hey, sugar pie. Guess the storm's here, huh?"

"Yeah, I barely beat it."

Megan laid her things on the bar and used a toe to ease off one damp Ked, repeated the process on the other.

Mom waited till she finished. "Will you cut off the TV when you go by? My head hurts."

Worn out, poor thing. Catering to the Packs and their entourage always left her exhausted.

Megan turned off David Brinkley in the middle of a sentence. "Bad news?"

"The usual. George Wallace is still mouthing off. England wants John Profumo to resign. President Kennedy's set to sign off on the equal pay thing—"

"Good! If I get paid the same as the men, that'll boost my—"

"—and the Pope died."

"Really? I didn't think he'd been pope that long."

"Four or five years."

Mom's eyes were red and her complexion blotchy. A staunch Baptist, she wouldn't be this distraught about a dead pope.

"You've been crying. What's wrong?"

"Just exhausted after seeing Sondra and Theo off." Mom waved a crumpled handkerchief. "First she forgot her train case and sent Henry back for it. Then she realized she wasn't wearing her new sapphire bracelet. I tore that suite apart, finally found it on their bathroom's top shelf. Heaven knows what it was doing up there. Then Peachie ran away before they could board and Sondra had hysterics. The usual stuff."

"Everything's always a circus with them."

Rain dashed at the sliding doors. Lightning flashed. As a *boom* rattled windows, both women jumped.

Mom shivered. "Lord-a-mercy, it's pouring buckets."

"Yep." Mom was used to the Packs' foibles. Something else had brought on the tears. "Okay. What is it?"

"Nothing. Really. Just all this rain. I declare, it's going to plumb beat down the flowers I laid on the graves yesterday."

June marked the deaths of Robby and David and Mr. H, so Mom always decorated the cemetery.

Megan squatted down so their faces were level. "It's more than rain. Tell me."

"Oh, Meggie." Mom's face puckered. "Theo's tearing down the gazebo to put in a fountain." She twisted her handkerchief. "Livvy's rose garden will be destroyed. They already took half of it along with the croquet lawn for that silly golf course."

"Tearing down the gazebo?" Her lungs wouldn't work for a kaleidoscope of memories. Tree frogs chirping. The surf's distant pounding. David's warmth. The hard wood against her back while a radiant moon shimmered between openings in the latticework.

"Uh-huh." Mom smoothed her handkerchief. "Sondra fell in love with a fountain over there in Europe so Theo's going to surprise her with a copy. He hired some foreigner to do it, and I have to make sure it's finished before the yacht races in September."

Megan resumed breathing, slipped into the role she'd perfected. A capable, sensible, imperturbable attorney. "So this fountain's going where the gazebo is?"

"That's the plan. But the fountain's so big it'll cover what's left of the roses. The design calls for eight bushes left. Eight!" Mom sniffled. "When Livvy died, she had near two hundred."

"I'm sorry. I know how much they mean to you."

"Livvy loved that garden. We once drove to Macon for cuttings off a rose some woman's great-grandmother had brought from Ireland." Mom dabbed an eye. "My, I'm being silly."

"No, you aren't."

It was only a gazebo.

From where she knelt, Megan rubbed her mother's neck.

Fritz and Dorchester are buried there, too.

She must have spoken because her mother said, "They'll pave over them." The side of Mom's forehead touched Megan's. "No graves for the boys. Now none for their dogs."

Drat Theo. He never thought about anything but his own whims.

Not about the work he dumped on Mom. Nor about people's ties to things he bulldozed so cavalierly.

They sat, leaning together, remembering. Then Megan inhaled, stood. "What if we move the dogs to our yard? The rose bushes, too. Chauncey would do it for us, I bet. The Packs won't care."

"Here?" Mom brightened. She hopped up and went to peer through the pelting rain. "Do you think the backyard will hold what's left? We don't use it much. The dogs can go by the sun dial."

The gazebo would be gone, but why not?

It was old and dilapidated, maybe dangerous. Nothing stayed the same, so why should it?

In her room, even before unbuttoning her jacket's large buttons and taking off the A-line skirt, Megan dropped her pearls and earrings into a trinket holder on the dresser.

Her music box sat beside it, and she caressed the carved roses adorning its top.

No more gazebo.

She turned the crank. The cylinder tinkled out Chopin's "Tristesse" as she lingered before a framed black and white photo on the wall.

Snapped in 1945 with a 620 Flash Brownie Mom and Dad had given her on her twelfth birthday, it showed David and Robby standing in front of the gazebo, behind a chaise where Miss Livvy, painfully thin but smiling as though nothing was wrong, lay among budding rose bushes. Mr. H knelt to the side, holding her hand.

The Harmony boys with their father and dying mother, back on the island at the end of the war.

The morning had been mild, the sun bright and the sky blue with lamb's wool clouds. Theo, just out of the army, had helped Mr. H carry Miss Livvy outside before he went over to the mainland to pick up the new nurse.

Megan had been alone with the Harmony family.

The five of them had laughed and joked like Miss Livvy wasn't sick. Mr. H sat at his wife's feet. Megan picked her daisies. Robby brought her pretty rocks. David, home for the summer from his hated boarding school, recited parts of a Longfellow poem.

Something about a skeleton and armor. He'd brandished a stick for a sword, imitating Tyrone Power but air-carving an H instead of the Z for Zorro.

They had laughed and laughed, Miss Livvy most of all.

Now Megan was the only one to remember.

Miss Livvy had died that fall. Then the next June, her family followed. As the search for the boys dwindled, Mr. H's coffin had been lowered beside her grave.

Megan pressed her closed eyes, but funeral scenes slashed as vivid as this morning.

A dark canopy of live oaks and loblolly pines. Spanish moss drooping over chipped gravestones like mourning crepe. Mom and

Dad flanking her. Islanders and mainlanders and strangers crowding the island cemetery in tribute to Mr. H and his sons.

Theo, distraught and pacing, saying over and over, "It's all my fault. I should have made sure the boys were in bed."

Sondra in black, fragile from her vigil at Mr. H's deathbed, but already gravitating toward Theo. "Don't. You aren't to blame, Theo. You couldn't know they would disobey James."

A searcher, grim and weary, standing with Megan's father. "After four days, we'll be lucky to spot their heads. About the size of a couple of floating coconuts, they'll be."

David's beautiful head . . .

She squinched her eyes tight. Her heart cramped.

Don't think of it.

David didn't have to be so foolish. Mr. H had forbidden him to take the cruiser out at night. If only he'd listened.

But that was David. Much as she loved him, she knew what he was like. Funny and tenderhearted and persuasive. And the most headstrong, obstinate person there ever was. Telling him not to do something was the surest way to make him do it.

Ah, David, I miss you so much. If we'd run away like you begged, you wouldn't have been here to go out that night and die.

No use regretting the past.

Better change and help fix supper.

The music box chimed Strauss's carefree "Blue Danube Waltz" while she hung up her damp suit.

Stripping off stockings, she put on an old shirt and shorts to stand, deliciously free of petticoat and girdle, barefoot on pine boards. She was no longer a confident attorney but a woman wondering whether she'd made another wrong choice about Ron.

Nope.

Breaking up with him had cured her stomach aches, hadn't it? Now she didn't dread leaving home, living in Atlanta, seeing him every day.

She'd done the right thing. Sighing, she shut the music box down.

In the kitchen, remodeled after a pine crashed through the roof, Mom sliced meat. She glanced up. "Leftovers from the Big House tonight."

"Again? I'm sick of marsh hens shot by resolute hunters."

"Intoxicated hunters more like. And Bertie took the last hens with her, Miss Smarty. No, we'll feast tonight. One of 'em shot a boar yesterday. Ulie dug a pit and cooked it all night."

"Sure it wasn't somebody's hog being fattened up?" One of Theo's cronies had killed Mrs. Sipskee's milk cow last year. Theo had reimbursed the widow, but she still held a grudge. "I don't want to make anybody mad by eating their pig."

"Chauncey promised it's okay. Though he wondered why anybody would hunt marsh hens with a rifle."

"Elementary, my dear mama. Someone wanted boar."

"Or deer." The knife paused. "Meggie, do you think the Packs will sell the island?"

Megan, taking out two cobalt blue Fiesta plates, exchanged a chipped one for another. "Cap'n Towle asked me that same thing. Did Sondra say anything to you?"

"Lord-a-mercy, no. I doubt she even knows Theo's plans. It's just unsettling to everyone, wondering what's going to happen."

"Guess we'll have to wait and see." She put the plates on the breakfast bar and got out glasses and silverware.

Mom started slicing again. "The island depresses Sondra. Especially in June. Because of James and the boys. That's why she always makes sure they're gone before That Day. I think Theo hopes the fountain will pacify her. He'd like to hunt longer. If he can't, he might sell—"

That Day.

"Mr. H didn't die on the island."

That strident voice couldn't be hers.

Come on. You're a no-nonsense attorney, remember? Tone it down.

"Sondra and Theo aren't here that much."

There. She sounded like herself.

"And Theo loves playing plantation master in front of his drinking buddies. Besides, what difference would it make? This house belongs to you."

"Yes, but I can't afford not to have a job."

"I've got one. We'll be fine. Especially with this equal pay law. You know what a stickler Lawrence is for the law so I'm sure he'll put me on the same terms as the men."

Mom sighed. "You could have been in Atlanta with Ronald and my grandbabies."

"Don't start on that. Please."

"But he was so perfect for you. Both lawyers and all."

"And I'd have to sleep with him every night, see him every morning. Ugh."

Mom put down her knife. "That's what marriage is about, Meggie."

"I know. But not with Ron. Sorry. You're stuck with your old maid daughter. You should be glad I'm here to help you out with the Packs."

"The Packs," Mom hissed, unlike herself. "Sometimes I wish they'd up and fall off the face of the earth."

"Wouldn't it be nice? But nothing's going to change anytime soon. Probably not till after you retire. So stop fretting."

She wouldn't repeat Lawrence's fears about Theo selling local businesses. No need to upset Mom.

Besides, he hadn't mentioned the island.

But Theo might do away with the island amenities James Harmony had provided that Lawrence allowed to continue. The generated electricity, the water taxi, the small school Miss Livvy had started, the library, the gas pump, the clinic.

Even the island telephone system came from Harmony charity.

And Theo wasn't philanthropic. He might waste money on himself and Sondra, but forget everyone else. Why, he'd tried his best to end the educational fund the Harmonys had set up.

"Okay for white kids but colored people got no business going to college," he'd argued.

Lawrence had put the kibosh on that right quick. He was from the old school who believed a client's wishes, even a dead client, should be honored.

A shame he couldn't transfer his scruples to Theo.

Hah. Theo hated Lawrence just for making him and Sondra live within their means.

She emptied ice trays and put cubes into glasses.

Theo might be forced to sell the island someday, but even the extravagant Packs couldn't run through James Harmony's fortune in a few years.

Plenty of time to worry.

Maybe Mom had the right idea. A shame the Packs wouldn't up and disappear.

CHAPTER 9

"Big House Blues"
As Performed by the Harlem
Footwarmers (1930)
Music by Duke Ellington

FROM THE BEGINNING of 1963, Lawrence, bearing more photos, dossiers, and homemade movie reels, flew back and forth to England four times, timing his visits to coincide with Nick's days off.

At the office, he dropped a hint about another supposed claimant to the Harmony fortune but told no one about his trips to England. Everyone knew he hated planes and usually hired people to check out such contentions. Any conjecture about this one being different might warn Theo.

He didn't hide his trail though. The trips, when Theo checked later, would be explained as consultations with an agency investigating this latest pretender, the same agency that had originally dug into Nick Downing's background.

After Nick's play closed in July, he advanced the actor several thousand pounds to live on so Nick could focus all his energies on studying David Harmony's life and habitat.

When he handed over the banknotes, Nick examined him quizzically. "Aren't you afraid I'll run off with the lolly?"

By that time, he had a handle on Nick. "And lose out on the big payoff? The chance to burst onto Hollywood?"

Nick laughed. "What an astute reading of my motivation, Whitey."

Lawrence both anticipated and dreaded summer's end. But when September arrived, he was resigned, if not eager, to the irrevocable step of bringing David Harmony back to life.

The final rendezvous in London took place in yet another of the out-of-the-way hotels where he and Nick had delved into particulars, gone over facts, and perfected their story. Nick, tanned and ebullient after a Riviera holiday—on Trust money, but never mind—bounced into the room.

"Oh my." Lawrence forgot his snit about wasted money. The beach sun had bleached Nick's light brown hair to blond. Not quite as pale as David's but close. "The hair's good except for the length. You can wait till you come over to get it cut."

"Why thank you, Whitey. How gracious of you to let me wear it like this till then."

Mocking devil.

"This is the last run-through. We'll bring you in the week before to force Theo into moving right away. Any questions, problems, last-minute qualms? Speak up now."

"No. None." Nick, in jeans and oxford shirt, dropped into a chair opposite Lawrence, tipped his head back, and plopped his feet on a low stool. The inevitable smoky odor hovered. "My poor brain is crammed to bursting. I'm ready to nab Theo and be on my way to California."

Lawrence sniffed. Nick was mighty sure of himself, but he had cause. Even for an actor, his recall was amazing. He had occasionally corrected Lawrence himself on some minute item.

How fortunate Nick resembled David so much, and how more than fortunate he was intelligent.

If he'd been stupid . . .

Lawrence shuddered. He had grown almost fond of Nick during this past year.

No, not fond. Respectful. That was the word.

Not many people could lose themselves in a role the way Nick had done. The actor had become David Harmony. He was everything Lawrence could have hoped for.

Time for more photographs. "All right. Give me the name and a brief summary."

Nick groaned. "We've done this far too often."

"Last chance to brush up."

Nick removed his feet from the stool. "You're a slave driver."

He tapped the first picture. "Tell me."

"Theodore Rhodes Pack. Six years older than me." Nick picked up the snapshot. "Second cousin to Dad by virtue of their grandfathers being brothers. Theo's maternal, my father's paternal. He came to live with us when his parents died before his first year at Vanderbilt. When he enlisted in the army, Dad got him a liaison posting with our factories to keep him off the front. I admired him when I was young. Now, of course, I see him for what he is. A parasite who lucked into everything my father had."

"A bit strong, don't you think?"

Nick dropped the picture. "Don't worry, Whitey. I'll hit the perfect balance between affection and contempt."

Whitey.

Today, for some reason, David's pet name for him brought to mind a slim boy with tender mouth and merry eyes like Livvy's.

What would James have thought of the lies? What would he have made of Lawrence's actions?

James was dead. What he might have thought didn't matter.

What did matter was the future.

Either this charade would work or it wouldn't. If it failed, his life would be destroyed. If it succeeded, Theo's interfering would end.

No matter what happened, everything in his world would change. He'd made his bed.

Sensing his mood, Nick leaned over to pat his arm. "I'm an award-winning actor, Lawrence. Our plan will go over slick as butter. I promise."

As if the word of a temperamental, egotistical hoodlum could mean anything.

But he had been raised from his mother's knee to hide misgivings and publicly accept a man's assurances. Besides, he'd gone too far. He had to believe in Nick.

"I'm sure you will be excellent. After all, you have a lot of money riding on our success, don't you?"

"How well you understand me." Nick waited a beat. "You can confide in me. Who's paying the tab for our show?"

He stonewalled as he did each time Nick broached the subject. "The less you know, the better. You have your contract with my signature. If I renege, you can ruin me."

"I'm not worried about my money," came the easy denial. "Although I do wonder if it's coming from the estate and if so, whether the Packs know they're paying to prove Theo is a murderer."

"It isn't their money. Not yet. It belongs to the Trust." Confound the man. Always pushing. "You'll get paid, never fear. Let me worry about where the money's coming from."

Nick arched one brow, but Lawrence had played the silent game for years.

At length, the actor threw up his hands. "All right. Keep your secrets. Just bear in mind that I won't be happy if I'm thrown into the joint because of your schemes."

American slang in an English accent. Absurd. "You won't go to jail. You're doing nothing illegal." No, jail would be his fate and his alone if this didn't work. "Your only obligation is to be David Harmony. I suggest we use our time to tie up loose ends."

He flashed another picture.

Nick glanced at it. "Sondra Ann Sellin Harmony Pack. My dear stepmother, and a sexy bird she is."

Lawrence sputtered, choked.

Nick chuckled. "All right, Whitey. I'll be good. Father hired Sondra straight out of the army nurse corps when my mother was dying. She and Father eloped eight months after Mother's death. I figured he was lonely and so what the hell. Robby didn't like it, though. She was extravagant, but Father said it was because she'd always been poor."

Humph. Sondra's still extravagant. Both she and Theo.

But if everything went as planned, Theo would incriminate himself, and in Georgia a murderer couldn't benefit from his crime. Sondra would inherit the bulk of the Trust, and without Theo's influence she'd be amenable to guidance. He could salvage something of James's legacy once Theo was out of the way.

Not that he'd admit any of this to Nick. Sondra without Theo would be a vulnerable, wealthy woman, and she attracted men like a honey pot drew bees.

Including amoral men like Nick.

Best not to give him any ideas.

"All right." He picked up a snapshot of a pretty teenager in a sailor blouse and slacks. "Let's try this one."

"My first girl friend, Rochelle Tollison. Daughter of our mainland plant manager. I'll have to wing the physical aspects of their relationship since we don't know how involved she and David were."

The dead quiet of the hotel room emphasized his severity. "You're David."

"How involved she and I were. Sorry, Whitey."

He bit his lip.

Oh dear. Would—could!—this insane scheme work? One slip, one lapse and the charade would be over. Then he would be disbarred and ridiculed along with being indicted. His family would be disgraced. The firm his grandfather had founded would go under.

He must have been mad. If only he'd never seen Nick's photograph.

Maybe he should call it off.

No. He couldn't.

His blood pressure rose every time he thought of that idiot Theo bleating about his attorneys looking into sloppy fiscal oversight once he got the estate.

Lawrence squared his shoulders.

Far too late to turn back. Maybe it had been too late from the moment he'd seen David's lookalike in that *Life* magazine.

Nick, exemplary after his lapse, rattled off more names and information as they sorted through friends and servants linked to the Harmony family seventeen years before.

"Good. Very good." He started putting away the photos.

Nick reached over to the stack and plucked out a snapshot of

Megan and David on the water taxi. They leaned over the rail, Megan's braids falling over her shoulders.

"What about the Mulrennons? You said Megan didn't get married as expected. You've made arrangements to get her out of the way? And her mother?"

"Yes. JoBeth will be on an extended vacation with her sister for the critical period."

"And Megan? David's best friend from nappies on?"

"*Your* best friend."

One side of Nick's mouth lifted. "*My* best friend."

Lawrence sighed. Too many slips, too many uncertainties.

"Megan won't be there when I show up, will she?"

Beneath the idle question, Lawrence scented a subtle change. Was that anxiety?

It was. Ah, so some things could bother the actor.

"No. The firm is sending Megan to a retreat seminar. She leaves the day before you arrive and will be incommunicado for a week." He didn't like the way Nick kept studying Megan's picture. "No need to worry."

"I'm only concerned that I don't meet her."

"You won't. This particular class promises total seclusion. No newspapers, no radio, no television, and no telephones. She won't hear a thing till she gets back."

Nick gave his lazy smile. "Perfect."

Lawrence startled himself by bursting out with, "If only this was over with."

Nick lounged in the overstuffed chair with the virtuous air that made him seem so innocent and unassuming. "Why, Whi-teee," he drawled, his voice sheer silk. "It's going to be a hoot, don't you know?"

Humph. Lawrence didn't know anything of the sort.

CHAPTER 10

"It Keeps Right On A-Hurtin'"
As Performed by Johnny Tillotson (1962)
Music by Johnny Tillotson
Lyrics by Johnny Tillotson

Harmony Island
Off the Georgia Coast
September 22, 1963

THE MULRENNONS' DOCK lay shadowed as the sun emerged from its bed to begin a lazy climb over the Atlantic.

Megan, carrying her mother's luggage to the runabout, stepped from early morning light onto shaded rough planks where the small boat rocked gently at its mooring. Fresh red paint masked the runabout's age, but the Evinrude motor was brand new.

When she set down the big suitcase and climbed into the boat with the overnighter, a cormorant lighted on a nearby post and spread its wings to dry, all the while eyeing Megan.

"Hoping for an easy fish? Sorry, guy." Hefting the suitcase into the boat, she stowed it by the overnighter between the seats. "Come on, Mom! You'll miss the train!"

Good thing she'd worn Levis and a windbreaker. The breeze ruffling her hair was cool.

Her mother, who had stopped to paw through her pocketbook, waved papers aloft triumphantly. "My airline tickets. I thought I'd lost them. I still can't believe it. Sadie and me in Europe. It's like a dream. I just hope the Packs can manage while I'm—"

"You and Aunt Sadie will have a blast," Megan cut in. Given half a chance, Mom's misplaced sense of obligation would convince her to stay. "But not if you miss the train."

Mom danced over the boardwalk. "We've got plenty of time, Miss Early Bird." She flapped a hand. "We can even eat breakfast at the diner before you drop me off at the station."

"I hope so." Megan pushed the runabout against the pilings so Mom, in Sunday dress and flats for the boat, could step in. "You're going to have a long day. Worse if you miss breakfast."

Mom grimaced. "Sure enough. All day on a train to Atlanta. But

Sadie'll meet me, and tomorrow!" She squealed. "Tomorrow we'll fly off to Paris. My first plane ride and it's to Paris."

"Look out, Europe. Here come the Hayseed Sisters."

"Sounds like sour grapes to me."

Megan laughed. "I'm teasing. You deserve this."

Once JoBeth settled on the front bench seat and straightened the old-fashioned cloche perched on newly permed waves—Mom believed train rides called for hats and gloves—Megan reversed the runabout until they were clear of the dock.

As they entered the saltwater inlet and the marshes that lined it, she relaxed. No need to listen as Mom went over instructions repeated every day for the past months, ever since Lawrence had first broached the cruise.

White clouds in blue sky made a picture-perfect Sunday. She let the motor hum and watched the line of pelicans zigzag over the reeds.

If George hadn't gone home sick Friday, she would have taken tomorrow off.

Just like him to get a stomachache and spoil her plans.

Come on, it wasn't poor George's fault. And it was more than an achy stomach. He'd run to the restroom four times before he left.

"Did you hear me?" JoBeth slid round on the front seat to peer back. "There are casseroles in the freezer so you won't starve. I do hope Bertie can manage the Big House. I feel bad, going at such a busy—"

"Mom, Sondra assured you they'll be fine. You just have a good time and don't worry."

"You won't forget the cemetery?"

"No, Mom. I'll put flowers there on Robby's birthday just like always."

"Make sure you do. You know, Sondra and Theo were really nice about the trip once Lawrence explained the situation." Mom snorted. "Though I'm surprised they'd care he'd be out so much money if nobody went."

"Sondra told me it's a way to thank you. Without you, the whole island would go under."

"But all their yachting friends will be here next week. And tropical storms are brewing in the Bahamas. What if there's a hurricane?"

"Mom. Really. A hurricane hasn't hit here in over fifty years. If one hits, it hits. There's nothing anybody can do about it. As for the guests, the Packs always hire extra staff. And Bertie's been here forever. She knows what needs to be done better than you."

"I know, sugar pie. You're right."

"Stop worrying."

"I'll try." Mom turned around to rummage in her purse. "Did I remember my gloves? Yes, thank the Lord." She flourished them, then scrunched up her face, exulting. "Lord-a-mercy, I never dreamed I'd be taking a trip like this. And with Sadie. Wasn't it sweet of Lawrence to think of us when his daughter and son-in-law couldn't go?"

"No refunds so someone might as well use the tickets. But yes, it was kind of him."

"Flying to Paris, then eighteen days on a ship. A luxury liner. Why, I'll be so cosmopolitan when I get back, you won't recognize me."

"Hoity-toity."

"Why, Megan. I think someone's jealous."

Megan laughed. "Maybe a little. If Lawrence hadn't booked me for this seminar, I could have gone with you instead of Aunt Sadie. Never mind. I'm looking forward to Salt Lake City."

Behind them the sun gained strength. The sour marshes didn't quite hide the tang of salt. With a brisk east wind, the inland waters were rough enough that Megan clung to the tiller.

On the mainland, they stowed JoBeth's bags in Megan's six-year-old Golden Hawk Studebaker before going to the diner.

Inside, a city councilman and the mayor nodded at them from a table in the back. Megan waved but chose a front booth with scarred plastic seats overlooking the pier. They watched the bobbing boat masts as the waitress brought coffee.

Mom sipped at hers. "Ruby told me Clive Ankeson asked you out the other day."

Nuts. "Yep."

The waitress returned to take orders, but Megan, opting for bacon, eggs, and grits, knew Mom wouldn't drop it.

Sure enough, as soon as the waitress sashayed away, Mom asked, "Are you going to go out with him?"

"Nope. I saw him kick a dog once."

"Oh, Meggie." Mom forced a smile. "You know best. As long you're happy."

Long after she waved her mother off at the train pulling out of the station, long after she drove back to the garage at the pier where the Studebaker stayed, even after she tied up the runabout at their own dock, Megan kept hearing her mother's last words.

As long as you're happy.

She was.

Being assigned this Utah trip proved how successful her work was. And she'd chosen to be an old maid, turning down three chances. There was no reason not to be happy.

On the way up to the house, she paused at the garden sundial where Chauncey had reburied David and Robby's dogs amid Miss Livvy's rescued rose bushes.

"Lucky Mr. H and Miss Livvy were planted in the island cemetery or the Packs'd be digging 'em up and moving them, too," Chauncey had joked when he transplanted the bushes.

Mom kept the roses trimmed and blooming, a memorial to the boys. Other than the music box, the roses and graves were all she had left to mourn David.

If only he hadn't taken the boat out that night.

But he had. And he was gone. No matter how her heart ached, nothing would change that.

****

"Brokenhearted Melody"
As Performed by Sarah Vaughan (1959)
Music by Sherman Edwards
Lyrics by Hal David

ON TUESDAY AFTERNOON, two days after seeing her mother off, Megan's airplane from Savannah set down smoothly at the three-year-old Atlanta Municipal Airport terminal. With an hour to kill before the plane to Salt Lake City left, she headed for the ladies' room where she weighed the merits of free toilets against pay ones.

A woman emerged from a pay stall and held the door open. "Go on in, honey. If they charge us a dime to pee, I'm gonna darn sure get my money's worth."

Megan laughed. "Thanks," she said as she went in.

Later, hands washed and dried, she stopped at the long mirror in front to survey herself. Pearls at throat and ears. Neat gray suit. Leather purse. Businesslike except for the baby face.

She might be thirty-three, but she always had to show a driver's license to get into night clubs.

Nor did her unruly hair help her appearance. No matter how she plaited and pinned her chignon, tendrils still escaped. She tucked them back, wishing she had listened to Mom and worn a hat.

Tugging down the three-quarter sleeves of her suit coat, she twisted to check her calves in the mirror. Was that a hint of white under her kick pleat? Yep. She adjusted her petticoat. There. The very picture of a poised professional.

She owed Lawrence. Usually the men went to seminars, and she stayed in the office. True, Utah wasn't New York or San Francisco, but Salt Lake City was a big deal to her.

Other than her senior trip to Washington, D.C., and Florida or

Alabama vacations, she'd never been out of Georgia. This was only her second airplane ride, the first taking place when she'd visited an old college friend in Huntsville a couple of years back.

Checking her wristwatch, she gasped.

Oops. Later than she'd thought. Better find her gate. No time for stomach queasiness.

Back in the terminal, she merged into the scurrying throng. Blaring loudspeakers, lively conversations, hurried footsteps. All the energy of a place for arrivals and departures charged the air. Smells of hot dogs and popcorn nauseated her.

Nerves. She needed to settle down.

She refused to get sick.

Not after Lawrence had chosen her for this retreat instead of one of the men. The attorney hired a year after her had gone ape when he heard. "Bet if I filled out a sweater like you, they'd send me on a seminar, too."

Toad. She worked as hard as he did, harder because she was a woman. But jealousy was the least of her worries.

As long as you're happy, her mother had said.

That was the main thing, wasn't it? Her career was coming along. She'd built a modest client list. Here she was, taking a jet to a seminar retreat across the country.

Things were going fine without a man, thank you very much.

There was her gate.

She spotted him sitting on the floor by the wall and froze.

David!

Someone slammed into her from behind. She stumbled, recovered, and brushed off the angry woman's rebuke. Noise around her abated. She might have stood in a vacuum.

He wore aviator sunglasses, a button-down madras shirt, and jeans. His head lolled back against the wall as if he was asleep. A worn duffel bag lay beside him. Under the flat fluorescents, hair barely darker than new corn gleamed. His chin, his mouth were just as she recalled.

Megan, oblivious to the crowds swirling past, couldn't breathe.

Finally, the sounds in the terminal pushed at her. People hurrying by jostled her. Someone's strong perfume sickened her.

She remembered where she was and shuddered.

You turkey. It's not him. It's never him. It can't be him.

Her mind knew this, but her heart always leaped when a man with a certain build, a certain color hair crossed her path.

Tightening her grip on her briefcase and purse, she turned her back to the stranger and found a seat in her gate's waiting area. Taking long slow breaths calmed her.

She was fine. Or was she?

After David's death, she'd recovered by making plans for college, law school, a job. But now she felt lost.

If the Packs sold Harmony Island, Mom talked about moving closer to Aunt Sadie.

Megan wouldn't go; too many memories were tied up on the island. If Mom sold their house, she'd have to find a place on the mainland. Then who would she have for company? Cats?

She didn't want to grow old alone. She wanted a family.

If only she could have married Ron.

But she couldn't. Nor any of the others. Three times she had ended an engagement because of some deficiency within her, some defect she couldn't change.

Losing David had done that to her.

Mom's right. I expect too much from a man.

No one could measure up to a lover who was dead. Not that she was sure she could give any man what he would expect anyway. Total obeisance to somebody because he was male . . . Hah! That was for the birds.

She really would end up like Miss Millicent India Asbury, living with ten cats and changing her will every six months.

Oh, flitter. There were worse things.

Like throwing up. She stood when an attendant opened the boarding chain and people started filing past. Her stomach threatened to upchuck.

Ugh. She shouldn't have worn this dratted girdle.

The flight evolved into a nightmare.

By the time the plane landed at Salt Lake City Municipal Airport, she was on first-name terms with the tiny lavatory and could barely stagger into the terminal without collapsing.

Not airsickness. She couldn't stop puking even on land.

Drat George. She'd caught his stomach bug.

One thing was for sure. She was in no shape to get on the bus for the retreat.

A kind taxi driver took her to a nearby hotel where she spent the next day retching in the toilet or passed out in bed.

Her first trip for the firm.

Whoopee.

CHAPTER 11

"Nobody Knows You When
You're Down and Out"
As Performed by Bessie Smith (1929)
Music by Jimmy Cox
Lyrics by Jimmy Cox

WEDNESDAY, WHILE MEGAN lay sick in Salt Lake City, Lawrence boarded a motor launch to Harmony Island and the Big House.

He'd been in and out of the Spanish Revival mansion frequently when James Harmony was alive, but the island had changed under the Packs' jurisdiction; it had become a place best avoided.

When the golf cart brought him up from the pier, they passed some kind of immense rococo fountain where once the fragrance and colors of Livvy's treasured rose garden had flourished. The mansion's interior had been gutted and redone after Sondra and Theo married. Now the outside grounds reflected their tastes, too. There was little left of James and Livvy.

Nostalgia vied with anticipation as he climbed the front steps.

This was it.

He should be on tenterhooks, not anxious to tell Theo he wouldn't inherit. Not exhilarated.

When the maid directing him to the library grinned broadly, Lawrence blinked, startled; she was responding to a smile he hadn't even been aware of.

He wiped it off. No need to seem too chipper.

In the library, the Packs and their attorneys, John Wilkins and Amos Lovett, waited.

Four days earlier Theo had landed on the island air strip so he and Sondra could prepare for their annual yacht races. At Lawrence's request, the other two men had flown in yesterday. All displayed beaming faces that rivaled the one Lawrence had discarded.

Humph. Expecting to work on details of receiving the Trust. Were they in for a shock.

Sondra perched on the leather sofa with her small poodle, Theo and Amos on either side of her. John claimed a matching club chair.

Lawrence laid his briefcase on the library table but remained standing, disdaining the last chair. He did straighten his tie.

Best to be blunt.

He drew out the photograph, exhibited it so all could see. "This man came forward last year claiming he's David Harmony. I'm happy to say it's true. He really is our David."

The lilt to his voice sounded real. He projected total confidence. *Heaven forgive me.*

Shocked silence; then John Wilkins sat up straight. "You can't be serious!"

Amos Lovett jumped up. "What the hell do you mean?"

Blood rushed into Theo's face. "I don't believe you."

Only Sondra remained composed.

As mayhem broke out around her, her dog whimpered and tried to scramble out of her arms. She shushed it.

Theo jumped up to rant and curse so that he drowned Amos's excited demands.

John rose more slowly, pulling at his partner. "Calm down, Amos, Theo. We can't hear if you don't quiet down. Let's find out what's going on before we besiege Lawrence."

After he succeeded in hushing the other men, he donned his lawyer's expression, blank and wary. "Please go on, Lawrence. What led you to such a, such an extraordinary conclusion?"

"Ahem." The air, crackling with enmity, charged up the old fires. Lawrence had never shied from confrontations. "Though the dental work is not identical, considering work done over seventeen years, it is consistent. And the fingerprint evidence is quite clear. Here." Still standing, he pulled out a paper and pushed it across the table. "See for yourselves."

The attorneys leaned over as Theo crowded behind them.

"I think, John, Amos, Theo." He looked across to the sofa. "And Sondra. From these photocopy blow-ups, even inexperienced laymen such as ourselves can find identical points between fingerprints the sheriff took from the boys' rooms after the accident and this man's prints taken last year when he came forward. Other than the scar on the right index finger, they match those of David Harmony perfectly."

Theo strained to see over his attorneys' shoulders. A giant of a man, he was normally genial. Not now. "A hoax. If it was anyone but you, Lawrence, I'd call you a crook. As it is, someone's playing you for a fool. David's dead." He slapped the table. "Dead!"

Amos kept looking at the papers. "Everyone knows that. This has to be a mistake."

John said, "Let's hear Lawrence out."

"Ahem. Your sentiments are quite understandable, Theo. I felt exactly like you at first. We've had many imposters since the accident claiming to be one of the boys. Most of them we could dismiss immediately. Others took longer. None were legitimate."

He had sat with James in the library of the Harmony mansion countless times before it became so alien. The Packs had sacrificed three walls of books to Theo's hunting trophies and a well-stocked bar, so that only one small bookcase gave credence to the room's name. James would have been annoyed.

Today, dead eyes of the stuffed animal heads looked down at Lawrence accusingly.

What if he was doing the wrong thing? What if, in his zeal, he had erred? What if James would disapprove?

No, James would understand. Surely he would.

Lawrence had not been a good caretaker. Lord knew he was no businessman. He hadn't the knowledge or personality to run James's companies, but he couldn't let Theo destroy James's legacy.

And Theo could have killed those boys. Right now, he looked capable of anything.

Too late for second thoughts. Nick would arrive tomorrow.

He shifted from one foot to the other. "I dispatched an underling to get this man's fingerprints last year, certain he was another imposter. When I compared them, I was shocked and launched an investigation. I still believed it a hoax. Then I interviewed the man myself, asking about his childhood, about the island, about his parents, trying to trip him up. I could not."

He pulled a thick folder from his briefcase. "The details are here. David's life is accounted for by independent sources from after the boat explosion till now."

John took the folder. "Independent sources?"

"Yes. They don't corroborate every part of his story, but neither do they disprove it. I don't understand why he stayed away for so long, but with the evidence, the only possible conclusion is that this man is David Harmony."

"Bullshit." Theo snatched the enlarged fingerprint copies, wadded them up, and threw them, barely missing Lawrence's forehead.

He was too surprised to flinch.

Theo's eyes glittered. "David is dead." After the temper fit, his calm was unnatural. "He and Robby are both dead. I know it and you know it, Lawrence. What're you trying to pull?"

Lawrence, erect in his five-year-old gray suit his late wife had bought in Savannah from Belk-Beery's during their annual half-price sale, straightened his bowtie.

He needed every ounce of authority he could summon.

"A man who says he's David Harmony, who can recite intimate

family details, who looks like David, talks like David, writes like David, whose teeth could belong to David, and whose fingerprints match David's, is here for his inheritance. I've no alternative but to give it to him."

John started. "Give it to him?"

Lawrence began to repack his briefcase. "On October second."

"That's next Wednesday!" Amos protested.

"I have no choice. The man is David Harmony."

"I'll hire my own investigators." Theo Pack clenched his hands. "Amos, get started on that right now. John, get stuff together for a lawsuit. This sonofabitch isn't going to get a penny of my money."

John wiped his forehead. "We don't want to rush into anything, Theo, but we'll certainly make our own inquiries. In the meantime, there can certainly be no question of turning the estate over to anyone until the man's identity is clearly established. Lawrence—"

"I've spent the past year establishing his identity to my satisfaction." Lawrence snapped his briefcase shut. "The Trust will be turned over to him next week."

"Oh, come now," Amos said. "This is outrageous."

"What about blood tests?" John asked.

"You'll find details about all that in your paperwork. David's blood was never typed so far as we could find, but James's was O positive. Theo was kind enough to give us a blood sample last February. It was also O positive. The same as this man's."

"That sample was meant to prove my relationship to James!" The deception incensed Theo. "You told me the test was to close any loopholes!"

"I told you we wanted to cover all possibilities in case another claimant came forward to contest the division of the estate," Lawrence said. "I didn't tell you a claimant had already come forward because, back then, I still wasn't convinced he was legitimate."

Theo started around the table. "You goddamned crook! You knew all the time this stinking bastard was trying to horn in on my money? What's he promised? To leave you in charge of the estate so you can keep using it for your personal bankroll?"

"Theo!" his attorneys said in unison. Both caught his arms, held him back.

Theo tried to shake them off. "I know damn well he's spent Trust money! *My* money!"

"Theo, calm down," John said.

Lawrence tugged at his bowtie. What a good thing the table was wide and solid.

"Theo! Baby, please."

Sondra, who'd shot up at her husband's outburst, held her dog in one arm and laid the other manicured hand on Theo's chest. Large diamond ear studs with a matching pendant and bracelet contrasted with her casual tennis outfit.

Thank heavens Theo heeded her.

Sondra, unrefined and with trite interests, wasn't a woman Lawrence esteemed. Her kitten face always reminded him of an actress who'd died during World War II. Carole somebody or other.

But she had courage, to confront Theo like this. A shame she had no class.

Stroking Theo's arm, she said, "This is no time to lose control, baby. You're saying things you don't mean. We must figure out what to do, not blame poor Lawrence."

"He *is* to blame!" Theo glared, but she kept hold of him, murmuring soothingly until he got himself under control.

When he broke away to go to the bar, she shivered and clutched her poodle.

"Lawrence, you must wait before you do anything." John, the more intelligent of Theodore's attorneys, stayed on track. "There's no reason you can't delay distribution until we do a thorough search into this man's background."

Lawrence kept an eye on Theo; the man might erupt any second. "Go through the reports, John. We've researched the man's story thoroughly. There are no inconsistencies. He is David Harmony, and I've reapportioned the Harmony Trust on that basis."

"That seems premature. The courts should decide whether or not you need to reapportion," John said.

"Fine. I'm confident the evidence will hold up in court." He hid his satisfaction at being able to add, "Of course, if you choose to go that route, you remember that I, as directed by James's will, have complete power to determine who has use of what part of estate income."

Theo splashed something into a glass.

You'll need more than one drink today.

"Theo, your and Sondra's individual trusts will provide you with ample funds. You may have to adjust your lifestyle, but you won't starve. David will, of course, begin drawing the estate interest you and Sondra have used until now."

Anger mottled Theo's face. He put his glass down and took a step with fisted hands. "My money? This is—"

"Don't, Theo," John said sharply.

Lawrence took a step back as Sondra almost threw the dog down. Her getting between him and Theo saved him from a physical attack.

"Ahem. You'll be happy to learn David isn't asking for repayments of monies already disbursed." He gazed out the large windows toward the sea to mask anxiety.

Sondra might be plucky enough to stand up to Theo, but he could easily throw her aside. John and Amos certainly wouldn't come to his rescue. "You will vacate all houses for David's immediate possession, but he's kind enough to allow you use of any residence except this one. He's being most—"

Sondra clung to Theo. Her dog's barking almost drowned out his shouting. "My ancestors settled this island! I'm not giving it up to some asshole claiming he's David."

"—magnanimous, considering the circumstances." Lawrence ignored dog and man, picked up his briefcase. "I'll leave you all to discuss it. John and Amos can explain my position."

Sondra said, "Please, Theo."

Theo breathed heavily but finally shook off her hand and headed toward his glass.

She turned to Lawrence. "I'll see you out. Come, Peachie."

They barely made it out the door before Theo started up again. "Amos, you gutless piece of shit. Both of you! What use are you if—"

Hah. Theo's so-called friends were already hedging their bets. Almost enough to make him cackle.

If he weren't so worried.

As she led him through the hall to the front, Theo's harangue faded through the plastered walls.

They passed into sunshine painting the veranda, its light revealing fine lines in Sondra's neck at odds with the lithe figure under the tennis dress.

Despite having no fondness for her, he softened. "It will all work out, my dear."

Her chuckle was dry. "Do you think so? Theo's been so excited, planning what to do with the money. This is a shock."

"Naturally, it is. It's to be expected."

"I know." She bent down, picked up the little dog. "But it's quite a big shock."

He pitied her, unusual for him where Sondra Pack was concerned. He patted her hand with its pretty rings. "Things will work out."

Her faint smile recognized the empty comfort. "I wish I could believe that, Lawrence."

He wished he could believe it, too.

Mentally drained, he left. The brief triumph from pointing out that he, as sole trustee, controlled the Harmony estate fled along with his feigned confidence.

Nick Downing would arrive tomorrow.

After that, anything could go wrong.

The actor could fail in his role. Lawrence's own part in the charade would be exposed. He'd be disgraced, ruined, disbarred—maybe go to jail—and the firm his grandfather had founded would be ostracized or dissolved. His children and grandchildren would be devastated.

Was he doing the right thing? Was gambling on Nick wise?

When the ferrying speedboat dropped him off at the mainland pier, he welcomed the sight of Curtis waiting with the Lincoln.

They rode beneath great live oaks to his office as the stench from the paper mill crept into the car. Visitors hated the odor, but to locals it meant jobs and money to feed families.

All due to James, who had seen a way to take advantage of access to yellow pine forests and easy shipping offered in the area.

"I remember after the Great War," he said to Curtis. "Before the steel plant and paper mill and cloth factory were here. This was farm country with few jobs."

Curtis turned the wheel smoothly. "Mam talks about those days sometimes."

Young people were always so indifferent to the past. Curtis, caught up in Dr. King's dreams after attending the march on Washington last month, cared more about the national scene than the local.

Ah well, the boy was bright enough to get into Yale's law school.

A shame he was too green to appreciate how James had shaped the region and country.

Lawrence had helped, too, in his own small way. James ignored Lawrence's advice as often as he took it, but he would always clasp Lawrence around the shoulder and say, "You're the only honest lawyer I personally know, Whitey."

The joke originated the day James strode into his office after quarreling with the Atlanta attorneys dealing with old Mickey Harmony's estate. "I need an honest lawyer to help handle my inheritance, Lawrence." James had looked him straight in the eye. "Is there such a thing?"

He'd been affronted at the time. Now . . .

What would James think if he were here today?

Damn and blast. I'm getting old.

Nowadays change distressed him, making it harder to accept. He hoped he was not too old for what lay ahead. If only James were here to advise him, to bulldoze over his fears and prod him into action.

James had thrived on challenges.

Seven days until October second. Seven days in which he would have to be extra careful, extra watchful.

Though not as careful as Nick Downing.

Theo had looked murderous when he learned David Harmony had shown up.

Absolutely murderous.

A *frisson* ran up Lawrence's spine and culminated in a little smile that couldn't be restrained.

Such a good thing Curtis was too busy driving to notice.

CHAPTER 12

"With These Hands"
As Performed by Jo Stafford
and Nelson Eddy (1951)
Music by Abner Silver
Lyrics by Benny Davis

FROM THEO'S SIX foot five inches, puny John Wilkins looked like a sour pygmy.

Stupid little ratface. He shouldn't take it out on John and Amos, but dammit! He was angry. So fricking angry. Not since he was a child had he been this angry.

Amos, tall enough to look him in the eye like a man rather than a grumpy dwarf, had retreated to the bar.

Drinking when he ought to be planning.

"Sit down, Theo," John said. "And calm down."

Dyspeptic asshole. He couldn't be as good a lawyer as Amos boasted, not after the way he'd dealt with Lawrence.

Or not dealt with him, the chicken-hearted bastard. "Calm down? Lawrence brings in a goddam imposter and you want me to calm down?"

"Now, now Theo." Amos added vermouth to gin for martinis. "Don't flip your wig."

He whirled. "Amos. How many men have shown up in the past claiming to be David or Robby? Fifty? A hundred? There's no way in hell David could be alive."

Amos let the stirrer clang. "You'd think not. Damn poor timing, you ask me."

Behind him, John sniffled.

Theo curled his lip.

John's nose had been running ever since they'd gone out on the new Ski Nautique this morning. Spindly-legged namby-pamby who didn't know Dick Pope from Toni Sailer. Only reason Ratface came down was to take care of all the paperwork for Amos.

Yeah, and Ratface can't wait to get his hands on my money.

John and Amos. Both of them had been all smiles, all assurances. They'd invest his money. They'd audit every transaction of Lawrence's dealings with the Trust. They'd look after everything.

Now they'd fricking better start doing it.

"Still, Lawrence does have proof." Amos looked up. "You want a drink, Theo?"

"No!"

Goddam Amos. He was as much use as tits on a boar.

Theo paced, breathed in and out. His head was about to explode. He had to get hold of himself.

Try persuasion.

"Look. Even if David by some miracle survived that fire and then the ocean, he would have come to me. I was like his brother. Hell's bells, Amos, use your head."

"Oh yeah, he would have come to you." Amos dropped into an easy chair across from John and tossed back his drink. "Helluva situation though, with fingerprints and all."

Shit, Amos acted like this was nothing! Like he was some disinterested onlooker.

And why not? Amos had inherited money and a place in his father's law firm. He had nothing to lose from some jerk pretending to be David.

From their days together at Vanderbilt, Theo knew Amos's intelligence was not above average. But like him, Amos was a great sportsman. And his trusted friend.

Now it looked like his *friend* was an idiot. He was sure no help now.

"Why didn't you call Lawrence's bluff instead of sitting there like a lump? I hired you to take care of my interests, not to let a country bumpkin run over you."

Amos widened his eyes. "We'll do our utmost for you, Theo, but if this fingerprint evidence holds up—"

John blew his nose. "If Wykerton says the fingerprints are David's, they are. Everyone knows he goes by the book."

Theo ground his teeth, blood pounding.

Amos, smoothing recently clipped hair, didn't notice. "I don't see that we have a case. From all the times we've gone over the will, trying to get Lawrence out of the picture—and he may be a country lawyer but he's damn clever—I can tell you he's right about one thing." He gestured with his empty glass. "He has absolute say-so over the Trust. Including your allowance."

"Screw Lawrence Wykerton. By God, I'm so sick of that oily bastard, I'd like to wring his neck. He knows I'm turning everything over to your firm. Can't you see he's brought this man in to keep control of the money?"

John hopped up, pocketing his handkerchief. His big nose twitched. "I advise you not to repeat that. Basis for slander."

A red haze rose. The stinking rat. Theo took a step. "He's brought in a fricking fake!"

John winced but held his ground.

Theo almost hit him. Instead, he grabbed up an antique side chair and smashed it over the library table.

Wood splintered. Papers and pens flew into the air.

"A goddam fake!"

He swept everything left on the table onto the floor.

Amos gaped.

John did, too.

Good. He liked seeing John frightened. He'd still like to punch the shitty little rodent.

Sondra, at the door giving Peachie to Janie, gasped. Tan legs flashed as she rushed over. "Baby, baby! Don't. We know he's a fake and we're going to prove it. We'll hire detectives."

"We most certainly will," John quickly said.

Ratface had paled, the sniveling coward. He ought to poke him in the eye.

Theo shook off Sondra's hand and went to the bar.

She addressed the others. "If he's really David, there's no discussion about what to do. But if he's another adventurer hoping to cash in on our heartbreak . . . It's a question of protecting our interests. Amos, John, you do understand our concerns, don't you?"

So diplomatic, so poised. Christ, he loved her.

He poured himself a martini.

"Of course we do." Amos went over to hug her.

Theo snorted. The fool had always lusted after her, even during both his marriages. He and Sondra laughed about it.

"And we share your concerns," John put in. Ratface was partial to Sondra, too, though not so blatant as Amos. "I can't tell you how sorry I am you have to go through this."

Men flirted with Sondra, hanging onto her every word. No reason to get annoyed.

Except today he was. After all he'd done to get her, he couldn't stomach this.

"Dammit, I've got to get out of here."

Before he lost it and beat them both to a pulp.

He heard Amos as he went out the patio doors.

"Jesus H. Christ. I've never seen old Theo act like—"

Maybe you don't know old Theo as well as you think. Ever consider that, friend Amos?

Away from them, on the sunny steps leading around to the front pool, he tossed back the martini and set the glass on a marble pillar.

If he had to listen one more second to those two pompous assholes talk about what they could and couldn't do, he'd explode.

Christ. Their faces when he'd busted the chair. You'd have thought he killed somebody.

Memories flashed: David's slack form; Robby, neck twisted, lying on the floor.

He almost gagged.

Calm down, calm down. Think about what to do, not what you did.

John and Amos.

He paid those cretins good money to guard his interests, but it wasn't their money at stake here. It was his. He could see the handwriting on the wall.

The rational part of him murmured: *You may have to kill him.*

No! He'd killed the boys, but that was in the past. He didn't want to kill anyone else.

Christ, he couldn't go through that again. There had to be another way to fix it.

He lit a cigarette and leaned against a life-sized nymph statue beside the pool.

The smell of new-mown grass overpowered the usual chlorine. A faint scent of ocean wafted in on a breeze. Seagulls flew overhead.

This would have been a perfect day for sailing or going out with his bow. Maybe shooting some doves.

Ruined now.

The cigarette was half-finished when Sondra came out.

"Theo? Are you okay?"

"Sure."

"I've never seen you like that before. I've never known you to be so out of control. You scared me." She looped her arm through his and leaned against his shoulder with an easy familiarity that today seemed especially poignant.

He caressed her hair with one hand before taking a drag. "I've never had the rug pulled out from under me before."

"We have to talk about what to do."

"There's nothing to talk about."

It wasn't fair. After all his work, all his planning and contriving. The boys had been blown to bits. They were dead. He just needed a way to prove it.

People thought him stupid, but he wasn't. Slow, maybe, but not stupid. And nerve and determination more than made up for slowness. He'd proved it seventeen years ago.

That was how long he'd waited for James's money.

"Theo."

"It'll be all right. I'm not about to let us lose out at the last minute. Not because of a scheming country lawyer."

He'd contained his temper. No more need to rip out at someone, something.

Time to plan. For himself and Sondra.

"I hate to see your pretty face so worried." He traced the worried lips. "It'll be all right."

"You promise?"

"I promise." Like he'd promised so long ago to take care of her. He kissed the corner of her mouth. "Have I ever broken a promise to you?"

"No," she murmured. "Never."

When James had sent him to pick up Livvy's nurse from the mainland, he'd expected a drill sergeant. Instead, he'd found an angel with eyes that promised him the world.

Until Sondra, life had been bland. He'd dropped out of Vanderbilt to enlist after Pearl Harbor, but James's string-pulling made him a liaison with Harmony plants and factories.

Not what he wanted, though he changed his mind pretty quick after seeing the crippled vets return.

If he'd died in the war, he'd never have met Sondra.

Christ, how young they'd been. Him twenty-two, her twenty-four. Two kids with impossible dreams he'd made come true. For her.

She still turned heads, but his obsession was no longer a frenzy. The years had bonded them closer than ever.

Some people thought their marriage was based on convenience, an effort to free up the Trust, but they were wrong. Their connection was far stronger than money.

She belonged to him. Like everything else James had owned.

The island, the houses in Palm Beach and Washington.

Sometimes he imagined his life if things had been different. He'd have kept working in the plant, plodding along like all the other poor fools. The boys would have grown up, still looking up to him.

But he'd have lost Sondra. He'd had to kill them to get James's money and her. If only James had left a conventional will, the arrogant shitass. Leave it to James to screw everything up.

There had to be a way around Lawrence's latest ploy. If not, he'd have to . . .

God, he couldn't do it. Not again.

"What are you thinking?" Sondra moved to lean against the statue and face him.

"Remembering when we fell in love. How I told you I'd take care of you. How we'd be together always."

Her expression softened. "It's all come true, hasn't it? Our life has been good."

"And it's gonna stay that way."

"But this man. David." Her forehead puckered.

What the hell. Was she doubting him? "David's dead."

"I know that, baby. But it may take time to prove it."

"Time we don't have. My Hinckley yacht's on order. And the Florida stable remodeling starts next month. Then there's your chateau we put the contract on. I'd counted on us getting the fricking money next month."

"Me, too." A tiny pink tongue wet her bottom lip. "This man. It's weird how much he looks like David. You don't think . . . ?"

He stiffened. "Hell's bells, how many times—The boys are dead."

"I know, I know." She put her fingers on his mouth. "But with Lawrence vouching for him, I can see where someone who didn't know better would believe he's David."

"This fricking bastard's the only thing in our way." He took another drag from his Camel. "If it wasn't for him, we'd have it made. We've waited too long, Sondra."

"I know, Buccaneer."

The pet name reserved for sex diverted him.

Caressing his throat, she stepped back. "We won't let him cut us out. We'll find a way. *You'll* find a way."

She leaned against the statue, hip cocked, one breast thrust out.

He caught her chin with one hand, kissed her greedily. "No, he won't cut us out. You can bet on that."

Without releasing her, he flung the cigarette butt to the side before lifting her and carrying her inside the conservatory that enclosed the indoor pool, where the tile was cool, the air harsh with chlorine.

Her hand ruffled his hair, clasped his neck. A small den lay off the side, redolent of furniture polish and gardenias.

He stopped, listened. No voices in the library.

Good. Amos and John had gone.

Blood surged.

When the opening of her tennis dress snagged, he yanked it down so hard tiny buttons flew across the room. He caught her breast. His head bent and his teeth closed around her nipple. He bit lightly, then harder until she whimpered.

Groaning, he fell to his knees, found her navel, tongued its edge. "We won't lose everything now."

He pushed down her tennis panties, inhaled the L'Air du Temps she loved mixed with her damp musky scent. "We'll have it all. I swear I'll never let that bastard Wykerton take everything away from us."

He parted the curls, found the tender flesh. When he pushed her down to the rug, she gasped at his invasion, then met his strokes until she shuddered and arched and cried out.

She was his.

Only then did he climax.

As he lay collapsed on top of her, face pressed against her throat, she finger-combed his hair. Her breath warmed his ear. "We can't lose everything now, Theo."

"We won't. I promise."

"I believe you." Her hand caught his hair, made him look at her. "But don't do anything rash. I love this life, but I love you more. You're my everything. I can't live without you."

"You won't have to."

That was an easy promise to make.

CHAPTER 13

ON FRIDAY MORNING, three days after her arrival in Utah, Megan had improved enough to put on clothes so she could, wobbly-kneed and bleary-eyed, check out of the hotel.

Why, she wondered as she staggered across the lobby's black and white tiles, were women such slaves to fashion?

Men complained about ties. Ha!

They ought to spend a day in brassieres and high heels.

Even with small kitten heels, hose were mandatory. At least, she'd packed a garter belt. A girdle would have killed her today. The gathered suit skirt was bad enough, with its waistband unbuttoned beneath the matching short jacket.

Good thing Ruby had been able to cancel the seminar. "They won't refund but we'll get a voucher for a future session. Mr. Lawrence insists you stay put at the lodge—"

Megan had opened her mouth to say she hadn't made it that far, but Ruby never gave her a chance. "—since you can't travel for at least a week," she prattled on. "You know George had it and he still isn't back at work. The doctor said . . ."

Kind Lawrence. She wasn't about to take advantage of his offer. Maybe if she hurried back, he'd let her return for the postponed seminar. It wasn't her fault she'd gotten sick.

The airport was buzzing. President Kennedy had been in town and it took forever to get her return ticket switched for a current one. Her seat was on the aisle, thank goodness.

Ugh. Fastening the seat belt over her poor tummy brought on more nausea.

A burly man paused at her row, looking at his ticket. "I've got the window seat. Not as much room as the aisle. Wanna swap so you can see out?"

"No." She wanted to be close to the toilets. "But thank you very much for asking."

She let him squeeze past to his seat. Lucky no one took the middle one. He'd be okay.

When the Boeing 707 was securely airborne, she loosened the seat belt, then picked up the local newspaper bought at the terminal.

The front page was full of President Kennedy speaking at Salt Lake's Mormon Tabernacle.

On the second page, two photographs lay side by side.

Her heart swelled like a balloon and beat so wildly her eardrums nearly burst.

David Harmony's school picture at St. Paul's, taken before he'd come home that last summer, looked out at her with his sweet smile. The other picture showed someone else, a stranger with a haunting, impish grin.

The headline blared: ACTOR CLAIMS HARMONY MILLIONS.

She couldn't read the article, couldn't see the words. The years rolled back.

Rain-scented woods and long summer evenings, golden days and shimmering water, the flash of tanned bodies diving and the sunshine dappling on brown pine needles.

All the memories so painstakingly stored away.

Alive! David's alive! He's alive!

Over and over the words repeated themselves.

She stared at the paper for ten minutes as a dark haze washed over her. Her cheeks grew wet, but she didn't swipe at the tears. Nothing mattered except that David was alive.

Alive. David's alive.

The refrain hammered inside her.

Finally, the dizziness passed and her heart's tom-tom slowed and she wiped the tears away and focused on the small black letters.

David Paine Harmony, eldest son of . . .

It was all there, the old tragedy rehashed, including how Theodore and Sondra Pack were due, on the second of October, to inherit the Harmony Trust.

Next Wednesday. Five days away. Not even a week.

"When pressed," she read, "attorney Lawrence Wykerton acknowledged that David Harmony is alive but insists final settlement of business magnate James Paine Harmony's estate will be completed as scheduled. The alleged heir has been living and working as actor Nick Downing in London. The family, in seclusion at their island home, had no comment. Sources say the Packs, until now considered the main beneficiaries, plan a suit to block disbursement. No reason was given to explain Mr. Harmony's absence or why he chose to return at this time."

Why he chose to return? Were these people imbeciles?

David had to come back or lose his inheritance.

She pushed her head back into the headrest and took a straggly breath. Then another.

Alive, alive, alive.

The words sang to her throughout the flight.

The stewardess handing out drinks and dinners returned her radiant smiles.

The man beside her, recovered from his annoyance at losing the roomier aisle seat, made conversational overtures. She beamed at him and gave incomprehensible replies until he turned his back and pretended to go to sleep.

So she came off as a lunatic. So what?

David was alive.

Every detail of their last night together came back.

"Meggie, Meggie," he'd kept saying. "I didn't know. They said it was great. But I didn't know. I didn't know it'd be like this. Did you? Why didn't we know?"

She'd kissed his neck.

He smelled of dried sweat and wood smoke and liquor with an undertone of Old Spice.

"Stupid. How could we? But we know now."

They'd laughed. The velvety darkness had covered them, her heart had expanded into the stars, the murmuring pines had lulled them almost to sleep, and he had been warm against her in their nest of clothes flung onto the gazebo's wooden floor.

The plane was halfway back to Atlanta before her deliberate mind began to question.

How can David be alive?

It didn't matter. The paper said he was alive.

Can it really be David?

Of course it could. Lawrence had said so.

Next came reproach.

Oh, David! How could you leave me? After that night, how could you leave me and stay away with never a word?

She studied the man in the other picture. Nick Downing.

Yes, he did resemble David. An older, jaded David. She frowned. He looked almost cynical. Calculating. But he was definitely David.

Or was he?

Her happiness slid a notch.

She wanted him to be. Oh, how she wanted him to be!

****

"Make Believe" (1921)
As Performed by Nora Hayes
Music by Jack Shilkret
Lyrics by Benny Davis

WHILE MEGAN FRETTED, willing the 707 to hurry to Atlanta, Lawrence hosted the Packs and their attorneys on the mainland. Though a Friday, he had canceled all appointments after lunch and sent everyone home, including his nosy son George and affronted secretary Ruby.

The Victorian house turned law office was empty except for the five people waiting for a sixth person expected momentarily.

Despite Lawrence's best efforts, conversation flagged. Adding to the strained atmosphere, a thunderstorm had flared. Flashes of lightning and booms of thunder moved through quickly, but the beat of raindrops against the bay windows remained.

As Theo walked a circuit from sofa to window to doorway to sofa, Amos said, "Lawrence, I beg you again not to do this."

From his leather chair, Lawrence looked across his scarred desk. "I regret you don't agree with my decision."

Theo snorted. "You can't possibly think we would."

Under the tall ceiling of what had once been the old house's dining room, now lined with floor to ceiling bookshelves, his large frame wasn't out of scale. In golf shirt and slacks tailored to his athletic form, he looked ready for eighteen holes. Amos and John wore suits appropriate for the occasion, but Sondra's lowcut dress . . .

Never mind Sondra's dress. Theo's composure was worrisome. Lawrence had expected anxiety, even the naked fury from two days ago.

But except for his restlessness, Theo remained controlled. "Some man says he's David and you accept him with open arms. I won't lie down and play dead, Lawrence."

Far too controlled.

"I understand your sentiments."

"Do you? Where is he anyway?" Theo eyed a wristwatch that probably cost the earth. "I'm anxious to get this over with."

Lawrence touched his tie. "Dodging reporters, I daresay."

John gasped. "Reporters? Here? Don't tell me that."

A first-rate attorney like John Wilkins would consider the publicity intolerable. No one, not clients nor a firm's reputation, would benefit from this kind of publicity.

In normal circumstances, Lawrence would share his concern. But this was different.

He had squared his shoulders, gritted his teeth, and alerted a close newspaper friend in Atlanta.

As an anonymous source, of course.

"It's regrettable the news leaked out." He steepled his hands. "But I'm anxious to get it done, too. I'm satisfied with David's credentials, so we need to move on."

"We aren't satisfied." Amos waved a hand sporting a large star sapphire. His immaculate shirt and tie screamed expensive. "Reminiscences about the past might convince you, Lawrence, but it's only fair that we have the courts rule on whether Downing is James Harmony's son."

"Reminiscences may mean little, but dental and fingerprint evidence is incontrovertible."

Sondra cut off Amos's retort. "If he is David, we can't go to court." She sat on the sofa, long legs crossed, one spike heel swinging. "I think we all agree on that."

She was costumed with the simplicity that takes money, but there were discordant notes. The white dress trimmed in red might emphasize her bleached hair and honey tan, but no respectable woman would show such cleavage. She looked like a fashion model or actress.

Like a lower-class woman aping a refined woman of wealth.

Humph. Had he voiced his opinion, Sondra would likely raise her brows. An old man was no fashion expert.

John said, "A settlement might be best if—"

"No settlement," Theo snapped. "The man's a fake."

Sondra shifted on the sofa. "Do sit down, Theo. You know how I hate it when you pace." She patted the seat beside her. "We want to try to avoid publicity, so don't broadcast your misery. We agreed to hear the man's story."

Plump sofa cushions whooshed under Theo's weight. "Lawrence is talking about handing millions of dollars over to someone we know damn-all about. *Our* money, Sondra."

"Theo. Baby." She brushed his thigh. "If he's David, it's his money. Let's wait and see."

Lawrence hated this, hated himself for being involved. His head began to ache. From the humidity. No. From guilt. "I do understand your views, Theo. I hope meeting David today will convince you who he is. If not, I'm afraid it makes no difference."

Theo caught Sondra's hand, rubbed it. "Don't you think it strange, Lawrence? David would never have stayed away all this time. He would have come to me."

"I was incredulous, but after months of questioning him and having the finest detective agency research, I am convinced this man is who he says he is." Time to tighten the screw. "Come, come, Theo, you've seen the reports yourself."

"Reports can be faked."

"I don't see how." Lawrence sat back. "I sent Curtis to London to obtain his fingerprints. Curtis kept them in his possession until he turned them over to me. I then had them compared to David's. It was providential the sheriff took prints from the boys' rooms in 1946, more providential that those records still exist. Theo, I have no choice." The words came out glibly. "David is alive. So long as he's alive, James's estate is his."

Heaven forgive me, how many more lies will I have to tell?

"It's so strange." Sondra's husky voice could have been discussing a best-selling novel. "It seems so out of character. David had to know we'd believe he was dead."

"Has he ever said why he ran away?" Amos asked.

Theo cracked his knuckles. "I need a drink."

Lawrence lowered his eyes. "I apologize, Theo. I don't keep alcohol for guests." Unless one counted the rare Armagnac in his desk drawer reserved for very special occasions of which this was certainly not one.

Sondra leaned forward. "Lawrence, why *did* he run away?"

"Why? I don't pretend to understand. Whether or not David acted wisely is questionable, but we must remember, he was a mere boy when it happened."

Theo's laughter was mirthless, but the sound of the outer door opening spared them whatever he might have said.

"Ah, good." Lawrence sprang up. "Back here, David."

The slender man of average height strolled into the room and paused. Quizzical eyes swept over the two lawyers belatedly rising, briefly lingered on Theo, then settled on Sondra.

Nick Downing had arrived. Without any fanfare, any noticeable effort, he became the center of the room.

Confound it, he's wearing those tight pants. And what kind of shirt is that? Wembley 1961? I told him to wear his suit. He looks like an idiot.

Never mind.

The important thing was that Nick in the flesh overwhelmed any other person around him. Including Theo's imposing bulk as he unwound himself and stood.

Lawrence hurried toward Nick.

Please, please don't overact.

The man was wonderful onstage, but there was no place today for irreverence. Lawrence mentally crossed his fingers. "Come in here, my boy, come in. Give me that dripping umbrella."

"Thanks, Whitey."

Theo started at the childish nickname.

Lawrence, suppressing a smile, stuck the umbrella into a converted bronze spittoon.

Nick said, "Hullo, Sondra, Theo. It's been a long time."

"David," Lawrence said, "meet Amos Lovett and John Wilkins, the Packs' attorneys."

Nick nodded and murmured a greeting, dismissing both men before turning back to Theo and Sondra.

Lawrence took a deep breath.

And we're off.

****

"The Stripper"
As Performed by David Rose (1962)
Music by David Rose

ACTING WAS HIS profession, true. But this role presented problems that had kept Nick awake. As late as this morning, he'd had jitters.

Not anymore, not once he began to strut his stuff.

After all, he was an award-winning actor.

This was rather fun. Whitey had been right about Theo. The bronzed Titan was like a cat waiting beside a mouse hole.

Dressing down had been the right thing to do. Theo didn't bother with a suit, not him. The lord of the manor wore what he liked.

So did Nick. Now he just had to stay within his lines and not get caught out in ad libs.

He tackled Sondra first, whose eyes had grown big. Two steps brought him to the sofa. "Sondra, you look not a day older. I swear before heaven, you're as beautiful as ever."

"Hello." She ignored his outstretched hands, but her lips parted the slightest bit. That might signal shock, but he doubted Sondra was the type to be shocked about anything.

Her reaction might simply be that of a woman greeting a stepson thought long dead. Or, that of a woman meeting an attractive man.

One thing for sure. Whitey's photographs hadn't done her justice.

In person, she was a bloody stunner. A man could drown in those midnight pools that promised all manner of forbidden delights. Neither James Harmony nor Theo Pack would have stood a chance.

Lucky he was made of stouter stuff.

"No, I lie." He captured her hand in both his. "I am indubitably, utterly, wrong. You're even more beautiful."

With an alarmed glance toward Theo standing to her left, Sondra tugged at her hand.

Nick held tight.

Theo eyed them but took a spread-leg, crossed-arm stance. "You used to be shy, not nearly so effusive. And you sound so veddy, veddy British. Unlike David."

"Did you really think me shy?" Nick used the beatific smile. "Ah, but you weren't around enough to judge, were you? I was at St. Paul's, you were at Vandy. And the army didn't leave you much time for socializing. As for the accent, I've been living in England for ten years."

Sondra tugged at her hand, but he took his time letting go. "You're looking good, Theo. Put on a little weight?"

Theo's lips thinned. "I'm ten pounds over what I weighed at twenty-two. Not that it's any concern of yours."

Amos put in, "I believe Lawrence arranged this meeting so that you could tell your story, Mr., Mr. . . ?"

Nick waved his hand. "Call me David. I've been Nick for so long, it'll take getting used to." He heaved a theatrical sigh. "But I suppose it's something I must bear with."

Whitey's jaw twitched.

Poor old Whitey. He didn't approve of Nick having fun.

Theo didn't like it either. Mouth thin, eyes narrow, old Theo looked ready to kill.

"Right." Amos ran a hand under his collar. "David it is. We're anxious to hear your tale."

"I'm sure you are. May I?" Without waiting for Sondra's assent, Nick plopped down as close as he could get to her.

She edged away.

Theo's face darkened.

The sofa shifted as he claimed the other side of his wife.

A dog guarding his bone. Perfect.

"Now. Shall I answer your questions first? I'm sure you must have millions."

Sondra peeked over at him.

No uncertainties now. She was wondering the same things about him as he wondered about her: what her naked body was like, what kind of sex she preferred, what kind of lover she'd make.

Hmmm, maybe Sondra wasn't as totally wrapped up in her husband as Whitey believed. How interesting. And Theo didn't like Nick being attentive to his wife.

Let's see. What mischief can we stir up?

When Sondra opened her purse and took out a cigarette, he stuck out his engraved gold lighter. One smooth flick of his thumb opened the lid and sparked the flame.

Her cigarette hesitated. Then soft fingers touched his wrist, steadying the flame.

"Lovely lighter," she said, blowing out smoke.

"A gift from a countess." He used the one hand close.

"Really?" Widened eyes communicated willingness to hear more. He let the opening slide to inspect her.

Exquisite nose, tiny ears, smooth skin. Bloody hell. He'd met hundreds of memorable women, some pretty, some not. Few compared to Sondra Pack with her sultry sexuality.

Theo drawled, "David didn't smoke."

Did Theo recognize that dewy edge around Sondra? Did he care that it was aimed toward another man?

A glance encountered total hatred.

Oh, yes, Theo cared.

Nick took out his case, chose a cigar, and lit it. "I was young when I last saw you, Theo. At sixteen, one is still experimenting. I picked up this habit in Cuba."

"Cuba?"

Three pairs of inquisitive eyes swung toward Whitey.

Theo kept his on Nick. Nick blew smoke at him.

Whitey cleared his throat. "I did tell you he's led a rather varied life."

Nick changed his sneer at Theo to a slow, insinuating smile for Theo's wife.

She inhaled and edged toward Theo.

John Wilkins, a serious man with a narrow face and large nose, said, "We would love to hear about your varied life." His level gaze didn't waver.

He might be wise to avoid John Wilkins. Nick stretched out his legs, crossed his ankles, and leaned back comfortably. "Shall I begin at the beginning? On the night Dad died?"

Theo ground his teeth.

Nick smiled at Sondra.

"Please do," John Wilkins said.

David Harmony had come home.

CHAPTER 14

"My Happiness"
As Performed by Connie Francis (1959)
Music by Borney Bergantine
Lyrics by Betty Peterson Blasco

AS HER PLANE neared Atlanta, an increasingly doubtful Megan Mulrennon examined the newspaper for the hundredth time.

No, no, the whole thing is illogical. This can't be right.

David wasn't alive so how could he come home?

He was dead. David and Robby were both dead. Everybody knew they were dead.

Now some opportunist had shown up to revive those brain-numbing days after the accident, raking up all the old conjectures and innuendos, and churning up the pain.

Such awful, gut-wrenching pain. She bit her lip till it bled and she had to dig for a hankie.

If David were alive, he would have come to her. Had he survived the fire and the ocean, he would never have left her believing him dead all these years. Not after that last night together.

Would he?

She studied the actor's features, trying to see something that might reveal the truth and displace her doubts.

How she wanted to believe.

Yes, there was a marked similarity between the boy and man in the pictures. What if it really was David? What if he had somehow escaped drowning?

No. Impossible. It didn't make sense. He would have let her and her parents know. Or Theo. Even Sondra. He would never have disappeared without a word.

Would he?

Then again . . .

She peered at the grainy face.

David had always been rash. There was the time he'd run away during the war. And again after victory in Europe, when he'd hitchhiked to New York, leaving his parents to agonize for five days. They'd called in police and hired detectives before he turned up hungry and unrepentant.

"I wanted to be in on the celebration," he'd explained to Megan and her mother. "And I needed space to breathe. You don't know what it's like to be James Harmony's son. Now that Mother's sick, Dad hovers over me and Robby. He even shows up at school without warning, just to check up on me."

"He cares for you, David," Mom remonstrated.

He made a face. "He expects too much. And I . . . At school, guys I barely know wanna be friends. I never know if they like me or Dad's money more. Some of them are rich but some of them are leeches. Real creeps."

David could be very perceptive at times, but he could also be insensitive. Even Megan's mother, much as she doted on David, admitted he was self-centered. "Not selfish," Mom qualified. "I don't think David has an ungenerous bone in his body. But he doesn't consider how his actions affect others. Of course, lots of you kids don't."

She had looked meaningfully over her reading glasses at Megan.

Yes, David had his faults. He could have run away again. Maybe it was true. Could it be?

No. Not after that last evening with him. The impromptu beach cookout with three of his visiting school friends and a few mainland kids. They'd eaten hot dogs and roasted marshmallows and drunk Cokes and beer. A few even sampled a smuggled bottle of liquor.

They'd sung. "Mairzy Doats" and "People Will Say We're in Love" and David's favorite, "Don't Fence Me In."

He'd smooched with Rochelle Tollison while Megan sat on a blanket with one of his friends from school. What was his name?

Brian somebody from Boston. He drank too much. When he fumbled with her shorts, she got scared and ran away. He caught her beneath a mimosa by the boardwalk.

Fastened into her seat on the airplane, Megan could almost hear the laughter echo over the sand, smell the wood smoke mixed with the yeasty breath of the boy pinning her down.

Heaven knows what would have happened except for David. David had jerked him off her and beat him senseless.

Afterward, stiff with outrage, David had walked her home, too furious to speak or even look at her. She'd thought he blamed her for making him fight Brian and finally snapped at him because it wasn't her fault.

That was when David had grabbed her and shook her until . . .

She refused to remember. With her protective armor shattered, thinking about that night was agony.

How quickly anger had turned to desire.

Better not remember that kiss and its aftermath. Better to focus on David and his impulsive charm.

Yes, David could have left her without a word, despite the new twist in their relationship. Yes, he could have left her the same way he'd run away from school.

What's more, Megan hadn't worked with Lawrence Wykerton for seven years without learning The Old Man was too cautious to commit himself to the press or anyone else unless he was absolutely certain of his facts.

Aha. David's return explained why Lawrence had taken so many trips lately. His excessive poring over the Harmony files would be for the necessary revisions.

She smoothed the paper creased by her continual reading and rereading of the article.

Lawrence must have known for the past year that David was alive. Why hadn't he told her? He knew how close she and Mom had been to David. He knew she could keep her mouth shut. Why hadn't he given her a hint of what was going on instead of packing her off to a retreat in Utah?

Where she should be right now, cut off from radios and televisions and newspapers. Locked away where she'd never have found out David was alive.

"How could he? How could he?"

Her seatmate asked if she was okay.

"What?!"

Meddlesome man. Why was he bothering her?

He put as much distance between them as he could. "I asked if you're okay. I didn't—"

"Yes! I'm fine. Just peachy keen."

He went back to hiding behind his magazine.

She went back to adding up facts.

Lawrence wanted her out of the way.

Along with her mother. That all-expenses-paid cruise on the Mediterranean, offered Mom and Aunt Sadie out of the blue by Lawrence, was no kindly favor.

Lawrence had meant to send her and Mom both away.

Slow down. Think this through.

Lawrence was a good person. He wanted to spare her and Mom all the turmoil. He knew how close they were to David.

That was the obvious reason. Sure it was.

Lawrence should have told us. He should have let us know.

The rest of the article rehashed the facts that ended with a terse statement about the only evidence recovered from the charred debris:

one life preserver with the lyre emblem denoting Harmony Island property. Both boys were assumed to have perished.

Until now.

Megan laid the paper on her lap and stared unseeingly at the seat back in front of her.

The day after she and David had pledged their love, she and her parents had left to visit family in Alabama. Four days later, they had cut their trip short to come back to a forever changed Harmony Island. She'd cried for days, wanting to die herself, unable to believe she would never see David again.

And all the time he was alive, taking a new name, starting a new life, doing heaven knows what.

No. Doing what he always wanted to do.

She'd always prided herself on seeing both sides of a situation.

So look at it from David's viewpoint.

He always swore he'd never end up tied to work like his father. He wanted to travel and see different countries, do different things. He'd shared those fantasies with her lots of times: his plan to hike through Europe, his crazy ideas about working his way to Japan and Australia on a cargo ship, his curiosity about countries behind the Iron Curtain.

Even that last night he'd begged her to run away with him. She'd promised she would when they were older.

But she'd turned seventeen alone.

Had he deliberately used the accident to follow his dreams? While hers died with him?

By the time her plane began circling Atlanta, Megan's annoyance at Lawrence for not telling her about David's reappearance, had shifted to David himself.

How could he have stayed away so long and not let anyone know he was alive? How could he have done that to Sondra and Theo and JoBeth and, most importantly, to her?

Damn him. Damn him for the selfish ingrate that he was.

Damn him for leaving me!

No, no, she didn't mean it. The joy of having him return easily overwhelmed resentment at his running away.

David had come back and that was all that mattered.

CHAPTER 15

"Little White Lies"
As Performed by Annette Fanshaw (1930)
Music by Fred Donaldson
Lyrics by Fred Donaldson

WHILE NICK DOWNING, not one whit dismayed at the rippling antagonism and avid scrutiny around him, told the rehearsed story, Lawrence sat on tenterhooks.

Pray heaven his anxiety wasn't obvious.

Not that anyone noticed him. Nick held the stage.

"I'm sure, Theo, you remember how upset Robby and I were about Dad. You tried to console us." Through drifting smoke, Nick aimed a pathetic half-smile at Theo. His eyes misted and his lower lip quivered. "You fixed Robby some chocolate milk, even mixed me one of your martinis. My, I remember as if it were yesterday."

All done in the most theatrical manner. Why in heaven's name couldn't the man play it straight? If Nick botched this opportunity, they wouldn't have another.

Confound it, he was gritting his teeth.

Lawrence forced himself to relax.

"You know most of what happened." Nick waggled fingers. "Robby and I went out in the boat to take our minds off Dad's death and the boat exploded. I was hanging over the front, untangling some line, and the blast threw me clear. I'd put on a life vest, something I didn't ordinarily do."

He frowned. "I don't know why I did that night, but it saved my life. I popped right up but the entire boat was ablaze and pieces of it were raining down everywhere."

John Wilkins paid close attention. "And your brother?"

"I heard Robby screaming. Then nothing. The fire was blazing hot. I yelled till I was hoarse but didn't hear anything else and couldn't see anything either. Just the fire, till it burnt down to the water."

The right amount of distress showed, and the screwed-up eyes made a nice touch.

Theo snorted, but that didn't fluster Nick. "I still dream about yelling for him. I hope he died quickly. There was no way to get to him."

Skeptical John asked, "How long were you in the water?"

Nick raised one shoulder. "Seemed like forever. It was dawn when a ship going out spotted me and picked me up."

Theo leaned past his wife. "One small speck out in the ocean, and a ship saw you?"

"You don't believe me?" Nick's raised brow mocked Theo's scorn. He spread his hands. "Yet here I am."

Theo smoldered.

Lawrence held his breath. If Nick wavered . . .

Nick didn't.

"The captain made me work for my passage. I intended to get off at the first port, find a way to get back home. That's honestly what I meant to do. I could have when we reached the Panama Canal. But working on a ship was kind of exciting. Robby was dead. There was nothing I could do for him. Dad was gone, too, so I went on to Acapulco. That's where a difference of opinion with the captain made me jump ship."

John saw an opening. "What kind of difference?"

"Acapulco?" Theo's lip curled. "What kind of cargo ship goes into Acapulco?"

Nick answered John first. "The captain thought I had a career as an indentured servant. I thought I'd labored enough. I was ready to see the sights on steady ground."

He leaned past Sondra to answer Theo, brushing her bare arm.

Theo noticed and flushed.

"In this case, Theo, the ship carried agricultural equipment. At least it wasn't chickens or cows." He shuddered dramatically. "I can't see me mucking out stalls."

"So you jumped ship in Acapulco." John Wilkins made notes on a pad. "How did you manage that without a passport?"

"Ah. That could have been a problem except for Nick. I met him after I sneaked off the ship. Nick was, um, trying to convince certain people he'd left the country. I needed a passport and I resembled him. A lot. You might say our mutual needs brought us together."

Theo pounced. "You exchanged places with a man you'd just met?"

The slower Amos chose a different tack. "What kind of trouble was this Downing in?"

"Dowserman. When I got an agent, he changed it to Downing. He had something to do with opium. Nick Dowserman, that is. Not my agent." He frowned slightly. "Although I can't swear to what my agent gets up to when he's not agenting."

Everyone stared at him blankly.

Lawrence choked.

Nick sneaked a wink his way. "Anyway, Theo, I agreed to swap places when Nick gave me a wad of cash to go with the passport and an airplane ticket to Cuba. All I had to do was be on the plane so I'd lead them away from him."

He grunted. "Stupid arse didn't know they were already onto him. When he left the cantina where we met, they started firing. I was right behind him." Indignation gathered. "I nearly got killed."

Amos blinked. "And this Dowserman?"

"Nick? Oh. He did get killed."

At Sondra's gasp, Nick waved a cheerful hand. "He was not a good person. He was bound to come to a bad end."

Amos and Sondra exchanged horrified glances.

Lord help me, this man will get us both jailed.

"You were left with Nick's passport?" John concentrated on jotting notes.

"Exactly. I was lucky again. I had his passport and the ticket so I headed to Cuba. Great place to be, way back then, before Castro came in and made everyone equal."

"You didn't come home when you could have," Sondra said. "Why not?"

Nick pulled out the beguiling smile for her. "Why should I? There was nothing for me here. I'd always wanted to see the world and this was my chance."

"You were only sixteen," Amos objected.

Nick laughed. "Ah, the eternal optimism of youth. Isn't it a pity we have to grow older and wiser? Yes, that's right, Mr., um, Loving, is it?"

"Lovett. But call me Amos."

Theo glowered at his friend.

Nick's tactics were perfect. Except . . .

What was Theo thinking?

Lawrence gripped his knees to hide a tremor. No one noticed because everyone's attention was on Nick.

Who, despite Theo's unblinking stare, neither trembled nor faltered.

"In Cuba, I hired on with a German yacht, went back to Vera Cruz, got into some trouble there, later ended up in Argentina. Went to Japan, then Cape Town, New Zealand, and Australia. A British BBC crew there took me back to England."

"Have you found any proof of this, Lawrence?" John asked. "Such as the ship that picked him up off Harmony Island?"

Thankfully, he had regained his equilibrium.

"Ahem. No traces of it. I have a detective working on it but Nick couldn't remember the flag it sailed under. He thinks the crew may have been Greek although he heard some Slavic phrases. All he remembers is that the name had 'Star' in it. Have you any idea how many ships sail between here and Mexico with 'Star' in their name?"

"I see." John drew out a handkerchief. "Wouldn't the captain have radioed at some point to the authorities after picking him up?"

"Good point." Nick leaned forward, put an elbow on his knee and his chin in that hand. "Personally, I think he intended using me as slave labor from the beginning."

"We're still trying to track the ship down, John," said Lawrence. "However, we do have passport records from Mexico to Cuba. And working from David's memories, we've found the yacht owner. So we have verification from Cuba on."

John blew his nose quietly. "And the real Nick Downing is dead?"

"Nick Dowserman," Lawrence said. "My detectives found a newspaper report of an unidentified foreigner shot to death near the cantina where David says they met. The police report gave a description that was likely Dowserman's. Copies of the clipping and report were in the folder I prepared for you earlier."

Thank heavens his hirelings were able to come up with an unclaimed body at the right time.

"So there you go." Nick settled back, crossed his legs. "As I said, a man like that was bound to die sooner or later."

Lawrence gagged at the repressed twinkle. Blast him. What was the man playing at?

"How convenient." Theo's flat tone matched his stare.

Nick's Cheshire cat smile beamed. "Wasn't it?"

Sondra put a warning hand on her husband. "You never got in touch with us. Why not?"

Nick hung his head, guileless as a child caught in a cookie jar. "I meant to, I really did. But everything was so exciting. Things kept happening and I . . ."

He chuckled and got up to crush the remains of his cigar in an ashtray stand by John's chair. "Let's be honest. I loved it. I loved being on my own, going where I wanted, doing what I wanted. Nobody peering over my shoulder telling me to behave. Nobody making up to me because I was James Harmony's son."

He stretched languidly. "If I came home, I'd have to go back to school. Then what? College and the family business that I loathed? Besides," he said somberly, "when I was busy I didn't think of Dad and Robby."

He dropped down beside Sondra.

Amos frowned. "It would be hard to check your story after so many years."

"As I told you, we did trace him back to the German yacht owner," Lawrence said. "Despite how long ago it was, my investigators got me a copy of the log with Nick Dowserman's name in it. There's also a copy in the files I gave you, John."

A ray of late sunshine broke through the window blind, its brilliance surprising after the thunderstorms and gloomy drizzle. It dazzled Theo, and he put up a hand to fend it off.

"So there it is." Nick stretched out his legs, planting his thigh against Sondra's. "The story of my life."

Too much enthusiasm. He should tone it down.

Sondra eased away from Nick.

"Not exactly." Theo moved out of the sun. "There's no proof."

"Unless you count the teeth and fingerprints as proof," Lawrence said dryly. "But I assume you've inspected them, John, Amos?"

"The whole thing's unbelievable." Amos shook his head. "This is like a movie."

"Isn't it?" Unoffended, Nick gave his elegant half-shrug. "D'you think Hollywood might be interested? I'd love to star."

Theo snorted. "Fiction like this? Hollywood should snatch it up."

"I still wonder," Nick mused, staring into space, "whether Dowserman intended those men to kill me so they'd think he was dead. He was bad. Quite bad. That was my first experience with a really bad man."

He gave a sanctimonious shake of his head, disapproving of how bad a man Nick Dowserman had been.

Lawrence barely stopped himself from rolling his eyes.

Incorrigible. Absolutely incorrigible.

Nick said to Sondra, "I was lucky. I got into some fights, went hungry, but I survived."

John continued taking notes. The others sat, Amos overwhelmed, Theo in frank disbelief, Sondra fascinated.

"Poor David." Her words rang with compassion.

"It was hard," Nick said to her sadly. "Very hard."

An alarm went off. Flirting with Sondra was not part of the plan.

Theo cut in. "Save your pity, Sondra." Then to Nick, "Why didn't you come home?"

Nick paused, no longer genial.

Lawrence couldn't breathe. He could almost read Nick's mind: Time to throw a little scare into Theo.

The people in the room did not know how it happened, but quite suddenly Nick Downing became a very dangerous man.

Even Lawrence, knowing firsthand how quickly the actor could revert from angel to devil, was caught by surprise.

The planes of the smiling face rearranged themselves into harsh lines. The body tensed like an animal at bay. Genial eyes turned icy. Menace exuded from every pore.

John stopped writing, pen immobile on his pad.

Amos slid forward to the edge of his chair, ready to run.

Sondra shrank toward her husband.

Despite himself, Lawrence's blood thrummed.

Without a doubt, this man would stop at nothing until he got what he wanted.

Theo was the only one unmoved.

"Why didn't I? That's a good question." Nick's velvety voice clashed with the unforgiving demeanor. He cocked his head. "Why wouldn't I, Theo? My home. The businesses. The money. Everything waited for me here. Can you think of any reason I wouldn't come back?"

Nick continued to lounge. He made no threatening gestures, yet the ambience between him and Theo suggested two cobras.

Theo blinked first. "Hell's bells, I asked you, didn't I? How can I explain your reasons?"

The gentle curve of Nick's lips banished the dangerous air and laid a softness in its stead.

A different person sat beside Sondra.

The people around him unconsciously relaxed. Even Lawrence, who had seen Nick manipulate audiences, felt his stomach unknot.

"Why, you couldn't, of course."

The actor spoke so softly that the others had to strain to hear.

"My reasons for not coming home were simple, Theo. My parents had protected and cosseted me all my life. They never allowed me to test my own limits. I wanted to be young and carefree. I wanted to live life on my terms. I wanted to stand on my own two feet. But mostly I wanted to forget that Mom and Dad and Robby were dead."

"Bullshit." Theo got to his feet. "You're no more David Harmony than I am. You may favor him, and someone"—he shot a poisoned glance at Lawrence—"may have fed you details of his life. But you're damn well not David Harmony."

Lawrence sucked in his breath, but Nick's smile widened. "Yes, I am. You don't want to admit it because of the money, but really, Theo, you know yourself Dad never intended to leave you more than a nest egg. Why, I remember him saying several times to Whitey here—"

Theo winced at the nickname.

His acting was better than good.

"—that it wouldn't do for you to have a great deal of money, that you'd only waste it." Nick leaned forward. "You see, Dad had a theory that a person's character needs adversity to develop. He didn't want to contribute to your going bad. You remember Dad saying that, don't you, Theo? That time you lost money at the tracks and asked Dad to bail you out?"

The angelic smile softened the words, but Theo's face turned white, then red.

Nick waited a beat before giving the screw another turn. "Do you still bet, Theo? If so, bet on this. I'm alive, and the money's mine. No matter how much you wish I lay deep in that watery grave with poor Robby. I'm alive and I'm here, ready to take what's mine."

He sat back, crossed his legs, and swung his foot back and forth as he complacently examined the vaguely familiar shoe adorning it. A shoe that looked like those handmade brogues from London James favored. From Trickster's? Tricker's?

He can wear an expensive shoe but not a suit to an important meeting like this? The man is—

Theo stood motionless, but his fist clenched.

Sondra touched her husband's rigid forearm. "Theo."

Her husband moved away. "Let's go. I've had enough of this prick and his explanations. Lawrence, we'll discuss this further. After I've heard from my detective agency."

"Theo." Sondra got up. "You're behaving like an asshole."

Vulgarity from Theo was a matter of course, but Lawrence winced at it coming from a delicate creature like Sondra.

She might seem fragile, but she wasn't afraid to tug at her husband. "You haven't given David a chance. We agreed to think this over before making up our minds. Theo, please."

"I don't know who the hell he is, but everybody in this office knows he isn't David."

Theo stalked out.

Amos sighed while John looked disapproving, Sondra bit her lip, and Nick smirked.

Lawrence relaxed.

The first round was over.

CHAPTER 16

"Race with the Devil"
As Performed by Gene Vincent
and His Bluecaps (1956)
Music by Sheriff Tex Davis and Gene Vincent
Lyrics by Sheriff Tex Davis and Gene Vincent

THEO RUSHED OUT. He wouldn't give in to his temper. Not again. Not in front of Lawrence.

Outside, he splashed through a puddle. Damn it, his new loafers were soaked.

He'd always loved walking around after a thunderstorm had passed. The clean, sweet smell of wet plants and earth revived him.

Now he could barely breathe.

This shitty fairy was not David Harmony. He'd known it all along, but seeing the man in person, drooling over Sondra like a slobbery dog with a bone . . .

And her smiling and encouraging him.

A fricking nightmare. Face-to-face, he should have been able to rip the fricking poseur's lies apart and be done with him. But someone had primed him.

Lawrence, just as he'd said all along. It had to be.

No one else would have known about James's reaction when he'd asked for a loan to cover a few measly bets on the horses.

James, the arrogant bastard, curled that upper lip and gave him a lecture. Before getting him the stinking plant job.

"Pay your debts, then save your money," James had said. Like Theo was a green adolescent having to be told what to do.

His mouth was dry. He needed a drink. Naturally, the old fart wouldn't have alcohol in his office.

Two-bit, small-town lawyer.

He hit the hood of the island car with his fist. The pain traveled from his knuckles up his arm. "Hell's bells, I'll kill the little turd."

Then he groaned. *I can't. Not again.*

His hand throbbed. He shook it, trying to defuse the pain.

Take it easy. The voice that had counseled him in other unthinkable situations showed up, clever and perceptive. *No need to think about killing now. Figure out how to show him up.*

That's what he needed to do. This shitass was lying through his teeth. Oh, there was some truth—yes, he had given David a martini, made Robby milk—but this, this sonofabitch had woven his own version of that night.

Like why he'd been at sea.

The boys weren't out in the boat because they were grieving for their father; the boys didn't even know James was dead. They were in the boat because he'd put them there.

But someone had taken his story and twisted it. And there was no way he could prove it without revealing he had killed the boys.

Sondra was right. They needed to make pretty with the bastard and probe for a weakness. Maybe they could find someone who'd known David, someone who'd realize this wasn't him. There had to be somebody.

Like the Mulrennons, except they were gone.

Because of Lawrence.

He cursed.

Lawrence had forestalled him there. But what about someone else? Who else had known David well enough to recognize a fake? Surely he could think of someone.

Failing that . . .

You can always kill him.

****

"Showboat Shuffle"
As Performed by King Oliver and
His Dixie Syncopators (1927)
Music by Barney Bigard and King Oliver

AFTER THEO LEFT Lawrence's office, the silence dragged on until, with a muttered farewell, Amos ambled after Theo. "He'll calm down," he said hopefully.

Lawrence doubted it and was glad.

"Of course he will," Sondra murmured before shaking her head ruefully at Nick. "We thought you were dead, David. It's been a shock to Theo." She held out red-tipped fingers. "You'll have to make allowances."

Nick took her hand. "I understand perfectly."

She didn't pull away. "Where are you staying?"

"The motel in town near the river."

"That dingy old motel? You can't stay there. Come to the island. We're hosting the yacht club this week but there's a cottage vacant. You must take it."

Nick gave her an appreciative once-over.

Ogling her!

Lawrence clamped his mouth together.

At a time like this.

What in the name of heaven was wrong with the man? He'd break up this little tête-à-tête right quick.

"Ahem." As he rose, the observant John hopped up, too.

The actor had eyes only for Sondra. "Theo wouldn't appreciate my presence there."

"Don't be ridiculous. Theo and I have already talked about it. We agreed you should stay at the island until this is sorted out. He'll be cooled off by the time you get there. I promise." Delectable lips curved invitingly. "Please, David."

John eyed the still joined hands. He looked as worried as Lawrence.

"You'll have to put in an appearance sooner or later," Lawrence said. "Things will be easier with you at hand. You can move over there tomorrow after the press conference.

Nick patted Sondra's hand. "All right. I'll come. For you."

She rewarded him with a brilliant smile. "Wonderful. We're having a barbecue and low country boil tomorrow afternoon. We'll turn it into a party to celebrate your homecoming."

John stepped forward. "Sondra. If you're ready to go?"

Nick made a show of his reluctance to release her.

After John hustled her away, her scent lingered.

In a reverie, Nick looked at the closed door. "That woman is dangerous."

"Strange," Lawrence said tartly. "I was thinking the same thing about you."

He wished he didn't like Nick Downing.

Underneath his arrogance, the actor was intelligent with enough confidence to tackle anything.

Regrettably, he was also egotistical and had a reprehensible sense of humor. He refused to take anything seriously. Though time might take care of that weakness.

But because he had warmed toward the actor, Nick's attraction to Sondra agitated him. He knew firsthand Sondra Pack's effect on men; see how his own son George turned into mush around her! They couldn't afford such a diversion.

"Stay away from her."

Nick shook off his trance. "Yes, that is certainly quite a woman. Her invitation solved the question of where Theo might strike. What do you think, Whitey?"

"I think you're stirring up stagnant waters."

"That's the idea, isn't it? Can you get a guest list? I don't want any unpleasant surprises."

"Nor do I. I have some work to do this evening. I'll call Sondra's secretary, get the names of the people who'll be there in the next few days."

At Nick's silent question, he shook his head. "No. Linda, the secretary, is from the Midwest and has only been with them a few years. But some of the island help will remember David. We went through them all so you should be able to carry off any unexpected meetings. As for the Packs' set, none knew James or the boys."

"Oh? Were James's friends a little too, um, sober for the Packs?" Blue-gray eyes danced.

"No doubt. And I meant what I said. Try not to slaver over Sondra," Lawrence snapped. "You were quite obvious to me. And to Theo. This affair is complicated enough without that."

Blunt words, but he needed to drive Nick's thoughts back to the business at hand.

"You cut me to the quick, Whitey. Was I slavering? I thought I was simply admiring the view. And such a nice view it was."

Confound Nick Downing. "I mean it, Nick. Hands off Sondra."

Nick laughed. "Even to rattle Theo's cage? All right. I'll be good, Whitey. There's no need to worry, you know. This is what I do for a living. I'll carry it off perfectly."

Worry about Nick's reaction to Sondra faded, replaced by a more imperative one. "You must take care once you're on the island. There's no telling what Theo might do."

Nick yawned. "Not in public. I'm safe so long as there are people nearby. You made good choices for my bodyguards, too. They've been around. I like that."

"I asked for men who could handle themselves."

"I think they can, and I'll be careful not to go into dark corners unless they know about it. This will work out. You'll see. I'll join the party and rub a little more salt on Theo's wounds. From his reactions today, it won't take him long to blow."

"I only wish we knew what he'll do."

"Does it matter?"

"I don't want you hurt."

"How lovely of you, Whitey."

Lawrence led the way out, not sure if Nick was being sarcastic.

Outside, the clouds were gone and the rain had left everything smelling clean and new. Puddles glistened in the late sun. Blue hydrangeas hung over chrysanthemum clumps, verdant with white blooms and more buds about to open.

Beneath a live oak with revived resurrection ferns, a gray Lincoln awaited the actor so he didn't have to wade the water.

One large unsmiling man sat behind the wheel while another held open the back door for their passenger.

Nick's protectors were on duty.

Lawrence watched the car pull away.

Dear Lord, let everything go all right. Let Theo give himself away without anyone being hurt.

It would be a shame if anything happened to Nick Downing.

If something did . . .

The risk was unavoidable, but he hated taking it.

One more thing on his conscience.

****

"I Gotta Know"
As Performed by Elvis Presley (1960)
Music by Paul Evans
Lyrics by Matt Williams

ONCE DISEMBARKED AT Atlanta Municipal Airport, Megan's kitten heels clicked on tile as she searched the concourse for a phone.

Never mind her stomach. She had to talk to Lawrence.

Passing under a row of bright banners that passed as art, she veered toward a bank of pay phones. A suited businessman headed toward the one not in use. She sped up, cut him off.

He glared and mumbled something about pushy broads.

Tough stuff. She had to find out about David. After laying out her coins and dialing zero for the long-distance operator, she realized it was seven o'clock.

"Lawrence'll be home. Drat." She hung up.

Her irate phone competitor started forward.

"Sorry. Not finished," she said crisply as she searched her purse for her address book.

He retreated, glowering.

She got the operator, gave her Lawrence's home phone number, put in her coins. A man in a Navy uniform vacated the phone two places down from her. The businessman behind her, grumbling under his breath, dashed for it and beat out a matron in a full-skirted print dress carrying a clutch purse like a battering ram.

Good. His hovering was irritating.

No answer at Lawrence's home. Her coins clinked in the return. She dialed zero, repeated it all with the office number. Kind of late for him to be there, but maybe he had things to do.

Of course, he had things to do. The Trust wouldn't be turned over to someone who showed up out of the blue. There'd be paperwork. Lots of paperwork.

"Hello." Lawrence's voice, as always, was mild.

He would be wearing his long-sleeved white shirt and bowtie, sitting with military posture. His white hair was likely standing out as he pored over the Harmony estate file.

Mr. H had appointed an ideal executor and trustee in Lawrence. He was not only intelligent but decent. A good man. She was pretty sure he hated having to convey Mr. H's estate to the Packs.

David's return came at the perfect moment.

Unexpected good luck for Lawrence. She shook off the thought.

"This is Megan, Lawrence. I've seen the papers."

"Megan? Papers?" He exhaled audibly. "I'd hoped you wouldn't hear. Newspapers tend to exaggerate, my dear. I wouldn't put too much stock in what they say."

"Is it really David?"

"I suppose it's too much to wish you wouldn't ask about this." He waited but she didn't say anything. "Yes, it's David. But there's no need for you to rush home. Stay on at the retreat lodge and get over this virus George gave you. It can be dangerous, you know."

Lawrence sounded like exactly what he was: an educated southerner molded by a lifetime of dealing with people from different places and classes. Usually his calm reassured. Not today. "I'm home, Lawrence. Or almost. I'm at the Atlanta airport waiting for my flight to Savannah."

"Atlanta! How did you get there? I told Ruby not to let you come back!"

Ha! That had shaken him up. "I never made it to the retreat. A hotel near the airport was as far as I got. I guess Ruby didn't understand that. But it all worked out for the best. I want to see him, Lawrence. Where is he?"

Dead silence. She gripped the receiver.

Was he not going to answer?

Finally he said, "David's secluded. We're having a small press conference here tomorrow morning to placate the reporters. After that, he'll be on the island."

"Harmony Island? With Theo and Sondra?"

Why did the idea sound so absurd? Certainly David would want to go home. And Harmony Island was his home.

Even if Theo and Sondra were in the Big House.

Megan unfastened her chignon and twisted its braid, a long-broken childhood habit. "Are they okay with this? Sondra and Theo, I mean."

It would take getting used to, David being back. Sondra and Theo had been the ones in charge for so many years. What would this mean to Mom's job, to all the other employees?

Nothing. David wouldn't fire anyone on the island. Mom least of all. He adored Mom.

"Ahem. Theo and Sondra's acceptance will come, I'm sure."

So the Packs weren't holding out open arms. "I want to see him."

A hesitation. "I can understand that."

"I'll be home tonight."

"Megan." No wariness now, just intensity. "Don't be foolish. It'll be late when you land in Savannah. Then you'll be driving down alone. No, no, it's too unsafe. What if your car breaks down? It'll be midnight before you reach town, and then you have to get to the island in the dark. Far too late to see David, my dear. No, best stay in Savannah tonight."

Why so many excuses?

"I want to see him right away. He'll want to see me, too. I know he will."

He would, wouldn't he? She held her breath, waiting for Lawrence to agree.

All she heard was Lawrence clearing his throat. Then: "Megan, David doesn't have much free time right now. When he finishes the press conference—"

"I can see him afterward."

"Part of Theo's yachting bunch is here with more of them due tomorrow. You know how they are. They'll be everywhere. You don't want to meet David in front of them. Wait. Have your reunion in private. Maybe Wednesday or Thursday when things are more, er, settled."

Wednesday? Thursday?

Her uneasy stomach roiled with an unwelcome thought. "Doesn't he want to see me?"

Lawrence coughed. "Of course, my dear. After all, you and JoBeth are the closest thing to family he has. Other than Theo." He sounded tired. "We've had so much to handle the past few days, and so much is still to come. I wanted everything finished before you got back."

As if it were her fault she'd caught George's stomach virus.

"I understand." She didn't, but no matter. She had to see David. "Listen, Lawrence, I don't care about anything but David. I'll catch him tomorrow."

"Oh, my. If you feel you must, I suppose you must. But Megan, I must warn you."

She had to prod him. "About what?"

Lawrence chose his words. "He's not the same boy we knew, my dear. He's a man and he's greatly changed. You may be disappointed."

"Disappointed? How could I be disappointed? I'm certainly not the same person I was back then, Lawrence. How could I possibly expect David to be? I'm just so thrilled he's alive, there's no way I'd be disappointed."

When she hung up, she wondered if she'd sounded as brittle to him as she felt inside.

Of course she expected David to be the same, and of course that was foolish. If he was the same now as when he'd left, he would never have stayed away without letting her know he was alive. Never.

Mind awhirl, she made her way to the gate where the small plane to Savannah would depart. Her heels made a sharp rat-a-tat on the tiles as she paced and visualized the two faces in the newspaper.

After all these years, David was returning to her.

He's greatly changed. What exactly did Lawrence mean? She sought an answer by studying the photos in the paper.

Nick Downing, an actor she'd never heard of.

David Harmony, her first love.

****

"Worried Man Blues"
As Performed by the Carter Family (1930)
Traditional

AFTER HE HUNG up, Lawrence put his forehead in his hands. "Damn and blast. Why in the world couldn't that girl stay at the retreat like she was supposed to?"

A list of people coming to lunch on the island tomorrow lay in front of him. He had, after talking to Sondra's secretary, circled two names on it, two people to warn Nick about.

Megan would make three.

Confound it, if only she had stayed out of the picture. There had to be something he could do to stall her, keep her away from Nick for a few more days.

Though he ruminated until the sun slanting through the bay windows gave way to dusk and the book-lined office grew so dim he had to turn on a desk lamp, he came up with no plausible way to keep Megan from confronting Nick.

Finally, reluctantly, he put a finger in the phone's dial. Was keeping an unspoken promise to James worth all these risks?

He was frightened.

Over the soft dial tone, he could almost hear James's contagious belly laugh. "Don't turn tail on me, Whitey. Hush up and handle it like the honest fellow you are."

There was nothing more Lawrence could do. The play had started. It was up to Nick.

Resigned, he dialed.

A bodyguard answered but put Nick on the phone. "Everything all right, Whitey?"

"There'll be people at the party tomorrow you'll need to recognize. May Addison was Livvy's closest friend. Theo's invited her but so far, she hasn't responded."

"Auntie May. I remember. And you thought I wasn't paying attention."

"It's good you were. If she shows up, you'll need to remember every word about her. And Rochelle Tollison will definitely be there."

"Ah. The old girl friend. She's a threat, isn't she? We've no idea how close they were."

"Brush up on what information we have. I'm confident you can carry it off."

He paused to regroup. He'd assured Nick that Megan would be gone. While he searched for words to admit his failure, Nick said, "I've been thinking about Sondra."

"What?" He stiffened. "What about her?" All he needed was an infatuated Nick.

When he opened his mouth to say so, Nick forestalled him. "It's easy to see how she made two such advantageous marriages."

Lawrence gritted his teeth. "I told you. Leave her alone."

"But her interest in me was so flattering. I never particularly liked blondes. Brunettes are so much more complementary on my arm, don't you think? No competition for my own fair locks. But Sondra. My, my. She's enough to make any man change his preferences."

The man's conceit knew no bounds. "Leave. Sondra. Alone."

A chuckle. "Whitey, Whitey. It's so easy baiting you. Almost as easy as baiting Theo. Are you sure you don't want to tell me who you're fronting for?"

"No!" Lawrence forced himself to take deep breaths. "All right. You've had your fun. There's one more thing you need to know."

He related Megan's illness and unexpected return. "She'll be in tonight, but I persuaded her to wait till tomorrow to approach you."

Silence. "I see. I have to meet her?" Amusement was gone. "You didn't say much about her, only mentioned her when she fitted in with some of the other people."

Ah. Nick recognized the problem. "Yes, and she's a bigger danger than anyone. I'll run over a few of the things you'll have to know."

Though he talked himself hoarse, he feared the information was too late and his memories were inadequate.

Confound the woman. Why couldn't she do as she was told?

Nick was quiet when Lawrence finally trailed off, when there was nothing else he could think of to add about Megan.

"Ahem." What was Nick thinking? "I'm sorry. I tried to avoid this. Can you manage?"

Nick's answer seemed long in coming, but when it did, he sounded confident, even cocky.

"Oh, yes. I have an idea or two. She was in the home movies so I know quite a bit about her relationship with David. Maybe I can keep her from focusing on what I don't know by proving I'm the same boy who drove her crazy. Don't worry, Whitey. I keep telling you, I'm an award-winning actor."

"So you claim."

"Here, now, I don't appreciate—"

Lawrence hung up. He should never have started this.

Resting his elbows on his desk, he clasped his hands together almost like praying.

CHAPTER 17

"Jealousy" ("Jalousie")
As Performed by Frankie Laine (1951)
Music by Jacob Gade
Lyrics by Vera Bloom

IN THE LIBRARY of the island mansion, Theodore Pack waited for Amos and John to come down. They were probably discussing Lawrence's shitty charade.

Pretending that frigging actor was David.

Stupid assholes. Any fool could see what was going on.

At the bar, he poured gin into a pitcher. Then a splash of vermouth and some ice. He and Amos always shared martinis before dinner. Or any other time.

Alcohol blurred the nasty past and his part in it.

He forced himself to stir the mixture smoothly. All in the wrist, his favorite bartender said.

How the hell could this guy look so much like David? The likeness was uncanny. He didn't know where Downing came from, but Lawrence had to be behind it. He'd bet his butt Lawrence was skimming from the Trust.

Or George. Lawrence might be honest, but he'd protect his son if he was stealing. Sondra had mentioned how much money George's wife spent. More than any small town lawyer's wife should.

Theo slapped the stirrer down and picked up a glass.

Didn't matter. George or Lawrence. Whoever'd brought this guy in would be sorry.

God, he didn't want to kill anybody. Not again. Maybe he could offer Downing more than Lawrence was paying. Buy him off.

He poured his martini, took a big swallow.

The telephone in the hall rang. Peachie yipped, but shushed at Sondra's soft voice. As she said, "Hello," he dropped onto the leather sofa across from the head of a whitetail buck bagged with a bow.

He'd relocated sixteen families to increase the hunting preserve on the island's north end. Normally, the twelve pointer in its place of honor over the mantel elated him.

Not this afternoon.

There had to be a way to prove Lawrence and the actor were lying, but he needed time. He tossed back the martini. From the hall, he caught Sondra's breathy, little-girl voice: "Okay. Everything's copacetic, then."

Talking to one of the other wives. Muffin or Billie?

"Theo." Sondra stood there holding Peachie. "I thought you were changing clothes."

"Not yet." She looked damn good in another one of those sexy tennis outfits that hinted at curves and showed off her long legs. "Who was that on the phone?"

"Billie Charlton." She put Peachie down, wandered over to the big globe standing in the corner. "They're driving down from Savannah and want me to meet them at that seafood place on the mainland in about an hour. I said I would. Do you want to come?"

"No. You know I despise the Charltons. Both of them but especially her." He got up to revisit the bar.

Her glow dimmed. She didn't like him drinking but never nagged. He loved her for it.

She twirled the globe. "I know Billie talks too much, but she and I need to discuss the start for next week's races. You might want to be there, too. Last year, the cannon kept firing before—"

"I'm not going to listen to Billie Charlton's yammering." He swung from the bar with a fresh drink. Why did she keep pushing it? What the hell was going on?

The actor. He'd flustered her.

She left the globe, held up both hands in surrender. "Okay, okay. Stay here, then. I have to meet them though. I told them I would and they're on the way." Stopping at a mirror, she smoothed her hair back. "I look a fright. I've barely got time to shower and fix my makeup."

"You're always gorgeous."

He hadn't missed Downing's reaction to Sondra.

He didn't mind other men ogling his wife, but Nick Downing was different. Downing's flattery had brought that telltale radiance to her cheeks. He wanted to kill the two-bit sonofabitch.

He hid his jealousy. "Don't stay out too late. More rain's supposed to come through tonight."

"You know how Billie loves to drag out dinner. If it's raining, I'll leave the car and ride back with them." Frowning, she came over and touched his cheek. "You're all right, aren't you?"

He melted.

It wasn't her fault the stinking fairy hung over her like a dog after a bitch in heat. She might put out the charm for Nick Downing, but until they could figure out the next step, they had to keep things on an even keel. She was doing her part like they'd agreed.

He had to do his.

When he kissed her, she kissed him back fervently before pushing him away with a husky laugh. "Later, Buccaneer. I don't have time now. Did Amos hear from the investigators?"

"Not yet."

"He will, I'm sure. If not, we'll figure something out." She picked up Peachie and threw him another kiss before leaving, back straight and hips swaying.

Hell yes, he would figure something out. He'd told Amos that, too.

Amos, the shitty bastard. Sucking up to the asshole. Once this thing got settled, he'd replace the stinking sonofabitch along with his rat-faced partner and hire someone loyal. Someone eager to take on anything or anyone.

And you can go to hell, Amos.

As for Downing . . . If Downing wouldn't be bought off, he'd do whatever he had to do. For Sondra.

He drained his drink and tapped the empty glass. Too bad his story was on record. He could have pretended to be on the boat.

No. They'd have suspected. He'd done the right thing.

Anyway, there were people who'd known David and who could recognize this man was a fake. Two of them would be at the party tomorrow. He'd made sure of that.

I'll wait and see what happens. If they can't expose the goddam faggot, I'll try money. If that doesn't work, I'll do something else.

He didn't like to think of what that something would be.

By the time Amos and John got downstairs, Theo had started on a new pitcher of martinis. He could hold his liquor, though. He sure could. When Sondra appeared in capris and a sleeveless top cut to reveal her taut midriff, he walked her down to the cruiser.

"It'll be all right," he promised her again before they got within earshot of the boat driver. "If May and David's old girl friend can't expose him, I have another plan."

She kissed him. "I'm not worried. I trust you, Theo."

He waved as the cruiser took her toward the mainland.

Lawrence had to be behind this. Either by himself or with George or someone else.

****

"My Boyfriend's Back"
As Performed by the Angels (1963)
Words by Robert Feldman, Gerald Goldstein,
and Richard Gottereff
Lyrics by Robert Feldman, Gerald Goldstein,
and Richard Gottereff

AFTER AN ENDLESS wait at the Savannah terminal, Megan's navy Samsonite train case came out into the baggage area, with the weekender and larger suitcase close behind. She pulled them out with mechanical precision and looked for a bellman. Ten thirty, but she was almost home.

Her gas tank was full, so the lights of a still-open Dairy Queen Brazier beckoned. She stopped to get a Coke and use the restroom. While there, she changed clothes.

Off with her gathered skirt and blouse. Off with the petticoat and garter belt and hose.

Aaahhhh. She could breathe.

Donning a shirt and capris, she exchanged heels for flats and took off her pearl set. Her business chignon had long since given way to the braid hanging down her back, but she wet the escaped wisps around her face and combed them back.

There. Much better. All set for the rest of the drive in the dark and unforgiving night.

After she navigated Savannah streets to route 17, driving should have been easy except that rain began, at first gentle, then worsening.

While she concentrated on the road, she reviewed the phone call.

Lawrence had said he didn't want her driving alone at night—and her mother would've had a fit, sure enough—but her gut said he didn't want her to meet David.

Why not? Surely David wanted to see her. He might not be as anxious as she, but still. They'd been best friends all their lives. Up till that night he left.

Anger had fled. Now she alternated between elation at having him alive and the fear that he didn't care about her anymore, that she meant less to him than a stranger.

By eleven, the rain lessened but her radio got only static. She turned it off and drove on. Windshield wipers kerthunked back and forth. Had she not been so wrought up, their hypnotic rhythm would have put her to sleep.

The storm passed, stars emerged.

She turned the radio back on. The local stations were long signed off the air, but the Cincinnati Top 40 station came in loud and clear.

Yay! You could always count on Cincinnati.

Singing along with the songs she recognized kept her awake. When a catchy tune came on, she turned the volume up. "Please Please Me." The disc jockey said he'd gotten the record from a friend and touted the group as big in England, but the Beetles?

Come on. Who'd name a group after such disgusting insects?

Cincinnati lasted the rest of the way home. She pulled into the lot she'd left three days earlier, turned off the Studebaker, and put her head on the wheel. The Packs owned a mainland house she could sleep over in if she woke up the caretaker.

But she wouldn't. She wanted to get back to the island. To David.

A nearly full moon hovered in the sky as she got out and stretched tired muscles.

The rain was gone. That was something, at least.

It might be midnight, but the moonlight and pier lamps outlined her runabout in its corner mooring, and she could find the way to the island blindfolded. The river breeze brought the welcoming smell of the marshes. She left the larger luggage in the car for later retrieval, but transferred her briefcase, train case, and purse to the boat.

David, David, she thought as she pulled out, I'll see you tomorrow.

The boat lights cut a puny path on the black water. The winds had disappeared with the cessation of the storm, but tiny waves in the inland river bombarded the boat prow.

Not that bad. She'd navigated rougher waters.

Nearing the island, she headed toward the right side where her dock lay. Would David be staying at the main house or one of the cottages? Mom would know.

Except Mom wasn't here. David had come home, and Mom was on a dream trip.

And Megan should have been away, too. Both the people who knew David best were gone.

A boat engine came to life from the direction of an old pier near her house. It had once serviced an island cannery though no one lived in the area now. The plant was defunct, but sometimes locals fished around there.

No lights visible, but the motor swelled. An inboard.

She scowled. It better not be any of the yachters. They were okay sober, but this time of night they'd be soused.

The engine got louder, from somewhere behind her.

Her running lights were on and the night had cleared. The boat driver should see her.

A dark silhouette appeared not fifty yards distant. It skimmed over the water, aiming directly for her. She gunned the motor and turned.

The speedboat showed no lights and didn't slow. It swerved, too, following her lead.

"What—"

It was going too fast.

The runabout's small engine didn't have the power to outrun it.

"Stop!" She stood up and waved her arms.

The shape bore down.

One dizzying moment and a sleek bulk closed in.

Straight for her boat. Straight for her.

No time to gather belongings. No time to grab a life jacket.

No time.

She dove to the side. The water clobbered her like a cold wall.

She tumbled head over heels for hours except it must have been seconds before she came up gasping and spitting.

The remains of her runabout lay several yards away. Broken boards and more junk.

The other boat was circling back. Still no running lights, but a powerful flashlight aimed over the wreckage, then began to sweep the surrounding waters.

Searching for her. She opened her mouth, closed it again.

They should've been yelling, calling to see if she was hurt. Why wasn't its lights on?

Instinct drove her, primal and unreasoned.

She went under and swam away from the boat debris. Holding her breath, she looked up through the water. No longer cold but warming as a fluid blanket.

After the bright light cleared her location, she came up, took a gulp of salty air, and dove again.

I'm being stupid. They're probably drunk, didn't see me. Now they've realized what happened and are looking for me.

Her common sense snorted.

Oh, yeah? Why aren't they in a frenzy? If they're drunk, they'll kill me trying to rescue me. Better stay out of sight.

Common sense won.

She kept swimming away as the speedboat made wider circles. It might be searching for her but she'd be crazy to trust anyone that careless. The shore wasn't too far.

Finally, the shadowy boat left, heading back in the opposite direction from where it had emerged. Not till it disappeared into a reedy channel did Megan relax.

She floated, done in, mind churning.

Idiot. She should have signaled the boat, shown herself. Now she had to swim, and lifejackets were back with what was left of her boat.

Why didn't they say anything?

Swimming and treading water got her to the closest land. She staggered ashore through the reeds, hoping no snakes or alligators were nearby. The marshy sand sucked at her feet.

At least it was still September. The water hadn't been cold, but the night air was.

She should have waved her arms, called for help.

Or maybe not. She was lucky she wasn't hurt.

Dripping seawater, she limped home.

The other boat's driver had to be one of the Packs' guests. Their yachts were anchored on the other side of the island near the main dock, the same direction where the speedboat had disappeared. Whoever it was ought to have to pay for the runabout.

My things.

They were gone. Her purse with car keys. And billfold, driver's license, checkbook, and travel money. Her briefcase with notes on Miss Millicent's latest will revisions and the voucher for the seminar fees. Her train case with her makeup and jewelry and toilet items. And her pearl necklace and earrings in her purse; a set Mom and Dad had given her for high school graduation.

Everything in the runabout. Lost. She passed time by mentally listing things to replace.

Nearly dry by the time she got home, she let herself in with the spare key kept over the kitchen window. Adrenaline had long since turned to exhaustion.

Once she gulped down a big glass of water with two aspirins, she fell into bed. Salt, sand, dirt, and all. Tomorrow was soon enough to clean up. She could deal with the accident and her lost things and the destroyed runabout then.

David, too.

CHAPTER 18

"The Crowd"
As Performed by Roy Orbison (1962)
Music by Roy Orbison and Joe Melson
Lyrics by Roy Orbison and Joe Melson

EXHAUSTED, MEGAN SLEPT past noon. When she got up, she was sluggish but determined. She had stuff to do that didn't include brooding over lost possessions.

Like chase down whoever was responsible for sinking her boat the past night.

And find David.

After taking a long, soaking shower, she fixed herself a piece of toast that, thankfully, stayed down. Then she braided her hair and put on her bathing suit under a pair of Bermuda shorts and a sleeveless button-up shirt tied at the waist.

If David was in a pool or the ocean or wherever, she'd be ready to confront him.

Setting off for the Big House, she took a longer route. Lawrence had said David would be busy till this afternoon so she had time to see what she could find out about the boat with no lights and a reckless driver.

The speedboat that ran over her had disappeared in the direction of the yachts, but the Packs often loaned their cruisers to guests, and these were berthed at the island's main pier near the yachts. Her little detour should prove whether one of them was damaged.

The more she thought about it, the madder she got.

Her personal possessions were lost. She could have been killed. And Mom's boat was destroyed. Running over her and leaving like that was low even for the fast crowd that gravitated to the Packs.

Emerging from the pines that separated the Mulrennons' cottage from the main pier area, she stopped for a golf cart to pass.

A tanned man and a gorgeous girl twenty years younger necked in the back while the uniformed driver aimed a stolid gaze straight ahead. From a dory and three runabouts lazily bobbing beside the pilings, the couple weren't the only yachters on the island.

A second golf cart stood by the ramp, waiting to transport anyone the quarter mile to the house. In the driver's seat, another of the

Packs' employees in the mandatory white golf shirt and khaki Bermudas reclined with a baseball hat pulled low to keep off the sun.

She walked over. "Hey, Chauncey."

He scrambled upright and pushed up his hat bill. Alarm died. "Megan. Wasn't expecting nobody from the woods."

"Uh huh. That's what happens when you take a nap."

When she'd started attending school on the mainland, Chauncey was the oldest kid riding the water taxi. Once in town, she walked two blocks to her high school while he and the other islanders walked three miles to theirs.

Once the integration ruling came down, that practice was supposed to end the past year. But Negroes as well as whites objected to the schools' merger, arguing about everything from which one would be a high school or junior high, to what name the new, united school would have.

Lawrence had been helpful in ironing out those problems, but some white parents had sued anyway. With the courts slow as they were, no one knew when it would get settled.

Now Chauncey yawned and stretched. "Just resting my eyes. Most of the yat-chet people's still in bed. Not much for us to do yet."

She grinned at the deliberate mispronunciation. Chauncey felt the same way she did about the visitors. "Listen, a motorboat without lights ran into me when I came across the sound last night. Have you noticed any damaged boats come in?"

Chauncey froze, hands over his head. His eyes opened so wide the whites showed. "A motorboat hit you?"

"Yeah. I couldn't see it too well but it sounded like an inboard. Tore Mom's runabout up and sank it. My pocketbook and suitcase and everything went into the sound. I had to swim in. Do you know anything about it?"

His hands came slowly down. His face returned to the usual blankness. "Mr. Theo and one of 'em come down early this morning to use his new ski boat, but it was all mangled up."

"His Ski Nautique they delivered last week?"

Chauncey nodded. "Mr. Theo quizzed me about it, but I didn't know nothing."

She started toward the boathouse. "I want to see it."

"The marina folk already come and took it off. Mr. Theo put in a report with the sheriff."

She stopped. "So he didn't take it out last night?"

"Don't reckon. He'd of said, wouldn't he?" He paused. "It had some red streaks on its bow. Like it might of hit something."

Mom had had the runabout painted bright red at the beginning of the summer, but Megan didn't say so. Chauncey knew. "If it wasn't Theo driving, it had to be someone on the island."

"One of the visitors, I 'spect."

"I expect you're right. So drunk they might not even remember hitting me today if the sheriff asks."

He guffawed. "Mr. Theo may of reported it but he ain't gonna let Sheriff Attaway *im*-pose on his guests by asking 'em questions. Reckon we'll never know for sure."

"No. I guess not." She'd say something to Theo, though. Mom shouldn't have to pay for what one of Theo's friends had done. "Guess I'll go on to the house. I want to see David. Have you met him yet?"

Chauncey got out of the cart. "Yeah. When he come over before lunch with the Wykertons. Had a couple of other men with them, too."

Her heart pounded. "What did . . . ? How did he look?"

Chauncey scratched his head. "Same as always 'cept about fifteen, twenty years older."

"It's been seventeen years."

"Yeah."

"Did he remember you?"

"Sure did. Once I told him who I was. He looked me over pretty sharp and said, you the Chauncey who told me how to raise that baby squirrel? I say, what squirrel was that? He say, the one that got out of its cage and bit my daddy. I say, yessir but I never did own up to it though, cause Mr. H, he sure had a temper."

He slapped his thigh and cackled.

She couldn't help but grin, too.

"Then he eyes my middle and says, I remember Chauncey being tall and string bean skinny. So I say, I still tall, man. And then he laughed, the same way he used to."

"So he's really David." The weight on her vanished.

Chauncey's teeth flashed. "He couldn't of knowed 'bout that squirrel otherwise. I about forgot it myself."

"So had I. But we always brought hurt animals to you, Chauncey. You always knew what to do for them."

"Yeah, 'bout the only time any of you needed me."

She heard the slight edge. The islanders had reason to resent the Packs, but the Harmonys? Maybe her?

He read her expression. "Hey. Didn't bother me none then and don't now. Y'all had your friends and I had mine. Still do. But say, can I ask a favor?"

"Sure."

"Leodicea Bodkin's grandson Curtis worked for y'all the past few summers, but I know he's off to school up north. Reckon Mr. Lawrence might think about hiring my girl?"

"Your girl?"

Chauncey's laughter boomed. "My daughter. Don't look so shocked. She ain't dumb like me. She's smart, so smart her teachers say she might even make valedictorian."

If she doesn't have to go to school with the whites, went unsaid. Law or no law, the blacks worried they'd still be put down.

"I'm not shocked at her being smart. I'm shocked at her being old enough to want an office job when she can catch crabs and sell them for extra money. And any man who knows when the fish are running and where, who can take an engine apart and find out what's wrong then put it back together, is not dumb."

"Don't take brains for that. That's basic. What about it? Will you put in a word for her with Mr. Lawrence?"

"How old is she?"

"Sixteen. She's saving money for Morris Brown College."

"She's been accepted at Morris Brown?"

"Yep."

"Good grief. I had no idea." She clicked her tongue. "I'll say something but I'm just a peon, Chauncey. You'll be better off asking George to put in a word."

"I didn't want to say nothing in front of Mr. Lawrence. You used to work there after school when you was in high school so I kinda thought you might jog his memory 'bout that. 'Sides, Mr. Lawrence might be more inclined to listen to you than Mr. George."

"Don't get your hopes up. But I'll ask. Right now I want to see David."

"Figured that." His bland expression gave nothing away.

Why should it? She and David were friends. Nobody had known otherwise. There'd been no time to tell. No time for anything except one night. And regret.

"See you later."

Squaring her shoulders, she started up the sandy trail. Late-blooming lilacs heated by the sun bathed her in a sweet fragrance as the house came into view. Mr. H had completely refitted a nineteenth-century house for Miss Livvy. Set among live oaks, pines, cedars, and sycamores, the Spanish Revival flaunted a red tile roof that rose between forks of a circular drive paved with oyster shells.

Megan, once on the driveway, strode past the front swimming pool ringed by seven life-sized Grecian maidens with urns. Two couples lounged on the pool steps, drink glasses held above water.

David wasn't with them.

She bypassed the porch where spiral columns and arched double entry doors gave visitors a restrained welcome and went to the side toward the cedar wood.

The golf fairway Theo had put in over part of Miss Livvy's cherished rose garden was empty and afforded a good view of the sound and the sailboats anchored there. At the edge, Sondra's fountain lay in sparkling glory.

Skirting the house, Megan reached the edge of the piazza that stretched between the cedars and the patio leading to the inside pool. Music from the back speakers met her.

Frank Sinatra, singing the romantic ballads that Sondra preferred.

There wasn't a big crowd yet. Most of the Packs' friends didn't get moving till late afternoon. Then they partied all night. Loudly.

Luckily, the races only occurred once a year. The hunting parties weren't nearly as raucous, and since Theo had moved the islanders on the north out, no one was close enough for the gunfire to bother.

Though resentment still rankled from the forced move.

Not that Theo cared.

Oh well. The past was the past. Except for David.

She scanned the terrain, seeking him.

A couple of women admired Sondra's fountain while a foursome on the tennis court included George Wykerton and his wife. The glass doors enclosing the indoor pool had been thrown open to the outside. Laughter punctuated the air from people in shorts, sundresses, and swimsuits spilling out onto the patio.

One man lay without a shirt, several beer bottles lined up beside his chaise. He'd be a lobster later today. The coastal Georgia sun, even in late September, was unforgiving.

Megan breathed deeply.

Lawrence had warned her there'd be a lot of people here.

Okay, there were people. So what else was new? There was always a mob when the Packs were in residence, and a lot more partiers would show up before the week was out. From the looks of this bunch, an unexpected heir wasn't about to spoil their good times.

Her stomach flip-flopped.

Too bad her first encounter with David had to be like this, but it didn't matter. Nothing mattered except that he was alive.

Once she edged past the fountain, she could see more of the grounds. Theo stood on the piazza, drink in hand, towering over two women who chattered and gestured with their hands.

No sign of David.

Perhaps she should have waited as Lawrence suggested.

No, darn it. She deserved to know why he'd stayed away without a word. Why he'd left her to begin with. He owed her that much.

Beyond the walks, a sweeping view of the beach stretched past the pavilion and salt water pool Miss Livvy had loved. No one enjoyed it today, but several people romped on the sands, throwing a ball and dashing into the surf.

A lone swimmer made for an anchored dock.

His strokes were relaxed, the shape of his head familiar.

Goose pimples rose on her arms and legs.

"Lawrence said you were coming."

She whirled. "Theo! You shouldn't creep up like that."

"Sorry." He swept off dark glasses, his gaze passing over her bare legs. Though he managed to convey interest, the whole thing was impersonal, an ingrained habit. "I just wanted to say hello." His tone was light.

Was he flirting? She didn't know him well enough to decide.

He studied her. "I expect you were summoned back to greet our prodigal."

"No. I got sick and canceled my seminar. I saw the news about David on the plane."

"Oh?" A flash of something—surprise? triumph?—flickered. "Is that right?"

In the ocean, the swimmer climbed up on the anchored swim dock. He wore navy swim trunks. Water glistened on bare chest and legs. A vigorous headshake sent droplets sparkling.

"A little strange." Theo watched the swimmer, too. "Your family was so close to the boys, I would have thought Lawrence would have told you and JoBeth first thing."

The swimmer sank down on the boards and lay down, stretching out on his back.

"My trip was planned last January." Megan would never admit bewilderment. "And Mom's cruise was booked in May." When Lawrence's daughter had scheduled her holiday. "I'm sure Lawrence didn't want to upset our plans."

She took a half step toward the pavilion path. "Besides, it isn't as if we're kin."

"No, but y'all were always close to him. Like a second family." Theo held his drink in one hand and sunglasses in the other as he watched the dock. "David always loved the ocean, but that's the first time that man's been in it since he got here before lunch."

Megan followed his gaze. "You've met him then?"

"Yes."

"How does he seem?"

Theo put his sunglasses back on. "Strange. The whole deal's strange. You remember how David swam all out, churning up the water? Did you see how sluggish that man's stroke was?"

"You're being obvious, Theo. You don't believe he's David."

Theo didn't take offence at her bluntness. "He isn't."

"Lawrence says he is. The newspapers say fingerprints and dental records match. Why do you think he's not David?"

"Ah, Megan, Megan." Taking her arm, Theo led her toward the steps going up to the piazza. "Do you think David would have waited so long to come home?"

She didn't like her own doubts thrown back at her. "People change. All of us change."

"You believe it, too? And you haven't even met him. I don't understand why everyone is so anxious to accept some two-bit actor as David."

Megan hung back. "I thought it was a fact. Is there any reason to suppose he isn't David? Lawrence would be hard to fool."

He stopped, too. "Lawrence would say the devil himself was David if he could keep his claws on the Harmony Trust."

"Theo," she rebuked.

"It's true." He was matter-of-fact. "My attorneys are lined up to take charge of it on Wednesday. Then every penny will have to be accounted for, not to mention every closed factory, every failing company, every sum paid out to consultants who happened to be friends or clients of Wykerton Perth and Ross. Every outlay, every loss will have to be explained. And Lawrence knows it. This man was a godsend for him. Don't you wonder, Megan?"

"Lawrence is one of the most honorable men I know." And Theo was a pain in the neck. Had been for years. "He'd never accept this man as David if he had any doubts at all. Never. Anyone auditing the Harmony Trust will find it in perfect order."

"Lawrence wouldn't be the first attorney who let temptation get the better of him."

"Some other attorney. Not Lawrence."

"Okay, maybe not Lawrence. But suppose George needed money and skimmed from the Trust. He'd have years to hide it because the money was tied up. Nothing to keep him from nipping in and taking some." Theo grasped her upper arm. Faint alcoholic fumes suffused her. "Then when time came to pay up, he couldn't. So he scrambles for a way out and comes up with this."

"No." She edged back. "George wouldn't do that either."

"Don't play innocent. Lawyers and banks get away with that kind of thing all the time."

"You're saying Lawrence or George is a criminal."

"I'm saying this so-called David turned up at a very convenient time for them. It'll take years to get this mess straightened out. By that time, God knows how much more they'll have plundered from the estate."

"Theo. Really. You just don't want to admit that David's come back."

"Wait till you meet him, Megan. You'll see. There's no way in hell that man is David."

"I hope you're wrong."

"Do me a favor. Keep an open mind, okay?" Theo draped an arm around her shoulders.

"Sure."

Theo had to be wrong. He was bound to be upset and suspicious, but Chauncey said it was David. And she trusted Lawrence. Lawrence of all people would know.

On the piazza Sondra, Peachie at her heels, talked to a cluster of men and one woman. Rings flashed as her hands gestured. "—in London. Their hair was so shaggy it flew everywhere! Their music's different, but they'll never be as big as Sinatra or even Elvis. Not over here."

She spotted Megan with Theo.

The smile on the perfect lips become a trifle fixed.

Megan sucked in her breath. Oh lord, she'd let Theo lead her back to the house. And he had his arm around her.

She tried to slide away, but Theo didn't let go. "If you of all people agree he's David, no one will say different no matter what they believe. No matter what the truth is."

Sondra pointed a portly man in slacks and button-down collar toward the bar. "Phil, Hubert over there is a big contributor to the Democrats. Go and introduce yourself."

To the others, she said, "I need to see my husband."

Protests ensued from a muscular man in swim trunks and jeers from another in tennis whites. She frowned prettily. "You boys behave. They'll be serving food pretty soon and the bar's always open."

Megan freed herself from Theo under the pretense of dumping a stone from her sandal.

Not that she was doing anything wrong, but Sondra might not see it that way. Sondra adored Theo. She might get prickly about seeing his arm around another woman, even if it was plain Megan Mulrennon in shorts and shirt, with flyaway hair and sweat beads on her lip.

Sondra always made her feel like a ragamuffin.

Like today.

Despite the sun and breeze, Sondra was as dashing as ever. A floppy hat protected a honey complexion while a halter top vaunted full breasts over a flowered sarong skirt. Most women would look awful in such an outfit.

Sondra looked like a pinup.

Peachie rushed at Megan, but obeyed when Sondra told her to sit down and stay.

Megan leaned over to pet her.

"She gets so excited she may wee on you," Sondra warned. "So good to see you, Meggie. JoBeth keeps us posted on what you're up to but I never talk to you. Aren't you sweet in those shorts. Like a little teenybopper."

She hugged Megan, whispered, "David's asked about you."

"I'm anxious to see him."

But Sondra had already turned away.

"Theo, did you tell the kitchen we needed more ice? Warm drinks on a day like today won't do. And, baby, could you check on the lieutenant-governor and make sure the Highburns aren't boring him?"

****

"You Belong to Me"
As Performed by Jo Stafford (1952)
Music by Chilton Price, Pee Wee King,
and Redd Stewart
Lyrics by Chilton Price, Pee Wee King,
and Redd Stewart

IF THAT DIDN'T take the cake. Theo hanging onto JoBeth's daughter. The housekeeper's daughter!

She'd take care of that right quick.

When Sondra adroitly steered him toward the lieutenant-governor, Theo didn't protest.

Suspicion faded.

What a lamebrain she was being. No need to be jealous of mousy little Megan Mulrennon who couldn't keep a man.

JoBeth said the last engagement was kaput, too. The one that snagged her that huge ring. This had to be the third or fourth chance poor Megan had lost.

Not that she cared about a poky lawyer's love life. Too much was at stake today.

Would Megan, or would she not, identify this man as David?

Christ, her head hurt. Smoothing her forehead, she turned back to Megan. "Low on ice. Of all things to run out of on a day like today.

Sometimes, I think I'm losing my mind. Of course, with JoBeth gone and everything else that's happened, I guess I have an excuse."

"He really is David?"

Oho, kiddo. You aren't fooling me. You've got doubts.

Little Miss George Washington never could hide anything.

What tack should she take? Better play it cagy till they met.

"Lawrence checked dental records and all those stupid things." She adjusted her sarong. "I'm sure he was thorough."

"You think he's David." Transparent relief showed.

Women so ingenuous really had no business trying to be lawyers.

"Lawrence says so."

Megan leaned forward. "How is he?"

"I really can't say." Wait and see which way Megan leaned. Then she'd know what to do.

Ah, there were Amos's friends. Perfect. She beckoned.

"Let me introduce you to the Joneses, Megan. They're from Charlotte but want a getaway house down here. Maybe you can help. Lawyers always know about local real estate." She picked up Peachie and murmured, "Tobacco money. You'd be wise to get in with them."

There. That should keep her out of Theo's way for a while.

Sometimes sweet things like Megan were the ones a wife needed to worry about. Sometimes they exerted an irrational fascination for even the most world-weary sophisticate.

And they did it without anyone realizing what was happening till it was too late. Oh, yeah, she knew all about those self-effacing women who stammered and blushed. She'd seen too many divorces come about because of some mealy-mouthed snot.

Not that she believed Megan posed any danger. For one thing Megan was too goody-goody to make a play for another woman's husband. For another, she wasn't Theo's type.

Searching for Theo, she found him engrossed with a slutty brunette, the kind of woman she understood at all levels. The kind she could handle with her hands tied behind her back.

Her shoulders relaxed.

Now to see what happened when Megan caught up to the actor.

CHAPTER 19

"Don't Let the Stars Get in Your Eyes"
As Performed by Perry Como
with the Ramblers (1952)
Music by Slim Willet aka Winston L. Moore
Lyrics by Slim Willet aka Winston L. Moore

MEGAN KNEW NOTHING about the real estate market, local or otherwise, but it took several minutes to convince the Joneses of that and make her escape. Then, as she headed toward the beach, Sondra's secretary caught her at the bar set up on the far side of the piazza.

Would she never get to him?

She could absolutely scream, but politeness meant she had to stop.

Linda wasn't pretty, but she camouflaged the deficit with cosmetics and style. The Packs' social secretary for several years, she worked closely with JoBeth to make sure the Packs' events succeeded. Caterers, invitations, entertainment—Linda took charge of all the details the Packs couldn't be bothered with.

Megan's mother said Linda knew exactly what she wanted and laid out exactly what she expected. "Not like that last flibbertigibbet who told me to do this and that, and ended up with a disaster. Linda lets me know what's going on."

Mom had added smugly: "She also leaves people alone who are doing their job."

Megan liked Linda, too. "Hi."

"Megan." Linda touched her arm in concern. "I heard someone ran into your boat last night. Are you okay?"

Megan grimaced. Chauncey must have blabbed. She didn't want to talk about the accident. Not now. "Except for being sore. And losing my transport to the mainland."

"Use one of the Packs' boats. They won't care."

"Ah. But then you have to ask, are the boats really the Packs' to loan?"

"Oh, screw it." It was Linda's turn to grimace. "Isn't this right out of a soap opera? No one knows how to treat him. They don't want to get in bad with the Packs, but they don't want to burn their bridges if he's really David Harmony. So everyone's taking a wait-and-see attitude. Except the press. They caught two reporters disguised as caterers this morning. Goodness knows how many more we'll have to fend off before it's over."

"Plenty, I bet."

"There was a swarm of boats out yesterday, too, with reporters shooting pictures." Linda waved toward the open sea. "Sondra got the Senator to intervene and the Coast Guard herded them back, but it's almost impossible to keep them away."

"I guess it's a big story."

"You could say that. God knows what's going to happen." Linda smiled and waved to someone before muttering to Megan, "The Packs are upset."

"Yeah, I saw Theo. He's convinced this man isn't David."

"No kidding." Linda simpered. "He's got too much to lose. How'll he pay for his new yacht and the other toys? Not to mention the safaris and sailing trips."

"Sondra doesn't seem too disturbed."

Linda raised her brows. "You know Sondra. She'll make lemonade out of lemons. But she can't be happy. I guess I should start looking for another job. Lawrence said David doesn't plan any staff dismissals, but I doubt he'll need a social secretary."

"Sure he will. To keep the reporters away if nothing else."

Linda looked over her shoulder. "Uh oh. The Flaherties are stranded again. Duty calls."

At these affairs, Linda didn't swim or water ski or use the pedal boats, though she did make up an occasional fourth at bridge or tennis.

Like JoBeth Mulrennon, she was hired help.

With a supportive wave, Megan started down to the beach. She could hardly wait to confront David.

If he was really David.

Drat. Theo's insinuations were getting to her.

An osprey circled as she walked toward the pavilion, the first time she'd seen one this year though when she was younger there had been lots of them.

The soaring bird made her overlook, until she'd climbed the ramp to the pavilion, two large men in Bermuda shorts and loose sport shirts seated on a bench. They held beer bottles and smoked.

Both nodded to her.

She nodded back but paused, reluctant to strip to a swimsuit in front of the Packs' friends.

No choice if she wanted to see David. At least she wore the modest black suit with the high boat neck.

Turning away from the men, she undressed and left her outer clothes on the bench beside a red knit shirt. His? An embroidered

"Wembley" with a crest beneath suggested yes. He'd been living in England, hadn't he?

Up at the house, Theo stood alone, drink in hand. Watching her meet David.

Poor Theo. Waiting all these years for nothing.

The sand was warm and so was the sea. Waist-deep, she dived. Salt water rippled over her skin.

David, alone on the swim dock, lay supine, one bent knee pointing up. His profile stood out sharply against the sky, with eyelashes closed and jaw firm.

An odd panic assailed her, akin to the one when he had jerked his friend off her. Before he grabbed her and kissed her himself.

Remembering that brought back the disoriented anger, then the shock that anger could so quickly turn to desire.

She treaded water quietly so as not to disturb him.

His lips were the same, the bottom fuller. The nose—was that kink there before? The hair was fine and straight, but longer and darker, not the new corn color she recalled.

The reedy boy had changed into a man with muscular thighs and flat stomach. A man who bore signs of hard usage.

A round scar the size of a half dollar stood out on the near shoulder while a short thin one ran across the inner thigh of the bent leg. Another jagged mark streaked down the side of his ribcage and disappeared under swim trunks.

This was someone who'd challenged life and survived.

The sick feeling in the pit of her stomach refused to go away. Her treading water sounded like ripples lapping against the dock but roused him.

His head pivoted. She gazed into stony eyes. Suspicious eyes. Stormy gray. Not the clear blue she remembered.

A fringe of lashes veiled them before they instantly reopened, bland and guileless.

Had she imagined the harshness?

"Hullo," he said.

Other than that quick turn of his head, he didn't move.

So that was how it was to be. No apologies. No delighted welcomes. She should have expected nothing more since she knew better than anyone what he was like.

Had been like. Cocky, oblivious to other people's feelings.

Her mouth dried. "Hello."

Straight-on, his mouth was cynical. It wasn't bowed and tender, but a little . . . brutal?

Her back tingled.

He watched her.

She took a breath. "Do you know who I am?"

His mouth twitched, gentling it, making it more like that of the boy she'd loved.

"It's hard to say. It's been a long time."

His voice had a British tinge. Its timbre was familiar but strange.

Because he'd been gone seventeen years. He was older.

Swimming to the ladder, she pulled herself up onto weathered boards where she sat cross-legged, dripping seawater and pushing back hairs that had escaped the rubber band. "Easy question. Do you or don't you know me?"

He remained motionless. "The braid gives you away, Meggie. You're the only girl I ever knew who wore braids from the time she was two until the time she was sixteen."

He didn't have to make fun of her. "You didn't recognize me without it?"

"I expect I'd know that face anywhere. Braid or no braid." With a mischievous grin, one hand snaked behind her neck to pull her mouth down to his. The other moved down her back, pressing her to him.

Stunned, she smelled the salty water and a faint sweet hint.

Old Spice?

The aftershave scent Miss Livvy had bought him for his sixteenth birthday; that same year she'd given Megan Evening in Paris.

The scent mingled with another, headier smell. His skin, sun-drenched and sea-soaked.

David was the one to push away. "Megan Mulrennon. Cute as ever." He brushed back her wet tendrils. "And hair as messy, too."

Reason returned. How could he do that to her in public? And then taunt her!

She slapped him. Hard. "You smug bastard."

"Learned some new words, Meggie?" Amused, he touched his reddening cheek. "You used to be prudish."

"I've learned more than a few words." *Deep breaths, deep breaths. Don't let him do this to you.* "I've learned about people, too. I should have known better than to expect common civility from you, David Harmony."

"Ah, Megan. Don't be upset." Penitence oozed. "There you were, begging to be kissed, and I never could resist temptation. You know that. You've turned into a bloody pretty woman. After all these years, can you wonder I lost my head? Don't be mad with me."

She almost took his proffered hand. Almost let him cajole her into overlooking such gall.

Except for the impudent twitch of his lips.

What a fool she was.

Why had she believed he cared about her? He'd never cared. If he had, he would never have left. She'd love to wipe that superior smirk off his face.

"You haven't changed, have you? You go your own merry way, never bothering about the mess you leave behind."

How could she have thought everything would be the same after he'd gone away and left her? Without a word! What an idiot she'd been to think she'd meant something to him.

"I'd like to say it's good to see you again, David, but I can't. You'll never change. I wonder I didn't realize that years ago."

"Megan." He captured her wrist. "Listen."

She was no longer a sixteen-year-old virgin, but a thirty-three-year-old lawyer trained to rational thought and conduct.

So why did she feel so panicky?

"You don't have anything to say I want to hear. I was a fool to expect you to be different. I grieved because I thought you were dead, but now I can stop. Thank goodness for that."

Twisting away, she jumped into the water before she revealed how much she had imagined a different meeting.

So much for cool, collected reason.

As she swam away, his low laughter followed. Tears welled up, their salt blending with the waves where she buried her face.

Fool. She had cried for him seventeen years ago and there was no need to do it again.

She despised him for going away without a word. She despised him for coming back for his inheritance and not because of her. But she despised him most for making her react to his touch.

He had behaved as if he could do whatever he wanted with her, and she had let him. He was the one to cut off that kiss, not her.

Damn him!

Damn him for such arrogance and conceit. And damn her for being so naïve.

Shaken, she swam awhile before wading out of the surf. The two men still smoked in the pavilion. Avoiding their curious eyes, she turned on the shower to rinse off. Then she made sure to drip on the red shirt before sitting down in the sun.

When the figure on the swim dock executed a neat dive, she yanked on her shirt.

Theo came up from the boardwalk holding two drinks. "I see you've succumbed to the consensus."

"What's that?" She picked up her shorts, worked to get them on over her damp suit.

"That it's truly our David home from his travels. No one missed your eager welcome."

"Great." She seethed, found the zipper on the side of her shorts.

"I'm surprised at you, little Megan." He waited till she zipped up to offer a drink. "Here. I thought you might need a bracer after that interlude."

He might be teasing or he might be annoyed.

"If you were watching, you also saw me slap him." She pushed back stray tendrils. On the dock, David had brushed her hair back. Always neat himself, he never understood why she couldn't keep her curls in check.

Never mind what he did to my hair.

Theo still held out the umbrella-garnished glass. The gin on his breath enveloped her, but Theo, even a juiced Theo, was a pain she could handle.

"Thanks." She took the pretty drink, glanced back to where David waded through the surf to the beach.

He was the one she couldn't handle.

"I was counting on you," Theo said plaintively. "I thought you of all people would see this man's a fake."

Megan sampled the fruity concoction. She could barely taste the rum. "Mmm. This is good."

"Sondra likes mai tais, too. But this man—"

"Theo, I'm sorry. He's David, the same smartass he always was." She stalked off.

"Megan, wait." He trotted behind her.

She stopped.

Over his shoulder, she could see the trim figure stroll up the steps to the pavilion and say something to the men there, then pick up a case and remove a cigarette.

A common habit. David hadn't smoked, but Mr. H had enjoyed an occasional cigar.

Theo said, "You can't be sure he's David. You barely spoke."

David, half-naked, had wide shoulders and narrow hips and muscular legs. He flicked open his lighter and lit his cigarette with a fluid movement of one hand.

He's an actor.

She swallowed. Keeping fit was part of an actor's trade.

"Megan. You don't know for sure—"

Back to earth. "I do know, Theo."

David turned his head toward her and Theo. He blew out smoke that drifted up. One corner of the soft mouth curved.

He was laughing at her again.

Flushing, she resumed walking. "He's David, Theo. He's changed, but he's really David."

Theo strode ahead, cut her off. "If you talk to him long enough, you'll see he's lying."

Megan shook her head. "He isn't. Let me by."

Theo didn't move. "He's good. I'll grant you that. But he plays parts for a living. Megan, in four days Lawrence will give him the Trust. It's wrong and you know it."

Her heart was broken and Theo was whining about the Harmony Trust. She held herself together but barely. "Theo, you can't do anything about it. It's his money."

"No, it isn't. It's mine. This man is not David. He's some two-bit actor Lawrence hired so he could keep dipping into the Trust."

She couldn't argue. Theo was too desperate and she was too emotional. "I'm sorry. I can't talk now." She pushed past.

When she peeked back, Theo still stood on the boardwalk, watching the pavilion where David stood under the shower with arms out and cigarette between his teeth.

He is David. He is.

But not her David. The David she loved had gone away without a word. This David had killed any feelings she still harbored for that boy.

****

"Shotgun Boogie"
As Performed by Tennessee Ernie Ford (1950)
Music by Tennessee Ernie Ford
Lyrics by Tennessee Ernie Ford

THEO WATCHED THE fairy awhile, then trailed Megan back to the piazza.

What did he do now? Dithery May Addison or that stupid girl friend of David's might come through, but it was Megan's denials that would count most. He and Sondra had agreed on that when they found out she'd be here today.

You need her on your side.

The shrewd voice was right. If he couldn't bring her around, he and Sondra would be out.

Forget the Megan problem for a moment. Maybe he could buy Downing off, pay him more than Lawrence.

About that time, the little shit strolled up from the beach with his fricking bodyguards and sneered at him before stopping at the bar.

Sneered!

That did it.

No chance in hell he'd give anything to any sonofabitch who kept coming on to Sondra. He'd never let this asshole waltz off with any of his money.

Only one way to fix it.

Hells bells. He hadn't wanted to do it.

You may have no choice, said the cold voice in his head.

Once he accepted that, calm settled, the same kind of calm he'd used all those years ago to get everything he wanted. But there'd be no remorse this time. This Downing was a stranger, not a boy who'd worshipped him.

Again he was on the slanted catamaran beside David, soaring inches from the sea, screaming with excitement, saltwater whipping over him.

Forget it. Forget David. Think about Downing.

A knucklehead actor. And Lawrence of all people, behind it.

Never mind. He could handle Downing. Follow the plan. Pick at Downing until he tripped over his lies.

Or find a way to convince Megan, get her to expose Downing for the fake he was.

If he could.

Okay, he was a sportsman, used to death. All it took was nerve. He'd found that out seventeen years ago.

David's weight on his shoulders. Robby's body on the floor. The creak of the ramp. The whine of the dory's motor. The explosion that brought home what he'd done.

Christ, did he still have it in him?

If he wanted to keep Sondra, he'd better.

And he couldn't lose her.

Not after what he'd gone through to get her and the money.

You know how to fix it, the shrewd voice told him. *You'll do what you have to. Just like before.*

He finished his drink, trying to quell the sickness inside his gut. He couldn't quite wipe the memories out.

CHAPTER 20

"Lipstick on Your Collar"
As Performed by Connie Francis (1959)
Music by George Goehring
Lyrics by Edna Lewis

DURING MEGAN'S SWIM, the crowd had swelled to a stifling horde of revelers where she was an alien. Her stomach, still sensitive, churned.

Maybe she should leave.

Through the cedars, she saw David's red shirt as he came up from the beach with the two men from the pavilion.

She put up her chin. No. No running away. Not after everyone had witnessed her humiliation. No way would she give David the satisfaction of knowing he was the sole reason she'd come to the stinking picnic.

Avoiding Theo and his pathetic arguments, she found a chaise lounge beside a table to hold her mai tai.

Autumn clematis clung to an overhead lattice, its fragrance mingled with perspiration and sun lotion and cologne from the milling crowd. Stereo speakers cascaded soft ballads that didn't hamper nonstop babbling.

At the bar, David took a bottle of beer and looked around. He headed her way, but a sunburned man cut him off, shaking his hand heartily and talking a mile a minute.

David listened without a hint of impatience.

Under the palms, white-coated bartenders held sway on the piazza. People thronged by, in cheerful sun suits, sporty shirts, swimsuits plain or with vivid cover-ups. Some stood and chatted, but others took advantage of accommodating chairs or lounges. A few flirted shamelessly, some wearing wedding rings and others not.

A red-faced and sweating George Wykerton, tennis racket in hand, dragged up to get a drink at the bar. Then he came over to her. "Hi, doll. Howya doing?"

"Great." Megan dredged up a smile and tried to ignore her unsettled tummy.

"Dad was worried about you."

"About me? Why?"

"About your meeting David, I guess. You know how the wheels

turn in the Old Man's head, always picking out any little thread that might unravel his well-laid plans. When it comes to smoothing out obstacles, he can still teach a thing or two to his juniors. Including me."

"And me."

Well-laid plans.

"I'm no threat to Lawrence's plans. Where is he, anyway?"

"Probably parked with Mayor Randall in a cozy corner. You know how he hates these things. Say, I'm bushed. Is that chair taken? Or are you saving it for someone in particular. Like a certain actor the women are swooning over."

"No!" Had everyone seen David manhandle her? "Sit down, George, but for heaven's sake, let's not talk about David."

George might foist his work off on her and call women *doll*, but he was okay. Not quite as polished as his father, or as shrewd. But he had a whimsical sense of humor.

One time he'd sneaked a whiskey bottle into a teetotal secretary's desk drawer. When she'd looked for her notary stamp, she nearly fainted; then she had promptly quit.

And after he'd filled out a card for a dance studio in Savannah under his father's name, the bewildered Lawrence had barely escaped signing up for a twenty-hour course in merengue and samba.

George possessed little of his father's gravity.

He dropped into an Adirondack chair next to her. "Okay, forget David Harmony. I'm sick of him myself. So. Getting right to the sixty-four-thousand-dollar question. Is he for real?"

"I thought we weren't going to talk about him."

"Never hurts to try." George guffawed. "Changing the subject. You let a bug do you out of ten days in beautiful Salt Lake City, eh? My, my, my. Don't know what to think about young attorneys nowadays, giving up a free trip to Utah. No stamina."

Free trip. George was always worrying about money. If he'd stolen money from the Trust, he'd have to be in better financial shape. Wouldn't he?

Drat Theo, putting thoughts like that in her head. He was grasping at straws.

A whiff of low country boil penetrated through smoke from fires where pigs were laid out to roast. Megan's gut rolled. "Yeah, we neophytes aren't tough like you old codgers. I guess they don't make lawyers like they did in your day."

George's head swiveled toward the bar. "You think we might see a fistfight?"

Hostile giant Theo confronted David, all innocent good will. The two big men from the pavilion purposefully closed in, focused on the antagonists.

No. Focused on Theo.

Megan straightened.

And they weren't guests. She'd seen assertive men like them before, when Mr. H invited the President and other notables to the island. Those loose shirts concealed guns.

"Why does David have bodyguards?"

"Dad hired them, doll. Just a precaution." George fanned himself with his visor. "Boy, the sun's too hot for tennis in the middle of the day. I should have known better but Mona insisted. She says I'm getting fat. I say, if true, it's not from her cooking."

He patted his stomach, then took a long chug.

Sondra, Peachie trailing, approached her husband, said something, and gestured. Theo turned to the bar. She thrust her arm through David's, chatting as she drew him away.

George grunted. "Well?"

"Well, what?"

"Sorry, doll. I know I said I wouldn't, but I can't help it." George's banter fled. "Is he really our long lost heir?"

She said cautiously, "Your father says he is."

"I know what Dad says. What d'you say? Since you have firsthand experience."

"You don't have to leer," she said coldly. "I say he's very arrogant." She took a sip of her mai tai.

"Wasn't he always? If I remember right, David could be a real shit. Pardon my French."

Megan choked, trying not to laugh.

It was true. No matter how much she'd loved him, David had not always been easy to deal with. But however conceited, imperious, and stubborn he was, he could also be tender, funny, and magnanimous toward people he cared about.

That last autumn, he'd driven all the way to Waycross to get a peck of muscadines for Mom because she'd lamented the wet summer had ruined the vines' yield and she didn't have enough to make into jelly.

Of course, being David, he'd taken off without a driving license or permission and had been late getting back to school. But still . . .

She expected too much. She ought to be happy he was alive.

Sondra abandoned David on the piazza. He aimed dark glasses toward Megan and George for a moment. Then he turned his back.

Oddly let down, Megan took a sip. "Why do you suppose he went away like that?"

"Didn't he tell you?"

"I didn't ask."

George grunted. "No time, eh?"

"What happened that night, George?"

George ended a condensation of David's story with: "He told Dad that he wanted to see what life was really like." He snorted. "That's a pretty lame excuse for abandoning home and family for seventeen years if you ask me."

True, but . . . "He didn't have a family anymore except for Theo. And they weren't that close. Maybe he was running away from the memories."

If she allowed herself, she could understand.

David would have forgotten his half-promises to her, given a chance to escape what he saw as his future. He'd hated all the baggage that came with being James Harmony's son. Mr. H hadn't been easy to get along with, but trying to live up to his reputation after he died would have been worse.

And no Miss Livvy to intervene.

She shivered, imagining the boat afire with Robby trapped inside and David struggling in the sea as it burned.

Years ago, she and Mom were on their way to Savannah when another car broadsided theirs. They had avoided the intersection ever since, but the detour still reminded them.

David's ordeal must have been a thousand times worse than a car wreck. She could understand why he'd been in no hurry to return home. But why hadn't he sent word to someone? More specifically, why hadn't he sent word to her?

"He's sown his wild oats." George laid his head back against the chair. "I guess you heard he's an actor."

"The papers are full of it."

"I've read the tabloids. He's been to court for assault and was the other party in a messy divorce involving an earl's wife. In his spare time, he attends soccer matches and cavorts around France and Italy. Settling down here will be dull, don't you think?"

Dull.

While she went about her—go ahead and admit it—her dull life, David had adventured all over the world. He'd come back only because of the inheritance, apparently feeling no guilt that people had mourned him. "He'll have the Trust to keep him busy."

"Oh, Dad'll take care of business." George yawned. His complexion had resumed its normal color. "I'm sure David knows we'll look after his affairs."

Affairs meaning money.

Her mai tai tasted watery. Darn Theo for planting these suspicions about the Wykertons, and darn David for being so smug and selfish. She ought to be furious.

Instead, she reclined on her chaise, hiding behind sunglasses. The warmth of the sun soothed her muscles, relaxed her body. Swimmers splashed, producing acrid scents of pool water. David sat down a few yards distant to take out a cigarette.

What was she doing, staring at him like a lovesick teenager?

She closed her eyes.

Anger had fled. Hazy contentment took its place.

David was back and she had let him know what she thought of him leaving her like he had.

They'd make up eventually. They always made up. On the dock, he'd offered overtures and if she wasn't mistaken, only George's presence had kept him away just now.

She'd get around to accepting his apologies. Sooner or later. Just like she used to.

If I'd run away with him like he wanted, he'd never have been in the boat that night.

She heard a man asking him about British actors. "Do you know Sir Laurence Olivier?"

"I once met him at a dinner party. I said hello and so did he. That's the extent of our relationship, I'm afraid." The accent no longer sounded weird but reminded her of the past.

German, Spanish, British, Scottish, French. David could make her and Robby howl with laughter when he mimicked a foreigner.

She opened her eyes.

As his questioner expounded on Olivier's directing efforts, David smoked and watched Theo stride toward him, towing an ash blonde with lacquered hair pinned up into a French half-twist. Jamaica shorts and white crewneck top revealed a buxom figure.

"David, here's someone you'll want to see." Theo pressed the woman forward.

Megan sat upright.

"Hello, David. Remember me?" Rochelle Tollison clearly expected the answer to be *yes* and wasn't disappointed.

Throwing down his cigarette, David sprang up. "Don't be absurd, Rochelle! How could I forget my first love?"

An enthusiastic kiss ensued where Rochelle clung to David's neck longer than necessary.

Megan sniffed, sat back.

The group on the patio let out a unified sigh.

They knew about her, Megan thought. Theo planned this.

Theo didn't quite gloat.

George gawked. "Who the heck's that?"

Megan said, carefully neutral, "David's old girl friend. The last I heard, she'd married a doctor and lived in New York."

When she'd asked David why he was dating the biggest nitwit in her school, his ears had reddened. "She has a, um, certain, um, reputation."

"Reputation?"

He'd been forthright. "She puts out if she likes you."

She hadn't understood till he'd put it in graphic terms. Incensed, she'd blessed him out.

He'd laughed at her. "Don't be a dip, Meggie. Aren't you curious what it's like?"

The laugh was still on her. Except for that one lapse, she was the good girl—even through her entire first engagement she'd postponed *that* part—but bad girl Rochelle was the one with the happy ending.

So much for Mom's dire predictions about giving in to horny boys.

George grunted. "The Packs brought her in, betcha a nickel. Theo ought to know Dad's always sure of his facts."

"Yes, he is." Lawrence's penchant for accuracy was proverbial.

"Oh, David." Rochelle's excitement eclipsed all music and conversations. "I can't get over it. After I heard you were alive, I squalled like a baby. Almost as much as when they said you'd drowned. When Theo offered to send his plane to pick me up and fly me down today, I jumped at the chance. And look at you. The same dreamboat you were then."

"No, look at *you*." David drew her to a bench beneath too-large crepe myrtles where they sat down side by side. "Still a dish after all this time."

Enough to turn your stomach.

People went back to what they had been doing. Theo's jaw set. Across the piazza, Sondra entertained a burly man wearing suit pants and dress shirt without a tie.

What did Sondra think about David? She generally went along with Theo. If they sued, there'd be years of preparation, briefings, hearings.

One big mess.

Oh well. Lawrence couldn't be worried, or he'd be sticking close to David.

Taking center stage, Rochelle played *way back when* while David nimbly responded.

"—but I never got over you. I swear, David, if you'd written me one teeny weeny note, I'd have waited forever."

"Why, lovely girl, I never dreamed you'd give me the faintest thought. If I'd known—"

"Do you remember our last date? The beach party when a bunch of us came over from town and spent the night?"

"Ah, all the skinnydipping and drinking that went on." He chuckled. "We knew everything at that age, didn't we? Nobody but us had ever done anything like that."

"That was the first time I tasted hard liquor."

"Um, bourbon, wasn't it?"

"Southern Comfort. We were so ignorant we thought it was the same thing. I got bombed and passed out. The next day I had such a hangover, I barfed all over the boat going home."

"I remember you as the life of the party and the cutest girl there."

Megan tensed. He couldn't have forgotten the party's aftermath.

Then why did he leave her? How could he flirt with Rochelle Tollison in front of her?

Because she meant nothing to him?

"And that was when you gave me your Key Club pin." Rochelle patted his cheek coyly. "We were sitting by the fire."

"The fire? Was it that night?" David's brow creased. "With all the others around? I rather recollect us being alone when I gave it to you. But maybe I didn't notice them. I only had eyes for you."

Rochelle shrieked and clapped. "You haven't forgotten! I still have it, David, and I don't know that I'll give it back. It has so many memories."

"Rochelle, poppet. Consider it yours." He lifted her hand to his lips, instigating a squeal.

More recollections. More laughter. More furtive stares from nearby people.

George bent over to her ear. "Look at Theo. He hoped for a lot more from her, I bet."

Sure enough, over to the side, Theo glowered.

"—craziest thing I ever did," Rochelle cooed beside David on the bench, their hands entwined and bare knees touching.

Theo walked over. "I just noticed, David," he said with studied casualness. "You're not wearing your druid's ring. I never saw you without it. You got it at what? Ten?"

His ring. Theo was right. Both hands were bare.

David's sunglasses pointed at Megan for an interminable moment.

"I remember that ring," George said. "He was pretty proud of it, wasn't he?"

She murmured, "Yes, he loved that ring."

Rochelle looked puzzled.

"You do recall the ring, don't you?" Theo purred. "It belonged to one of our ancestors who was a druid?"

The sunglasses turned away. "I doubt anyone in our family ever worshipped trees, Theo. A druid supposedly gave it to one of our ancestors. I was twelve when Grandfather left it to me."

"Then where is it?"

The answer was quiet, hard to hear. "I don't have it."

"No?" Theo's teeth slashed white against his tan. "I find that hard to believe. David Harmony would never have let that ring out of his possession. Never." He pointed with his drink. "How curious. If you don't have his ring, it does make one wonder who you are."

David stood, slowly took off dark glasses.

And turned into an animal with muscles poised to strike.

The hum of conversation died.

Close observers involuntarily stepped back.

Rochelle looked uncertainly from one man to the other.

The bodyguards edged closer.

David wasn't as tall as Theo, and was so slender as to appear delicate against Theo's bulk.

But David was the one who dominated, the one to be feared.

Megan caught her breath.

David could never look so cruel.

His icy eyes could have frozen fire, but his voice remained perfectly smooth. "I'm David Harmony, Theo. Don't you doubt that for one instant." The words spun a silken cord that could choke the life out of a man. "Even if I don't have the ring."

"So you admit it." Theo clenched his glass. "Where is it then?"

Absolute silence. Not even a breeze stirred.

David shrugged one shoulder.

It wasn't a gesture she remembered.

"I lost track of it. Many, many years ago."

"Hah!" Theo scoffed. "David would never have lost that ring. Never."

David surveyed Megan and the other watchers, taking his time before answering. "How would you know what I'd have done? There were times I'd have sold my mother's soul for one decent meal. Murdered for one decent night's sleep. Don't tell me what I would or would not do. You've never had to fend for yourself among thieves and murderers so you have no right to judge me. If selling a ring could keep you from starving, you'd sell it in a heartbeat."

Theo took a step forward. "If you don't have the ring, you aren't David."

"Will you prove me a liar?" The gentle voice contrasted with the dreadful face. "I wonder how. The only way would be to produce the ring yourself. Can you do that, Theo?"

Theo's triumph faded. "It's difficult to disprove your story."

"It's impossible. Because it's true. I *am* David Harmony. Like it or lump it, Theo." The beatific smile cancelled none of the sting.

Megan shivered. Next to her, George wheezed.

Theo's fists clenched. Then he spun on his heel. The bodyguards melted into the murmuring bystanders.

"Round one to David," George said.

As if hearing, David looked at them and laughed.

Megan breathed deeply.

She was in no mood to gossip but George, craning to watch David and Rochelle, didn't care. He couldn't stop grinning. "Theo sure ran off with his tail tucked between his legs. I'll bet he hoped for a lot more than a lovers' reunion."

David and Rochelle got drinks and sat down on the shaded stone wall with heads together. Why were they chortling like that? David hadn't seemed half as happy to see her.

Because he didn't care.

Be fair. He's had other loves since then. Like me.

The sadness didn't go away.

From the speakers came a subtle switch. Ballads gave way to jazz. The more alcohol, the more demand for jitterbug or bop. Even rock and roll. Sondra would prevail after a while, but for the moment everyone gyrated. On the piazza and the patio beside the pool.

No dancing for the reunited twosome, though. David and Rochelle chattered without running out of steam for over an hour. When they finally parted, David stood and stretched, then raked a victorious glance over the crowd till he found Theo.

He smirked.

Theo turned his back.

"Guess the interesting part's over with," George said.

About that time, his wife appeared and gestured. Sighing, he struggled to stand. "There's the better half. I have to check in. Gosh, I hope she won't make me get back out on the courts."

Once he left, Megan risked a peek.

David headed directly toward her.

CHAPTER 21

"Heebie Jeebies"
As Performed by Louis Armstrong (1926)
Music by Boyd Atkins
Lyrics by Louis Armstrong

LAWRENCE SAT IN a lawn chair beneath a great oak with several of his cronies and tried to behave normally.

Like everyone else, he'd watched Nick confront Rochelle, then Theo. He silently applauded when Nick triumphed but didn't relax until Rochelle left. Linda said she was flying directly back home for some kind of shindig.

One problem solved.

David's old girl friend had worried him; they knew so little about her. But Nick had pulled it off without a hitch. The man was a marvel.

Where was he going now?

What? Heading toward Megan? After their heated encounter on the dock, was that wise?

Ah, well. He'd have to face her sooner or later. Maybe Nick knew what he was doing.

The group around him discussed some new television program. "M'wife loved it," the funeral home director said, "Did you see the beginning when the girls threw their petticoats over the fence? Reckon they had on anything behind it?" He didn't wait for an answer. "But I still like the Clampetts best. That Granny tickles me to death."

Odell McNamara never did have the sense he was born with.

Lawrence got up. "Gentlemen, I've got to stretch my legs. My bones won't let me sit for long. Old age, I suspect."

"Don't coddle yourself. You're the same age as my brother," Berriman said, "and he just finished roofing his new barn by himself."

Yes, and his brother had been the same neck-or-nothing fool in grammar school.

"A better man than me," Lawrence murmured.

He visited the bar, dodging shrieking women and laughing men but keeping a sharp lookout. Nick may have convinced Rochelle Tollison, but Theo could have found others who might be more skeptical.

Like May Addison.

Maybe she'd declined Theo's invitation.

But when he got his ginger ale—he didn't care what these people did; he'd abide by the old rules: no alcohol before five—he saw her.

Her neat rust-colored dress with round collar and bell sleeves stood out in the maze of bathing suits and shorts and revealing sundresses. Its old-fashioned flavor caught his eye, but he didn't know who she was. Only when she paused in a vaguely familiar stance, head cocked, one hand clasping the other elbow, did he recognize her.

Yes, she was plump and her hair was snow white, but she was May Addison. Her belted waist might be wider, but her impeccable posture kept her back straight as ever.

Oh my. His heart sank, but he hurried over. "My dear May. How delightful to see you."

She ignored his hand to hug him. "Lawrence Wykerton! I was hoping you'd be here. I couldn't believe it when I heard about David. I sat down and cried with joy. I know you must have done the same. It's truly a miracle."

Age wrinkled her skin, but she seemed to possess all her faculties. Her glasses were thick, though. Problems with her sight? Not a bad thing considering the circumstances.

"A miracle. Ah, yes, indeed. It's been quite a, er, quite an experience." He stepped back. "It's been so long since you were down here."

"James's funeral. That was the last time we met."

"Ah yes. Such a sad occasion. I was sorry to hear about your husband—"

Theo butted in. "May. Linda said you'd arrived. So glad you could make it. Ready to meet David?" He took her arm with no polite greeting to May or *Excuse us, Lawrence.*

Theo couldn't wait to throw May at Nick.

Lawrence drank half his ginger ale. Like Megan, May had known David all his life. If Nick slipped up , she'd be on him.

Nick won't slip up. He can't.

He should have gotten a highball.

****

"He's So Fine"
As Performed by the Chiffons (1963)
Music by Ronnie Mack
Lyrics by Ronnie Mack

MEGAN'S STOMACH FLUTTERED as David bounded up.

He took off his glasses. "I'm sorry, Megan."

"No need to apologize."

"Ah, but there is. My only excuse is that I couldn't resist. I looked up and there you were, a dripping mermaid, begging to be kissed."

Megan jerked upright hotly. "I was not begging—" His chuckle stopped her.

She schooled her twitching mouth.

"It's still easy to rag you. I'm glad you haven't changed." He added with charming simplicity, "I'm sorry. For everything. Won't you accept my apologies and let's start over?"

She'd forgive him anything. For the kiss earlier and all the miserable years she'd thought him dead. "You could always talk me around, couldn't you?"

"Not always." He made himself comfortable in the chair George had vacated. "I didn't have time to say everything I wanted to on the dock. You ran away."

"Like you?"

His hand moved to touch hers but changed directions to settle on his chair arm.

"I never forgot you, Meggie. The entire time I was gone. Whenever I thought of home, and believe me, there wasn't a single day when I didn't think of home, I always thought of you and JoBeth."

She started to tell him it was all right.

Pride forbade her. "Then you should have let us know you were alive." She wouldn't forgive him. Not right away. He deserved to suffer. She had for years. "A phone call would have been enough. Even a postcard."

He rested an ankle on the opposite knee and one hand massaged the calf. "I couldn't." He sounded tired. "I'd made my choice. I had to live with it."

She wanted to believe him, almost as much as she wanted to pat his hand.

The fingers were the same, long and tapering. Except that when he moved them a certain way, a thin white scar was visible, running from the side of his little finger up to the wrist. Imagining how he got it and the others on his body made her blink back tears.

He didn't notice. "I thought of ringing hundreds of times through the years. But I didn't."

"I know," she snapped. "Believe me, I know. It would have been a lot easier on me—and Mom—if you had, David Harmony."

He rested a hand on the back of her lounge, leaned over to push down her sunglasses. "If you knew how long I've dreamed of your eyes, all soft and trusting. Only now they're not. They're detached. Wary. Did my leaving do that?"

"Don't flatter yourself." She shoved her glasses back on. "You've traveled the world and become an actor. I've gone to school and become a lawyer. We've led different lives. As we should have. Nothing's forever. Everything changes."

Hoping he'd contradict her.

He didn't. "Whitey says you were engaged but not anymore. Is that right?"

"What business is it of yours?"

He laughed in his throat, that sound that made her ache, before covering her hand with his. "None, Megan. How could it be when I left the way I did?"

Each golden hair, each clipped fingernail stood out clearly.

A shadow fell between them. An elderly woman stood there, in a dated dress conspicuously out of place in the sun-worshipping crowd. "David? Is it really you?"

David jumped up. "Auntie May?"

Megan got up, too, but more slowly.

More of Theo's work. First Rochelle. Now May Addison. He had to be desperate.

Rochelle had been David's girl friend only a few weeks, but Auntie May was Miss Livvy's dearest friend from school days and had known David all his life.

Maybe she could convince Theo to give up.

Petite Auntie May wore a pixie cap of white hair but retained the artless air Megan recalled.

After hugging David, she peered at Megan from behind thick spectacles before offering a cheek to be kissed. "Dear child. How nice to see you again. Livvy used to say you'd have to be her daughter since she never had a little girl. She was very fond of you."

"I loved her very much."

After asking about JoBeth, Auntie May faced David. "Let me look at you, you rascal."

David obliged, saying wryly, "It appears our Theo has been diligent with his invitations to my homecoming. Here, Auntie May. Sit down."

"Yes, so kind of Theo to think of me." Inspection over, Auntie May settled herself.

Megan reclaimed her chaise. She didn't protest when David moved her feet aside and perched on its bottom.

"Theo has his motives," he said, "but I hardly think *kind* is the right adjective."

Auntie May didn't understand.

"I believe his intent," David explained delicately, "was to expose me as an imposter."

"An impost—? No, dear. I'm sure you're wrong. He told me you were alive and wanted me here to welcome you. I tried to beg off—I don't get out much. So he sent his car. Imagine that! All that trouble just so I could spend a few minutes with you."

Auntie May had never been clever. When David once made fun of her, Miss Livvy, in a rare show of temper, had sent him to his room. "You should be ashamed of yourself. I hope you have such a good friend one day, young man. Maybe then you'll understand."

Today's insinuations passed over Auntie May.

"Tell me, how is it you survived that boat accident? Why didn't you come home? Where've you been? Tell me all."

"All right. But let's get you a drink first." David stood. "D'you want one, Megan?"

She got up, too. "You visit with Auntie May. I'll play waitress."

When she returned, he was wrapping up his tale to an attentive Auntie May. "—then I sent Lawrence word and he did whatever lawyers do. And here I am."

She handed him his beer and gave Auntie May her gin fizz, then sat back down on the chaise. He gingerly took his place at the bottom.

Like old times.

"Unbelievable." Auntie May sipped her drink. "You were always lucky, David, but I'm sure your mother had to be watching over you." That brought up reminiscences of Miss Livvy and Mr. H which led back to Theo. "I don't understand why you say he thinks you're an imposter. Surely he recognized you. You and he were always very close."

"I was a gullible kid and Theo was like a big brother. He was a great athlete, someone to look up to. And he wasn't unkind. But since he lived off my father, he couldn't be, could he?"

The damning words in their dulcet tone passed over guileless Auntie May, but Megan's stomach, which she'd hoped a Coke would ease, roiled.

"You adored Theo." Auntie May cocked her head.

"Hero worship, Auntie May. Boys are prone to it. Till they grow up."

"Dear, dear. I hate to think of you two being at odds. You're the only blood family left."

"We'll work it out. Are you still at Hilton Head?"

"Yes." Auntie May talked about her life. Then: "Is it strange, being a guest in your own home?"

David held up his bottle. "My home half a lifetime ago."

"A long while has passed." Auntie May nodded. "But aren't you glad to be back?"

"I have some good memories." He drank. "But at the end . . . I'm not sure I am glad."

"I see. And then there's Theo." Auntie May knit her brows. "I can't believe he has any doubts. Not with Lawrence Wykerton vouching for you."

"Oh, I can't blame Theo. He has a lot to lose."

Megan listened drowsily. David was back.

Around them spread the hum of voices and music. Somewhere a girl squealed and a man laughed uproariously. Overlaying the pool's chlorine, island scents of salt water and musty trees and sun warm on stones wafted by.

Auntie May abandoned Theo. "It was nice that Rochelle came. Your first love. You know, your parents thought you were too young for girl friends."

The chaise shifted when David stretched out a leg. "Just Mother. Dad advised me not to unzip my pants unless I had a rubber handy."

Auntie May gasped.

Megan nearly overturned the chaise. "David!"

"What?" Puzzled, David realized his gaffe. "Oh. Sorry, Auntie May. I've forgotten how to behave in polite society. Dad was always blunt. I guess I got it from him."

"He was blunt, but he was never crude," Megan muttered.

David started to defend himself.

Auntie May intervened. "James fumed when you gave Rochelle your Key Club pin."

"Ah. Yes, that's true. Strange she held onto it all this time." He rested his elbows on his knees and cupped the bottle with both hands.

Auntie May sipped at her drink. "Not strange at all. Most women do cherish keepsakes from their first loves."

David winked at Megan. "Do they? Sounds like you have a keepsake yourself."

Auntie May gurgled. "I do. A flower holder I still treasure."

"A flower holder?" David's smile glimmered. "A vase?"

Contentment filled Megan.

Was this what she'd waited for all these years? Why she couldn't be happy with anyone else?

How illogical.

Absolutely irrational.

Auntie May explained her keepsake. "—and pins to a dress. The flowers are long gone, but not the silver holder. I suppose you never saved anything like that."

"Young men aren't as sentimental as girls."

No matter that he'd stayed away. He was back now.

He said, "Sentiment comes to men as they get older, when they realize what they've let slip away."

She hadn't felt so lighthearted in years.

What a dope she was.

Lawrence was right. David was a different person from the boy she remembered. But here she was, acting like an infatuated schoolgirl.

Auntie May rearranged the napkin round her glass. "I remember the first thing your father gave your mother. Only a week after they met. A darling antique music box with a diamond ring inside. He always claimed he knew the first time he saw her that he wanted to marry her."

David looked at her indulgently. "Love at first sight."

Auntie May chuckled. "On his part, certainly. Livvy wasn't so sure though. She made him wait six weeks before she said *yes*. I wonder where that box is now."

Megan pictured it on her dresser, waited for him to say she had it.

"I'm sure it's around here somewhere."

Auntie May worried aloud. "James wouldn't have given it to Sondra."

He ran a finger up the side of his bottle, flicked a glance toward Megan. "Heavens, no."

Why didn't he admit he got the box after Miss Livvy died?

Why doesn't he say he gave it to me? Has he forgotten?

No, he'd never forget.

It was private, between the two of them. Maybe that was why he didn't say anything.

Unless . . .

The sunny day darkened. Her stomach cramped.

He didn't know.

Auntie May had brought up the music box. He'd been noncommittal. And the engagement ring part was new to her. Did he know about it? Or was he just pretending?

Auntie May persisted. "You do remember the box I'm thinking of?"

At the dock, when she had soundlessly approached him and caught him by surprise, she hadn't recognized him.

Because of the eyes.

These eyes could be secretive gray or clear blue or hard ice, all within a few minutes.

Her David's eyes were sky blue, like Miss Livvy's.

Sparkling. Unaffected. Optimistic.

"I was never much for knick-knacks," the man calling himself David Harmony said with an apologetic smile, "but if you ask me about my horse Bunch, or the catamaran Dad gave me on my thirteenth birthday, I can describe every detail."

He knew nothing about the music box.

He wasn't David Harmony.

CHAPTER 22

"A Blossom Fell"
As Performed by Nat King Cole (1955)
Music by Howard Barnes, Harold Cornelius,
and Dominic John
Lyrics by Howard Barnes, Harold Cornelius,
and Dominic John

HOT SUNSHINE SLANTED through the overhead clematis, but a chill enveloped Megan.

How could she have believed he was David? Now she could see the differences so rashly dismissed. His nose was wrong. The long face resembled David's, but the features were harsher. David's pliant mouth could never be so severe.

And his mannerisms. That one-shoulder shrug. She'd never seen David do that.

They had been inseparable when young. No matter that he was a boy and she a girl. Even after he went off to school, they were together summers and holidays.

They played hide-and-seek and roller bat, rode bicycles and horses. They fought pretend wars on the beach and played Tarzan on the vines hanging from the great oaks. They sailed in the sound, swam in the pools, chased butterflies in the gardens, caught lightning bugs on the lawn. They watched movies in the upstairs ballroom and bowled in the basement alley.

When David got his driving license, she had been the first person to ride with him.

They were friends. Best friends. Their last night together hadn't changed that.

Someone had told this man a lot about the Harmony family and a lot about David, and he was good at regurgitating it.

But he wasn't David.

Lawrence should have realized it. He'd known Mr. H forever and was fastidious at research. But people make mistakes, and Lawrence was human. And old. He couldn't possibly be as sharp as he used to be. Unless Theo was right.

Nausea rose. She sipped at her Coke.

Auntie May was completely taken in. "Of course you wouldn't be interested in things like music boxes, David. Boys never are. Didn't you have a dog?"

The stranger looked over his shoulder at Megan as if to say: See, everyone believes me. Everyone accepts me as David Harmony.

She hated him.

He was oblivious. "Two. Dad got a bulldog for me—Fritz— when Robby was born. I suppose it was a kind of consolation prize. When he died, we got a golden retriever, but Robert laid claim to Dorchester. By then, I was fifteen and had discovered girls."

"Ah, I remember now. Livvy picked out Dorchester, didn't she? Is he still around?"

"He died just before Dad. Robby was heartbroken. Do you remember how Dorchester once tried to bite a painter and Mother found out the man had struck him and got so mad she fired the whole crew?"

Someone had briefed him thoroughly. Someone knowledgeable about the Harmony family and David.

Lawrence? Surely not Lawrence.

"Livvy was such a good person," May said. "And Theo was wonderful when she was so ill, coming so often to run errands and check on her. His attentions meant a lot."

"I think she knew his attentions were for her nurse." David's mouth had never set in that thin line.

She should have known better.

Oh dear God in heaven, she wanted so much to believe.

"No," the stranger calling himself David Harmony went on in his British accent, "Mother never had any illusions concerning Theo. Or anyone. She was a realist. She saw people as they were. But she forgave them their failures and loved them anyway, something I can't do. She, of all people, shouldn't have had to suffer. It wasn't fair how she died." His bitterness seemed real.

My, he was good.

It's been so long. Maybe I'm wrong. He could have forgotten the box.

But she wasn't and he hadn't.

He was an actor. His job was convincing people to believe his lies.

People like Auntie May, distressed at his feigned grief. "Life is unfair, my dear."

"Cold comfort." He stood. "I think I'll swap this empty bottle for some water."

"And I must go." Auntie May pushed herself up. "I tire quickly nowadays and there's a long ride ahead. Even with a chauffeur, it's not been easy. But I had to come. Welcome back, David." She stood on tiptoe to peck him on the cheek. "I'm glad you're home."

She kissed Megan, too. "Goodbye, dear. Take good care of him now that he's back."

Auntie May's reservations were gone, brushed aside by a facile tongue. The brilliant smile awarded the elderly woman infuriated Megan.

"It's good to be home, Auntie May. Here, I'll walk with you past the pool."

He couldn't get away with his lies.

She watched Auntie May depart, then hopped up and cornered him at the bar. Behind them were the golf fairway and masts gently bobbing on the distant ocean. Straggler blooms from a nearby gardenia scented the air. "Theo was right about the druid's ring. What did you do with it?"

He nodded at the fairway past her shoulder. "Wasn't the rose garden there?"

"Forget the rose garden. Where's your ring?"

The whir of motorboats in the cove, the tinkling of glasses from the bar, the buzz of conversation around them, the rustling leaves from the light wind—all dissolved into hazy background. Even the beach music faded against the pounding of her heart.

She asked about the ring, but this was his chance to tell her about his mother's music box.

Please, please, be David.

She prompted. "You would never have sold your ring. Where is it?"

Brows rose over his sunglasses. "Didn't you hear? I said maybe I sold it."

"Not that ring."

He considered. "Have it your way. Maybe I gave it to a woman. There. Satisfied?"

She shook her head. "You'd never have given it to anyone. What happened to it?"

Ice tinkled when he swirled his glass. He drank, watching her. "You get dehydrated when you're in the sea for two days. When you're picked up, you don't remember a ring slipping off your finger. Strangely, being alive seems a lot more important than things."

"Oh." He could have lost it in the water that night, but that didn't explain the music box. "More important than things? Things like your mother's music box?"

"Megan." The knuckles holding the glass turned white. "Why do you care so much?"

He didn't know about the box. She clutched her midriff to keep from gagging.

"Meggie." The mouth softened, like that of the boy she'd loved. "I really am David."

Not David. He was not David.

Somehow she got control. "I never said you weren't."

"You're thinking it. Please don't spread doubts about me." His voice became husky. "I suppose I'd be foolish to hope this is purely a feminine response to Rochelle Tollison?"

He was so like David she could hardly bear it.

I'm the fool.

"I don't care about your relationship with Rochelle. I do care that nothing—your ring, Miss Livvy's music box—nothing seems to matter to you."

"I learned long ago that material things are meaningless."

"This was the first thing my father ever gave my mother," he had told her that morning, gasping from the run to their house.

He had risen early because he knew they were leaving at sun-up for her grandparents' home in Alabama, and he wanted to give her his mother's music box before she left. He wanted her to have something that meant so much to him.

Because she meant so much to him.

She would have died for him. When she'd taken his box, she hadn't known he would be the one to die.

So she stood mute, giving this man in front of her every opportunity to bring up the music box, to tell her he still cared the same way he had cared seventeen years ago.

Or to laugh and say he knew she had the box and that she could keep it, that he didn't care. About it or about her. His indifference would crush her, but she would survive. If he was really David, alive and healthy, nothing else mattered.

"Megan." He stopped, frowned. "What do you want from me?"

This man said nothing about Miss Livvy's music box because he didn't know about it.

Her own breathing filled her ears. "If material things don't mean anything to you, what does? If you've learned which things in life really matter, would you have stayed gone all those years without letting Mom and me know you were all right? Would you have been so selfish as to let us think you were dead all this time?"

"Megan." He looked away. "I'm not . . . I can't—"

"If you're David, you've admitted that nothing at all, not Mom, not me, nothing matters to you anymore. If you're not David, then you only want the money. Either way, you lose."

She wheeled and dove into the crowd, hearing him swear softly behind her.

He was not David Harmony, and what was she to do?

****

"Stumbling"
As Performed by Frank Crumit (1922)
Music by "Zez" Confrey
Lyrics by "Zez" Confrey

LAWRENCE WYKERTON, RELIEVED at May's departure with no outcry about Nick being a fake, remained on guard.

Who else would Theo come up with?

He couldn't think of another person who might present a danger, but Theo might. He sorted through faces in his mind, most of them dead, trying to convince himself his plan was invulnerable.

He hadn't succeeded by the time Theo's attorneys waylaid him. They wanted him to postpone the Trust disbursement. He was politely rebuffing their arguments when a distraught Megan dashed past.

What the devil was that all about?

She disappeared around the house before he could extricate himself. He caught Nick at the edge of the patio beside a white-clothed table of empty bottles and glasses and pulled him behind a trellis spilling over with fragrant pink roses. "What did you say to Megan?"

"Nothing. Everything. It's a bloody mess." He pulled out his gold case. "I'm hopeless, Whitey."

Nick dejected was a new sight. And alarming. "If I believed that, you wouldn't be here."

"You're wrong. I saw it. When I was talking to Auntie May. Megan realized I'm not David." He chose one of his small cigars and tapped it against his hand.

"You mean she suspects?"

"Ohhhh, I'm pretty sure she knows."

"What? How? Everything was going so smoothly."

"Yes. And if I'd handled it differently . . ." Nick bit his lip, staring into space. "No," he said, almost to himself. "I couldn't have done other than what I did."

"We knew there'd be occasions where you'd have to make split-second decisions. And we also knew some of them might not end well. Can you gauge how bad this is?"

Nick snorted. "Of course I can. That adorable face is as easy to read as a printed page."

Lawrence started. "See here, this interest in Megan—"

"That isn't the problem." Nick lit his cigar and inhaled. "Somehow we have to persuade her to keep quiet." Smoke billowed. "It looks like she's gone home to think about it so we have a bit of time to decide what to do."

Lawrence studied the distant masts silhouetted against the blue sky. "This is not going the way I hoped. Why in the world couldn't she have stayed in Utah? All right. I'll try to pacify her, figure out how to keep her quiet."

"Keep her quiet?" A breeze ruffled Nick's hair and blew smoke toward Lawrence. "You sound like an American gangster. Exactly what does keeping her quiet mean?"

"Exactly what I said," Lawrence said tartly. "You do your job and I'll do mine. Leave her alone. And blow that smoke somewhere else."

Nick showed his teeth. "Megan's being here today means you haven't done your job. I can't leave her alone when she and David were like this." He crossed his fingers.

Lawrence fanned the smoke aside. "I told you, I'll take care of it. You stay as far away from her as possible. I saw you grab her on the swim dock."

"I hoped to throw her off balance. And it was working until . . ." Nick threw the barely smoked cigar onto the sandy path leading down to the beach. "I just hope she doesn't go to Theo. How do you mean to smooth this over? It doesn't involve any rough stuff, does it?"

"Goodness gracious, what do you think I am? Go away and let me think." He didn't like the way Nick scowled at him.

"I mean it. I don't want her hurt."

"You're a fool." Lawrence bit off the words. "Megan's almost family. Go away."

In the end, Nick did as he was told.

After the trim form sauntered away, anxiety replaced irritation. Nick had a way of ignoring directives he didn't agree with.

But he was right.

They were sunk if Megan approached Theo with her suspicions. Confound this inexplicable interest Nick had in her! Well, they would have to go on as best they could.

At least the bodyguards were on duty, discreetly watching over their client as he took center stage among several men and women. Emotions were building, fast and furious. He could almost see them roiling the atmosphere, particularly around Theo.

Nick was doing a splendid job of baiting Theo, taking every opportunity to flaunt his ownership of property the Packs had previously considered theirs.

He'd nearly laughed this morning when he and Nick walked into the library.

The actor had lifted his hands in exaggerated shock at Theo's stuffed trophies. "Oh, no no no no no! They'll have to go. I can't possibly concentrate with those pitiful heads staring at me. I'd spend all my time feeling guilty that some thrill seeker with a high-powered scope on a high-powered rifle shot those poor defenseless animals simply to decorate my library."

"I shot those animals myself," Theo snarled. "And it was a fair contest."

Nick raised a brow. "Oh. Beg pardon, cousin. I was unaware that the wildlife had armed themselves. Nevertheless, they still must go."

Theo had been livid.

Yes, Lawrence thought with satisfaction, Theo Pack was rapidly working himself up into resolving the problem of David Harmony.

Egged on by Lawrence, of course. He was taking every opportunity to point out that only a live David stood in the way of Theo keeping all he had and getting all he'd expected to inherit.

Not that it needed pointing out.

Soon everything would come to a head.

Lawrence sighed. Get back to the problem at hand.

Megan.

Confound it, he liked Megan, mostly because she had a nice, balanced disposition. She was a sensible woman and a conscientious lawyer. But like her or not, right now she was smack dab in the way.

If only she hadn't come back. What on earth was he going to do?

As he saw it, there were two options. He didn't care for either.

After mulling over the situation, he started off with a purposeful step.

CHAPTER 23

FLEEING, MEGAN'S ONE thought was to get as far away as she could.

Past the front pool amid the rhododendrons lining the side driveway, she slowed.

Here she was, running away when so much was at stake. Wetness trickled down her cheek, but she swiped it impatiently. This was no time for tears.

Had she exposed herself? Maybe not. The fake David might suspect she knew, but he couldn't be sure.

Could he? What had she said?

No matter. She needed to sound the alarm, to tell someone what was going on.

Lawrence could advise—

No. What if Theo was right?

She didn't believe it. But someone had put this man up to it. Someone who'd known the Harmonys well. And there weren't that many intimates left.

Theo. He'd lived with them several years, but he had too much to lose. So did Sondra.

Auntie May? But if she was behind the fake David, she wouldn't have inadvertently caused him to slip up. Besides, she wasn't a beneficiary of the Trust and, after Miss Livvy's death, she'd stopped visiting the island altogether.

How about islanders from back then? The most likely prospects were dead, but there were still a few old-timers left. Cap'n Towle, Miss Bessie, Chauncey.

They'd all been here, but they didn't work inside the Big House. They wouldn't know enough, would they? Plus they seldom left the county. Hard for them to find a David lookalike from Europe.

Then there was Mom, but she'd never do something like this.

Her head hurt.

Forget it. She had to tell someone, but who?

Lawrence was out. Because—and she loathed herself for her

suspicions—Theo might be right. Lawrence could have brought in this phony.

After all, he was the one to state positively that the man was David. Without Lawrence's backing and approval, this imposter wouldn't have a leg to stand on.

And because of Lawrence, at this crucial time, Mom had gone on an extended cruise of the Mediterranean with Aunt Sadie while Megan should have been incommunicado in Utah.

Of the people who had known David best, the ones most likely to spot an imposter were, or should have been, absent.

All Lawrence's doing.

But Lawrence was so honest. And she owed him so much. It couldn't be him. Unless Theo was right. Lawrence's administration of the Trust meant he could easily siphon off money.

Or George. George complained about always being short, but Mona spent plenty. If George had somehow embezzled money, would Lawrence help him cover?

Surely neither of them could be behind this.

She pressed her throbbing temples. She could go round and round for days and still have only conjectures. Right now, she needed help to expose the man, help from someone beyond suspicion. Someone who wanted the truth.

That meant Theo and Sondra.

They had everything to lose and nothing to gain by bringing David back to life. They would have resources to open an investigation headed by someone other than Lawrence. And they certainly wanted to prove this man was not David.

"Guess it'll be the Packs."

Drat it. Too bad there was no one else.

When she plodded back to the patio, Lawrence was talking in low tones to George.

Telling George that she suspected them?

How would Lawrence know?

Because whoever this man was had told him what she'd said.

Whoa. Slow down.

She didn't know the Wykertons had anything to do with this. Not for certain. She mustn't lose her head. There was no reason to become paranoid. After all, she hadn't accused the man outright.

Nor was there any proof the Wykertons had hired him. There might be an old servant or someone else involved she didn't know about. Someone like Bertie's mother, who'd worked in the Big House for decades.

No, she was reaching.

None of the islanders was conniving or sophisticated enough to come up with this impersonation.

Theo was right. Lawrence had to be involved.

As she stood indecisively, the Wykertons both spotted Megan.

Were their expressions apprehensive or was it her imagination? She tried to remember her conversation with the actor, what he might have repeated to Lawrence.

The sweat on her forehead and neck came not entirely from the heat. She spun in the other direction, searching the crowd.

By the inside pool, several women flirted with the fake David. In the distance, Theo, shoulders rigid, walked back from the barbecue pits on the edge of the golf course.

Theo. She skirted Sondra's fountain to intercept him but stopped out of sight behind a bleeding heart bush.

Theo was easygoing but slow. She could imagine him getting excited, blurting out accusations that no one would believe. Accusations that would alert Lawrence.

Then Sondra Pack appeared on the piazza.

Sondra.

She was the logical one. In spite of her self-absorption, or perhaps because of it, Sondra could be depended upon to act when her lifestyle was at stake. Theo might bluster and threaten but never do anything constructive. Sondra would. Mom said she was tougher than people realized.

Yes, Sondra was the one to tell.

Despite her impatience, Megan had to wait to get her quarry alone.

Joining the fringes of a group on the piazza talking about a big bash some Greek tycoon had thrown on his yacht, she shifted from foot to foot while Sondra finished beguiling a couple of men.

Then Lawrence pulled Sondra aside.

Keeping her from talking to Megan?

She really was paranoid. Maybe he was saying his goodbyes.

On pins and needles till the two parted, Megan made sure Lawrence was out of sight before she cornered Sondra. "I have to talk to you."

"In the middle of the party?" Sondra raised her brows. "What about?"

"I don't want anyone to overhear. It's important to you and Theo. Very important."

"Oh?" Sondra picked up Peachie, murmured excuses to an approaching couple. "Why don't we go inside?"

She led the way to a back door and into a den off the conservatory.

A vase of sweet gardenias topped a console. The single window framed a view of the back pool where several people cavorted, but the den was empty and hushed.

"Ah, it's cool in here. Christ, this air conditioning is worth every cent we paid to get it installed." Sondra put Peachie down, took off her brimmed hat and laid it on a table. "What's so important, dear?"

"Sondra, that man out there isn't David."

"Of course he isn't." Sondra sat down in an overstuffed chair and removed her sunglasses. Her painted face could have been that of a doll, its expression eternally bland. "Theo and I knew from the beginning. What made you decide?"

Megan paced. "Because I, I . . . Because of things he's said."

Sondra appraised her. "Hmm. Lawrence swears he's David. We'll need more evidence than a vague 'things he's said' from you."

"Lawrence is wrong, I know he's wrong. I can prove this man isn't David."

"You can prove it?" Sondra stiffened. "How?"

"I—" To tell the truth would mean revealing all her bittersweet secrets. She licked her lip. "I don't want to go into it, Sondra. Just take my word."

Sondra widened kohl-lined eyes. "Oh, I believe you, Megan. You were always truthful." She stuck a leg of her glasses into her mouth. Perfect white teeth bit at the plastic. "But I doubt anyone else will. What do you have?"

"I can't tell you. Not now. When the time comes, I'll have to go into it, but not now." Megan swallowed. "Sondra, you have to find someone to get to the bottom of this."

"I take it you don't mean Lawrence."

"No! Especially not Lawrence. Sondra, has Theo told you what he suspects about the Wykertons?"

Sondra's features flattened. She looked out at the pool. "I know everything Theo thinks."

Through the decorative palm in front of the picture window, Megan saw Theo approach a bikinied brunette half his age and hand her a towel.

"He's my husband, Megan. We share everything."

Megan's cheeks burned. "Like he suspects the Wykertons appropriated Trust money?"

"Theo thinks it a possibility. I have no cause to believe anything like that of either Lawrence or George."

"Still, maybe you should get someone else."

Sondra sighed. "You don't want to take your proof to Lawrence in case it's true."

"Exactly." Thank goodness for Sondra's quick understanding.

Sondra massaged her temples. "So what do you propose we do?"

Megan stepped nearer. "I think you need to get your own attorney."

"Other than Amos or his partner, you mean? Yes, something like this would be over John's head. And certainly Amos's. What about you? Shall I hire you?"

Megan managed not to shriek. "I work for Lawrence, Sondra. Besides, I have no experience in anything like this. You need a criminal attorney."

"I see. All right. Bobby Bairdston can recommend one, I'll bet. Now who did he hire when he accidentally shot that stripper?" One red-tipped finger tapped her chin. "His yacht's already here so he should be arriving soon. In the meantime, Megan, let's keep this quiet. You haven't talked to anyone else, have you?"

"No. Just you."

"Okay. Good." Sondra thought. When she spoke, she used her *do-as-I-say-with-no-questions-asked* voice, as Megan's mother called it.

Mom also complained Sondra in that mood was hell to cross.

"I don't want you talking to anyone about this, Megan. Including Theo. At least for now. He's prone to leap without thinking, and I'd rather have everything arranged before we confront this man." Sondra wrapped her arms around herself as though cold. "I may be wrong, but there's a certain, um, ambience about him that is positively frightening. Did you notice?"

Megan remembered the icy stare and the cruel mouth. "Yes. All right, we'll keep this between the two of us until you can consult an attorney."

"Good. I wish you would reconsider, dear, and tell me how you know he isn't David."

Megan picked out parts of the truth. "There was a note. David left it the night he died. This man doesn't know about it. David wouldn't have forgotten."

"A note?" Interest lilted. "A love letter? To you?"

"Not, not really. But it was private."

"It *was* a love letter! Well, well. How you amaze me. I didn't realize the two of you were that close. I always thought you and David were at odds all the time. But sexual tension often takes that outlet, doesn't it? Especially at that age. Poor dear, his death must have been horrible for you." Sondra rose. "And us never dreaming. Poor, poor Megan."

Megan hated having Sondra suspect what she and David had shared. Examined under the cold light of day by a woman like Sondra, their interlude would seem childish, foolish.

She stuck out her chin. "It was a long time ago and I'd rather forget about it. Anyway, it wasn't a love letter. Just a note David wrote to me before he—before it happened. About some money he borrowed from me. But he would have remembered, said something. And he didn't."

Sondra patted her arm. "All right, Megan. I'll look for a lawyer."

"Are you sure we shouldn't tell Theo?"

"I'll give him a hint of what's going on. Later. I've never seen him this upset, and I don't want him to go off the deep end." Sondra frowned. Her pansy eyes clouded. "Listen, Megan, this man doesn't suspect you know he's an imposter, does he?"

"I don't think so. Maybe not. He can't know for certain."

"You're not afraid of him?"

"Afraid?" She shivered. The room was cold. "Why should I be afraid?"

"Oh, I don't know." Sondra put her hat back on. "There's so much at stake. And he strikes me as dangerous. You've led a sheltered life. There are people who would kill without a second thought to get the kind of money James left. And you're all alone. It worries me. Shall I send someone over to stay with you?"

"I'll be fine."

Sondra's smooth forehead creased. "I suppose you're right. But JoBeth will never forgive me if anything happens to you."

"Nothing'll happen to me."

Other than being run down by Theo's drunken guests.

Not the time to bring up the smashed runabout. She'd ask the Packs to replace it later.

Sondra snapped her fingers for Peachie to follow. "All right, dear. But once you get home, lock up tight for the night."

When they left the den, Megan skirted the piazza where the stranger who called himself David stood with the Wykertons. They were so engrossed in conversation they didn't notice her.

Plotting. She couldn't hear what they said, but it didn't matter. Her burden had lightened. Sondra would do what was necessary.

Servants had put out buffet tables on the patio and were setting steaming dishes on them. Sausage, shrimp, crabs, potatoes, corn, onions, and seasonings, cooked together for low country boil, had been lifted from tubs in large strainers to be laid on wooden tables where guests didn't have to worry about the mess. The tangy aroma of barbecue overlay everything.

Too bad she didn't feel better. She hadn't eaten since her brunch. Her head ached and her stomach cramped. Though the day was still bright, the sun hovered over the west marshes. Better leave before she threw up.

Despair overwhelmed her. She was halfway home before she identified it.

This was the same way she'd felt seventeen years ago when she learned David was dead.

****

"Forever and Ever"
As Performed by Russ Morgan (1949)
Music by Franz Winkler
Lyrics by Malia Rosa

LIKE MEGAN, SONDRA had noticed the Wykertons flanking the actor and wondered what they were saying. She had things to do after her tête-à-tête with Megan but lingered, watching him.

Such animal magnetism.

There were other men here, men with better physiques and handsomer features. But Nick Downing was the focus of the gathering, and not because he was supposed to be David. His presence commanded attention. That restrained virility coupled with a primitive aura of danger was irresistible.

No wonder women flocked to him.

One of their guests came up behind her. "He's fascinating, isn't he?" The tipsy woman sipped at a cocktail but watched Nick greedily. "Have you screwed him?"

She was a knucklehead, but her husband was okay. Very attentive to Sondra. And he hosted a lot of Theo's hunting trips. "Don't be smutty, Millie. You know I'm a good wife."

Millie shrieked with laughter. "Good wife. Is that slang for prick tease, dear?"

Bombed, the bitch. "You should watch the alcohol," Sondra said sweetly. "You know Bill detests women who can't hold their liquor. In fact, I understand it's about to cause another divorce."

Millie bridled at mention of her husband. "What's that s'posed to mean?"

"Guess, dear. Come along, Peachie."

If the sow couldn't figure it out, she deserved what was coming. Sondra headed toward Theo. He'd abandoned that pouting sexpot and was deep in conversation with an officer of their bank in New York.

Good. He'd better be discussing the payment on their loans, persuading Carl not to make a hasty decision about calling them in. Lucky Theo got along with Carl. But then he got along with everyone.

She sighed.

Her golden giant paled in comparison with the elegant actor. Not by much. Just a tiny smidgeon. Theo was still the daring buccaneer she'd fallen in love with. The man who'd swept her off her feet. Who'd sustained her and given her everything she'd desired.

The fear of losing him nearly paralyzed her.

Oh, Theo. If only I didn't love you so much.

CHAPTER 24

"Wipeout"
As Performed by the Surfaris (1963)
Music by Bob Berryhill, Pat Connolly,
Jim Fuller, and Ron Wilson
Lyrics by Bob Berryhill, Pat Connolly,
Jim Fuller, and Ron Wilson

THE MULRENNONS' COTTAGE was quiet after the bustle of the mansion. Kicking off her sandals, Megan fixed herself a glass of CoCola—a surefire cure for queasy stomachs according to Mom—and plopped down on a bar stool.

Before he died, her father had expanded the kitchen by adding a dining room. A breakfast bar divided the new part from the old kitchen. Modern sliding glass doors beside the bar opened onto a concrete porch overlooking the backyard. A creek leading to the sound lay beyond.

The view was usually relaxing. Not today. The empty house pressed in.

Too bad Mom wasn't here to dispense her ever-practical advice.

Was this man scheming with the Wykertons? Did he suspect that she knew he was a fake?

She laid her head on her arms and thought of David, a luxury she hadn't allowed herself in a long, long time.

If he'd lived, Mom wouldn't have had to put up with Theo and Sondra. Megan wouldn't have had to worry about the island's future, or whether or not Lawrence and George were dishonest.

She and David would have married and had a family, lived here and been happy.

Lengthening shadows finally got her up.

The cottage felt strange without Mom.

She turned the television on. Static interfered with both the Jacksonville and Savannah channels they received so she tried the radio. All it got was the local station.

Better than silence.

As she pried open a Mason jar of homemade soup, Elvis wondered whether an ex-lover was lonesome tonight. While the soup heated, Patsy Cline followed with more despair.

Maybe silence wasn't so bad.

She turned the radio knob to *Off* and sat down on a heavy wrought-iron bar stool to eat.

The soup had no flavor. By the time she washed up her half-empty bowl, she was dragging. After bathing and donning threadbare baby-doll pajamas, she went to bed with Mom's copy of *The Glass Blowers*. Barely eight o'clock, but the day's events coupled with the past night's accident and her illness had left her exhausted.

She dozed off before finishing the first chapter.

A clatter jerked her awake.

Was that glass breaking?

The bedside lamp reflected from the dark windows. Her heart's drumming drowned every sound. When she sat up in bed, the heavy book thudded to the floor.

Her heartbeat slowed, normalized.

No, everything was quiet.

She must have been dreaming. Quarter to nine by the clock. She hadn't been asleep long.

Loud pops broke the smothering silence.

Held breath hissed out.

"Partying at the Big House."

The fireworks were supposed to be tomorrow, but some of the merrymakers must have set them off early and woke her up. Could have been worse. Last year, in the middle of the night, they'd fired the cannon used to start the races and scared everyone to death. Dimwits.

She turned off the lamp to go back to sleep, but a peculiar smell made her sniff.

Was that gas? Had she not turned off the stove eye after heating her soup?

"Drat." She didn't want to get up.

But that odor was gas, all right.

She made herself get out of bed, walk down the hall, and reach for the light switch inside the breakfast nook.

Brightness. Pain. Darkness.

Later: *My head. Something's wrong with my head.*

She could hardly lift her lids.

Something was wrong.

A moan came. One faraway moan.

What's that?

She dragged her eyes open. Another moan came.

Someone's hurt.

What in the world was she on that was so hard and cold? It felt like a floor.

Yes, there was their speckled linoleum under her. Why was she lying on the kitchen floor? Had she fallen?

Someone groaned again. Someone must be in real pain.

No, it's me. My head hurts so bad I can't stand it. That stink.

Ugh. Gas.

Gas!

She had to move, get to fresh air. She tried to crawl, but her legs collapsed. With a sob, she slid one knee up toward her chest.

Rubber. Her arms and legs were rubber. They refused to obey.

The sliding glass door lay inches away.

She couldn't reach it. What was wrong with her body? *Move, move.* Finally she got her hand to respond.

Cold metal met her fingers. One of the bar stools.

She marshaled her reserves and with her last bit of strength shoved the heavy wrought-iron stool into the sliding door.

Glass shattered. Fragments sprayed at her face and shoulders.

Blessed cool air rushed in.

Blackness.

****

"My Heart Has a Mind of Its Own"
As Performed by Connie Francis (1960)
Music by Howard Greenfield and Jack Keller
Lyrics by Howard Greenfield and Jack Keller

OCCASIONAL WORDS FILTERED through bone-shattering misery.

"—have her head seen to—"

"—think she'll be all right once—"

"—need to tell Lawrence what—"

Each word hammered at her skull. She could not get comfortable. Impossible to move her feet and legs. If she could pound her head against a wall, put it in a vise—anything would be better than this excruciating pain.

Open your eyes.

"—won't like it—"

"—her hand moved—"

"Good, she's coming around."

David!

Sickening clarity rushed in. No, not David. Someone else. An actor she didn't know.

He hovered over her, anxious. Behind him two men held the same steady regard.

"Wha—?" Her mouth didn't work either.

Relief suffused the actor's face. "Cor blimey, I was beginning to think you weren't going to wake up."

She lay outside, half on the patio slates and half in his arms.

What was he doing here? Why was she on the ground?

"My head." Was that croak hers? She touched her forehead. "It's killing me. What did you . . . ? What happened?"

"It appears you tried to gas yourself."

"Gas myself?" Nothing made sense. "How did you get here?"

"You didn't eat anything at the picnic today, so on our way to our cabin we brought you some food. I hoped we could have a late supper and talk things over."

He added enticingly, "I brought barbecued chicken and white wine."

She groaned, the image of barbecue making her stomach do horrible things.

"Don't care for chicken? We can always send back for pork. Or low country boil."

"Shut up." Her tongue was thick as cotton. "I may puke on you."

"Gawd forbid." He made no attempt to move out of danger.

In fact, laughter lurked under the concern, but she was too nauseated to lash out. "I'd never eat with you. You had no business coming here."

"Lucky I did. Such gratitude overwhelms me. We found you inside the house, covered with slivers of glass and looking like death warmed over."

She labored to turn her head.

The screen of the sliding door was ripped and folded aside. Broken glass shimmered under the artificial yellow light spilling onto the patio. The floor inside held other shards. A bar stool lay amid the wreckage.

Dav—not David; Nick Downing—shifted her so that her head moved and his shirt momentarily smothered her face. It smelled of Coppertone and Old Spice and sweat.

I'm going to be sick.

She struggled weakly.

"Stop it." He resettled her in his lap. "You're all right. I'm stretching out a leg. It has a cramp in it."

"A cramp—Oh." His belt cut into her cheek while her shoulder rested on his hip.

The steady beat of his pulse filtered through his shirt. She felt comfortable, calmed. The nausea abated. Even her headache dulled.

"I heated up some soup. I guess I left the burner on and the fire went out." She fought the sensation of drowning. "I smelled gas and got up to see. I must have passed out."

Somebody behind them snorted. "In the first place—"

A big man in front of them shook his head. "Not the time, Danny."

He was powerfully built, with a thick neck and heavy shoulders. His bovine face wore a puzzled expression.

The men from the pavilion. The bodyguards.

A stone dug into her. She tried to switch her weight around, but her arm brushed a bare leg. Recoiling, her elbow hit Nick's hip.

"Ouch! Watch what you jab. Stay still."

She tried to jerk away. "I have a rock sticking in my butt." Drat! She could bite her tongue for whining.

He shifted her. His hand slid underneath her hips.

She gasped. "Don't do that."

"Be still and I'll get the rock."

"There's no need to paw at me."

"I am not pawing you. I am simply . . . Ah, there it is. No rock, though. Just an acorn." He extracted it and threw it to the side. "Is that better, my princess with a pea? Or to be exact, princess with an acorn."

"I'm all right. Let me get up."

He withdrew the comfort of his arms.

One of the other men helped her to her feet. Nick Downing got up, too, brushing off his shorts.

She was dizzy. Her head felt as if it would split in two.

Nausea returned with a vengeance. She stumbled against a steadying shoulder. A reassuring arm encircled her waist.

"Don't touch me." She couldn't fight him.

"You can't go back into the house," one of the big men said as she took an unsteady step. "We opened the windows and cut off the main valve, but the place still reeks. It's dangerous."

"Hal's right, Megan," the actor added his persuasions. "Come sit over here."

He and Hal helped her over to the wooden yard swing and deposited her in it. The chains creaked as he sat down beside her.

"I could clear up some of this glass," the other man said. "You got a broom?"

She tried to think. Her head would surely explode. "By the kitchen door on the side."

The two bodyguards went around the house, leaving her with Nick Downing.

Her head throbbed. She must have fallen hard, but she could bear it. Courtesy was engrained. "Thank you for getting me out of the house."

The unpleasant smile, seen before, curled. "I couldn't let you die, even if it would solve a lot of problems."

Moonlight silvered his hair, reminding her of David and making her heart ache. "Would it solve them?"

"You couldn't go around telling people I wasn't David Harmony if you were dead."

"I didn't—"

He put an arm around her.

She was too weak to argue or even be scared. All she wanted to do was go to bed. "Is the house aired out enough for me to go back inside?"

"No. You can't sleep here tonight. I think we'll take you with us."

Despite her weakness, her antennae went up. "I'm not going anywhere with you."

"Just for tonight."

"I don't want to spend the night with you."

"You won't be *with* me," he said patiently. "In fact, I wonder if we don't need to take you over to the mainland first, get a doctor to tend your head."

"My head?" It was hard to think, with the hammer pounding inside her skull and her stomach wanting to spew. She'd rather lie back and let him make the decisions.

"Yes, love. You've got a bump the size of a goose egg right . . . back . . ." He gently threaded his fingers through her hair and touched her crown. "Here."

"I'm not your love." How pathetic she sounded.

He ignored her. Though he was careful not to press too hard, his touch caused her to cry out. "Sorry. You're bleeding and you could be concussed. Better get it seen about."

"Let me feel."

He took her fingers and guided them.

She gingerly patted the lump. Her fingers came away sticky.

"I guess I hit my head when I fell. I don't know. I remember waking up and smelling gas and coming to the kitchen to check the stove. Then I must have blacked out."

"You need to get it treated. And while your pajamas are charming, I don't think they're suitable for visiting the mainland. Shall I run inside and get you a robe?"

She was so far from being herself that her worn-out baby-dolls failed to embarrass her. Annoyance at having to think shuffled everything else aside.

In the end, she steeled herself and went inside for shorts and a shirt, but the smell of gas was so strong that she barely made it to the bathroom before throwing up. Afterward, she wasn't so adamant about not leaving.

But she refused to go to the mainland. "Bessie Alcock is Dr. Lowe's nurse for his colored patients. She lives across the island and can look at my head in the morning."

"I remember Miss Bessie. She won't care if we roust her out tonight."

"You don't remem—" She caught herself.

"You were always her pet. She won't mind."

They helped her to a golf cart and drove it across the island to Bessie Alcock's little cottage half-hidden by shrubbery and a riot of flowers that couldn't be appreciated in the dark.

When one of the big men pounded on her door, Miss Bessie herself, gray hair pulled tight in a bun and tying a bright red house coat around her ample middle, opened it. Her coffee-colored face peered up at the man towering over her. "What the hell you mean banging on my door like that in the middle of the night? And who the hell are you?"

"Miss Bessie Alcock." Nick Downing stepped up. "You haven't changed a bit. And it's barely ten thirty. Nowhere near the middle of the night."

Miss Bessie dropped the hand held behind the door. A shotgun glinted before she disappeared. When she came back, unarmed, she was adjusting glasses on her nose so she could look them up and down. "Is that David Harmony?"

"In the flesh."

"Hah. They said you were back but I didn't believe it. Not with the Packs all burrowed in like ticks in a dog's ear. You still a troublemaker, eh? You didn't recollect I keep early hours?"

Miss Bessie had always pretended to dislike David. Megan could do no wrong, but Miss Bessie never held back from giving David a piece of her mind, whether it was about him trampling flowers along her driveway or jumping over her garden fence or riding his bicycle through her yard.

But the stick candy she kept for them was usually clove, David's favorite. And she always offered them the peach fried pies he loved.

Megan preferred peppermint candy and apple pies.

Nick stepped back, put a hand over his heart. "You cut me to the quick. I was never a troublemaker. I was filled with *joie de vivre*."

"Filled with joy of devilment more likely. What you want? And Megan. That you? What you doing back there?"

"She hit her head and won't go to the emergency room. Can you look at it?"

"Her head? Oh my land. You always did get her hurt, even when she was a little bitty thing. Come in here, child."

"Me! Me get *her* hurt? See here, she was always the one daring me to do the dangerous stuff. I never wanted to jump off the top of the garden barn but she—"

"Stop blaming her." Bessie examined Megan's lump and washed it with soap and water. "Not a big place. No need to cut the hair for a bandage. Don't think you got a concussion but you might better stay here with me tonight so I can make sure."

"We'll keep an eye on her," the actor said.

Under Miss Bessie's disbelieving glare, he added, "There are three of us to nurse her. You don't want to stay here, do you, Megan?"

She opened her mouth. He was right, drat him. He wouldn't have helped her if he meant her harm. If she went with them, maybe she could find out who'd put him up to this. "I'll be all right, Miss Bessie."

"Huh." Miss Bessie gave her Easter Island imitation. "How'd your head get bashed like that to start with?"

Megan told about smelling the gas and going to check the stove. "I must have passed out and hit it when I fell."

Miss Bessie snorted. "Uh uh, sugah. People fall forward. They scrape the forehead, the chin, one side of the face. The back of they heads don't get hurt like yours."

"Maybe I hit something when I fell."

"More like something hit you."

Something? That meant someone. "No." The idea was preposterous. "No. It was an accident. I fell."

No one had any reason to hit her. No one but the man standing right beside her, and he had pulled her outside into the fresh air.

Miss Bessie stood akimbo. "First your boat gets smashed to bits. And now somebody hits you on the head. If them's accidents, 'pears to me you need to be more careful."

Trust Chauncey to spread it around about the boat. "I'm all right. A drunk boat driver is a different thing entirely. And no one hit me. I just fell, and now I have a headache. Are y'all ready to go?"

Outside, ensconced in the golf cart, Nick Downing said, "Tell me about your boat."

"One of the Packs' friends ran into it. Probably drinking." No need to mention her unease. "I wasn't hurt but our runabout was totaled."

He questioned her some more as the golf cart went through the woods, dragging out an admission she'd hidden in the water as the boat circled.

"Because you thought they'd rammed you deliberately?"

"Because I thought they were so soused, they would run over me trying to pick me up."

He kept digging for details until she rebelled. "I'm tired. My head hurts. I'm nauseated. I don't want to talk about it. I just want to forget it all."

Including you, whoever you are.

Except she couldn't.

Low music covered the forest sounds as the golf cart meandered toward the guest cottages. Bursts of laughter floated over the woods. A few hardy souls still partied in the distant mansion but only muted lighting from pools and fountains glowed in the night sky.

Next to her, the actor shifted restlessly. Crunching wheels against the pebbly trail hypnotized her, made her sleepy.

"Miss Bessie was right, you know," he said after a while. "Someone did hit you tonight."

"That's crazy. Why would anyone hit me?"

He didn't answer.

A lurking apprehension flared. She was alone with three men she didn't know. Drowsiness fled.

By the time they passed the huge magnolia tree that gave its name to the cottage that housed Nick and his bodyguards, she was less shaky and less afraid. One of the big men suggested food for her. Her stomach rebelled.

"I can't eat anything. Really. I still feel sick. All I want to do is go to bed."

Hal, the older man, said, "I'll move in with Danny and put her in my room, David."

The actor shook his head. "I'll bunk there. She'll be more comfortable in my room."

"I don't want your room."

"Mine has its own loo. You'll be happier there."

So she took his room, decorated like the other cottages with chintz curtains and rustic furnishings. Reading lights with large circular shades hung on each side of the cypress bed. A small table with two chairs was stuffed into a corner.

Everything tidy, with no clothing strewn on chairs or shoes tossed to the side. Not even a brush and comb rested on the bureau. It might have been a vacant room.

As he disappeared into the bathroom, she looked at the roughhewn bed longingly. What she would give to fall down on it.

He reappeared with a toilet case, went to the chest and, with the spare movements of a soldier or ascetic, retrieved clothing. "All right, princess. You can go to sleep now. You'll be safe here with us."

"Will I?"

"I promise."

A certain tenderness in the words puzzled her. She didn't want to like him. She didn't. Or did she? If only she felt better, then maybe she could think straight.

He touched her shoulder. "Sing out if you need anything."

"I won't need anything."

Fifteen minutes later she was in bed but not asleep.

What should she do? She couldn't be angry with him, not when he looked so much like David. Not when he'd pulled her outside the gas-filled house and braved Miss Bessie for her.

She had been happy to cling to him tonight.

More than happy.

You're a nincompoop, Megan Mulrennon.

Just because he looked like David didn't mean he was anyone she could trust.

Use your mind.

CHAPTER 25

"It Had to Be You"
Performed by Ray Charles (1959)
Music by Isham Jones
Lyrics by Gus Kahn

MAGNOLIA COTTAGE HAD one telephone in the living area with a twenty-foot cord. Carrying it into the room Hal had vacated for him, Nick Downing dialed Lawrence Wykerton.

"Someone hit Megan Mulrennon over the head and tried to gas her tonight. They broke in through a window, snuffed the pilot light, then turned on the oven and all the burners."

He was furious but spoke calmly because he was a great actor. "And last night, when she was crossing the sound, someone rammed her boat and destroyed it. She could have died. What do you know about either attack?"

"Attack? What?" Whitey squawked through the lines. "My heavens, why would anyone try to hurt Megan? And why do you ask if I know anything about it?"

The protests sounded genuine. Maybe they were. But . . .

"Because you said you'd keep her quiet. I'd better not find out you were involved in this, Whitey. I may have bargained for rough stuff, but I never expected anyone besides Theo or me to get hurt. Certainly not Megan."

For long seconds he heard only heavy breathing. Then Whitey said, "It had to have been Theo. He must think she'll testify you're David."

"You think so?" He mulled it over. "You may be right. But why should he think her testimony would do more harm than the evidence you've already shown them?"

"Because she grew up with David. Because she'd pass a polygraph test. Because she's a lawyer. How the devil should I know what's going through his mind?" Whitey asked testily.

"Hmmm." He wrestled with his conscience. "I'll have to tell her the truth."

"No! Surely we can think of something else."

"I don't see any way around it. We have to keep her from confirming to Pack I'm not David, and she's got to be warned to be on her guard."

"Oh for the love of heaven." Whitey sighed audibly. "Confound it. Do what you think best."

Nick hung up and stared into space, jaw set, clenching and unclenching his fists.

His life had changed the moment he saw Megan's picture. Past disappointments and crimes, his shortcomings and cowardice—all washed away in a resurgence of optimism.

He'd enjoyed affairs before, passions intense while they lasted but forgotten the day they ended. When that candid face looked out of that bleeding photo, he knew this woman was for him. He was downcast to learn she was engaged, elated to hear she'd broken it off.

After weaseling her flight schedule out of Whitey, he'd flown into Atlanta early to see her in person. He'd hoped he'd be disappointed. After all, what would a woman like her see in a happy-go-lucky nomad like him?

But when she came tap-tap-tapping up in her heels and pearls, looking like a kid playing dress-up, he surrendered. He was caught, like it or not.

Right then and there, he'd decided to approach her afterward.

Meeting her this afternoon hadn't changed his mind, but her presence here was pure bad luck. Now he didn't know if she'd even speak to him once the thing was finished.

Assuming, of course, that he was in any shape to be spoken to by her or anyone else.

****

"Trust in Me"
As Performed by Mildred Bailey (1937)
Music by Ned Wever, Jean Schwartz,
and Milton Ager
Lyrics by Ned Wever, Jean Schwartz,
and Milton Ager

ON THE MAINLAND, Lawrence fixed himself a stiff bourbon and water before going back to bed.

Contrary to Nick's suspicions and office rumor (of which he was well cognizant), he did not sleep in his white shirt and bowtie. He wore cotton pajamas broken in the way he liked by repeated washings. Despite their soft comfort, he still tossed and turned.

Nick's accusation had stung. How could Nick think he would harm Megan, of all people?

And such anger. It resonated over the phone. Because Nick was attracted to Megan?

That wouldn't do. No, no. Not at all.

But he had no time to dwell on that. Exposing Theo remained the big concern.

Had Theo attacked Megan? It made sense if he decided that she was one of the few people whose testimony might be believed in court. If he was desperate enough to attack an innocent woman, he would be ready to strike out at Nick.

And there was little time left.

Lawrence arranged his pillow, threw the light blanket down, pulled it back up, rearranged his pillow.

Nick said nothing about quitting. He wouldn't, would he? Not when they were so close.

Flinging the covers back, Lawrence got up and went to the open window where he could breathe in clean night air. The curtains fluttered when a wayward breeze ushered in the scent from moonflower vines. A night bird twittered.

He'd have to trust that Nick would stay on the job. He'd also have to hire a bodyguard for Megan. That was all there was to it. He'd call his contact in Atlanta first thing in the morning.

Would the week never end?

****

"Then He Kissed Me"
As Performed by the Crystals (1963)
Music by Phill Spector, Ellie Greenwich,
and Jeff Barry
Lyrics by Phill Spector, Ellie Greenwich,
and Jeff Barry

UNINTELLIGIBLE WORDS WOKE Megan. People talking.

Who's that? Where am I?

A man laughed. Another said something indistinct.

A large round lamp floated above her.

Bewilderment blurred into understanding. She was not at home. The fake David had brought her to Magnolia Cottage. He'd given her his room and his bed, and she'd accepted without a qualm.

Okay. Not much of a qualm.

Someone pounded on her closed door.

"Breakfast in five minutes," an English voice called.

She winced. "You don't have to sound so cheerful."

"Thought I'd warn you, let you wash your face or use the loo."

She'd neglected to bring toothbrush or lipstick. All she could do was wash her face and rinse out her mouth. She raked her fingers through her hair and used a lace from her Ked to tie it back. He knocked again, as she scrambled into shorts and shirt.

Before she could call out *come in*, he threw open the door. Dressed in a loose shirt and flowered shorts that had seen better days, he placed a cloth-covered tray carefully on the table.

"Fresh from the Harmony Island Café for mademoiselle." He whisked away the napkin to reveal a fresh pastry, ham biscuit, bowl of strawberries, orange juice, and two coffees.

"Did you cook?"

"Hardly. Danny made a trip to the Big House for victuals. We ate an hour ago. Hope you're hungry."

She was surprised to find that she was. Her stomach wasn't back to normal, but almost.

As she ate, he sipped coffee and told her he'd talked to Lawrence. "Whitey says don't come to work tomorrow. You're to take off as long as you need to recover."

And let the men joke about her being on the rag? No way.

"I'll go in. I feel fine."

He inspected her. "You look pretty raunchy."

Raunchy?

She hadn't looked that bad when she'd checked the mirror. "Thanks a bunch for the boost in confidence."

"How's the head?"

She touched the bump gingerly. "Tender, but the headache's lots better."

He smiled across the table. "I'm glad. I'd give anything to have spared you last night."

His unmistakable concern at first touched her. Then: *He's an actor.*

Finished eating, she laid her napkin on the tray. The manners drilled into her from childhood kicked in. "I must thank you. For taking me in and bringing me breakfast and everything else."

"Must?" He raised a brow.

Her neck heated. "That sounded ungrateful. I'm sorry."

Amiability gave way to the curious tight smile. "No need for thanks anyway. As I said last night, I couldn't let you die, even if it would solve a lot of problems."

She pushed the tray away. "You aren't David." She didn't mean to say it. Her rebellious mouth simply had to blurt the words out. "I was closer to David than anyone alive, and you aren't him."

"He. Mind your grammar. We were close, yes, Megan. Practically brother and sister."

Was he making fun of her?

She sat with every muscle tense, more aware of him than she had been of any man in her life.

Except one.

But she wouldn't think of David, not confronting this person who looked so much like him.

Nick Downing pushed his chair back from the table, his arm brushing hers accidentally. He sent an apologetic smile toward her. A smile like David's.

Warmth filled her. She covered her weakness by curtness. "Brother and sister. Yes."

He draped a bare leg, its foot sporting a foreign-looking loafer, over the chair's wooden arm. A churlish pose.

She pretended not to notice. "David and I played together from before we could walk. Until he died we were best friends. No one except his family knew him better than me."

From his case, he took out a cigarette that was brown, exotic. No, not a cigarette; a small cigar. As he stuck it between lips, soft and bow-shaped like David's, one thumb flipped the lighter open and flicked the flint.

Her mouth dried.

A straight lock of pale hair fell forward. Smoke wafted over his head as the lighter snapped shut.

"Who are you?" she croaked.

A faint smile twitched. "Don't you know?"

Everything about him was masculine, seductive.

So different, yet so much like David.

She coughed nervously. That way he sat. Arrogant. Inflexible. "You're very like him. But you're coarser than he could ever be. You're rough. Unkind. Maybe even cruel."

He inhaled, exhaled, never taking his eyes off her. Acrid smoke filled the air.

"David was never unkind, not intentionally. Unthinking, egotistical, insensitive, yes. He could be all those things, but he was never unkind." She coughed again.

He lifted his cigar. "Does the smoke bother you?"

She made a moue. "Yes. No. I don't care about that. I want to know who you are."

He pressed the cigar, almost whole, very deliberately into the ashtray. "You ought not to pout like that. That kind of pout stirs the blood and heats the loins. It drives a man to throw over the traces and revert to his primeval origins. You should be careful who you use it on."

Was he crazy? "Who are you?"

"Does it matter?" He swung his leg down and rose in one smooth movement.

"Of course it mat—!"

He reached her with one long stride and yanked her up from her chair. His arms wrapped round her. His mouth took hers.

She melted.

She was still sick. From the virus, from the gas, from the headache. Excuses. All excuses.

She kissed him back, pliable, near-senseless.

I used to be proud to be rational. Lawrence hired me because he said I think like a man. Work like a man. Act like a man.

As he'd done on the dock, the actor broke away. "Gawd, Meggie." His eyes shone. His chest rose and fell.

She gave a strangled cry. "Did Lawrence Wykerton put you up to this?"

He shook his head. "You can't blame *that* on Whitey. That was entirely my own idea."

"You know what I mean. I'm going to have to tell the truth about you. Even if you, even if I . . ." She heard herself, gasping and hoarse, uncertain as she hadn't been in years.

Pull yourself together, ninny!

She took a deep, temporizing gulp of air. "No matter how I feel, I can't let everyone go on thinking you're David."

The foreign half-shrug came. "I expect you'll do what you think best."

That was the last thing she expected.

"Who are you? Please." Oh Lord, she couldn't be begging. "Who are you?"

"If I'm not David Harmony, I imagine I'd be Nick Downing." His drawl was British.

"That's your real name?" She tried to sort out the truth.

"My agent didn't care for Nick Dowserman." Underlying mirth belied the apologetic tone. "That's the name I started my career with, but he changed it."

Her legs wouldn't hold her. "Are you English?"

One brow lifted. "Didn't you hear my story?"

She all but fell into the chair. "The one you've been telling, yes. I want to hear the real one."

He laughed but the wheels were turning. She could see him assessing her, deciding how much to reveal, how much to conceal. "All right, darling Megan, let me tell you how it could have happened."

He sat down across the table. "Not that I'm saying it did happen, mind you, only that it could have happened. Nick Dowserman could have been on this side of the world in 1946. He could have been on his way to Mexico. He could have traveled around South America for a few years till he fell in with a movie company from England. He could have gone back with them, got in with an acting agent, and before long could have become king of the mountain. Or at least one of the crown princes."

He polished his fingernails and tried to look modest but wasn't altogether successful.

"Are you saying all that part of your story is true?"

"I've found it's much better to stick to the truth whenever possible. Don't you agree?"

"I wouldn't know. I try not to lie."

"In your case, darling Megan," he said between laughter, "that's probably wise."

She took a long swallow of her coffee. It had cooled. "What made you decide to pose as David Harmony?"

"Did I say I was posing?" He wagged one finger at her. "You weren't listening, Meggie."

If playing word games was the only way she could get him to talk, she would play them. "All right. If you were posing as David Harmony, what would have made you do it?"

"What would have made me do it?" He pretended to think. "If I were playing the part of David Harmony, it would be mainly because there's a resemblance, don't you suppose?"

She hated him, hated the likeness to David. No, that wasn't true. She couldn't bear to look at him, but neither could she bear to turn away. Her chest felt like it was being torn in two. She got up to pour coffee dregs down the bathroom sink, give herself time to calm.

"I can see your resemblance to David," she said when she emerged. "Go on."

He had got up to pace. "All right. It might be that someone saw my photo in a magazine and noted the resemblance. I could have been called upon with an interesting proposition."

"That you come here and pretend to be David? But why? Who hired you?"

He closed the door leading to the front room.

"If this were a story, then Whitey would be the one who asked me to become David Harmony, I should think. As for why." He kept his distance. "It might be because there are, um, discrepancies about the deaths of David and his brother. Someone could even have come up with a quaint notion that they may have been murdered."

Her lungs refused to function.

"L-Lawrence thinks David and Robby were murdered?"

Horror, disbelief, grief, emptiness, even anger. All the emotions that had raged when she lost David.

She had taken years to finally accept the explosion as a tragedy, an unfortunate accident, a hideous coincidence coming as it did right after Mr. H dying.

But David and Robby were deliberately killed?

Black dots swirled. A tremor started in her hands and spread up her arms and shoulders and down her legs till she shook all over. Her breakfast rose, pressed on her throat.

"Meggie." He was instantly beside her, overturning a chair in his haste. "Meggie, I shouldn't have been so blunt." He embraced her, held her upright. "I didn't mean to upset you. Darling, love, don't cry. It's only a story."

"Don't call me darling or anything else." When the sobs began, she couldn't stop them. "You don't know me."

"Don't know you? Meggie." He pulled her closer, his breath warm against her cheek. "Of course I know you. You and every other important person in David's life. I watched home movies where you and he wore a path in the front lawn with your bicycles and a Streak-O-Light wagon. I saw you throw David off the dock when he kidnapped your doll, and I know how yellow is your favorite color, and how you and David got in trouble because you wouldn't lie when his mother asked if you were fishing in the goldfish pond. No, Meggie, don't pull away."

She stilled, barely taking in his words. She didn't trust him but his resemblance to David fascinated her.

The shaking stopped when he began to kiss her. She let him, passively at first, held fast, unable to respond until, under his spell, time turned backward, and she was sixteen again.

His hand navigated its way into her shorts.

"We can't." She could barely get the words out.

"Then tell me to stop." His words warmed her skin, but he sounded breathless. A faint scent of soap and Old Spice and male perspiration spread over her.

She opened her mouth but only ragged gasps came out.

"One word," he taunted. "Tell me to stop, darling Megan."

All the time, his hand stayed inside her shorts. His lips were close and the temptation too great, and she pulled his head down. A brief regret for her long abandoned pills, but no time to think of consequences.

Only once before had she ignored the strictures of her upbringing with such abandon. With David.

His tongue touched the pulse at the base of her neck. No harshness in him now. Only the special muted softness of love. Or desire masquerading as love. "Is it all right?"

She shouldn't. "Yes," she whispered. "Yes."

He rolled away. "Unless you want to wind up pregnant, I have to get a rubber."

The bald words didn't faze her.

He came back and lay down, saying, "Help me, then."

Like another time in her life, she obeyed a man without question and touched him the way he wanted and guided him to her center.

Torment gave way to crushing sweetness as he gently began the rocking motions that filled her again and again.

She heard her own cry, felt him climax.

But David was the one who filled her mind.

CHAPTER 26

"It's Been a Long Long Time"
As Performed by Perry Como (1956)
Music by Jule Styne
Lyrics by Sammy Cahn

AFTERWARD, HE NUZZLED her shoulder and twisted his fingers in her hair, long undone from its makeshift holder. She lay beside him, breathing in earthy scents of sex and him.

What had she done? How could she have let this man, this criminal, make love to her?

Seventeen years ago she'd lain on the floor of a gazebo with a boy she'd known all her life. This morning she lay in bed with a stranger.

Why had she allowed it? Was he telling the truth about David and Robby dying or was he trying to keep her quiet while he claimed the Harmony fortune?

She was out of her mind. Had to be. Maybe she did have a concussion.

He propped up on an elbow. "What are you thinking, to look so solemn?"

A stranger with David's face.

"I'm wondering what's wrong with me, falling into bed with you."

And about what you said, who you are, why I feel this way.

"Nothing's wrong with you. I'd say everything's quite all right. More than all right." Sweetness changed to mockery. "At least so far as I know. I thought you enjoyed it, too."

She had to clench her hand to keep from slapping him.

Instead, she sat up and swung her feet down, then pulled the sheet up over her breasts. "I wasn't talking about that. I don't know you, I don't know anything about you and yet I went to bed with you without a second thought."

"Is this leading up to something I don't want to hear? Please don't tell me you hated it. I'd be terribly distressed. I daresay even devastated."

Was that a twinkle? Darn him. "You told me Lawrence Wykerton hired you."

"No, poppet. I said he might have. In my hypothetical explanation." If there had been a twinkle, it vanished.

She tugged at the sheet, wrapping it close so that it pulled away from part of his legs and hips. "Did Lawrence hire you so that he could put off turning over the Trust? Is he worried about the Packs' audit?"

"Bloody hell. Is that all you can think about?" He pushed the pillows against the headboard and sat up against them, knees bent unselfconsciously when the sheet fell. He didn't bother to cover his body, glowing and sated.

She looked away.

"Megan, I feel Whitey's basically honest. I assume he knows what he's doing. Besides, if I were pretending to be David, I could only carry it off for so long, wouldn't you think? I'd be bound to slip up one of these days, make some big mistake I couldn't just brush off with an *Oh, it's been so long, I simply forgot, ha, ha, ha!*"

She risked a look. "How long did you plan to carry it off?"

His smile was disarming. "As long as necessary. That is to say, if I were—"

"—impersonating David Harmony," she finished. "What is it you hope will happen? Obviously, no one has thrown up his hands on your return and said *Here I am! I did it! I killed David and Robby and left the bodies in the sea for the fish—*"

Her breakfast started to come up. Her hands went to her mouth. She bent over.

David, her spirited, lovely David, intentionally murdered.

"Megan. Megan." He scrambled across the bed to put his arms around her. She could smell their scents on him. "Darling, I'm so sorry." He stroked her hair, her bare arm. "Here I've unloaded all this on you and not even given you time to digest it before—"

Nausea subsided.

She pulled away. "Before taking me to bed. No need to sugarcoat it on my account."

Getting up, she searched for her clothes.

He lay among the rumpled bedclothes, comfortable in his nudity. "Don't be ashamed of it. Don't turn what we shared into something sordid."

"Isn't it?"

"No," he said quietly. "It isn't."

"Obviously, you and I have different standards. Mine say a woman doesn't do that with a man unless she loves him. What we shared was sex, pure and simple. I'm entitled to feel sordid."

She gathered up clothes and fled into the bathroom for a long calming shower.

Clean and dressed, she came out to find him, in garish shorts but no shirt, lounging in a chair. He smoked one of his thin cigars and watched gray rings dissipate under the ceiling fan.

"I need to go home," she said. "I have to wash clothes for work tomorrow."

He stubbed his cigar out. "I told you, Whitey isn't expecting you. He can vouch for me. As for his part in this, you'll have to work that out yourself. I trust him."

She hung her head. "Everything is so mixed up, D—No, I can't call you that, can I? What do I call you? Nick?"

"Nick, Fred, John, Bob, whatever the bloody hell you like." He snatched up his cigarette case and snapped it open.

"Oh, I forgot." Icy eyes met hers. "David's the one you're in love with, isn't he? The one you imagined in bed with you? Are you absolutely positive you don't want to keep calling me that?"

She took a step back. She hadn't called out David's name.

Had she? No, she couldn't have.

The vicious way he took out a new cigar scared her.

He'd been frightening before, but this was something different. She hadn't thought him capable of such overpowering anger. Not without a reason.

Sondra said he was dangerous. Had she seen him like this?

"There's no need for your tone."

"No? You're the one setting the tone." He jabbed the cigar at her. "All I did was make love to a pretty woman and, fool that I was, expect her to treat me with some kindness afterward."

Heat rose to her face. "I'm sorry."

"Are you? Because we went to bed unexpectedly? So you had a weak moment. That doesn't make you a bad person. And does it automatically mean we have to hate each other?"

"I don't hate you." The words, tumbling out, were true. She looked at her hands, at the floor, anywhere but at him. "I just don't trust you. I'm no good at games. I shouldn't have gone to bed with you, but I did. You're right. It doesn't mean anything."

"I didn't say that." He put the unlit cigar back in his case and snapped it shut. "For a lot of people that's true. You've already admitted you're not one of them." He pointed to the bed. "What the hell was it that went on there? What were you playing at? That I was David?"

She refused to cry. She blinked. Hard, to hold back the dam.

"Oh, shite." He took a deep breath. His body relaxed. Softness returned. "Listen, Megan. If you want me to, I'll throw myself at your feet and beg your forgiveness. You're right to be leery. I'm old enough to know better but when you started crying, all I wanted to do was comfort you. And then it escalated. Now all I've done is to further complicate an already complex affair."

"I don't know you or anything about you." Megan put her palms against her hot cheeks. She wouldn't break down again. She wouldn't. "I don't know if any of what you've said is the truth or not. What do you expect me to do?"

"I expect you to talk to Lawrence Wykerton. Afterward, I expect you to tell all and sundry that you are convinced I am David Harmony. You say you can't play games but this is important. Try just this once, Megan. Try to pretend I'm David Harmony."

She thought of Sondra and Theo, dangling in a situation not of their contriving while Lawrence and Nick spread their lies. "I can't. It's wrong."

His jaw set. "It'll be more wrong if you can't. If you give me away, David's murderer will do more than get off scot-free. He'll get David's inheritance."

"Who'll get—?" She gaped. "Theo? Theo murdered David and Robby?"

Nick remained unyielding. "Will you go with me to see Lawrence Wykerton?"

She agreed. What else could she do?

CHAPTER 27

"River of No Return"
As Performed by Marilyn Monroe (1954)
Music by Lionel Newman
Lyrics by Ken Darby

WHEN MEGAN RANG the doorbell, Lawrence, unchanged from his church shirt and tie but clutching a napkin, opened his front door. Bay rum aftershave met her nose. Verdi's *Il Travatore* filled the hallway behind him.

Lawrence seemed more worried than annoyed at her and Nick and two bodyguards storming his home. "I'm having lunch. Some of Mam's soup from the freezer. I can get out some more if you'd like to join—"

Nick, churlish man, interrupted, "No. Go ahead and eat. We won't be long."

"I see." Lawrence stood aside. "Come on back." He waved his napkin toward the living room, and said to the bodyguards, "Y'all might be more comfortable waiting in there."

Though Megan had visited here often, she felt ill at ease as she followed Lawrence's small figure.

No going back now. "I thought you ate Sunday dinners with George and Mona."

Lawrence paused long enough to lift the needle from the record player in the hall. Verdi was silenced. "Not when Mona's mother is visiting them," he said tartly, quickly adding: "She, er, gets to see the grandchildren so seldom, I hate to barge in during her time with them."

"That's very thoughtful of you."

Megan had met Mona's widowed mother and agreed with Mom that Mona was trying to matchmake. Lawrence was wise to be leery.

His home, a remodeled farmhouse on the mainland, was modest in design though some of the antiques chosen by his late wife might have been valuable. In the kitchen, shelves framing a bricked-in fireplace contained a variety of teapots, more evidence of the late Mrs. Wykerton's tastes and hobbies. Occasional panels of wallpaper sporting yellow cabbage roses reinforced the sunny yellow and white décor. The smell of vegetable soup permeated the air.

Reaching a dining table covered with a cutwork lace cloth, Lawrence pulled a chair out for Megan, then sat down to his barely tasted lunch. "Are you sure—"

"Positive." Nick sketched out why they were there.

Lawrence picked at his soup while he listened, then pushed away a half-empty bowl. His fingers drummed on the honey-colored table.

"So it was Livvy's trinket box that gave us away. Bless my soul. I knew you and your mother would be the ones most likely to realize Nick wasn't David, Megan, but both of you should have been safely out of the way. I hope you understand the necessity for secrecy."

"I don't understand anything. What are you trying to do?"

Megan wanted to believe Lawrence. That would make it easier to believe in Nick.

Lawrence folded his snowy napkin. "I'm sure it's hard for you. Believe me, hiring Nick was the last thing I ever thought I'd do. But I had no choice." Without haste, he placed the napkin beside his water glass. "You've helped with the Trust a bit, Megan. You know its provisions, that it must be turned over to the Packs next Wednesday."

"Yes."

While Nick stirred restively, Lawrence took off his glasses and rubbed his eyes.

"You also know the problems we've faced with James's will. After the boys died, Sondra and Theo had the largest bequests by far. They could have engaged in endless litigation about who should inherit how much. Instead, they fell in love, married, and agreed to accept equal shares in hopes the Trust could be settled right away."

Megan nodded. "Both Sondra and Theo gained a lot when the boys died."

"But Theo killed them." Lawrence rattled the ice in his tea.

Nick leaned forward. "I've asked you this before but you never answer. Why did you fix on Theo as the murderer? Sondra would have had just as much motive."

"Theo was with the boys the night they died. Sondra was in Washington with James." Lawrence set his glass down. "Also, James left her more than Theo. When she married Theo, they agreed both portions would be divided equally. If money had been her objective, there was no reason to split her larger share with Theo."

"You're assuming they weren't involved in planning the murders together," Nick said.

"Yes." Lawrence leaned back in his chair, put his fingertips together. "I have my reasons for believing that but won't reveal them now. Theo Pack is the one who killed the boys."

Megan traced a cutwork flower.

Theo. A murderer.

While he wasn't overly intelligent, he was the consummate sportsman. He hunted animals and mounted their heads. But calculated murder of two boys he treated like family?

He didn't have Sondra's personality and he might be heavy-handed with the islanders, but he was pleasant to her and Mom. He drank too much, but his crowd all drank too much. And he was crazy about Sondra. Did murderers have good marriages?

No matter. Lawrence said Theo had killed David and Robby, and she'd believe him over Theo anytime. At least the Lawrence she'd always known. This new Lawrence . . .

"Okay." She shifted in her chair. "Theo was the last person to see the boys. How does Nick pretending to be David flush him out?"

"Oh, we have hopes," Lawrence said vaguely.

She didn't miss the warning glance Nick shot him.

They thought because she was a woman, she was stupid.

"Ahem." Lawrence forestalled her protest. "Theo will have to do something before Wednesday. He's getting pretty desperate. Nick has been pressuring him and I've convinced his attorneys that the dental and fingerprint evidence will hold up. He'll have to—"

"How did you do that?" Megan asked, momentarily diverted. "The evidence?"

"Photocopies, my dear. The fingerprints supposedly taken from Nick actually came from the sheriff's files, doctored up a bit. Same sort of thing with the dental records. I had a little help from a friend of mine who works with that sort of thing." Pride briefly lit his face.

"As far as Theo's concerned, they're real," Nick cautioned.

"That's illegal."

"And I'm desperate." Lawrence's worried expression returned. "I've told Theo and his attorneys that I'm satisfied Nick is David and they think I intend to release the Trust to him."

"They'll sue," Megan said.

"But they think it'll be a long and costly fight. One they can't win. It's imperative that Theo continue to believe that." Lawrence grimaced. "I have absolute authority over the income until the suits are settled, so the Packs' funds will be cut off immediately if they fight it and Theo needs that money. I happen to know he's incurred obligations in anticipation of getting it this Wednesday."

Nick grinned. "So he has to discredit me before then."

Lawrence sniffed. "Yes. He's got to make a mistake, and when he does, we'll catch him."

"A mistake?" Megan's exasperation returned. "You've set Nick up as bait so that Theo, if he is a murderer, will try to kill him?"

"Don't be ridiculous," Nick scoffed. "Do you really think I'm the heroic type? What Whitey here means is that Theo will have to come up with proof the real David is dead. And once he formulates it, we'll have him."

She glared. "You think I'm a fool."

"My dear, believe me, we are taking no risks with Nick's life," Lawrence said hastily. "There are private detectives with him at all times. Hal and Danny have the best references."

"They might be supermen. But they can't be with him everywhere."

Nick grinned. "Worried about me?"

"Worried about—? Think a lot of yourself, don't you? Why should I worry about you? I don't even know you." Her indignation sounded authentic to her, but Nick only grinned wider.

The egotistical, insufferable jerk.

Lawrence said, "Nick will be as safe as we can make him."

Reality doused anger. "What if this isn't resolved? What if Wednesday comes and goes? Will Nick get the money?"

"Come, come." Lawrence frowned. "I hope you know the law better than that. I'll have to release it to the Packs, much as I dislike doing so. But Theo mustn't suspect that. It's vital that he believe you're convinced Nick is David Harmony."

"I can keep a secret." Megan's head spun. Her day had barely begun but it had already been filled with too many disclosures.

"Theo may be a little too convinced Megan thinks I'm David Harmony," Nick said dryly.

"Yes." Lawrence showed every year of his age and then some. "The boat accident and the gas you told me about. I understand your concern."

"I wonder," Nick mused, "how he knew to waylay her in the sound."

Lawrence raked at his hair until it looked like beaten egg whites. "I phoned Sondra after I learned Megan was coming home. I suppose she could have mentioned it to Theo or he could have overheard my call. Then he intercepted the runabout. But why would he go to so much trouble? What difference does it make if Megan says you are David?"

"Because she was close to him. Theo might convince people you're angling to keep control of the Trust by saying I'm David, but Megan has no reason to lie."

She said, "You could be wrong. Theo didn't know I'd accept Nick as David when I came across the sound. His Nautique rammed my boat, I'm pretty sure, but he reported the damage. Would he have done that if he was responsible? Isn't it more likely one of his visitors got drunk, went for a ride, and didn't see me?"

Ignore the instinct that had led her to hide in the water. No need to give Lawrence the impression she was flighty. "As for the gas, I could simply have forgotten to turn the stove off."

Nick looked at her scornfully. "With a broken window pane in the kitchen door? And the oven going full blast? If you believe that, you are a simpleton."

"A broken window pane! You didn't say anything about a broken window!"

So someone really had attacked her. Theo? It had happened after she confirmed to him that Nick was David.

Nick said, "Whitey, Megan ought to go away for a while."

Lawrence nodded. "That would be best."

"Sondra knows Nick isn't David," she said abruptly. "I told her. She asked me not to say anything. She wanted to keep Theo in the dark till she had a criminal attorney lined up. She was afraid of what he might do."

Nick's eyes narrowed.

"I understand her reasoning." Lawrence stared at his fingers. "I suspect she hasn't said anything to him, and that's why he acted last night. You need to get away, Megan."

"I'm not going anywhere." She pointed to Nick. "He's the one in danger. If Theo really did kill the boys, Nick's the one he'll be after."

A phone on the kitchen wall rang. Lawrence got up to answer. "Hello." He glanced at them, turned away, and lowered his voice. "Yes . . . I can't talk now. I'll be at the office later . . . Yes, I know it's Sunday but I'm going in for a few minutes. Give me half an hour . . . Fine."

When he hung up, he said, "Megan, I implore you. Stay here. I have spare rooms. Or check into the motel in town. It'll take several days to repair your doors and you mustn't be alone at your house until it's secure and this is over."

"I'll be all right."

Nick studied his fingernails. "She can stay with us. We've already rearranged rooms to accommodate her."

Arrogant and overbearing turkey. "I want to go home."

Nick pouted. "Then you'll have to take Hal or Danny with you. And that means I won't get all the protection I'm entitled to. Since you don't care what happens to me, then by all means, insist on going home with my bodyguard."

"I hate the way you make me—you're trying to—"

Come off it! Surely she had enough moral fiber to withstand him.

She would never have been seduced so easily this morning had she not been shocked to learn about David and Robby.

Nick shrugged. "I'm watching out for myself. If you don't care whether Theo gets me, fine."

"That isn't it and you know it!"

Lawrence disregarded their dispute. "If you won't come here or go to a motel, staying with them might be best, Megan. Just until I can hire another man. Will you?"

Withstanding Lawrence was impossible and that egotistical creep knew it. She unclenched her teeth. "All right. I'll stay in the Magnolia Cottage for one more night."

"Good. That relieves part of my worry. Nick, why don't y'all head back to the island, do whatever you need to get Megan settled?"

"Fine." Nick stood up too. "Megan, shall we go?"

As Hal drove the Lincoln and Danny rode shotgun, she and Nick sat in cold silence.

From Lawrence's home, the road to town wound through palmetto dotted clearings and cotton fields. When they entered a shady portion lined with the great oaks, Megan thawed. "Do you believe Lawrence?"

He kept staring out his window, one hand opening and closing his silly lighter. "Believe him about what?"

"About the evidence against Theo. What if Lawrence is using you to keep control of the Trust? If the Packs go to court, that means he'll be in charge for a long time. Maybe years."

Nick glanced at her, put the lighter in his pocket. "He said there's no legal way he can keep from turning it over next week. I'm inclined to believe him though I admit I had doubts to begin with. I do wonder what makes him so sure Sondra Pack wasn't involved."

"She wasn't here. Theo was. He must have seen his chance when he learned Mr. H had died, and . . ."

Her voice broke. "Mr. H had caught the flu before his trip. Mom and Sondra wanted him to go to the doctor, but he wouldn't. By the time they left, he'd improved. No one expected him to die. No, it had to have been a spur of the moment thing for Theo."

"I see. I'll accept your judgment." He used his sweet smile. A sunny patch lit his side of the car and gilded his hair. "In that case, I wonder if Sondra's the one behind Whitey's crusade."

"You think someone is behind Lawrence?"

"Surely you don't believe offering me half a million dollars to impersonate David Harmony was Lawrence's idea. He's much too cautious to dream up such a scheme. No, someone put him up to it. Besides, someone had to show him proof Theo was involved. I can't help but think that Sondra must be that person. Who else could get the proof?"

She stared. "He's paying you half a million dollars? Nick, what I said was right, wasn't it? Theo'll have to get rid of you before Wednesday or lose everything."

"Don't be such a worrywart, Meggie. Hal and Danny are constantly with me. He'll try something, but whatever it is, we're prepared." He raised his voice. "You blokes up there. We *are* prepared, aren't we?"

"Sure," Hal said.

"Yeah," Danny mumbled around his chewing gum.

"See?" Nick said to Megan. "No need to worry. I'm not in the least concerned."

"Of course not. You're an idiot."

"I resent that. I may not be Einstein but an idiot?"

"You could be hurt or worse. If Theo killed the boys, what makes you think he won't kill you?"

"He may try, but he won't succeed. I can take care of myself. I don't suppose this means you're beginning to care a little bit about me, does it?"

They were nearing town.

She could see the inland river winding between the mainland and Harmony Island. Its usual brown was dotted with tiny ripples, their sparkles showing the trail of the wind.

"I'm not sure. I thought I hated you and now I don't know. I should be furious. But I'm not."

"Ah. I'm growing on you. Good. I don't like playing second-fiddle to a ghost, love."

Love. Actors used endearments like that all the time.

Before she could complain, they pulled up to the mainland pier where their cruiser waited. Nick leaned toward the front. "Let's not go back to the island right away. We can walk over to that café across the street and have lunch. It's got a lovely view of the water and dock."

The bodyguards looked at each other, but like Megan, they got out and headed to the café without protest.

She didn't like being told what to do, but she was doing what he said just the same.

Including walking a path that promised disaster.

CHAPTER 28

"Suspicion"
As Performed by Elvis Presley (1962)
Music by Doc Pomus and Mort Shuman
Lyrics by Doc Pomus and Mort Shuman

SONDRA HAD AWAKENED that morning terrified. As always when Theo wasn't hunting, they'd slept in, meaning he didn't get showered and dressed to meet Amos until nearly noon. She'd fought her nerves until he left.

Then the terror came rushing back.

Theo suspected. She was positive he suspected.

Christ, sometimes she thought she had jumped into a whirlpool that kept dragging her down and down and down. She never should have gotten into this. Maybe she should back out. Maybe she could fob Lawrence off.

No. Too late. Then again, what if she could put things back the way they were? And right now that's what she wanted to do. Go back to the way it was. If she recanted . . .

She called Lawrence, but he couldn't talk.

Janie brought coffee and toast up to her room. She fed Peachie both pieces. She couldn't eat a bite.

A second call to Lawrence's office found him. He told her about Megan getting hurt.

Her heart hammered. "Christ, Lawrence, is she all right?" She wrung a panel of her silk peignoir.

"She's fine now, but she could easily have died. Do you think Theo could have gone over to her house last night?"

"I don't think so," she denied, then backtracked. "Maybe. I don't know. I was tired and went to bed before he did. This is too much to take in. I can't—"

"She remembers going to bed and waking up to smell gas. When she went toward the kitchen to check, someone hit her on the head. Nick and his men found her after ten, so as best we can tell, it must have happened between nine and ten."

She ran her tongue around her dry mouth. "I just don't know, Lawrence. Theo and I don't live in each other's pockets. I suppose that he. . ." She checked the door to make sure it was still closed. "I'm concerned. He's been looking at me in a peculiar way. And he's acting very strangely."

Silence from Lawrence. Then: "Does he suspect?"

"No, no, I don't think so. I'm sure he doesn't. But he acts like he's going to pieces."

"That's what we want, isn't it?"

The silence was on her part this time.

Lawrence repeated, "We did want him rattled, didn't we?"

"I never dreamed it would be like this. It's all so hard and I'm half crazy. Listen, I must talk to you, Lawrence. Can I come over?"

"Do you think it wise to come here?"

She would tell him she was mistaken. She would be so very apologetic, cry. Lawrence was a man. Face to face, she could persuade him. "He's with Amos and some others. They're going to the north end of the island to check tree stands or something. I'll leave now."

"Now? I don't—"

"Please, Lawrence."

She could barely hear his breathing over her own, but he finally said, "Very well. If you think he won't miss you, I'll be at the office."

"I'll dress and meet you there as soon as I can cross the sound."

After she hung up the blue Princess phone, Peachie stood up on hind legs to lick at her hand. Her baby knew something was wrong. She fondled the poodle's ears.

Peachie tried to kiss her, but she fended off the wet tongue by holding the small dog tightly. "Sweet baby. You know Mama's upset. Oh, Peachie, what have I done?"

The shift with the big flowers would be the quickest to put on. That and her leather sandals. "Janie!"

What would she tell Lawrence?

Christ, she should have known better. How could she ever have come up with such a ridiculous idea? She should have let things be. She'd talk to Lawrence, feel him out.

But Megan knew about Nick. And Lawrence. Was it too late?

"Janie! I need you!"

****

"The Mooche"
As performed by Duke Ellington (1928)
Music by Duke Ellington and Irving Mills
Lyrics by Duke Ellington and Irving Mills

AS HE HUNG up after Sondra's call, Lawrence frowned. Theo might be falling apart, but Sondra sounded like she was, too.

Which under the circumstances was surely understandable.

An hour later, she showed up at his office.

The gaily flowered sundress suggested a cheerful woman until a closer inspection revealed dark circles beneath the violet eyes.

She sank down in one of the visitors' chairs facing his desk. "Tell me about Megan."

He recited events of the boat and gas mishaps, ending: "It seems strange for Theo to attack her, but he must have. No one else has a motive."

She twisted her purse straps. "I suppose not."

"It makes sense if he believes she's the one person whose word would be taken as fact." He steepled his fingers. "If he believes she'll confirm Nick as David, that's his motive. Was there any time that he could have slipped off for a while?"

"Maybe." Sondra fumbled in her purse. "I was so exhausted, I went to bed early."

Tormented, poor soul. Despite everything, she didn't want to believe it of Theo. *She loves him.*

"Christ, I wish I had never started this." She pulled out a tissue, clenched it. "Lawrence, what if I'm wrong? The more I think about it, the more—"

"You aren't wrong. We have to see it through. But could he have attacked Megan?"

She took a shuddering breath, wet her lips. "He was gone for . . . We have a friend who . . . Bobby's crew brought his yacht down yesterday, but he flew into Savannah last night and rented a car. He phoned to say he'd be at the city pier about nine or so. Theo took the cruiser to pick him up. It must have been eight or after when he left. I was asleep when he came to bed."

"So he could have been the one who hit Megan and turned on the gas."

She smoothed her tissue on the corner of his desk.

Stalling. Not wanting to admit it.

She finally said, "I don't know. But he was angry about Megan saying Nick was David." Tears glimmered. "Megan told me before she left that Nick was lying, Lawrence. I couldn't admit what we were doing so I asked her to keep quiet about it till I could find an attorney. If I'd come clean then, warned her, then maybe . . . It's my fault she got hurt."

"Nonsense, you did what you had to do." Lawrence reached over the desk and caught her hand. Despite her pampered lifestyle, Sondra showed more grit than most men. "Courage, my dear. It's almost over."

One soft hand clung to his; the other daubed at her tears. "He suspects something, Lawrence. I didn't think so, but after . . . I think he suspects me."

"Oh, dear. Are you certain?"

"I don't know. Maybe I'm wrong. But he's been so peculiar lately. I've never seen him like this before. I'm frightened."

"Do you think you're in danger? If so, we'll think of an excuse to get you away."

"No." She pulled away and tried to smile, but the red lips turned lopsided. "It's just nerves. I'll hang in. As you said, it's almost over. Except that sometimes he looks at me and I don't know what he's thinking. He's going to do something soon, I know it. He has this rage in him, all bottled up. Maybe that's what makes me afraid. Maybe he doesn't suspect me at all."

She covered both eyes. "Sometimes I wonder if there's an innocent explanation. If I've made this into something that—"

A banging came from the front.

Sondra nearly jumped out of her chair. "Are you expecting someone?"

"No."

"Christ, what if it's Theo?"

"Why would it be? Stay put. I'll get rid of whoever it is."

When Lawrence went to the front, Nick, Megan, and both bodyguards stood outside. He opened the door a notch. "I can't talk to you now."

Nick shouldered his way in.

"See here!"

"No good, Whitey." Nick paid no attention. "We saw Sondra land at the pier and followed her here. I think you can talk to us now. In fact, I rather think you must."

"Oh, dear Lord in heaven." Lawrence closed his eyes.

What else would go wrong?

"Stay here," he told Hal and Danny.

"Wait," Nick countermanded. "Hal, pull our car behind the building out back. We don't want anyone noticing it."

Lawrence marched back, Nick close behind. Megan trailed along.

Sondra stood poised for flight. On seeing Nick and Megan, her face went through a range of emotions from fear to surprise to dismay to anxiety.

Poor woman.

"It's all right, Sondra," he said. "Nick's too clever by half. He's known for some time that I'm not the one who initiated this. When you called this morning, he and Megan were at my house. I'm afraid he guessed from my side of the conversation you might show up here and decided to barge in. He's like that, unfortunately."

He scowled at Nick, but Nick studied Sondra.

The rapscallion.

"Humph. It's useless to try to keep your involvement a secret."

Sondra collapsed into her seat.

Without being asked, Nick pulled up a side chair for Megan and took the visitor's one next to Sondra. He winked at Lawrence. "Now. Who's going to tell us what?"

For all the world like this is his show, confound him.

"What do you want to know?"

"As you said, Whitey, I guessed Sondra is the angel making my sterling impersonation possible," Nick drawled. "My only question is why?"

Sandra silently implored Lawrence.

He said, "I think you may as well explain. He won't leave it alone till you do."

Sondra closed her eyes.

Wishing them all gone to the devil no doubt.

Then she waved the remains of a tissue in surrender. "Someone sent me a news clipping with your picture, Nick. They had written *David Harmony's coming home* on it. Psychos send us junk like that all the time so I didn't think anything about it. Later, when I discovered Theo might have . . ."

She shuddered, nearly broke down again but controlled herself. "I remembered the clipping. I found a photo of you in *Life* magazine and brought a copy to Lawrence when I told him . . . when we decided to hire you."

"What did you tell Whitey?" Nick prodded.

She bit her lower lip. "That I was scared Theo had something to do with the boys' deaths. I couldn't believe it at first. I spent weeks agonizing. Finally, I decided I had to find out for sure one way or the other." She turned to Nick. "That's when I remembered the clipping."

Megan leaned around Nick. "You wanted Lawrence to prove Theo's a murderer?"

"I want to know. I have to find out if he did such an awful thing. I love him." Sondra's voice shook. "I do love him. But if he murdered David and Robby . . ." Tears reformed. "The uncertainty is killing me. Not just because I love him, but for the boys' sake."

The words came spilling out, as if she'd held them inside too long. "I know I wasn't a real mother to them. How could I be, barely older than David and them still grieving for Olivia?" A droplet trickled down to her chin. "But I liked them. They liked me at first, too. It wasn't till after James and I married that they—Everything went wrong. And I didn't know what to do to fix it."

When her purse couldn't produce another tissue, she used the sodden one she held.

"There, there." He offered his own handkerchief.

"Thank you." She blotted the tears and blew her nose.

Crying, in Lawrence's experience, usually turned women ugly, leaving swollen and red faces. Not Sondra. Her eyes looked like dew-drenched pansies.

She addressed him, ignoring Nick and Megan. "You know they disliked me, Lawrence. I was their stepmother. And stepmothers are always wicked, aren't they?" A laugh ended in a sob. "I did try. God knows I tried."

And now she had to deal with Theo. Pitiful. "Of course you did."

After a watery sigh, she pulled out a compact. When she'd inspected her face, she dabbed powder on her nose and cheeks to repair damage that wasn't there. "David finally started to accept me, I think. But Robby never did."

"Ahem. That's often the case with second marriages, Sondra. Livvy's death hit the boys hard. I'm sure things would have worked out between you and them had they lived. They were both reasonable children. James was quite aware of their feelings but never once blamed you. He blamed himself for eloping without considering the boys' state of mind."

The compact snapped shut. The lovely face contorted. "James was wonderful. I know you never thought I deserved him, Lawrence."

How the devil did she—?

"Come now, my dear. You were James's choice. He loved you. And he wasn't an angel, far from it. He would never have expected you to be one."

"It's okay. I know how you felt." She waved his efforts away. "A woman can sense these things. And you were right. I didn't deserve him. But I was determined to be a good wife."

She wasn't the class of woman Lawrence was accustomed to, but she was undeniably arresting. The only sign of her age was a certain texture in the skin that did nothing to detract from her beauty. And she showed more backbone than he'd expected.

"I tried with James. With the boys, too. I really did." She blew her nose again, then carefully folded his handkerchief. "You understand why I have to find out the truth, don't you, Lawrence? I feel guilty. I should've tried harder. James and I could have waited to get married. After all, their mother had been dead less than a year. I should have realized how they'd react."

"My dear, the world's full of people regretting lost opportunities. The fact is, most of the time it wouldn't make one whit of difference." He himself had played the *if only* game far too often. "You mustn't be so hard on yourself."

Megan, in Bermuda shorts and a shirt with one of those round collars that made her look like a schoolgirl, leaned over Nick to touch Sondra's arm. "He's right. Don't punish yourself for something you couldn't help. But what made you suspect Theo was a murderer?"

Sondra blinked several times but didn't cry. "He had the combination on the safe at the Palm Beach house changed. I wondered at the time. He said James's secretary knew the old one and he didn't trust him. But he'd let the man go so what difference did it make?" Her lovely forehead puckered. "I never used to think I was stupid. Now I think I must be."

"Nonsense," he interjected. "Naïve perhaps, but not stupid."

"The safe," Nick prodded. "Why did his changing the combination make you suspect he'd killed the boys?"

"Oh, changing the combination didn't." Her face cleared. She sat back in her chair. "But one day last year, when we were in Palm Beach, just as Theo opened it, he got called away."

She wound her purse straps so spastically that it fell to the floor. She barely noticed when Nick retrieved it for her. "The Club's Annual Ball was coming up, and I'd bought a Givenchy. Gold lamé with silk bodice and sleeves, and a bateau neckline in front that went down to a deep vee in the back. Fantabulous. It needed emeralds with the gold and when I saw the safe was open, I naturally—"

A rattle came as the front door of the house opened.

Everyone froze.

"Dad? Are you here? Hello, who're you? What're you doing here?"

"Waiting for Mr. Wykerton," came Danny's reply. "He's got somebody in with him."

"Confound it!" He shot up. Unbelievable. "What the devil is George doing here? Today's worse than a weekday, with everyone traipsing in. Stay still and I'll get rid of him."

In the reception area, he found Danny and George in a standoff.

"Dad." George turned in relief. "I ran Mrs. DeLacey home after lunch—she'd come to see Mona's mother—and noticed the Harmony Island car out front. Is Sondra here?"

"George." He couldn't deny it, but he could speak up clearly. "Sondra did drop by. Yes."

"Did something happen on the island? Is she all right? Is there something I can help with?" George came forward, craning to see past him into his office.

Danny edged in front of George, giving Lawrence a quizzical look. *I ought to let him throw George out.*

Instead, Lawrence shook his head at Nick's bodyguard and blocked George himself. "Everything's fine."

Sondra appeared. No trace of her earlier tears. No nervousness or guilt. "George, how sweet of you to worry. I'm fine, except for some jangled nerves from all the commotion getting ready for the party tonight. Everyone's wild. I simply had to get away. I'm going to lunch at that darling little place outside town, but when I went by here, I saw your father's car. We've not had a chance to talk about the allowance Theo and I can expect, so I stopped in to chat."

Hard to believe she was the same distraught woman.

George believed every word. "I didn't mean to butt in if you're talking business."

She touched his sleeve flirtatiously. "You could never butt in, George. Besides," she glanced at Lawrence, "we're done, aren't we?"

He managed a grunt.

George brightened. "Then why don't I go with you? I've had lunch but I can keep you company."

Sondra's musical laugh tinkled. "You are so sweet. I'd love you to keep me company. Why don't I ride out to the restaurant with you and afterward, you can drop me back at my car?"

No one else could have used such dexterity on George.

His son, escorting Sondra out, beamed like he'd won first prize.

Love-smitten saphead.

Once back in his office where Megan and Nick had eavesdropped on the exchange, Lawrence wiped his brow.

"That woman can act." Nick didn't hide his admiration. "There's a lot more to her than you'd suspect, isn't there? I bet most people don't see past the sexpot exterior."

"Sondra is certainly intelligent," Lawrence said acidly. "Never doubt that for a second."

"Anyone capable of coming up with this crazy plan to trap Theo must be intelligent," Megan said. "Or maybe not quite right in the head."

Nick grinned. "No, no. A crazy woman could never have talked the cautious Whitey into cooperating with her." He got up and stretched. "What did Sondra find in the safe that convinced her Theo murdered the boys?"

"That's not for me to divulge, nor do I have the time now to discuss it. It's sufficient to say that I believe her. You may ask her yourself at a later time if you like."

He did not sit down, a deliberate hint they should go.

"Oh, I'll certainly ask her." Nick held out a hand to Megan. "Will you be at the party tonight, Whitey?"

"Yes." Lawrence normally turned down the Packs' invitations but his presence at this one, like the barbecue the day before, was mandatory. Time was growing short. Anything could happen. "I've also hired another man to watch Megan. He's driving down now."

"Good. That'll take care of one worry," Nick said.

Megan frowned at him. "I think you need to be worrying about yourself."

Nick put a hand on Megan's back to guide her toward the door. "Humor us."

Lawrence didn't miss the gesture.

Oh my.

As much as he disapproved of the interplay between his son and Sondra, he abhorred the rising intimacy between these two more. The man was up to no good, and Megan was too gullible.

It was almost enough to make him wish Sondra would work her wiles on Nick.

Almost.

At the door, Nick said, "I'll turn up the heat on Theo tonight, Whitey. He won't like me making love to his wife. He'll do something soon."

Lawrence nodded, apprehension returning. "He only has two more days to do it."

CHAPTER 29

"No Other Love"
As Performed by Jo Stafford (1950)
Music by Paul Weston
(Derived from Chopin's Etude Opus 10,
No. 3, in E Major, "Tristesse")
Lyrics by Bob Russell

MEGAN WAITED WITH Nick and Hal outside her cottage.

"All clear." Danny, who had gone into the Mulrennons' cottage first, held the kitchen door for them. The window panel above the lock was broken, as Nick had said.

He didn't have to be right about everything.

She hung back. "I wasn't invited to the party. I don't know why I have to go."

"You have to go because we have to stay together so Danny and Hal can protect me, remember?" Nick said. "Unless you want to leave me short on protection."

Steaming, she stomped in. Know-it-all.

Nick trotted on her heels. "It's just till this other man gets here, Meggie."

"You're the one in danger. Not me."

"Considering the smashed boat and your bump on the head, that doesn't seem entirely true, does it?"

She flounced to her bedroom and pawed through her closet. "I doubt I have anything suitable to wear. I don't usually mingle with the swells."

He looked over her shoulder. "Surely you have something for lawyerly cocktail parties and dinners. What about that yellow thing?"

"I wore that to my last sorority dance."

"Outdated, eh? I see. Okay. What else do you have? What about that green thing there?"

"Get out. I don't need you kibitzing."

"You cut me to the quick." He laid a hand over his heart. "I have impeccable taste. Women value my opinion on clothes. Men often ask my advice on what to buy their girl friends. I've never been known to steer anyone wrong. They all thank me effusively."

"Get out."

She grabbed a royal blue crepe dress, cap-sleeved with round neck and fitted waist. The skirt looked straight in the front but flared in the back from waist gathers reminiscent of an old-fashioned bustle.

She'd bought it for an Atlanta reception she'd attended with Ronald during their engagement.

It would do.

Nick hadn't left as she'd ordered. He'd turned on her music box and was brushing his fingertips over the carved roses on the top. "This is very pretty."

She barely refrained from running over and pushing him away. "It was Olivia Harmony's."

"Ah. The one Auntie Mae asked about."

"Yes. David would have known I had it."

He lifted the lid and stopped the chimes.

"Be careful."

He didn't heed the edge in her voice. "I knew it couldn't be my acting that gave me away. Did I tell you I was an award-winning actor?"

"Several times. Your acting may be flawless, which I seriously doubt, but your lack of modesty's certainly not in question."

"Actors can't afford modesty. I've seen a box like this before. Is it Swiss?" He picked it up to look at the bottom.

She lunged for it.

"What's wrong?" He held it out of her reach.

"Put it down before you break it! It's fragile."

"You only had to ask." He put it down carefully. "How'd you get it?"

Her eyes stung. She hugged the crepe dress. "David asked Mr. H for it after his mother died. It meant a lot to him. Please don't handle it."

She wouldn't cry. Not in front of Nick Downing.

"So David gave it to you."

She nodded, not trusting herself to speak.

"He must have cared for you very much."

"Yes, I think he must have." She couldn't keep the wobble from her voice.

He took a step toward her. "Megan."

She quickly turned and hung the dress on her closet door. "I need my pearl earrings." From a chest drawer, she pulled out her jewel case and opened it. "Drat. I forgot. They're lost in the sound along with my necklace. It'll have to be the garnets, then."

He waited till she took them out. "Do you have everything else you need?"

Everything I need?

Laughter, hysterical and wild, bubbled up.

She'd never have everything she needed.

No time to give way. Just like a woman, he'd think. "Yes."

He eyed the dress. "That's what you're wearing? Looks like an old lady's dress. Don't you have anything more festive? Even a lawyer's allowed to dress up for parties."

"You're a butt." She rushed out of the room and reached the bathroom down the hall before letting loose. After she locked herself in and had a good cry, she splashed water on her face and assessed herself in the mirror.

What a mess. The music box stirred too many memories. Or was it Nick? Did her awareness of him make her feel guilty? Why should it?

Because he overshadowed David?

Come on. You can't seriously be interested in the likes of Nick Downing. A womanizer and worse. It's because he looks like David.

Calming down, she stuck out her chin and went back.

He was thumbing through her old photo album. "I didn't mean to upset you."

"You didn't." Wearing the earrings would keep her from losing them. She inserted one.

"You were in love with David."

She put on the other garnet. "What does it matter? David's dead."

"If you loved him—"

"Leave it alone!"

He took a deep breath. "All right. Is that dress what you're wearing tonight?" He turned up his lip. "Blue isn't your color. You'd be better off in yellow or lavender."

She fumbled with the pendant clasp. "I don't need or want your opinion. I'll be ready to go as soon as I get the rest of my things. Why don't you wait out front with Hal and Danny?"

He made a move as if to help her with the chain.

She shrank away.

"Wait out front, Nick!" She couldn't bear for him to touch her. "Please."

He huffed but left.

She gathered up shoes, gloves, makeup—the Merle Norman stuff she'd bought when she and her old roomie got facials before seeing *Hud*; she'd not used it since, and this was a party, wasn't it?—slip, bra, panties, stockings, and a waist pincher. She couldn't stand a girdle tonight. Some clean clothes for tomorrow, and she was done.

When they rode the golf cart back to the Magnolia Cottage, she and Nick sat in the back.

She stared out her side and he stared out his. Neither spoke.

****

"Somebody Loses, Somebody Wins"
As Performed by the Three Keys (1932)
Music by George Whiting, J. C. Johnson,
and Nat Schwartz
Lyrics by George Whiting, J. C. Johnson,
and Nat Schwartz

LAWRENCE DID NOT care for boats.

Shifting and swaying, they were invariably unstable. Even large, solid boats like the water taxi transporting him, George, Mona, and other local dignitaries to Harmony Island for the dress party marking the beginning of the Packs' annual sailing regatta.

The water emitted a brackish scent. The early autumn evening was lukewarm with a hint of southern sultriness, still light from the barely set sun. The river behaved, too, without the brisk winds and whitecaps that sometimes characterized trips through the marshes.

Still, he'd rather have been at home in his easy chair, listening to Verdi. Or Gilbert and Sullivan. Or some of the blues recordings his late wife had abhorred.

Between him and George, Mona tried to keep her new dress from wrinkling by sitting carefully.

He thought the green and gold brocade quite ugly, but she smoothed the skirt proudly. "I'm glad that hurricane petered out. It'd be a shame to spoil the races by having to evacuate."

The mayor and George started discussing the new storm Flora, not a serious threat but the possibility always lurking. Everyone living on the coast took the weather seriously.

Lawrence, in a black suit—he didn't own a dinner jacket (certainly not a revolting white one like the coat George sported) and wasn't about to rent one—didn't join in.

Hurricanes were the least of his worries.

How did Nick stand it, not knowing when or where Theo would strike? What if Sondra was wrong? What if his dislike of Theo was prejudicing his judgment?

The moldy smell of the marshes gave way to salt air.

No. Sondra wasn't wrong and neither was he. He'd stake his life on Theo having something to do with the boy's deaths.

Which was pretty much what he was doing.

At least his life as he knew it. Images of handcuffs, judges, and jails rose up but he'd deal with those fears later.

At the island dock, golf carts waited to trundle guests to the house on a path where Japanese lanterns dotted the trees and colored lights outlined bushes.

Alighting at the rear of the mansion, Lawrence and the others entered a celebration already underway. The patio and walks held small tables while the band, moody trumpet blaring, played on a temporary platform beyond the piazza. Swaying couples danced on the piazza itself.

Mona loved it. "Dreamy! Like a wonderland, isn't it? Sondra ordered those crystal candleholders for the tables last year when we went shopping in Savannah." She lowered her voice. "They cost nearly fifty dollars apiece. She's a marvel, so busy but still finding time to put this together."

Much his daughter-in-law knew. Spending might be Sondra's forte, but JoBeth and Linda were the workhorses responsible for arranging the Packs' parties.

From the crowd, the pasture airstrip had stayed busy all day with arrivals from distant places. The mansion and cottages sprinkled around the island could sleep about thirty people while the seafarers would stay on their yachts.

There must have been over a hundred people here already.

Like Lawrence's group, the men had donned dinner jackets and the women dressy frocks.

Sondra, Peachie nowhere in evidence, wore a hot pink dress with rows of fringe that hung past her knees and swung seductively on her hourglass figure.

No signs of distress as she kissed one man on the cheek and hugged another. She was the perfect hostess enjoying her own party, dancing and laughing as if she hadn't a care in the world.

"Don't you love her dress? Made especially to dance the Twist." Mona followed his gaze. "She never wears anything but designer clothes. I wonder if that's a Dior."

Lawrence harrumphed.

George, after one wistful look toward Sondra, had gone ahead to stake out a table. Lawrence and Mona followed.

"We need to circulate," Mona said.

George stopped in the middle of pulling out her chair. "I don't know anybody here."

"That's the purpose of circulating," she snapped. "And we need to at least say hello to Sondra and Theo before we get settled."

"They're dancing."

"The music will stop in a moment and we can catch them. Stop being unsociable, George. Papaw, are you coming?"

Lawrence shook his head. "I'll pay my respects to Theo and

Sondra later. As for the others, an old man shouldn't have to observe social niceties." Anyone he knew would gravitate to him sooner or later. "I'll hold your places."

Waving a glum George and an enthusiastic Mona off, he sat down in time to see Megan arrive with Nick, magnificent in a dinner jacket sporting brocade lapels and matching vest.

Humph. To be expected.

Megan wore a demure dress and evening gloves past her elbow and didn't look happy. Three watchful bodyguards followed.

Bo, the new man, as calm and steady as Hal and Danny, had arrived in time for the party. At least something had gone right today.

Nick took Megan's arm on the piazza steps and said something that brought a smile.

That actor. Something would have to be done before he turned the child's head. The last thing she needed was another failed romance.

Nick didn't stay with Megan. Her eyes followed his shoulders as he sauntered toward the long table where a cluster of men vied for Sondra's attention.

Why do all males, including my George, flock to her like that?

Bedroom eyes and attentive air couldn't explain the attraction. Maybe she exuded the same kind of scent female animals secreted to signal availability.

He sighed, beckoned to Megan.

She reluctantly turned her back to Nick and Sondra, and Bo detached himself from the other men to follow.

Damn and blast.

She knew that Theo was possessive of his wife and Nick was taking full advantage of it. Why must she look so forlorn?

Because she was falling in love with him. And that would never do. Nick would break her heart and JoBeth would never forgive him for bringing the man into their lives.

Pray God this would soon be over. If only Theo would do something. Bringing out his handkerchief, he patted his forehead and scanned the crowd.

Theo's big form stood out in a pale gray jacket with a red rose in the lapel. With the ever-present cocktail, he strolled through people like a monarch and ignored Nick's latching onto his wife. He conversed, socialized, and pretended to be a man without a care.

This had to be eating him up. He was never one to share possessions.

George and Mona finished their rounds and came back through the mob bearing cocktails for themselves and a highball for him.

By that time, Megan and her escort had waded through the crowd to his table where the expensive candleholder bought in Savannah mirrored a flickering candle surrounded by water with floating red orchids and carnations.

He rose politely.

"Hello, Lawrence. George, Mona." Megan pulled her bodyguard forward. "This is Bo. A friend from Atlanta."

"Bo?" Mona raised her eyebrows. "How do you do?"

George didn't hide his speculation. "From Atlanta, eh? Been holding out on us, doll?"

"Sit down, sit down." Lawrence resumed his seat.

The band broke into a soothing tune. Thank heavens. That loud Elvis the Pelvis music jangled already strained nerves.

Nick swept Sondra away from her followers for a tango.

Well, the music was a tango. How they danced was positively obscene. "Humph." Scandalous. With their thighs and privates latched together, they might as well be copulating.

Part of the act. Nick was doing a good job of pretending he was on the make for her.

At least he hoped Nick was pretending.

The dimly lit table seated four comfortably, but George, scowling toward the dance floor and the torrid tangoers, stole another chair for Bo. The sociable Mona asked if Bo knew her cousin who lived near Atlanta's Peachtree Road.

He didn't, but further digging revealed he was acquainted with one of her friends whose parents had died in the plane crash at Orly claiming many of Atlanta's art patrons the past year.

Over the snowy linen, that revelation carried conversation for a while. Then discussion about the tragedy languished, and Mona swayed her shoulders to the music. "The Packs always throw the best parties."

Megan's smile was forced. "No expense spared."

Mona eagerly took in everything. "And the band's so good. Are they a local group?"

"From Macon," Megan said. "Mom heard about them when Berriman Montrove had them at a bank reception last year."

"They're perfect for a shindig like this. Sondra always manages to find the best people, doesn't she? I wish I were that efficient."

Mannerly child that she was, Megan abstained from pointing out that JoBeth had made arrangements for the night's entertainments long before she left on her trip.

Lawrence couldn't keep from goading his daughter-in-law. "I think her secretary arranges these things, Mona. And of course JoBeth never gets credit for pulling them together."

He was rewarded by a subdued glimmer from Megan.

"JoBeth's a wonder," Mona quickly agreed. "Sondra's said gobs of times she couldn't make it without JoBeth. I swear, these singers sound better than the Platters, don't they? Honey, don't you want to dance?"

To the side of the patio, Danny and Hal kept tabs on Nick with Sondra. Two big men ready to act.

Theo won't do anything here. He'll wait till no one's around.

Lawrence wished he knew what Theo planned.

And when.

Like him, Megan couldn't keep from glancing at Nick and Sondra, cozied up like lovebirds.

Later, when he wandered to the bar, he overheard, through the buzz about the recent church bombing in Birmingham and anger at President Kennedy, Theo's voice. "We know he's not David. Sondra lived in the house with the boys before they died so she's going through her diary. She's sure to find something to prove he's an imposter."

"What could she turn up in her diary?"

"You never know. I think the more interesting question is who's behind the charade?"

"You mean you think they might—?" The other man nodded toward George's table before noticing Lawrence.

Lawrence gritted his teeth and collected his highball and went back to find Megan watching Nick flirt with Sondra.

Again.

"Here. I brought you a lady's drink. A brandy alexander. I think you'll like it."

She jumped. "Thanks, Lawrence. I'm sure I'll love it."

Mona claimed her attention, talking to her about the fire at the last Kiwanis potluck supper.

Good thing, too. Nick danced with Sondra, leaning his head over and pulling her close to murmur in her ear. Sondra herself scanned the crowd guiltily, searching for Theo.

No need. Her husband would track every move she made as long as Nick stayed beside her.

Megan glanced at Nick and Sondra as she replied to something Mona asked.

The devil. Why should he feel sorry for her?

She ought not ride herd on the man. And she certainly shouldn't wear her feelings on her sleeve.

He'd thought better of her.

When George and Mona got up to greet acquaintances across the piazza, he leaned over the table. "Nick's doing his job."

Megan traced one side of the crystal candleholder. "That doesn't keep me from worrying."

"Nor me. But try not to show it."

Her blank look gave way to realization. "I'm not doing my part, am I?" She put on a cheerful face and began to talk about the latest storm in the Bahamas.

He patted her hand. "That's the way. Ah, music I can dance to. Shall we try?"

All evening, Nick hung onto Sondra. They carried on openly while Theo pretended not to care. Only someone knowledgeable would note his tight jaw and careful avoidance of his wife and her admirer.

After Lawrence, Megan partnered George, Bo, and several of the local people who'd ridden over on the water taxi with them.

Lawrence danced with the wives of his friends.

Waltzes and foxtrots. No bebop for him.

Around eight, as food began appearing on the buffet tables, a man took the microphone during the band's break and droned about rules of the next morning's yacht races.

A loud boom shook the ground and tables.

Lawrence started. "Good God!"

People screamed and rushed for cover.

Bo sprang out of his seat to shield Megan.

She beat him off and rose, wildly seeking Nick. He had his arm around Sondra's waist, unharmed but vigilant, with Hal and Danny crowding each side of them.

No more explosions followed. Lawrence pulled at Megan. "Nick's all right. Sit down."

About that time, she saw Nick and sank like a marionette.

"'S okay, folks!" One of the guests in a captain's hat jumped up on the bandstand and nearly pitched off headfirst.

A young waiter caught him.

The inebriated man staggered upright and pushed the waiter aside. "Just checking out the starting gun. No need f'alarm. Everything's unner control!"

Everyone exploded in laughter or let out groans. People sat down. Some came out from under tables.

"That stupid cannon." Megan seethed. "Some idiot does this every year. At least this time he didn't shoot it off in the middle of the night."

"Bobby!" a man called. "Go soak your head and sober up!"

It took three waiters to lift Bobby down from the bandstand. The annoyed rules arbiter resumed his speech, but the crowd giggled and chattered so much he could hardly be heard.

When he finished and the buffet line opened, Nick met Lawrence and Megan.

"Sondra says Theo's brooding." He put pâté on a plate. "This is for her. She said just something to tide her over. D'you think she'll want some caviar?" He shoveled some of the said caviar on a cracker and popped it into his mouth.

"Try the lobster bites and crab cakes," Megan said.

"Theo?" Lawrence prompted.

Nick filled the plate with hors d'oeuvres. "Theo's furious about her flirting with me. She told me not to go near him without my bodyguards."

"That'll defeat the purpose, won't it?" Lawrence murmured.

Nick smiled tightly, picked up some napkins, and turned.

Megan clutched his arm. "What are you going to do?"

"Stay out of his way."

Lawrence bit his tongue.

She surveyed one and then the other.

Nick winked at her. "It'll be all right." He left, weaving through the crowd toward Sondra.

Lawrence led her into the queue around the tables.

"Lawrence—"

"Nick knows what he's doing. He'll be fine. Hal and Danny will see to it." He tried hard to believe his words.

The buffet made a splendid display with its ice sculptures and silver serving dishes.

People talked about how wonderful the shrimp were; someone explained it was because they were white Georgia shrimp.

A man raved about the she-crab soup; a woman said it was because they were those little blue crabs fresh caught from the sound.

Around Lawrence everyone stuffed themselves on the delicacies offered, but he filled his plate and forced himself to eat.

CHAPTER 30

"Quizas, Quizas, Quizas "
As Performed by Perez Prado (1957)
Music by Osvaldo Farres
Spanish Lyrics by Osvaldo Farres

LAUGHTER AND CIGARETTE smoke filled the night before dissipating overhead. The band came back from a break. Theo tried not to watch Sondra flirt with the shitty actor.

It didn't mean anything. She was just doing her part. But still, he'd enjoy ruining that sneering face. That'd teach Downing to make passes at Sondra, put his paws all over her.

Not much longer to wait. He finished a martini and started to get another, but an inner voice stopped him.

No more. You can't afford to mess up.

Christ, he dreaded tonight.

Nearly lost in the crowd, the Wykertons sat near the band with Megan and some man.

He recognized the type. Big. Confident. Wary. Another bodyguard. Lawrence was right to be scared for his lying stooge, but he could hire ten men and it wouldn't matter.

Megan didn't look happy. Perhaps she didn't know what Lawrence was doing. Perhaps she was having second thoughts.

Worth another try? If he could convince her, he wouldn't have to go through with it.

He made his way to their table. Mona was effusive, George jovial, Lawrence polite. He didn't give them a chance to introduce the stranger. "Dance, Megan?"

She hesitated but nodded. "Okay."

He led her out, away from Lawrence's ears.

The cha cha was swingy, not loud. Easy to talk over. He took her right hand with his left. Did a few steps, a forward and back, then moved so they were side by side. "Everyone knows Lawrence brought this actor in to keep control of the money."

Cha cha cha. Her shoulder dipped with his. "He didn't, Theo."

Defending the silly old windbag. One two. They straightened, came back together. Cha cha cha. "I saw you with Nick. You've been spending time with him."

Another side by side dip. "Yes. I, I . . . Yes."

Cautious, maybe uncertain?

One two, back together. Cha cha cha. "Are you sure he's David?"

Forward, back. Cha cha cha. "Yes." She didn't look up.

Back, forward. Cha cha cha. "Have you really put the screws to him?"

She stumbled. "What?"

He caught her, moved back into the cha cha motion. "You know. Asked him hard stuff. Private things that no one but family would know."

"Yes." Back step, forward. "Just like you did." She turned her back to him.

Cha cha cha. Was she laughing at him for bringing in May Addison and the old girl friend? Stupid little nobody. She had no right to criticize him!

He bit his tongue, followed in time to the music, turned. "Did he mess up on anything?"

"No, Theo. He didn't," she said to his back. A stronger denial.

Cha cha cha. Forward turn to Megan's back again. "He's acting."

One two. He didn't turn but she did. They faced each other, and he took her right hand.

She shook her head. "Oh, Theo." In that patient tone like he was crazy. "He's David."

Perhaps she was in on this hoax with Lawrence. That would explain a lot.

Might as well give up on her.

When he walked her back to the table, only Lawrence and the bodyguard were there. He didn't linger. Across the patio, he glanced back. Lawrence and Megan had their heads together.

Telling Lawrence what he'd said?

Not that it mattered.

On the terrace, Sondra whirled around with the asshole, laughing like she was enjoying every moment.

If he thought she really liked the son of a bitch, he'd . . .

No, she didn't mean anything by her flirting. She was just trying to pacify Downing.

What if she wasn't? What if she was falling for him?

Don't lose your focus now, warned the cold voice in his head. *Sondra belongs to you. You're bonded forever. Kindred souls.*

He wouldn't worry about Sondra.

If only Megan had come through for him, agreed the asshole wasn't David.

Could he do it?

You can do whatever you have to do, the voice assured him. *And you will.*

****

"It's Only Make Believe"
As Performed by Conway Twitty (1958)
Music by Conway Twitty and Jack Nance
Lyrics by Conway Twitty and Jack Nance

HOW CAN LAWRENCE eat like nothing's the matter?

Megan had filled her plate, but she couldn't take a bite. When Theo danced with her, she'd been careful. Even when he'd asked outright: "Are you sure he's David?"

She'd lied, wrong as it felt. Maybe she'd convinced him.

Theo hadn't seemed annoyed. Not even disappointed. Just resigned. Like her endorsement of Nick was expected. Would a murderer take her answers so calmly?

Sondra should have simply asked Theo about whatever she saw in the safe that made her suspect he'd killed the boys. He might have a perfectly innocent explanation.

George and Mona, either sensing her and Lawrence's tension or else having a marital spat, picked at their food, too. Neither had much to say to each other.

An argument seemed more likely, since George sulked and Mona's mouth was grim.

Not that she cared about their problems. She had her own. How did Nick stand it? How could he be so nonchalant while waiting for something to happen?

Around them, people ate and drank and danced. The laughter got louder and more raucous and the speech more slurred. Sambas, mambos, and bossa novas mixed in with jitterbugs, foxtrots, and twists. Twinkling lights stirred by a light breeze made the night surreal.

Nick and Sondra waltzed by, near enough that Megan could hear Theo when he appeared and cut in. "My dance. This is our song."

Nick relinquished Sondra graciously. "Be my guest." As they twirled away to the strains of "Forever and Ever," he pulled up a chair between Megan and Lawrence. He didn't say much but watched Theo and Sondra.

Megan did, too. They danced like a couple in love. Sondra pressed against Theo, her face nestled in the hollow between his neck and shoulder. He buried his face in her hair.

How could Sondra dance like that with him and believe he's a killer?

She couldn't ask in front of Mona and George.

When the music stopped, Sondra caressed Theo's cheek before

they parted. Amos headed toward her, but Nick had quietly left the table. Under Amos's nose, he made off with her.

During the night, Megan caught Theo watching Nick and Sondra. Most of the time he remained impassive. Maybe a little sad but not unlike his usual self. Not like a killer.

Could Lawrence and Sondra be wrong?

No. It was nerves getting to her. Not for herself but for Nick. She trusted Lawrence.

Smile. Pretend you're a guest at a party with an attractive man beside you and your best dress on. Pretend Nick means nothing to you. Pretend Theo didn't murder David.

She gulped, pushed her plate away, and tried to listen to the music.

After a midnight fireworks display, the band switched to slow numbers for the winding-down period, when dancers clung together and drinkers waxed sentimental. Couples strolled down to the beach as others headed toward the docks and yachts. A few comatose bodies were carried off. By one a.m., the crowd had thinned.

"I think it's time to go," Lawrence said to George.

"Awww." Mona pouted. The last frozen daiquiri had mellowed her into forgiving whatever George had done. "There're still people dancing."

George pulled her up. "Come on, woman, the party's over. We've got a twenty-minute ride in the water taxi with another fifteen-minute drive to the house. And you've had one too many. Let's go say our goodbyes."

Lawrence rose arthritically. "Megan, Bo. Take care."

"We'll be fine." Nick was the one he should be worrying about.

The Wykertons shook Theo's hand and found Sondra—Nick still dangling after her—before heading down the lantern lit path toward the waiting cruiser ferries.

Megan and Bo's table was one of the few still occupied. She was as exhausted as the night before, but she refused to go without Nick.

He and Sondra sat on the piazza wall, conversing in intimate tones interspersed with laughter as the orchestra softly played. He held her hand, sometimes slipped an arm around her waist. Once he bent so close to her neck he might have been kissing it.

In a group of men by the pool, Theo watched.

What was he thinking? He didn't seem aggravated. He was just . . .Theo. How could he be a murderer?

Sondra had to be wrong. Or confused.

Sondra confused? Not likely.

Finally, about two o'clock, Theo crossed over to the couple and said something.

Nick shook his head. Even from Megan's table, she could see him smirk as he took out one of his small cigars. Sondra got up to embrace Theo. Gray dinner jacket sleeve wound round her bright pink dress. She patted his cheek, said something to him, smoothed his hair.

Theo left abruptly.

Nick lit up and watched him walk toward the garages with Amos Lovett and several others. Sondra sat back down. Nick nudged her with his shoulder, then picked up her hand and kissed it. She leaned against him.

Shortly after, "Good Night, Sweetheart" signaled the last dance. Two couples, one staggering, swayed on the piazza. A few small clusters talked in hushed voices.

The band disassembled instruments and packed up. The waiters retrieved soiled dishes and tablecloths.

Nick at last abandoned Sondra and came over, Hal and Danny close behind.

"Has it been hideous for you?" he asked Megan. "Are you ready to leave? Theo's headed off with his pals. My cozying up to Sondra has lost its audience so there's no need for us to stay."

"Where did Theo and the others go?"

"They took golf carts and searchlights to flush out deer at the north end. He considerately asked if I wanted to come. I told him I wasn't so foolish. Not with him anywhere near a rifle."

Bo voiced her concern. "They were hunting? At two in the morning?"

Nick shrugged. "Why not?"

Theo with a rifle. Megan swallowed. How could Nick brush it off?

As they walked through the night toward the Magnolia Cottage, the bodyguards crowded close. To make it harder for someone to shoot Nick?

They were risking their lives, too.

At least someone besides her was worried.

Hal glanced up at the three-quarter moon. "Plenty of light to see by. Danny's taking first shift outside in the screen house. It has a good view of the approaches."

She asked, "You think Theo will try something tonight?"

"Not necessarily. He's got tomorrow and Tuesday to make his move."

Nick said, "Danny'll make sure he doesn't sneak in here to turn on the gas."

Like what had happened to her.

Once inside Magnolia Cottage, Megan brushed her teeth and washed her face. When she went to bed, she could hear Hal and Bo talking in the living room but couldn't make out any words over the tree frogs croaking outside.

She tried to stay awake, but the residue of illness and sleep deprivation of the past two days proved too exhausting. The familiar island sounds lulled her to sleep.

****

"All the Way"
As Performed by Frank Sinatra (1957)
Music by Jimmy Van Heusen
Lyrics by Sammy Cahn

NICK, IN RED silk pajamas that slid seductively over his skin, couldn't sleep. Lucky he'd brought the new script along that his agent had enthused over. "It's great! You'll love it! Perfect for you! And it films in Italy!"

Propped against piled-up pillow, he tried to read, but his racing mind wandered despite the snappy lines.

Dialogue in a saloon brought up images of what Theo might do and how he'd respond. In the middle of the heroine's rant, thoughts of Megan intruded.

Megan and her David.

Stupid to let that half-sighed "David" during sex bother him. But she should have been thinking of *him*, letting him consume her head as she had his.

Not fixated on an untried boy glorified by foggy memories.

Infuriating.

Why did it get to him?

Because she was still in love with that boy. What if she couldn't let go? He didn't know what her fixation meant for their future.

Yes, he did. Unless he could make her accept him for himself, there wouldn't be one.

Assuming he came out of this intact.

The phone in the alcove by the hall had a soft ring, but he heard it. The clock on the bedside table read three thirteen.

Time froze. Every nerve vibrated.

This is it.

He hopped out of bed.

So did Hal, hastening from his room fully dressed. Bo, who'd been playing solitaire in front of a television with the sound turned down, joined Hal hovering over the telephone.

Both men looked to Nick.

"I imagine it's time to earn my money." He picked up the receiver. "Hello."

"David!" Sondra, snuffling, was nearly unintelligible. "Thank God you answered. I have to see you. I've found out something terrible. Are those men listening?"

Those men.

And her voice. She sounded drunk.

"No."

"Can you—" she wheezed. "Can you come over?" Not drunk. Like she couldn't speak.

"Right now?"

"Yes. It's terrible. You won't believe . . . Don't bring those men. Come alone. And don't tell them anything. Please." She sniffled, coughed. "Please."

He could barely understand her.

Theo's with her. He has to be.

"You want me to leave Hal and Danny here?"

She made a choking sound. "Yes. Don't tell them where you're going. Come in through the conservatory. The door's unlocked. My rooms are on the left of the main hall."

"Do you think it wise for me to slip out without them?"

"David, please. Please! Theo's hunting. Don't worry about him. Just come." She choked. "It's important. It changes everything." She began to weep. "Oh, Christ, if you won't help me—"

"You know I will," he said soothingly. "I'll be right there."

"Come through the conservatory." The receiver clicked.

Hal was at his side. "Who was it?"

"Sondra. I'm to meet her in her rooms. Alone."

Hal's nostrils flared. "This is it then."

"She warned me several times tonight not to go anywhere without my bodyguards. Theo must be there with her."

"She was under duress?"

He thought about her panicky voice, the slurred words. "Undoubtedly."

"He'll be waiting then."

"And I mustn't disappoint him." He started toward the bedroom and his clothes.

"We'll go with you."

"No." He kept walking. "You and Danny hang back. He'll be watching to make sure I'm alone. If he sees you, he'll wait. Then we'll have to go through it all over again."

Hal exhaled. "What do you think he'll do?"

"Who knows?" He stripped off pajamas and found clothes.

Hal went to make his own preparations, came back with a holstered handgun and a loose pistol. "He might try hitting you when you're going up to the house. That path is exposed enough for a sniper to get a clear shot."

"I'll go by the docks. It's farther, but I can hide in the shrubbery, come up by the side."

He threw on jeans and a dark tee shirt. Rejected the tennis shoes in favor of leather Chelsea boots that could deliver a hefty kick to the nuts.

"I won't be out in the open long enough to give him a clear shot. The danger will be once I get inside. Their rooms are isolated from the rest of the house. She told me to go in through the conservatory. Very specifically. He'll be nearby."

"Danny can follow you."

"Yes." Nick put a switchblade in his jeans pocket. "But he needs to stay far enough behind to give me time to get inside and make Theo show his hand."

Hal had surveyed the house earlier. "If Pack's staking out the front hall, he'll have a narrow view of the conservatory. Danny can stay out of sight. I'll go through the staff wing to the reception area, come in behind the hallway leading to the Packs' suite. Here." Hal handed Nick the pistol. "I hope you weren't lying when you said you knew how to use it."

"Me, too."

An American-made Smith and Wesson Model 39, its magazine in.

A bullet showed in the chamber when he pulled back the slide. He left the safety off and stuck the pistol in the back of his jeans. "Gentlemen, we have a plan."

"You think it's enough?" Hal hesitated. "If he shoots you on sight—"

"Then Danny had bloody better be there to catch him in the act."

"I don't like this. It may not work."

Adrenaline flowed. "Won't be because of me. If he kills me, make bloody sure he pays. Shoot him yourself if you have to."

He didn't wait for an answer.

Tonight he'd be through with Theo.

One way or another.

CHAPTER 31

"Mack the Knife"
As Performed by Bobby Darin (1959)
Music by Kurt Weill
Lyrics by Bertolt Brecht

THE BACK DOOR of the cottage led into an enclosed yard. If Nick were Theo, he'd be at the Big House waiting.

Or out there in the dark, watching.

He shunned the yard's lone exit and scrambled over the top of the rock wall.

Bloody hell, it's good to finally do something.

The moon was almost full, bright enough to illuminate each post and shrub except that the canopy of live oaks and their mossy shrouds blotted out the light.

The gun at his back felt alien, heavy. He couldn't remember the last time he'd packed heat.

Best to take the circuitous route to the Big House, the one past the dock where he could blend in with the shrubbery. The one that gave him a view of several hundred yards and offered shelter all the way to the house.

Not that Theo couldn't be lying in wait to take a shot. He'd gone off with a rifle tonight. A hunting accident, he'd say. Terribly sorry.

Whitey would never let him get away with it.

Nick clung to that belief.

Like it'll matter by then.

Nearing the dock, he stopped. Water lapped at the pilings and the boats moored there. The shell path stood out, stark and white, inviting walkers up to the Big House.

Quicker, but no way in hell would he use it, make himself a target.

Nor would he take the strip by the dock and the beach. He hated the smell of mold and decaying organisms that comprised the marshes around the inlet and he hated the dock, too. Its dark interior offered a good place for a marksman to hide.

The trees away from the path and behind the shrubbery would be safer, but underbrush cluttered the ground. Hiking to the mansion took an eternity. Every shadow threatened an ambush, every rustle signaled a tracker.

He flinched with every crackling twig.

You're bloody terrified.

So what? Nothing wrong with that.

Fear had helped him survive before.

Theo didn't show, not even when he reached the unlocked door at the rear. He took hold of the pistol before slipping in, careful to keep his back to the wall.

The conservatory lay deserted, dark except for dim pool lights. A noise broke the silence.

He froze, lifted the pistol.

A fat shape snored at the bottom of a statue. A late partier passed out drunk.

Not Theo.

His stomach unclenched.

The reception area lay ahead. In the hush, each booted footstep tapped at marble tiles.

Should have worn the sneakers.

The main hall led to the Packs' suite. He turned that way. A grandfather clock in the reception room ticked.

No Theo in sight. Maybe he was wrong. Maybe Sondra wanted to take their flirtation up another step.

Yeah, sure.

Theo would be inside. What if he threatened Sondra, hid behind her while he stalked Nick?

Can I risk her life?

He touched the door.

"It's open."

Theo's soft voice came from behind.

He jumped.

Bloody hell, how did he sneak up on me?

"Theo." He started to swing his pistol around. The glint of a gun stopped him.

"Don't try it." A quick movement brought Theo so close Nick could touch the gun.

A revolver. A heavy caliber that would kill with one bullet.

Hal's not had time to get here, but Danny's following me.

Stall. Stall.

He raised his hands. "What's this about, Theo?"

"Stay still." Theo snatched his pistol.

I still have the knife.

A gaping closet door showed where Theo had lain in wait. Sidling over to it, Theo laid the pistol on a shelf, never taking his eyes off Nick. His hand was steady with its gun.

"All right, *David*. We've been expecting you. Do go in. Keep your hands up."

He sounds distant, aloof. Like Phoebe after a couple of joints. Can't reach the knife before he shoots. Danny should be right behind me. Got to get Theo to admit what he did.

Time for a stage voice. "Do you intend to shoot me with that gun?"

"Shut up. Not that it matters. No one's close enough to hear you through these plaster walls." Theo's revolver motioned. "Go on in."

Theo had better be wrong. Danny, Hal, you'd better be listening.

Without turning his back to Theo, he pushed at the door and edged inside a sitting room. Beyond a curio cabinet on the left, a feeble glow spilled from a doorway in the back where part of a rumpled bed could be seen.

No sign of Sondra. What had Theo done with her?

In the flickering half-light, Theo looked the hulking brute he was. The diminutive Sondra would stand no chance against him.

"Here we are, *cousin*. Alone at last. I'm so glad you could make it." Theo was calm, his eyes black holes. He had shed the dinner jacket and tie but still wore the white dress shirt. "Stupid of you to come, but Sondra has a way with men, doesn't she?"

The large revolver aimed at Nick.

Damn him to hell, I don't want to die like this. Not now.

"What did you do with her?" He cautiously lowered his hands. He needed his knife.

"Don't worry about her. Better worry about yourself. And if you don't keep your hands up, I'll kill you right now."

"If you do, everyone will know it's because of the money. You can't get away with it." He projected his voice.

Hal, Danny, where the hell are you?

"I told you to shut up." The gun swung, gesturing for Nick to move further into the room.

What was Theo waiting for? "If you shoot me, no one will believe it was an accident."

"You should never have agreed to play this part." Theo might have been a disinterested acquaintance, not a cold-blooded murderer. "Not a good way to end your career."

Can't see his eyes. Watch his hand. He pulls the trigger, I jump.

Time for a tiny step forward. "I was offered a great deal of money. Too much to refuse." He again eased a hand down toward the knife. "You knew I wasn't David, though, because you killed him, didn't you? Him and Robby both."

Theo winced. "It doesn't matter."

"It does to them. They're dead, thanks to you."

"I didn't want to do it." Theo swallowed. "I had no choice."

Almost to the knife. "Of course you had a choice. Lawrence knows you killed them. That's why he hired me. It's going to seem peculiar when I turn up dead, too, don't you think?"

The gun swayed.

He's about to do it. If I can jump him—

"Get back." The gun steadied. Theo's voice hardened. "And put that hand up."

There was no way in hell he could reach the gun before Theo fired, no way to get to his knife.

Keep him talking.

"How will you explain another David's death?"

"Easy. You attacked my wife when she confronted you with proof you aren't David."

"What proof?"

"Maybe a mole she remembered you had. Maybe something David told her long ago. It isn't important. You thought she had proof so you decided to kill her. I came in, found you attacking her, and you turned on me. You won't be alive to give your version."

"Bollocks. Do you think anyone will believe you?"

"Yeah. They'll believe me." Again the pleasant guise. "By the time I'm through with you, everyone will believe me. Just like before."

Theo stepped forward, forcing Nick against the wall and at the same time laying the revolver down on a console table.

My chance!

He jumped at Theo. Right into a fist.

Pain blasted his stomach, came out his spine.

He doubled over to a soft sound like a collapsing tire.

Not a tire. Him.

"You runty two-bit actor." Theo hit him again, this time in the face, sending him reeling. "You were stupid to think you could pull this off. I waited years to get that money."

Nick twisted, avoided a third blow.

Why didn't he shoot me?

A left-handed punch sent him to his knees. Somehow he blocked another and scrambled to get out of the way.

Hal. Danny. The switchblade.

Theo aimed for his chin.

He managed to turn. A fist went past.

He wants to beat me to death. And he just might.

A blind punch caught Theo's belly. The collision jarred up to his shoulder, but a grunt was Theo's only response.

I can't breathe.
Theo advanced again.
Nick inhaled noisily, retreated.
A bureau stopped him.
Theo swung and Nick ducked.
The bureau mirror shattered. The lamplight silvered a hundred splinters flying past. Glass stabbed his head and shoulders. Stinging cuts on his face.
Worry later.
A right cross to Theo's nose drew blood. He followed with a kick to the crotch.
Theo blocked his foot, swung a roundhouse.
He stepped to the side, caught the blow on his forearm, and jabbed at Theo's chin.
Not enough. Theo advanced again.
He stumbled into a straight chair, caught it, and flung it.
Theo batted it aside.
It hit the wall. Pictures cascaded, spun. More breaking glass.
He grabbed Theo's fist before it gathered momentum. They swayed together toward the console where the revolver lay.
If I can get it . . . No, don't give him a chance at it. Got to keep him away from the gun.
He hit at Theo's stomach.
Theo grabbed him by the neck and refused to let go.
He was tiring. His lungs burned.
Theo's too big. I'm no match. Where the hell are you, Hal? Danny?
The knife. No way he could dig it out. He had to breathe.
He pried one of Theo's fingers loose, heard it snap.
Theo howled, let go.
He gulped air.
The hands grabbed at him again.
He butted his forehead up into Theo's chin. Theo grunted but kept a tight hold on his shoulder.
From somewhere a woman screamed: "Theo, stop! Stop!"
Theo let go.
Nick backed into a stool, tripped, and recovered. Theo wiped his bloody nose with his elbow's crook.
Sondra, white nightgown cascading, stood in the dressing room doorway. She picked up the revolver Theo had laid on the console.
Could she use it?
"Theo," she called piteously.
The gun shook as she took aim with both hands. Her face was puffy and discolored. Her gown was ripped. Bloody.

Theo looked from her to Nick. His breathing rasped in his throat. His hands fisted

Nick, breathing as hard, edged away. Would she shoot?

She loved Theo. If she hesitated . . .

The gun boomed, spat flame.

A stream of acrid smoke drifted up.

The force of the bullet hurled Theo backward. He slammed into the wall, hung there for a long second, then slid to the floor. Sitting there, he looked down, touched his reddening chest.

Nick's head throbbed. His ears drummed.

Was that his heart? No, just reverberations from the shot.

Sondra.

The revolver slipped from her grasp. She put both hands to her bleeding mouth. He saw the gun tumble as if in slow motion but didn't hear the thump when it hit the floor.

He couldn't hear anything.

As she swayed, one tear and then another trickled down until rivulets wet both her cheeks and dripped off her jaws. She sank to her knees, hands still over her mouth. Her eyes, saucer-big, horrified, locked on her husband.

She was crying, saying something.

He couldn't hear what.

Movements at the door caught his eye. Danny, with Bo crowding behind him.

A white-faced Megan.

Ah, no, not Megan. She shouldn't see this.

No time to worry about her now.

He stumbled to where Theo sat propped against the wall with his hand over the wound. Red seeped through Theo's big fingers and over his white shirt.

People began to fill the room. Megan and Danny rushed over to where he knelt beside Theo. Others in various states of dress and undress peeked in.

Sounds trickled back. Voices, talking with distorted words. One sounded like Hal's.

Megan reached out, but he avoided her hand. "Later." Then to Hal, "Go to Sondra."

His words sounded like a mumble. Everything was hazy. The drifting smoke?

He wiped his eyes and that helped some. He lifted Theo's chin. The blood kept soaking the shirt. "Theo."

Theo stared at him. The normal blue of his eyes had faded. They were watery and dim.

He was still alive.

"Theo," he said urgently. When there was no response, again: "Theo! How could you do it to them? Why, Theo? You were like a brother."

Theo's eyes shifted as life sparked. "Sondra."

The barely audible word sounded like a plea.

Close behind them, Sondra screamed. "Theo!"

Weeping as if her heart would break, she shoved past Nick to cradle her husband's head. "Theo, I love you, I love you, I'll always love you! Oh, my darling, my darling buccaneer!"

Theo's eyes did not close but they dulled. His mouth grew slack.

Sondra continued to keen.

Megan, pale and scared, materialized to touch her arm. "Sondra, he's gone."

Sondra shook her head, frenzied. "No. No, he can't be. I won't let him be dead. He isn't dead! He isn't!"

Her hair-raising shriek penetrated to the core.

He tried to pull her away. "It's no use. Let him go, Sondra."

Hal took her other arm.

"No! Leave me alone!" She fought, grief contorting her face into someone he didn't recognize. Before they could force her away, she fainted, still clutching her husband's body.

"Oh, jeez," he heard Danny say behind him. "Bo, get those people out of here."

He got up clumsily. His knees hurt. His stomach threatened to spew. He ached all over. He could barely see. When he rubbed at his face, his hand came away smudged and sticky.

The bloody mirror.

Megan, in jeans and sweatshirt, came up beside him, a towel in her hand. She wasn't crying, but her eyes were big. She started dabbing at his face.

"It's over," he told her. "It's done."

"You're hurt." Her voice trembled.

He patted her cheek, stroked her unruly hair. "No. Not much. Just got hit with glass when Theo broke the mirror. Find something to cover Sondra. She's in shock."

Megan threw her arms around him and leaned against him for a second as if reassuring herself he was telling the truth.

He could hardly stand but he embraced her, patted her. "I'm fine, Meggie. I'm fine."

As quickly as she had hugged him, she let him go. Her hand touched his face and she gave him the towel. "Sit down and wipe off the blood. I'll get some blankets for Sondra."

What a woman. She ought to be hysterical.

No, not his Meggie.

Bo was pushing out the last of the gawkers. Hal crouched beside Sondra.

A boudoir chair had escaped damage. Nick sank into it and gingerly patted his face.

As Danny phoned the sheriff's office, Hal ministered to Sondra. "She needs a doctor."

Megan came back in time to hear. She handed Hal the blankets. "Use these for her. I'll call Miss Bessie when Danny gets off the telephone. Did you know there's a pistol in the linen closet?"

"The closet?" Hal swiveled to scowl at him. "You put your pistol down? When you knew he was waiting?"

"I thought it the safest place. Wouldn't want it to go off accidentally and hurt anyone."

Bo, back from shooing nosey parkers, looked at him strangely.

"Gaaah." Hal was used to his execrable humor. "Get it, Bo, and bring it to me."

When Danny had finished his call and the sheriff was on his way, Megan dialed Miss Bessie. "No answer. It's Sunday night. She may be with her daughter on the mainland."

Hal said, "Sondra needs medical attention right away."

Theo might be dead, but Sondra looked near death herself. Her nose and cuts on the forehead were encrusted where they'd bled. One side of her face and an ear had swollen to twice their normal size. A split bottom lip still oozed blood.

Bo came back in. "Oh, jeez. Those damn rubberneckers won't go away." He handed the pistol to Hal.

Houseguests drawn out by the shot crammed the hall, peering into the room and threatening to come inside.

Danny went over to confront them. "Sheriff's on his way. Yes, sir, someone's hurt. No, ma'am, nothing you can do except go back and wait. No, sir, I can't say till the sheriff gets here. Clear the area, folks."

He herded them back toward the reception room.

Nick said, "It'll take the sheriff half an hour to get here."

Hal set his jaw. "Sondra needs help. Now."

Gawd, he was tired. But Hal was right. "Let's take her across to the hospital. Danny can stay here to deal with the guests and," Nick glanced toward Theo's body, "and him."

Odd. He'd thought he would feel different.

Triumphant. Happy. Absolved.

Maybe that would come later.

Likely he was getting too old for fistfights.

CHAPTER 32

"The Party's Over"
As Performed by Tony Bennett (1959)
Music by Jule Styne
Lyrics by Betty Comden and Adolph Green

THEY BROUGHT A patio chaise to use as a makeshift stretcher to carry Sondra to the dock. Hal and Bo held the top as a couple of conscripted bystanders carried the bottom.

Nick was too drained to help.

He wanted to rest till he could walk back to the cottage, but Megan wouldn't let him. "You're going to the hospital, too, if I have to carry you myself."

Easier to give in. Even if he could barely stand.

In the end, he leaned on her as they trailed after the group transporting Sondra.

When they lifted Sondra into the cruiser, the jostling brought her to. She focused on Megan, standing near her head. "Is Theo really dead?"

Nick could barely understand the hoarse whisper.

Megan touched her arm. "I'm so sorry, Sondra."

Fresh tears flowed. "I loved him so much," she said brokenly. "I loved him so much."

She didn't gain consciousness again, even when they met the sheriff's boat and they had to stop long enough to explain and let a deputy climb into the cruiser to accompany them to the mainland. At the city pier, an ambulance and deputies waited to whisk them to the emergency room.

Megan, stricken and quiet, helped Nick into a patrol car.

He wished she hadn't seen Theo. "You should have stayed at the cottage."

She grimaced. "You turkey. You shouldn't have sneaked out." She might still be scared to death but at least her color had returned.

It was nice having her there. It was nice being alive.

Even if a man lay dead because of him. Not the first time, but he'd never had this aching emptiness before.

Did he regret it?

No. Nothing to regret.

The game was over. He'd won. Theo had lost.

He moved, grunted.

Bloody hell. He hurt all over from Theo's pounding.

Poor miserable Theo.

He must have been incensed, watching me make out with Sondra and unable to do anything about it. He wanted to hurt me, make me suffer.

Once the doctor had Sondra x-rayed for internal damages, she was admitted. Besides the obvious contusions, she had a nasty bump under her hair, a bruised kidney, and three cracked ribs. "A concussion, too," the doctor told the deputy. "She can't talk to anyone tonight. Come back tomorrow."

As the same doctor picked slivers of glass out of Nick, Whitey showed up. His hair stood out like a white bush while he wore a wrinkled dress shirt buttoned up wrong with baggy navy slacks. No hat. No tie. No suit. "Danny called me. Thank heavens you're all right."

"Whitey! I would never have suspected you capable of wearing such shabby attire." Nick swept his gaze up and down the old man. "Looks like yellow paint smears on your pants to boot. And no bowtie. Is there an immediate crisis?"

"Are you crazy?" Whitey grabbed Nick's arm. "What happened?"

"Owwww. Gently, please. I'm an injured man."

"Lawrence!" Megan, who had refused to leave during his examination, rushed to his aid.

Whitey shook her off. "Tell me, confound you!"

Humor wasn't lightening the situation so Nick abandoned it and went over expurgated events while the doctor examined him. As he finished the part where they'd left Danny to keep order in the mansion, the doctor, who'd been working with pricked ears, spoke up. "Mr. Downing, you need to be admitted, too."

"No. It's only cuts and bruises." He could feel muscles seizing up, but he'd suffered worse. "It's not as bad as it looks. I just need some sleep and some aspirin. It's been a long day."

The doctor argued.

He was too bloody wiped out to listen to this.

His adrenalin rush had come and gone. He could barely put one foot in front of the other, but he got down off the table. "I'm leaving."

The doctor talked about concussion.

"I know all about concussions. I'll keep an eye out." He headed for the door.

"I'll watch him," he heard Megan say before she rushed to help Whitey support him.

Why couldn't he manage a quip?

Too exhausted.

The sheriff, back on the mainland and coming up the hospital steps, stopped them. He looked like he'd put his clothes on in a hurry, too. "I'm going in to see Mrs. Pack. What happened?" He looked from Whitey to Nick.

Whitey harrumphed. "The man's about to keel over, Wadley. And they've put Sondra out. Surely you can take their statements tomorrow. They aren't going anywhere."

The sheriff agreed he could.

"I guess it helps to know people," Nick said as they left.

"Sometimes." Whitey sighed. "I never dreamed it would end like this when Sondra came to me. Perhaps I just didn't want to believe it would. I'm thankful you weren't hurt worse."

"Not as thankful as me."

Whitey had driven his Town Car to the hospital and refused to yield the wheel to Hal or Bo. By the time he dropped them off at the dock, Nick understood why someone always drove the old man.

Whitey wasn't reckless, no. But slow. Gawd, was he slow.

Stopping at stop signs at empty crossroads. Putting on blinkers with no one behind them. Keeping to twenty miles an hour when an open road stretched before them.

It took forever to get to the city pier.

"I hope he makes it home all right," he said as Whitey drove away.

Once the four of them loaded into the cruiser, Hal started the motor and they set off for the island. The roar made speech hard, even with Megan right beside him. And it was nice to be quiet.

For some reason, the night's aftermath left him down.

Took him a minute to recognize it: the same feeling after coitus. Sad, a little wistful.

Except with Megan. He'd been exhilarated, then angry.

But not sad. Maybe that was a sign. If she turned him down . . .

And she might. Depressing thought.

She must have sensed his mood because she didn't let go of his hand. Once she did lean over to tug at Hal. "Why weren't you there to keep Theo from half-killing him?" She had to yell over the motor.

Hal, shamefaced, shouted back, "I got in the staff door with my master key but someone had shot the bolt on an inner door. I couldn't get inside the main house. Hadda go back around to the pool side."

Megan, the darling, poked her lip out like she blamed Hal for him getting beat up.

He pressed her hand. "It worked out, love."

She didn't look convinced, but let it alone.

Dawn stretched its rosy fingers over the ocean's horizon before they reached the dock. Nick pointed it out. "Sometimes you forget how beautiful sunrises can be."

She laid her head on his shoulder.

He pursed his lips. "Did you know your sweatshirt is on inside out and backward?"

"I was in a hurry."

"What am I going to do with you?"

He had thought she'd flare up but she didn't. The anxious expression of the past few hours didn't change and that worried him. He preferred her cantankerous and confident, but he was too tired to think straight.

Tomorrow. Tomorrow they'd talk.

At the cottage, after he took a hot shower and several aspirins, he made her and the others promise to go to bed and then followed his own advice.

He slept like a baby until past two o'clock that afternoon.

CHAPTER 33

LAWRENCE, AT SONDRA'S request, came to her hospital bed late Monday when the sheriff questioned her.

Both men cringed at her injuries.

Scabbed-over cuts and stitches. Black and purple bruises on every visible part. A puffy face.

Worse, her demeanor was that of a woman who'd lost everything.

Under Wadley's questioning, she tonelessly related how Theo had hit her, forced her to call Nick. Then, he'd beat her into unconsciousness. When she came to in her dressing room, she heard Nick and Theo fighting.

"I knew I had to get up and help Nick. Otherwise, Theo . . . he meant to kill me, too, and blame Nick." The split lip, or maybe a loose tooth, distorted her words. "Nick couldn't deny it because he'd be dead. I couldn't believe it, not even after he told me what he planned. But when I saw them fighting, I knew it was all true."

Fat tears rolled down her cheek. "I never wanted him to die. I loved him."

"There, there, my dear." Lawrence patted her hand. "You have what you need, don't you, Wadley? If Sondra hadn't shot him, Theo would have killed both of them. Nick and the others will be in today or tomorrow to fill in the details for you."

Wadley, shocked and sympathetic, agreed more questions could wait. "We'll get a formal statement later, Mrs. Pack, once you're feeling better."

After the sheriff left, Lawrence comforted Sondra. "Now, now, my dear. I can imagine what you're going through. But you did what you had to do."

The room door swung open. George who had waited in the lobby after chauffeuring him to the hospital, peered in. "Sheriff Attaway said he was done."

He gaped at Sondra's appearance.

Megan and Nick crowded in behind him. Megan went immediately to the bed and took Sondra's hand. "Sondra, I'm so very sorry."

Sondra lay still. "Thank you, Megan. It's all so strange. I still can't take it in."

Megan patted her. "It's hard for all of us to understand."

Nick strolled over to stand beside Megan. "We've put most of it together. Are you fit enough to fill in the rest?"

Well! Nick certainly seemed chipper, considering his marks of battle. You would think appearance should be a primary concern. Battered features couldn't be good for a film actor.

Nick seemed to take his wounds as a matter of course. But then he had a history of brawling. Perhaps he was used to being beat up.

Sondra's monotone didn't change. "He meant to kill you and me both, Nick, then say he'd found you attacking me. The staff wing is way across the house and the guest rooms are all upstairs. After our parties most people are too drunk to know what's going on."

Pathetic, that's what she was; a word Lawrence never thought he'd apply to Sondra Pack.

With her head partly shaved and bandaged, she was a far cry from the rich sophisticate he knew.

Sondra's hand lay unmoving in Megan's. "After the band packed up, I told Bertie to send the help home, that they could finish up the next day. Theo and some others left to look for deer, so he said. I was doing my night routine, putting on face cream, when he came in. I asked if everything was all right."

She shivered.

Megan stood to pull up a blanket at her feet.

Sondra didn't notice. "He just hit me. I thought he'd found out about me and Lawrence. Then he made me call Nick. You know the rest."

George opened his mouth. "I still don't—"

"Yes." Lawrence put a stop to that nonsense; George was an idiot. "We do."

"He was crazy," George said. "He must have been."

"Not crazy." Nick pondered. "Avaricious might be a better word. Or obsessed."

"Certainly criminal," Lawrence said.

Sondra fingered the blanket edge. "When I came to you after I found that ring, Lawrence, I didn't, not really and truly, believe Theo had killed the boys. I hoped—"

Nick straightened. "What ring?"

Lawrence cleared his throat. "Do you remember David's family ring?"

"Theo baited me with it at the barbecue. Lucky you had briefed me. Was that what Sondra saw in his safe?"

Megan, horrified, looked from Nick to Sondra. "Do you mean David's druid ring?"

Lawrence nodded. "Sondra and I both agreed that the only way Theo could have gotten the ring would be if David was dead. Since Theo had it, he must have taken it before the boat exploded."

Nick's brows rose.

Megan clenched and unclenched her hands. "No wonder you were so sure Theo had killed the boys."

Nick's surprise abated. "This ring was so convincing, Whitey, that you paid me half a million dollars?"

Sondra closed her eyes. "I always hoped I was wrong, that I'd jumped to conclusions. I tried to think of an innocent reason he had it. But it kept eating at me. I thought maybe if we brought you in, we could discover the truth. All I wanted was for Theo to explain."

"He couldn't explain," Megan cried, eyes blazing. "David would never have given his ring to Theo. He wouldn't have given it to anyone!"

Poor child. The boys' deaths must be eating at her as much as it had him.

"He wouldn't have given it to anyone, eh?" Nick gazed at her thoughtfully. "I see. Hard for me to believe, but I must bow to your superior knowledge."

A new tear dribbled down to Sondra's jaw. "And I lived with him all those years never dreaming what he'd done."

Megan recovered herself. "You were very courageous when you had to be, Sondra."

Lawrence agreed. "If there's any consolation to be had from this whole affair, it's that you did what was necessary."

"I may have, but Theo's gone. And I'll never be the same."

"Bollocks!" Nick said cheerfully.

The man had absolutely no sense of what was appropriate.

Nick went on, "You may feel that way now, but you're not old. You're a beautiful woman, Sondra. Plenty of time for you to meet someone else. Think of this as a new beginning."

Is he making a pass? Blast him, the woman's grieving. Can't he show a little sensitivity?

"Don't! Christ, don't." Sondra covered her face to hide the tears. "You can't possibly understand. There'll never be anyone I love the way I loved Theo. Never."

Her body bore the brutal marks of Theo's hands, yet no one doubted her sincerity.

He would never understand women.

"Theo was part of me. He made me complete." Sondra took a quivery breath. "He's gone and I'll never be the same."

She asked Lawrence to get in touch with a lawyer for her. "Parrish Dungoode. Bobby Bairdston used him when he shot that Atlanta stripper. They say he's the best. I guess I'll need him now."

"You acted to protect Nick and yourself. I doubt you need to worry about charges, but I'll talk to him. It won't hurt to consult someone who specializes in these things."

She turned toward the wall. "Thank you, Lawrence. All of you. I'd like to be alone now."

****

"Sheik of Araby"
As Performed by Don Albert and
his Orchestra (1921)
Music by Ted Snyder
Lyrics by Harry B. Smith
and Francis Wheeler

AS THEY HEADED back to the law office in the Town Car, Lawrence sat in the passenger seat while his son drove. For once, George had little to say. Seeing Sondra had unnerved him.

Maybe that would spur him to get over this infatuation and take charge of his family. The way Mona spent money was a disgrace.

Not that he would butt into their affairs. Heaven forbid.

Nick and Megan rode in the back seat. Chauncey had dropped them off at the hospital before doing errands in town but would meet them at the pier for the return trip.

Conversation was subdued.

It was over. Lawrence would have to wait to find out what ramifications awaited him from the legal association. His gamble had been vindicated, but the price was still to be paid.

James would have been pleased. Maybe surprised by his actions—James had always been the rash one while he himself had been the voice of reason—but pleased.

To think how Theo had fooled him all these years.

Fooled everyone.

His death bothered Lawrence. The law should be allowed to take its course.

But perhaps it was better this way.

The boys were gone. A live Theo couldn't bring them back.

By turning slightly, Lawrence could see Nick behind George, one hand opening and closing his blasted cigarette lighter. The actor looked moodily outside the car window at the palmettos and trees dripping Spanish moss.

Was he still reliving his shave with death?

"He couldn't have got away with it," Nick said finally. "If he'd killed me, everyone would have known why."

George stopped too abruptly at a stop sign.

Lawrence clutched the armrest. Now he remembered why he never rode with George. "If he'd killed you and Sondra, then said he came in as you were attacking her, it might have raised doubts. But everyone knew—thought—he loved Sondra. No one would have suspected him of hurting her. Or he could have made it look as if you shot her and he happened to walk in. Yes, he might have got away with it. Either scenario would give him a perfect excuse for killing you."

Nick was unconvinced. "Why would I hurt Sondra?"

"Because she knew you weren't David," Megan said.

"But Theo must have guessed she was in it with Whitey. Whitey would know the truth."

Megan shook her head. "Not necessarily. And who would have believed Lawrence, with Sondra and Nick both dead? Or Theo might have thought he'd stay quiet. Hiring Nick puts Lawrence in a bad position if someone accuses him of embezzling from the estate."

"Unrequited passion," George threw out from behind the wheel as he pressed on the gas. "When she turned you down, Nick, you wouldn't take no for an answer."

Lawrence sniffed. At least George hadn't started off with a jerk this time. "Unrequited passion? Come now."

Nick snorted. "Do I really give the impression of some lovelorn stripling?"

"Sondra's broken a lot of hearts. Everyone noticed how hot and heavy you two were last night." George got the Town Car up to speed. "Nobody would be surprised."

"I would be," Nick said dryly. "She isn't my type. Blondes never are."

Lawrence considered George's theory. "Theo might have started that rumor himself."

Why couldn't George keep his eyes on the road and not weave back and forth? And he ought to slow down. Such a poor driver.

Unlike Curtis, long departed for Connecticut. He ought to hire someone else to drive and run errands for the firm. An intelligent boy like Curtis without the connection to Mam.

Not that he should be making office decisions. He didn't even know if he'd keep his license.

Back to Theo. "Him starting gossip about you and Sondra would tie in with his plan to accuse you of attacking her. Maybe muddy the waters a bit. I overheard him at the fete last night, telling someone Sondra was going back through her diary hunting proof you weren't David. He could say she'd found something. That would give you another reason to kill her."

"His whole plan was outlandish," Megan said. "Almost as absurd as yours, Lawrence."

Nick said sternly, "Don't be so judgmental, Miss Jurisprudence. Whitey's plan worked. Theo took the bait."

Lawrence jumped in before Megan could retort. "I admit I don't know what was in Theo's mind. But if things had turned out differently, Nick and Sondra would be dead, the bodies consistent with some sort of struggle. One between you and her, Nick, and one between you and him. Theo would have had bruises to corroborate him defending her, no matter what motives he would attribute to your attack on her. His story may have been suspect, but I don't know that anyone could have disproved it."

At the wheel, George shook his head and sighed. The car wobbled. He yanked at the wheel but overcorrected. The car thumped off the road. He jerked it back the other way. "I liked Theo. I thought he was a regular guy. You sure can't tell about people, can you?"

Lawrence let go the arm rest and opened his eyelids that had involuntarily clamped shut.

George didn't seem to notice they could have careened into the marsh. Sometimes he worried about George. His son had many fine qualities, but good judgment was not among them. Neither in driving nor assessing character.

He had learned nothing in forty-two years.

George drove on, unaware of disapproval. "I'll drop you off first, Dad, then take Nick and Megan to the pier in my car. By then, it'll be five so I can head on home."

"Fine." George always looked for excuses to leave work early. Another character flaw.

But at the law office, Nick got out and said, "I can walk from here to the pier. There's no hurry to get back to the cottage, and I want to talk to you, Whitey."

Megan immediately said, "I'll walk, too. I need to check my calendar."

Oh my, she couldn't let the actor out of her sight. This did not bode well. JoBeth would not be happy. Better get Nick paid off and out of town as fast as possible.

George sulked. "I guess I'll come in, too, then."

Like a child. Oh, what did it matter?

"Go home, George. It's nearly five."

Inside his office, the clerks were atwitter with the news of what had happened the past night. Even attorneys stuck their heads out, popping with curiosity until Lawrence ran them off with an astringent hint about people minding their own business.

Ruby was too good a secretary to pry, but she bustled around, so ostentatiously not asking questions that he finally told her that all they needed was privacy and to please see that no one disturbed them.

When she shut his door, he settled at his desk while Nick and Megan took the visitors' chairs in front.

Thank heavens it was almost time to close the office.

"Whitey," Nick said, "I'm curious. Once Sondra found the ring, why didn't you do a bit of safecracking?"

"For one thing, the ring was circumstantial evidence. I knew, as did Sondra, that David would not have given Theo the ring, but I apprised her of my doubts that a jury would convict on our beliefs. Even if we found it, no matter how certain we were, a jury might feel differently."

Megan's hand hid her eyes but not the lip she was biting.

Nick touched her shoulder. "Don't cry, Meggie."

She jerked away. "I'm not crying." A sniffle belied it.

Nick took her hand in both his, patting it. This time she let him. Oh dear.

Blasted sheik. Utterly deplorable. She'll succumb if I don't get him gone and quickly.

He hopped up and nudged them apart before offering his handkerchief. "Besides, Sondra contrived a chance to check later and there was no trace of the ring. Theo may have realized she saw it and got rid of it."

"After keeping it all these years?" Nick made a face. "And as attached to family possessions as he was?"

"Ahem. Then it's hidden. Anyway, Sondra and I agreed we had to flush him out. Make him show his hand. That's when she suggested we hire you to impersonate David."

"I knew from the start someone was behind you, Whitey," Nick drawled. "Such a wild scheme is simply not your style."

"I never approved of it. I just couldn't see any other way to bring Theo to justice."

"And of course, neither you nor Sondra realized he might attack Megan." The soft drawl belied Nick's steely face.

Discomfited, he moved back to his desk chair. "That was unsettling, yes. But Megan shouldn't have been here. When she showed up, I never expected Theo would go after her. I was more worried about her telling him you weren't David."

Megan had recovered her composure. "I'm still not convinced. Why would Theo want to hurt me?"

Nick raised his eyes heavenward. "Sometimes I wonder how you got a college degree, Meggie. How have you managed all these years without a caretaker?"

"It doesn't make sense, Nick."

"If someone knows something that another person is trying to refute, and that someone gets run down in a boat and then hit on the head—"

"Theo's yachting friends are always getting drunk and—"

"Ahem." Such wrangling. "Maybe Theo got frustrated. He was smart enough to surmise I'd hired Nick. He may have thought you were in league with me, Megan. It would have made more sense for him to attack me, but I doubt he was thinking clearly. Now, Nick, the job's done. You're anxious to leave so I'll personally advance your fee."

"Leave? When the hard part's over? Won't there be a hearing or something? After all, a man was killed. No no no! I refuse to be beholden to you, Whitey. I'd feel positively, um, dissolute, spending your money on booze and broads."

Lawrence huffed. "I don't—"

Nick held up a hand. "I won't hear of it. Megan and I are going back to the island. I think a well-earned rest is in order for both of us."

No getting rid of him so easily, confound it.

Lawrence held up his pocket watch. "It's past five. What time are you meeting Chauncey at the pier?"

"He only had a few errands," Megan said. "He should be through by now."

"Good. Dusk comes early. Best to get back to the island before dark. Everyone in the office should be gone so I'll see you out. I have work to do. Per James's will, Theo's share goes back into the Trust. That means reworking all calculations for the remaining beneficiaries. There's no way I can get them done by Wednesday."

He could curse, thinking about everything a recalculation entailed.

Maybe his petition to delay dispersing would be granted. That might give him enough time. After what he'd done, he couldn't risk too much delay. The state bar would consider it one more black mark.

Megan stood up. "I'll run by my office before we leave and check my calendar."

Lawrence called after her. "We're taken care of your Wolgood and Tamerkin filings that are due tomorrow, so don't even think of coming to work."

Nick lingered in his chair. "This has been tiring, Whitey. And I have a lot to think about. Do you have some free time tomorrow? I may need a lawyer. I know I could use some legal advice."

Advice, eh? Hmm. Wonder what that was all about?

Hal had mentioned a project Nick's agent was working on. Nick must be worried about some contract clause or other. Despite his loathing of Hollywood and the movie crowd, he did owe Nick.

"If I don't have an opening, I'll make one."

He would find Nick a contractual attorney in California. That might encourage him to leave.

"And, I'm sure you'll be happy to learn, I'll allow Sondra full access to her share of the estate as soon as my petition to extend administration is granted." Assuming it would be. "If you won't allow me to advance your pay, you'll receive your money then. It shouldn't take long before you're off to California."

"Excellent." Nick seemed abstracted.

Maybe a little encouragement. "Ah, the state of sunshine and beautiful starlets. How I envy you. Making films out there. Basking in all that, ahem, that land of milk and honey."

"You're overselling, Whitey, and very poorly. Is Sondra going to leave her inheritance with you?"

Blast.

"I have no idea. I'm old-fashioned, but she does know she can trust me, I think."

"After all this, I'm sure she does. A bit ungrateful if she changes attorneys now, wouldn't she be?" Nick stood. "Two o'clock okay? Megan and I plan to sleep in tomorrow morning."

"Two? All right."

Megan and him? Sleep in? *I knew it!*

"You've been seeing a lot of her lately."

"Yes." Nick gave a Cheshire cat smile. "I have. And I have hopes. I can't deny that I do have hopes. Of course, they all depend on Megan."

Humph!

Lawrence knew exactly what Nick's hopes involved.

Much as he owed Nick, and even grudgingly respected his talents, he distrusted him. The man was not the type of son-in-law JoBeth would welcome. Not a man who'd run around with painted-up women and who would always be short of money and make Megan miserable. She'd probably end up divorcing him.

He opened his mouth to say so but Nick, waving, gave him no time. "Thanks, Whitey. I'll see you tomorrow."

CHAPTER 34

"Chain Gang"
As Performed by Sam Cooke (1960)
Music by Sam Cooke and Charles Cooke
Lyrics by Sam Cooke and Charles Cooke

IN THE FRONT room, while they were still plainly within Whitey's sight, Nick deliberately put his arm around Megan's waist. "Let's give Whitey a show."

She tensed but allowed it to stay. Not till they were outside and walking down tree-lined sidewalks in front of old houses did she push him away. "You've scandalized Lawrence."

"Yes. Isn't it fun?" Almost as much fun teasing the old man as provoking Megan.

"No. You should stop ragging him." She didn't sound annoyed.

"Killjoy."

The sun weakened overhead. Stink from the paper mill touched down, then lifted.

Would she gripe if he took her hand? Better not. They walked toward the dock in comfortable silence.

His good mood didn't last long. Too many things to consider.

Sondra in the hospital. Whitey proving not to be the fraud he'd half expected. A missing ring responsible for his whole performance. A dead boy standing between him and Megan.

And all that lovely lolly hanging in the balance.

There must be piles of it, though Whitey was too closemouthed to say how much. Might be interesting to find out.

Okay. He could play it out to the end. See what happened.

Or he could leave as he'd intended. Why not? Staying meant the same old cycle. Taking too many risks, trusting too many wrong people.

Why shouldn't he just vamoose, run away, abandon it all, and do his own thing?

Megan.

He wanted her. That meant staying, telling her the truth about his life and the things he'd done.

She'd be shocked, maybe never want to see him again. But if he didn't confess, and she agreed to come away with him, she'd find out sooner or later. And that incurable streak of morality in her would never forgive his dishonesty. He'd lose her anyway.

Bloody hell.

In the end, he supposed, there was only one thing to do.

C'est la vie.

He'd talk to Whitey tomorrow, cajole him into going along. The money alone would be enough to persuade most people, but Whitey was that anomaly, an ethical man.

What a drag.

Maybe he should lie.

Might be easier to persuade the old man. What if he told Whitey that he. . . ?

No, he couldn't. Could he?

Oh, you git! And here you are, trying to change your wicked ways.

He might end up in the big house yet.

****

"Fare You Well, Old Joe Clark"
As Performed by Fiddlin' John Carson (1924)
Old Mountain Folk Song

LAWRENCE LOOKED FOR Nick after lunch Tuesday, but it was four before he showed up.

"Sorry I'm so late, Whitey. We sat up last night talking. Then Danny and Hal and I stopped by the sheriff's office this afternoon to give statements."

We? Who was "we"? Megan.

"Quite all right. Sit down, sit down."

Tsk tsk. With his scabbed-over and bruised face, Nick looked like a thug. While the golf shirt and sharply creased pair of twill slacks might pass muster for their business appointment, the battered boots showed a total disregard for appearances.

Never mind. The man's clothes were no longer his concern.

"Ahem. Matters are moving to a satisfactory conclusion. My petition to delay the Trust disbursement has been tentatively approved. Wadley, of course, won't bring charges since Sondra acted in self-defense. So, unfortunate as this whole affair was, it's over. Hal and the others can leave and things will go back to normal. I must confess I'm glad."

"I'm sure you are." The toe of his boot preoccupied Nick.

"You know, I had my first good night's sleep since Sondra came to me last year. Nothing can bring those boys back, but their murderer hasn't gone unpunished."

He shot his snowy cuffs in satisfaction.

With a slight smile, Nick abandoned his boot study. "You were determined to avenge the boys, weren't you?"

"Avenge is perhaps too strong a word." On his scarred desk top, Lawrence made a steeple of his hands. "The least they deserved was to have the truth brought out."

"Will you ever know exactly what happened?"

"No, but we can guess. When James died, Theo saw his chance to inherit by killing the boys."

Dwelling on the old tragedy didn't ease the sorrow, but at least he—with Nick's help—had exposed Theo.

James would have approved.

"I would not have thought Theo was—" Nick pondered. "Um, *enterprising*, enough to take advantage of James's unexpected death."

"Oh, he had nerve. Lots of it. He was never physically afraid of anything, Theo."

Nick stood and went to the French windows framing showy yellow dahlias. "Nerve. Yes, he proved that. But he never struck me as being clever. Yet when James Harmony died, he planned and carried out everything on the spur of the moment."

Lawrence leaned back. "Even unintelligent people can be cunning at times. When James died, everything must have come together for Theo. The gasoline leak already suspected on the boat may have given him the idea, and I imagine when he heard James was dead, he realized what his future could be. So he took the chance."

"Don't patronize me, Whitey. I understand that."

Nick plopped back down. He smoothed his slacks.

"It just seems to me an explosion on a boat is a little harder to manage than, say, a gas leak at the Mulrennons' where a large propane tank stands beside the house."

"Ahem. When Sondra came to me, she said some months after James died, Francis Mulrennon complained about dynamite missing from his farm shed."

Lawrence fingered the tome on his desk that offered a legal route to extend his custodianship of the Harmony Trust.

"She remembered because Francis was quite put out at having to buy more to blast a beaver dam. He told her he was sure the same person who'd stolen his fishing boat earlier that year must have taken the explosives. The boat eventually turned up on the mainland, but the dynamite never did."

"So you think Theo took them."

"That seems the most likely explanation."

Nick shifted in his seat, unconvinced. "Was he familiar with dynamite? You can't just set dynamite off, I would think At least not without chancing getting blown up yourself. Don't you need fuses or something like that?"

"I have no idea, but it doesn't matter. Not now. You heard him admit he killed them."

Lawrence pushed the law book aside.

"You must be anxious to get your money, Nick. You've certainly earned it. Unfortunately, I'm about to request a stay on final disbursement of the Trust due to Theo's death. I've been granted an extension, but the other details will take longer to wrap up. I'll be happy to advance you part of your pay so you can be on your way."

"No worries. I'll wait. I trust you."

Oh my, not good. He should be itching to get his money and go.

Nick was hard to read. While unconventional, he could be high-handed, persuasive, and sometimes entertaining. But at times he did exactly opposite of what was expected.

"Ahem." What was the man up to? "I don't mind."

Nick leaned back, thrust his legs out in front of him, and drew out his cigarette case. "No, there's no need for you to hurry matters because of me. I'll be here for a while yet."

Damn and blast. What can I do?

As Nick chose a cigar, Lawrence wondered if he knew of the studies about the danger of smoking.

Presumably that included cigars. He might mention them. For the man's own good, of course. After prodding him on his way. "This movie your agent was talking to someone in Hollywood about. Is it still viable? This negative publicity won't hurt your career, will it?"

"On the contrary. Any publicity helps. And the movie deal seems promising. Very promising." Nick morosely tamped the small cigar on the case. "I talked to my agent this morning. They've started negotiations. Tell me, Whitey. Has the ring turned up?"

"David's ring? No. No trace so far, according to Wadley. Sondra gave him permission to search all their houses. That's going on now, but I suspect the ring's at the bottom of the ocean. Fitting, considering the boys are there, too."

Nick took out his lighter and flicked it open and shut. Finally he lifted it to his cigar.

"Ahem. I read an article about tobacco leading to lung cancer."

"Megan showed it to me."

"I see. In that case, I'll say no more."

"Good."

"Well, then. This movie contract. You'll be heading straight to Hollywood if it works out?"

"Hollywood?" Nick lit his cigar and blew smoke rings. "Of course I'm heading for Hollywood, Whitey. That's been my goal all along, don't you know?"

Then why couldn't the man leave?

Once they saw the end of Nick, things would get back to normal. Megan might nurse a broken heart but she'd soon get over it and find someone more settled.

Though she might have to settle for a divorcé or widower after waiting so long to marry. Probably one with children.

Danny didn't wear a wedding ring. Not educated but not illiterate. Maybe he ought to see if Danny could stick around a few more days. If Nick would just leave.

He pushed an ashtray across the desk.

His own plans were coming together.

If he got his petition passed so he could finish up the Trust, he could explore options. Being disbarred—he gave the odds as seventy-thirty against him—wouldn't hurt so much if he retired.

For some reason, the thought disheartened him.

"Ahem." He needed to dole out whatever advice Nick wanted and get on with his work. "Tell me about this movie contract."

CHAPTER 35

"Any Day Now (My Wild Beautiful Bird)"
As Performed by Chuck Jackson (1962)
Music by Bob Hilliard and Burt Bacharach
Lyrics by Bob Hilliard and Burt Bacharach

ON WEDNESDAY, ROBBY'S birthday and the day when the Trust should have been disbursed, Megan got up at dawn and put on her gardening gloves.

The afternoon before, once Nick got back from the mainland, they had strolled around the grounds, then sat up late, listening to records. They'd talked a lot but touched gingerly on Theo and what he'd done to David and Robby.

That part hurt too much.

Theo. She hadn't really believed Theo was guilty until he'd battered Sondra and nearly killed Nick.

How could he have murdered the boys?

She'd opened up to Nick about how she still couldn't fathom it. Mr. H and Miss Livvy had treated Theo like a son, and David had idolized him.

She'd agonized about never suspecting.

Nick had listened and sympathized. In fact, they'd talked about everything and nothing, almost like old friends meeting after a prolonged separation.

She was tired after their late night, but this was one of the days when Mom always took flowers to the cemetery; she'd promised to do it since Mom couldn't this year.

Scarce roses and dahlias sprinkled in with plentiful chrysanthemums and spider lilies made a colorful bouquet for the Harmony plot. After cutting them, she went on to weed. Foliage ran amok in the mild climate, and had to have constant tending.

Not that weeding kept her from thinking.

Theo had come close to killing Nick. If it hadn't been for Sondra, he could have died.

Thoughts of what could have been still scared her.

Sondra was improving and should be released in time for Theo's funeral. Since Sheriff Attaway wasn't filing charges, she'd be free to leave afterward.

Sondra had never liked the island anyway; Theo had been the one who loved it. Once she got her inheritance, she'd probably sell it.

Melancholy thought, but nothing she could do.

Nor Lawrence. His own conduct was sure to be reviewed by the Georgia Law Board, but he had friends in Atlanta. Maybe he'd get by with a reprimand. Then things would get back to normal.

As normal as they could be once Nick was gone.

I can't think about that. Think of David and Robby.

Robby would have been thirty today. David was nine days younger than her.

How old was Nick? Not that it mattered.

For a half hour, she snipped dead roses and cut back dahlias and staked up chrysanthemums beside where the boys' dogs were buried. When Nick, in frayed shorts and plaid shirt, came down the road, the sun was bright and she was hot and sweaty.

She'd have to have a bath before heading to work.

He spotted her in the yard and detoured to come up beside her. "You look sad."

"Today's Robby's birthday."

And Nick was leaving.

He cupped the back of her head and kissed her brow. "You can't change the past, love."

"I know." She inhaled the scent of soap. Unlike her, he looked fresh and clean.

"Whitey called this morning. Got me out of bed, the inconsiderate git. The coroner wants to hold some sort of hearing into Theo's death."

"What!"

"Gawd'struth. Looks like I'll be here awhile. Hal and Danny, too. Bo can leave, though."

"The coroner is holding a hearing?" Bewilderment dampened the joy that he'd be with her a little longer. "That's crazy. Sondra had no choice but to shoot Theo."

Nick bent over a bush to sniff at an overlooked rose.

She stripped off her gloves and rushed inside to call Lawrence. Not seven thirty and the man was already at work.

"What's going on? Odell McNamara has never held an inquest since he was elected to office. Why start now?"

"It's his prerogative."

Over the telephone, Lawrence sounded tired.

He ought to take some time off. He wasn't a young man anymore.

"But why?" she persisted.

"It won't hurt his chances for reelection next year."

"Reelection? Oh flitter." That explained it all. "He's making a mountain out of a molehill because of the people involved." Because the Packs were big news.

"Maybe so. In any event, Nick and his bodyguards will be staying at Magnolia Cottage till after the hearing. Are the reporters still hanging around the island?"

"Not so much as yesterday and the day before. I think most of them are at the hospital."

"The sheriff is ensuring Sondra's privacy. Megan, I need a favor. Don't worry about work this week. You and Linda make sure the remaining guests get gone without incident. And let me know if the reporters try to storm the island again. Both senators and Governor Sanders offered to help us out if they do. JoBeth won't be back for another week or so, and until Sondra is released from the hospital, you're needed there."

Her heart leaped. "Of course, Lawrence."

She wasn't a naive girl. Nick would leave the island and her behind after the hearing, but she could enjoy these last few days. Most of the Packs' friends had already departed. The ones who remained should be gone soon, and she'd be free.

Nick had followed her inside while she made her call. When she relayed what Lawrence had said, he nodded. "Good. We can do something today."

"Sure. Want to come to the cemetery with me?"

At the Harmony graves beneath the sheltering oaks, he watched her arrange the flowers. "Why is James Harmony's headstone smaller than his wife's?"

She got up and brushed off her knees. Between Miss Livvy and Mr. H's graves, the white chrysanthemums made a pretty backdrop for the red spider lilies, a handful of pink roses, and three purple dahlias.

"That was what he specified in his will. A plain flat marker. He chose the ornate monument for Miss Livvy, but he wanted only his name and dates on his. Mom suggested Sondra add 'Beloved Husband and Father' and she did."

Nick shivered. "So many dead people. Depressing place, cemeteries."

"Some people think so." She swung the empty flower bucket. "To me they're kind of restful. When I'm here, I feel people I loved are near me. My daddy's grave is there."

They wandered over so she could point it out. "Mom will go beside him. If I don't marry, there's room for me."

"And if you do?"

"Plenty of room for him, too."

"You don't think that's a bit macabre?"

"Nope. It's called planning for the future. It's reassuring. I'm the type person who likes to know where I'm going."

"And I'm not."

She didn't miss the melancholy. "No. I guess you aren't."

As they were leaving, he paused at the Harmony plot. "You and your mother must have cared for them very much."

"I loved them. Mr. H always tried to be so stern, but Miss Livvy could do anything with him. She was so sweet. I remember when we would listen to records, she'd pull us up and make us dance with her. She could even get Mr. H to dance. And she loved to laugh. She was like David, all full of energy. You could tell her anything and she didn't get upset or judgmental or angry. She just listened."

She'd started menstruating at the Big House. She and David had come in for lunch after bicycling all morning. When she went to pee, her panties were bloody. Miss Livvy had soothed her, found her fresh panties—step-ins, she'd called them—and a Kotex. She'd also showed her how to use it and explained what was happening.

Not that Megan didn't know. She and David had talked about their bodies like they talked about everything. She'd been too modest to tell him about her first period, but he'd wormed it out of her; he always tricked her into spilling whatever she tried to hide.

His eyes had got round. "You can have babies now."

"I'm not going to have babies!"

And she hadn't. Looked like she never would.

That afternoon, when the sound lay windless and glassy, she and Nick water-skied with Hal and Danny until dark. Theo's Nautique was still in the shop, but the old Chris Craft that dated from her youth worked. Even after her years off skis, her proficiency soon came back.

Nick could ski on one board. He'd learned in France. When he found a Dick Pope set of skis that included a slalom, he demonstrated and volunteered to teach them.

Hal and Danny refused, but he talked her into trying. At first, she couldn't hold the tow rope steady against the ski until the boat could pull her out of the water. When she finally did get up, she laughed out loud in the exhilaration of feeling the spray and wind in her face while zooming over the sea's surface.

She'd forgotten how she used to enjoy waterskiing.

That night they were exhausted.

Chauncey, who had seen to repairing the sliding door and cleaning up the mess, came by to invite them for leftovers at the Big House. "We got more of 'em than an army could eat. Bertie say y'all better help us out or we'll be eating till Sunday week."

When Nick walked her home afterward, he didn't try to kiss her nor did he stay long.

Thursday morning, he came by early again.

While Hal and Danny fished, she and Nick wandered the island. They picked up shells and driftwood from the beach, crabbed from the docks, swam in the saltwater pool, and collected wildflowers from the woods that they put on her dining table.

Nick was cheerful, entertaining, and made no effort to seduce her. She understood why.

He was planning his departure. He was an adventurer, a rambler, and she, no matter how she felt about him, was still a homebody.

No matter how much she enjoyed his company, a timid Tessie like her would hold no challenge for a fearless adventurer like him.

Hal and Danny, fishless but faintly buzzed from the beers drunk that afternoon, went up to the Big House for supper again. She and Nick fixed hot dogs and ate them on the porch. Afterward, they sat down in the glider overlooking the denuded rosebushes.

She talked about making the garden a memorial when Miss Livvy's roses were about to be discarded along with the boys' dogs, about how they'd moved bushes and reburied the dogs.

He asked about the dogs. "I saw them in Whitey's home movies. Dorchester couldn't have been very old when he died."

"No. Barely two." Thinking of David and Robby and their pets hurt. "Chauncey thought Dorchester got into some antifreeze, and the vet agreed. Poor thing. His kidneys failed first and then other organs."

"Sounds painful."

"It was. We never found out where he got it. Robby was terribly upset. He'd barely got over losing Miss Livvy. David—" She sighed. "David told Robby Chauncey would get them a puppy—Chauncy's always coming up with strays—but Mr. H said to wait till after his Washington trip. He and David argued. They always rubbed each other the wrong way. Then it was too late."

He laid an arm on her shoulders. "You loved David."

She inhaled his scent. "I told you that."

He turned her face to make her look at him. "You're going to have to let him go. He isn't coming back."

"I know." Old Spice cologne didn't make him David.

"Do you?"

"Of course I do."

"Then why did you call his name when I made love to you?"

She hadn't. She knew she hadn't.

Had she?

"You're imagining things."

He tilted his head. "Meggie, you're still pining for a lover who no longer exists."

"I am not."

He raised his brows.

"I'm not!" She grabbed him and kissed him.

He let her. He let her press his head to hers, brush his tongue with hers. But his arms didn't wrap around her.

She drew back. "There! See?"

He didn't move. "Was that for me? Or to make me stop talking about David?"

How does he know? How can he tell?

Then he laughed. "Maybe I don't care. See what you think about this one."

Then he pushed her back and kissed her so hard her teeth hurt.

She almost lost control. Almost.

Till his hand wandered to her hip and trailed around her stomach.

Shaking because she wanted him so much, she pushed him away. "Don't go there."

He chuckled, swept back a loose tendril of her hair, and put his hands around her face. "Your loss. I'm not David, but I'm good in bed."

She swallowed. "I admit you're wonderful in bed. Does that help soften the blow?"

His sweet smile almost made her change her mind, but better to face it now. They had no future together.

CHAPTER 36

"It's All in the Game"
As Performed by Nat King Cole (1957)
Music by Charles Dawes
Lyrics by Carl Sigman

FRIDAY, NICK BEAT on her door at dawn. The wind blew his hair across his face; his eyes sparkled. "Let's go sailing."

"Do you know how to sail?"

"I live in England! Of course I know how to sail."

They took out one of the smaller sailboats and spent the morning in the sound, zipping along the surface, leaning out over the side and screaming when they capsized.

A dolphin and calf swam alongside them for a while. Gulls wheeled overhead. A curving line of brown pelicans swooped down close to the water.

At one point Megan spotted a brown pelican overhead. "Oh, look!"

She told him why brown pelicans didn't live as long as the white ones. "They dive from such heights, their eyes go bad so they can't see to fish. The white ones fish close to the water and keep their eyesight longer. That's why there aren't as many brown pelicans around."

He grinned at her from the tiller. "Everyone knows that."

"No, they don't!"

They squabbled, nearly keeled the boat over again, and finally sailed back in, happy with their morning and each other.

After a late lunch, they went down to the beach to watch the surf. Taking off his shirt, Nick, skin browned and hair gold in the early October sun, stretched out on a blanket beside where she sat cross-legged and opened a script he'd asked her to review.

After an hour or so, she finished reading. "This is good. Which role will you play?"

"Hopefully the lead."

"Too bad. The sidekick has a much better part."

"You think so?"

She put down the script. "Yes. But I don't know much about things like this."

"Who does?" He had his eyes closed against the sun.

The marks from Theo's beating remained, but there were also the old wounds she'd spotted the first time she saw him. "How'd you get the scars?"

Lazy eyelids opened. "Which one?"

"All of them."

"Ah." He touched the wide one on his shoulder. "I got this one in a bus accident. This one," he brushed his thigh, "from a man who shot me. He thought I was shagging his wife."

"Which of course you weren't."

"I, um, may have been about to." He threw a sharp glance at her. Gauging her reaction.

"Nick, Nick, Nick."

"In my defense, I didn't know she was married."

"Did you ask?"

His lips twitched.

She picked up his left hand, with the threadlike line that curled from his little finger past his wrist. "What about this one?"

The harsh, inscrutable Nick came back.

Her spine tickled. "Another jealous husband?"

"No." He didn't look at her.

She let it go. He was the one who, after a while, pushed himself up on an elbow. "Meggie, it's time you learned. I'm not a nice person."

"Why do you say that?"

"Because it's true. I'm a thief. And worse."

"If somebody's hungry, he does what he must to survive. Wasn't it you who said that?"

"Probably. That's been my motto." He looked away from her, then back. "There's more. I've killed men."

"During the war."

"This was later."

"Oh." Her heart sank. "Why?"

He shrugged. "I had to."

"Was it justified? Like Sondra? Anyone can defend himself."

He took a deep breath, glanced at the sea. "I suppose so."

She pretended to look over the script but couldn't stand it for long. "Nick?"

"Hmm?"

"I understand."

"Do you? Before we go any further, I want you to know about me. I'm not a good person. I've done bad things. Things I don't like to remember, much less admit to you."

"Then don't admit them." Easily said, but now she'd always wonder about him, his character, his past.

He opened his mouth, closed it, and lay back down. "Tell me about you."

He'd started to say something else. What? "Me? Nothing to tell. Besides, didn't you hear it all from Lawrence?"

"Not much about the broken engagements."

"Oh. Those."

His eyelashes looked like black caterpillars on his cheeks. He smiled without opening his eyes. "Those. What happened? David get in the way there, too?"

"No!" She plucked at a page of the script. "The first boy I met in college. He graduated before me and moved to Minnesota for a job. I didn't want to go to Minnesota."

"Isn't that where it snows all the time? Good decision."

"The second one was an artist. Funny. Always joking." Like David. "He'd come down here to paint. I'd just started work with Lawrence. It took me awhile to realize he was depending on me to support his career. And his old girl friend in Vermont."

A smothered laugh. "I can imagine how that went over."

"Yeah. The last one had political ambitions. He had a better chance of getting elected with a wife and children. Unfortunately, he had absolutely no sense of humor."

"Revolting. Never would have worked."

"No." She liked sitting on the blanket with Nick lying in the sun beside her. They didn't even have to talk.

Except: "Your turn. Ever been married?"

He snorted. "No."

"But you've been in love?"

His head turned toward her. "In love? Yes. Once. Long ago."

"What happened?"

"Death." He looked as harsh as he sounded.

"I'm sorry. I shouldn't have pried."

He laughed unexpectedly. His facial planes softened. "It's all right. As I said, it was long ago. There've been a few women since. Just not any I could stand more than a few weeks. Now you. You grow on a man. I could get used to seeing you every morning."

"Liar."

"I'm not lying."

"You don't know me well enough to decide."

"Yes, I do."

His hand crept toward her thigh. When it went further, she slapped it. "Stop."

"This is making it hard on me," he complained. "Making *me* hard."

"Don't be crude."

"Was my lovemaking that bad?"

Tell him the truth?

"It was lovely. But you'll be better off with someone like you. Someone who wants to be fancy free and anxious to wander over the world."

"And you don't?"

She couldn't admit she was afraid. Afraid of loving and being abandoned. Afraid of leaving Mom and her home. Maybe afraid of leaving what little she had left of David.

"I don't think I can. I'm too bound up with the island."

Later, as they watched strings of orange butterflies flutter by, they talked about the movie role. He leaned toward taking it. "But you may be right. The sidekick part may be better. Maybe I should try for it. In any event, I have to make up my mind soon."

He was slipping away, and she wasn't sure whether she was sorry or glad. Perhaps she'd built him up in her mind as something fine and noble, but he wasn't. He'd admitted as much. Worse, he would go away and forget her.

An unfamiliar pang hit her heart.

She brushed it aside. She'd play the game till he left.

He didn't remark on her silence. "I want a role that'll make people sit up and take notice. I intend to be the biggest thing in Hollywood before I'm through. People are going to be begging for autographs and producers are going to be vying to get me for their films."

She groaned. "I'm dying laughing."

"What? Don't you think I can make it happen?"

She relented. "I'm sure you can."

And she'd never hear from him again.

Squawking sea gulls signaled Linda's approach.

Good. No need to pretend enthusiasm for pie-in-the-sky plans that didn't include her.

Sondra's secretary had come down to the beach to tell them Sondra was out of the hospital. "Theo's body will be released tomorrow so I've arranged the funeral for Sunday, in the church here. He loved the island and Sondra wants him buried here."

Nick stood, put on his shirt. "Have you heard when the inquest will be?"

"The day after the funeral." Linda echoed Megan's previous dissatisfaction. "Sondra saved both your lives. I don't know why they're bothering with an inquest."

Nick spread his hands. "Your guess is as good as ours."

Megan closed the script. "Lawrence says the coroner asked for it. He's up for reelection next year and someone's running against him."

Linda tossed her head. "Somebody wants to get his name in the paper? A man killed and a woman beaten half to death, but some silly politician sees it as an opportunity to promote himself? That's just plain disgusting."

Megan found her flip-flops. "I agree. It's heartbreaking for Sondra. But that's politics."

Linda sighed. "I don't know how she's held up. This is so terrible. They really loved each other. At least Sondra loved him. I would have sworn Theo loved her, too."

Nick finished buttoning his shirt. "You can't tell about people." He pulled Megan up.

Linda kicked at the sand. "I thought I knew him."

Megan folded the blanket. "You and everyone else. Poor Sondra."

They walked up to the pavilion together, but at the fork Linda took the path to the Big House. "Come up and eat with us tonight. We still have leftovers."

She hesitated, not wanting to hurt Linda's feelings but dreading another onslaught of conjecture and outright questioning from the other islanders.

Nick saved her from answering. "We're making an early night of it. Hal and Danny will probably come up though."

That evening, after she baked one of Mom's frozen casseroles and Nick praised it way too lavishly, they did the dishes, then put a stack of 45 records on the hi-fi.

Sneaky, who had been collected from her babysitter Tuesday, had finally forgiven Megan for abandoning her. She claimed her place on Mom's easy chair and dared anyone to move her. Nick didn't try.

Sometimes Megan was uncomfortable with visitors. Ron had managed, without uttering a word, to imply distaste for their old furniture with its scratched wood and faded upholstery. And he'd hated cats.

Not Nick. He took their lived-in home and Sneaky as a matter of course. She liked that. She liked a lot of things about him. Even his inability to stay still didn't bother her.

This night, he prowled the room until she patted the sofa beside her. "You're too fidgety. David was, too. Mom used to tell him to cut back on the CoColas so he'd slow down."

Nick sat down beside her but turned sideways to see her. "David." He stroked her arm. "We always come back to him. How much in love with him were you?"

Was he expecting her to lie? "When I saw the paper on the plane that said David had come home, I was, it was . . ."

She thought. "As if I'd come back to life after being dead."

He searched her face. "Then you found out it was me. That must have been a shock." A jaw muscle quivered.

"I hated you once I knew you weren't David. I thought you were a crook."

"You were right. I told you exactly what I am. How do you feel about me now?"

She wasn't certain. "If you would risk your life to get at the truth for two boys you didn't even know," she said slowly, "you can't be as bad as you like to think."

"Megan," he began and stopped.

The raw intensity in her name alarmed her. "What is it? Are you all right?"

He shook his head, then took her hand and kissed it. "I've done things I'm not proud of. A lot of things. This scar on my hand? I got it when I killed my second man."

His second man.

He waited for her to say something.

"Was it self-defense?"

He shook his head. "I planned to kill him."

Her heart stopped. She swallowed. "Deliberately?"

He nodded.

The room blurred. "You wouldn't kill someone unless you had to. I know you—"

"No, you don't know me. That's what I'm saying." He took both her hands.

"Listen, Megan, I did it because . . . He was a man I worked with in a, um, a smuggling operation in Mexico. Okay, what I did to earn my keep was outside the law. That's another strike against me. But this man beat his wife. I told myself it wasn't my business. Then I caught him with his daughter. She was only ten and he had other daughters."

He shuddered. "I decided to kill him."

"Because he was with his daughter?"

"He was having relations with her. D'you understand? And he used the other girls, too. Six of them. They ranged from two to fifteen. He rented the two oldest ones out."

Megan couldn't breathe. "That's horrible."

"Yes." He snorted. "I've seen lots of horrible things. Some of them I've done."

"Not like that. Not with a child. To a child."

"No. Never that." He leaned back against the loveseat, not looking at her. "I didn't kill him right away. I didn't want to get caught. I waited for my chance and shot him as he slept."

A murderer. Like Theo.

She couldn't deal with this. She fastened on his hand still holding hers. "He gave you that scar?"

"Not him. His wife." He showed teeth like a skull's grin. "I tend to act without thinking things through. Big fault of mine. I didn't consider her. All I thought of was those little girls. Afterward, their mother came at me with a broken bottle, screaming bloody murder and cursing like a sailor. I held up a hand and she slashed it. I had to knock her out to get away."

From the record player, Harry Belafonte sang about a banana boat. She listened to the lyrics, tried to make sense of them. Tried to make sense of Nick's words. "She attacked you?"

"I thought she'd be happy."

"Happy?" Her hand in his felt clammy. "When you'd killed her husband?"

"I'd killed her meal ticket. Never mind her daughters being raped every night. Never mind him breaking her nose, knocking her teeth out."

He let her go, turned to lean over his knees, head bowed and forearms resting on his thighs. "Like I say, I didn't consider her reaction. But I wasn't completely heartless. I stole the proceeds of our little smuggling operation and gave her the money before leaving the country."

What should she say? What could she say?

He jerked upright. "Don't look at me like that!"

She heard the despair.

Tenderness for him, for his anguish, overcame revulsion. "It's all right, Nick. Whatever you've done doesn't matter. You have a chance to start out fresh now."

"What I've done won't change. The dirt is still here." He tapped his chest.

"Nick." She cupped his face. "Don't torture yourself over something in the past. You're good inside. I believe that. I wouldn't be here with you otherwise."

He kissed her hand, held it to his cheek. "I think that must be why I love you, your complete confidence that whoever you care about is worthy of it."

Love her? If only he meant it.

"Don't say things like that."

"Like what?"

She almost said, "That you love me," but changed it at the last minute. "I couldn't care about anyone who wasn't good inside."

Deep down he was good. She'd recognized that about him, first when she thought he was David, and then when she'd gone to

Magnolia Cottage with him. He had a kind heart. Like Lawrence and Mr. H and her father.

Even if he did occasionally irritate her. Even if his character wasn't what she'd prefer.

He might have led a rough life, but it didn't matter. If he was a bad person, she wouldn't be so at ease with him.

She laid her head on his shoulder. "I don't care what you've done, Nick."

"You don't care because I remind you of David."

"No, that isn't it." Then she sighed, honest even when it hurt. "Maybe a little."

He touched his lips against her ear, then moved down to nuzzle her neck and throat. When he reached her mouth, she opened to him.

No roving hands tonight, just delicious, lingering kisses that warmed her all over.

After a while, she pushed him back, breathless with the unspoken desire that was always there. "I'm not going to give you what you want."

"You don't know what I want."

"Maybe not everything," she conceded. "But I'm not going to sleep with you."

"I don't want to sleep with you. I want to shag you till you forget everything and everybody but me."

She shook her head. "No."

"All right. But I won't wait long for you."

"What do you mean?"

"You know what I mean. You'll have to decide soon. When this inquest is over and I get my money, I'm leaving. Come with me."

She put her hands up to her cheeks. Her skin felt hot as fire.

He'd asked her to go with him. Did he mean it or was it just to get her to bed? She'd never been skilled at flirtations.

If only she was the type of woman who could throw aside what people might think and say, do what she wanted for once.

If only she knew what she wanted.

CHAPTER 37

THE DAY BEFORE Theo's funeral, Sondra Pack kept her maid and secretary busy as she tried on black dresses sent down from the Savannah Belk-Beery.

Janie and Linda hovered over her, being oh so awfully sympathetic and clucking at her appearance. Assuring her she'd get over her misery and Theo. "It just takes time."

Time! As if time would make any difference.

What the hell did they know about heartache?

Theo was dead and she almost wished she was, too.

Maybe they were right. Maybe once the funeral was over, this agony would get better. That had happened with the captain she'd lost in the war. And with James.

But the ache after James died had come from having to watch him suffer. She hadn't loved James. And even what she felt for her captain was infantile compared to what she'd shared with Theo. She'd never known what love meant until Theo.

The habit of careful grooming was too ingrained for her to abandon entirely, but no matter how she tried, she couldn't summon the old delight.

I'm still in shock. I should have left it alone. I should never have gone to Lawrence. If I hadn't, my buccaneer would still be here.

Strange how you can plan for the future and imagine the results, but when things actually happen, everything goes all topsy-turvy.

I had no choice, came from her brain.

But I did, said her heart.

If only she'd left it alone.

Linda brought her a cup of tea. "Black becomes you."

"Theo hated me in black. He said it was depressing."

The tea was hot, but it didn't help. No matter how much she sipped, she couldn't get warm. She plunked it down.

Linda was right. Black did become her, accentuating her

complexion instead of washing her out like it did a lot of blondes. The famous pansy eyes were clear, thanks to abundant eye drops. Facial bruises remained, but a judicious use of makeup should disguise them. Her lip was healing. The swelling was gone, and she could barely see the cut.

Images of Theo came. Crying as he hit her, hurt her. All those tears because he had to hurt her.

She couldn't think of that. Must focus on her appearance.

A black mantilla like the one Jackie Kennedy sometimes wore to mass would hide the bruises and the shaved spot above her temple. She'd had Belk-Beery send one down with the dresses.

At the mirror, she sat still while Linda brushed her hair. So many times Theo's face had been reflected behind hers.

Her heart would surely burst. "I miss him so much."

"Of course you do." Linda put down the brush. "You were married for years."

Janie stopped bustling around and made soothing noises.

Sondra flicked a fold of her skirt, trying not to cry. "Isn't this rich? Theo's dead and I have to bury him in an outfit from a hick town department store because there's no time to have a designer dress flown in."

After all they'd meant to each other, she couldn't look halfway decent at his funeral. And his closest friends had abandoned him. The only ones here were John and dear Amos.

Because of the money. They didn't care about Theo.

John didn't even care that much for her, but she could count on Amos. He'd been in love with her for ages. Theo used to tease her about Amos and his crush on her.

Not that Amos was any comfort now. If Theo were here, he'd kiss her and pet her and . . .

She put both hands on her abdomen. "There's this terrible emptiness. Right here. I'll never love anybody else the way I loved Theo. How can I go on without him?"

Linda massaged her shoulders. "You loved the Theo you thought he was. But he wasn't what you thought. Here, try the pearls. They should look good with that neckline."

The tears couldn't be denied. She angrily dashed them away. "But he *was* who I thought. At least up until the end. I should never have gone to Lawrence."

Janie and Linda exchanged glances over her head. Thinking she didn't know they thought she was half out of her mind, the stupid bitches. "Oh, yeah, life goes on. Everyone says that and it's true but it's so hard when it's my life they're talking about. He was my life."

She looked in the mirror. At least the sheath fit. It would do. Choosing a strand of pearls, she put them up to her neck and examined her reflection one way and then another. "No, they spoil the effect. Isn't there a cameo in there, Janie? I had one for James's funeral."

There. The black-ribboned cameo was much more in keeping with her grief. She wasn't going to a frigging cocktail party. She was a widow in mourning.

Black for Theo, black for her sorrow.

Linda and Janie hovered behind her, their images in the space where Theo belonged.

He'd never stand there admiring her again. Never brush his hand against her neck, lean over to suck at her ear, squeeze her breasts, screw her till she screamed.

Linda and Janie waited anxiously. "That's perfect for the funeral, Sondra."

Sondra bent over, hands over her eyes, the heartache unendurable. "What am I going to do without him?" she sobbed. "I can't bear it, I can't bear it."

If only the knife-edged grief would go away.

****

"The Wayward Wind"
As Performed by Gogi Grant (1956)
Music by Herb Newman and Stan Lebowsky
Lyrics by Herb Newman and Stan Lebowsky

SUNDAY, AS SOON as she got in from Theo's funeral, Megan took off her gloves and navy pillbox hat so she could undo the chignon and let the braid hang loose. Next she tugged off the fake lapis earrings and Mom's white pop beads. A poor substitute for her pearls sunk in the river, but the best she could do. Finally, she stripped off her clothes. Dark colors didn't mix with a sunny October day.

Neither did a girdle, hose, and nylon petticoat.

Drat it. She'd dropped mustard on her navy suit skirt.

Sondra had insisted everyone come back to the Big House for lunch, including her and Nick, though they could just as well have skipped it; Sondra had immediately broken down and closed herself up in her room.

It was for Sondra's sake she'd attended the service. She was glad she and Nick had gone because only a handful of people showed up. But she felt hypocritical the whole time.

She hated Theo for murdering the boys, and his death didn't change that.

But she'd done what Mom would expect: shown up for Sondra. Thank goodness, Mom was still away and could enjoy her cruise, ignorant of what had happened.

As for her, she would put on her shorts and sandals and pretend things were back to normal.

Or as normal as they could be.

She took her music box to the living room.

For some reason, Lawrence wanted her to bring it with her to the inquest tomorrow. She hesitated, then cranked it and turned it on. The silvery chimes brought David back.

If she'd run away with him, Theo couldn't have killed him. She could have had him all these years.

But now there was Nick.

He would leave after the inquest. And he wanted her to go away with him.

How could she? It was idiocy to even consider leaving home for a man who might tire of her before a week was up.

She sighed, put the box on the breakfast counter so she wouldn't forget it.

Nick, who'd swung by the Magnolia Cottage to change into plaid shorts and a navy oxford shirt after the rites, came in while she was in the bathroom.

She found him on a bar stool eyeing her music box.

Remembering his cavalier handling of it, she whisked it out of reach. "Lawrence asked me to bring it to the coroner's inquest. He said I might have to give evidence about how I knew you weren't David. Strange, don't you think? It had nothing to do with Theo's death."

"I suppose Whitey knows best."

"Whitey knows best? How sheeplike you've become." She put her hands on her hips. "This from the man who insists on having his own way all the time."

"I don't. Not all the time."

She snorted.

"How unladylike you are. Were you always a hoyden?"

"Yes. But that box. Sometimes I think Lawrence has put off retirement too long."

"I wouldn't worry about him. Whitey's saner than you and me put together."

"Speak for yourself."

She fixed glasses of iced tea, then led the way onto the porch overlooking the garden. There they sat on the glider, thighs touching.

She wished he would stay here with her.

He wouldn't.

Nick was as unreliable as wind in a sail. If she went with him, she'd end up heartbroken when he came across a woman more exciting.

Moving the glider gently forward and backward, they soaked in the sun. Among faded rose bushes, red spider lilies lined the walk in front of chrysanthemum clumps. Beyond the yard, a heron flew over the dark river that flowed between the marsh grass.

She'd be a fool to leave her safe life here to traipse after Nick Downing. Face it, she barely knew him. No matter how comfortable she felt with him.

He elbowed her. "What are you thinking about?"

"About how wonderful Lawrence was to do this for Robby and David. They deserve to have the truth known. I'm just glad you and Sondra weren't hurt worse."

His face shuttered. "Yes." He gulped at his tea.

He didn't want to talk about it. Troubling.

"Everyone's been so strange lately. Lawrence asking me to do things that don't make sense and you . . . One moment you're laughing and the next you're depressed. What's wrong, Nick?"

"Nothing, love." He set down his tea and stopped the glider. His heat warmed her when he took her hand.

"Is it the inquest? It'll be all right. You'll see. Everyone understands your part. It's because Theo died that it's being held. Sondra had no choice."

He tugged at her braid, pulling out the wayward curls and pushing them behind her ear. "Still, I don't look forward to tomorrow very much."

"Me either." She liked his gentleness. "I hope I don't get nervous if I have to testify."

"You'll do fine. Shall we have breakfast at the diner in the morning?"

"All right."

"You aren't going to work, are you?"

She made a face. "Lawrence said not to, but he can probably use my help. He got an emergency extension on dissolving the Trust and is petitioning to continue as executor. Refiguring the disbursements can't be done in a couple of days."

"Oh?" He entwined her fingers with his. "Have you thought about what I said? About going with me?"

She started the glider moving again. "Yes, I've thought about it."

No lie that. She had. Every minute.

She'd never known anyone like Nick. It was tempting to throw everything she'd worked for aside and go with him, but he wasn't the solid kind of man a woman should marry. He might try, but in the end he'd be gone and she'd be alone with another failed love affair.

That didn't keep her from considering it.

"And?" He stopped the glider, tightened his grip on her hand. "Are you still in love with David, or can you care for a great actor who might be a tad egotistical and ornery, but who has exceptional talent and who's terribly, terribly in love with you?"

"I do care for you, Nick."

"Good. Will you run away with me to Hollywood?"

"I don't know."

He sat back, moving the glider gently. "We're getting down to the wire, Meggie. I need someone to look after my interests. And you're perfect. You can read contracts and dole out money to me and make all the decisions. Keep me from doing stupid things. And acting means uncertain paychecks. If we're short of money, you can always pick up some legal business on the side."

She ploughed her feet down. The glider stopped. "You want me to support you?"

"Only when I'm resting."

Before she could formulate a blistering reply, she saw the twinkle. "You're incorrigible."

"I am not. I'm sensibly planning for the future. Isn't that what you like? To plan ahead? An actor's income is never secure, but everyone needs a lawyer. Will you go with me?"

Dear God, how she wanted to. "Let me think about it. We've known each other a week. That isn't long enough to make a big decision like this, is it?"

"It is when you know what you want."

When she started the glider again, he pulled her close. She liked his arm around her, and she loved his smell of Old Spice and him.

"I want you," he murmured at her ear. "The question is, do you know who you want? I can't be your David. So you'd better make up your mind about which of us to choose, Meggie."

"You're being silly. David isn't a choice."

"Just decide."

"I'll think about it. I promise."

****

"Song from Moulin Rouge (Where Is Your Heart?)"
As Performed by the Mantovani Orchestra (1953)
Music by Georges Auric

NICK BURIED HIS face in that unruly mop of russet hair. He only hoped that after the inquest was over, she would still consider his proposal.

If she ever forgave him.

Intolerable, the idea that she mightn't.

Strange how over the past years he'd never let any woman get close, and now this. Meggie. A brown mouse with a smile that cut through the dark. Who would have thought it?

Distrusting people had become a habit because he'd never wanted anyone to cling to him, never wanted to lean on anyone. He'd valued his independence. That was before.

If she'd only forget her David and look at what he had to offer.

"Which is exactly what?" he jeered at himself as he walked to the Magnolia Cottage that night in the moonlight. All right, maybe he wasn't much of a catch. But he could change. He would, for her.

She was bossy, irritating, and wonderful. Calm in a crisis, accepting without judging. With a moral compass lacking in him.

Just the woman he needed.

He'd give anything if he could replace that boy in her past.

Later, in the rustic bathroom, he squeezed out toothpaste and eyed himself in the mirror. "You bounder, it's time to settle down. Fun and games are fine when you're young, but there comes a time when certain basic responsibilities must be manfully shouldered. In a word, marriage catches each and every one of us male animals eventually. It's an inevitable course of nature. We can fight it kicking and screaming, or we can ride the wave."

Marriage to Megan was a thought so beguiling that he caught himself standing like a half-dazed idiot grinning at his pasted teeth.

"Not to count your chickens, old friend," he said to his reflection when he finished rinsing his mouth, "but you're not a bad sort. Megan could certainly do worse. If she'll stop mooning over David, and I think she's close. Once this is all settled, we'll see."

Once this was all settled.

CHAPTER 38

"I HAVE TO GET in," Megan pleaded in the dingy hallway.

The bailiff, a tiny gray-headed man with a pugnacious nose, blocked the door of the courtroom. "Are you a witness?"

"No. Yes." Her gloves tightened on her music box. "Possibly. I work for Lawrence Wykerton."

At that moment Lawrence put his head out the door. "It's all right, Walt. She's with me."

Relieved, Megan slipped past the little man.

"Nick's saving us a place. I apologize for leaving my keys at the office. Thank you for getting them." Lawrence led her to the front of the small courtroom. "Odell tried to keep the inquest quiet but you know how word gets out. I should have realized something like this would bring out every busybody in town and beyond. It's a wonder more reporters didn't show up."

The coroner, Odell McNamara, wasn't on the judge's bench yet, but six wide-awake and inquisitive jurors, chosen first thing, sat in their seats waiting to be sworn. Packed pews on both sides of the aisle seated the audience.

In their row, George sat on Nick's far side while a bored Hal and Danny took up the remainder. Megan ended up squeezed between Lawrence and Nick, spiffy in tailored suit and narrow tie. He emitted a citrus scent rather than Old Spice.

A pang fluttered, was quickly banished.

Senseless to miss the reminder of David. Nick wasn't David; he had his own cologne preferences.

She gave a quick hello to George and the others.

Nick winked at her. "Late as usual." He inspected the strands curling round her ears and made a face.

She bit back a retort and tried to tuck the hair under her mother's summer hat.

Not only had she borrowed the pop beads again, but she'd had to rummage through Mom's closet because four of her five hats were bought for weddings and teas and luncheons. The only one suitable for court was navy to match her good navy suit. Which, thanks to her carelessness, sported mustard on the skirt.

Fashion experts said no wearing navy with black, so it was Mom's unseasonable, outmoded gray straw with a turned-up brim. At least it didn't make her look like a socialite, and it went with her black and gray plaid suit that she liked because the straight skirt had a row of kick pleats in the back to make walking easy.

She gave up trying to poke the errant curls back. Nick was right. It was hopeless.

As she dug Lawrence's keys out of her purse, the tall courtroom doors opened and flashing lights popped.

A murmur went through the crowd as Sondra, Linda, and Amos Lovett entered. The bailiff hurriedly closed the doors against the flashbulbs and cameras.

Sondra, leaning heavily on Amos, had dressed for court all in black. Her small whimsy hat on teased hair, a clutch bag, and even three-quarter gloves were black.

Looking neither to the right nor to the left, she carried herself with great dignity. Her features could have been carved from marble except for the slash of lipstick. She was plainly ill. Probably still inconsolable.

Poor, poor woman. How would she live with what she'd done? Even though Theo had deserved it, she'd loved him. This had to be eating her inside.

Linda responded to Megan's slight wave, but Sondra didn't notice.

John Wilkes, the noted Atlanta attorney Parrish Dungoode, and an unidentified associate had claimed the bench on the other side of the aisle earlier. Now they slid down, making room. Moving like an automaton, Sondra went in first, to sit by John. Amos came next, with Linda on the aisle. Dungoode leaned over John to speak to Sondra.

Odell McNamara was a hard-hearted politician, putting a grieving woman through this. Serve him right if he lost the election next year.

She nudged Lawrence, gave him his keys. Her purse fit on the floor beneath the pew, but what about her music box? Wrapped in a towel, it shouldn't get scratched up, but at a foot long it was too big to hold. Especially since they might be here several hours.

After some indecision, she set it by the purse, behind her feet where it wouldn't get shuffled around.

There. She was fixed for the duration.

Maybe they'd be through by lunch.

Lemon yellow walls and light gold trim lightened the courtroom, too cheery a paint scheme for so solemn an occasion. A row of deep gold shutters gave the impression of several windows, but only one, directly behind the judge's bench, was drawn back. Motes floated in the sunshine it allowed inside.

The bald head of Tim Purley shone from the table facing the bench. He'd started his career with Lawrence but got elected district attorney before Megan was hired.

In a quick brush-up on Georgia law regarding coroners' inquests, she'd discovered he had the sole authority to question witnesses. Other attorneys or involved persons could present questions to him, and he could ask them or not as he deemed proper.

Not like a regular court.

Especially with Odell McNamara as judge. A tall, thin man, Odell was the funeral director and served as coroner.

Megan expected him to strut with importance when he came in. Or at least to march in with his usual sober dignity. Instead, he scurried in like a scared rabbit.

Maybe Odell was rethinking his decision to hold this travesty.

If not, he ought to be.

A verdict from a coroner's inquest in Georgia was not legally binding. Whatever was decided here would be strictly an opinion unless it was presented to the grand jury which, in this case, would never happen.

A lot of time and taxpayer money spent for nothing. Odell McNamara deserved to lose his silly election if this was how he ran the coroner's office.

Tim administered the oath to the jurors.

Outside the one exposed window, a big heavy lantern hanging from the eaves of the courthouse swung back and forth on its chain. It continued to sway gently throughout the morning, its presence sometimes a distraction, yet its rhythm oddly comforting.

Time would pass. This would soon be over. Nick would soon be gone. She could go back to her normal life.

Think of that later.

Sondra, stunning in her black sheath despite her pallor, was called first to testify.

The whimsy's tiny cap sat back on her head, leaving its frothy veil to partly hide her face. Her skin was drawn over etched cheekbones and the makeup didn't cover bruises.

Tim gently led her through testimony, first delving into the background of her marriage to Mr. H and the deaths of her first husband and stepsons, then her remarriage to Theo.

Finally he got to the newspaper clipping she'd received the previous year. "What did you do with this clipping that stated David Harmony was coming home?"

"I burned it. We received things like that all the time. People can be spiteful."

He led her next to the discovery in the safe. "What did you see there, Mrs. Pack?"

"David's ring."

"David Harmony?"

Sondra's hand twisted a handkerchief. "Yes."

Tim checked his notes. "How do you know it was David's ring?"

"It was a family ring that James's father had bequeathed David. He wore it all the time."

"Can you describe the ring, please?"

"It was gold. It was so worn you could hardly see the plume design on top."

Tim took a pace back. "Is it possible you made a mistake, perhaps mistook another ring your husband owned for David Harmony's ring?"

"No. There was no mistaking David's ring. He always wore it. James called it the druid's ring. I saw it constantly from the time I came to nurse Olivia Harmony. Before I found it in the safe, I last saw it when James and I left to go to Washington. David was wearing it at that time."

"So you drew certain conclusions from that ring turning up in your husband's safe?"

"Yes. I knew David would never have taken that ring off unless he was unconscious," Sondra's voice broke, "or dead. I don't think he even took it off to bathe."

Tim nodded sympathetically. "Since your husband had that ring in his possession, you concluded he had removed it from David's finger?"

"I—" The tip of Sondra's tongue wet her lips. She covered them with her handkerchief.

Megan wasn't the only one who strained to hear.

From the bench, Odell was apologetic. "I'm sorry, Mrs. Pack, the court recorder didn't understand you. Please speak into the microphone."

He ought to be apologetic. This was all his fault.

Tim asked again, "Do you believe your husband took that ring from David Harmony?"

"Yes." Sondra clasped herself like she was cold.

"And that would mean that he had seen David's body before he was lost at sea? In other words, David was dead before the boat burned?"

"Yes." The microphone barely picked up Sondra's words. "He

must have been. And if that was true, Theo must have been responsible for destroying the . . ." A tear glistened on her lashes tip before slowly dropping. "For destroying the boat with the boys."

For goodness sake. Why didn't that idiot John Wilkins do something? What about this vaunted Atlanta attorney? It wouldn't hurt them to speak up, help Sondra out. Tim would listen. He might even decide he'd heard enough.

Ah, he was looking toward Odell.

Tell him to stop, Odell.

"Would you like some water, Mrs. Pack?" Odell leaned over solicitously. "I know this is upsetting, but it has to be done. Please be assured that everyone here understands and regrets most deeply that you must go through this."

Hah! There was no reason for this inquest. No reason to dig into the boys' deaths and put Sondra on the stand.

She was going to vote against Odell McNamara and she'd make Mom vote against him, too. And anyone else she could persuade.

Twenty years was too long to be coroner anyway.

Nick must have felt her shiver because he reached for her hand and held it as the bailiff handed Sondra water.

Resuming, Tim Purley walked up to the stand. "Mrs. Pack, after concluding that your husband had killed your stepsons and covered up their murders by burning the boat, did you put into motion a plan that evolved from the news clipping you received anonymously?"

"I didn't know what to do so I called Lawrence Wykerton. I knew I could trust him. I remembered the clipping and found another picture of Nick Downing in a *Life* magazine. I took it to Lawrence." She brushed at her eyes. "We discussed me finding the ring before I showed it to him. We decided to hire Nick to pretend to be David."

After whipping through the details of Nick's hiring, Tim got to the night that Theo Pack died. "He beat you, forced you to lure Nick Downing to your rooms?"

She nodded dumbly.

"I know it's hard, but please speak up. The court reporter needs to hear."

"Yes." The words were barely audible. "He hit me, made me call Nick."

"Can you tell us what happened then?"

"I had been afraid he suspected me but didn't know for sure till then. He accused me of helping Lawrence. He said he was going to get rid of Nick and me both."

"How did he intend to explain your deaths?"

She began to tremble. "He planned to say Nick attacked me

because I told him I could prove he wasn't David. He—Theo—would pretend he had caught him—Nick—in the act of shooting me and then kill Nick. After Nick agreed to come to the house, he—my husband—knocked me out. He wanted to make sure Nick was there before he, he . . . when he killed me."

She held her handkerchief to her eyes.

"He admitted this to you?" Tim's tone managed to convey dismay and sympathy.

She lowered her head. "Yes. That's why he didn't shoot Nick right away. He wanted Nick's corpse to back up his story that he fought for the gun when he found Nick standing over my body. He'd say the gun went off as they struggled, killing Nick. Nick and I would be dead. There would be no one to tell the truth about what happened."

"I see."

There was a long sigh from the spectators.

Megan gripped Nick's hand, thankful he was safe beside her with no worse injuries.

Tim checked his wristwatch. "Mrs. Pack, can you tell us what transpired later that night? After you called Nick, he agreed to come over. Is that right?"

"Yes."

"Then what happened?"

"He—"

"*He* meaning Nick or your husband?" Tim interposed.

"Theo. He had left me unconscious in my dressing room. I came to and heard the fight. I managed to get up and went out. Theo was in a frenzy, pounding on Nick. He would have killed him. I saw the revolver on the console so I picked it up and called to Theo. I just wanted him to stop."

She didn't break down, but the tears rolled. The little bailiff refilled her glass, and she took several sips.

"You had the gun and called out to your husband," prompted Tim.

"He started toward me and I . . ." Sondra's face crumpled. "I shot him."

"Had you ever used a revolver before?"

"Theo taught me. He and I occasionally do—occasionally did—target shooting."

Tim paused dramatically. "Mrs. Pack, remembering you're under oath: Did you mean to kill Theo Pack?"

"No! Never!" The whimsy's beaded veil couldn't hide her anguish. "I only wanted to make him leave Nick alone. I was so scared. He kept hitting him and hitting him."

Tim paced. "Even though you knew your husband meant to

murder you and Nick Downing in cold blood, you had no intention of killing him that night?"

Tears streamed. "I never wanted him to die, I never meant him to die. I only wanted him to quit hurting Nick. I didn't know any other way to make him stop."

Odell gave her a moment to compose herself.

Tim shifted from one foot to another until she had quieted. "Afterward . . ." He rushed through the other details of Theo's death and appeared ready to release Sondra.

Odell called him over to the bench to confer in whispers.

What was that all about? Sondra's testimony was clear. She'd said everything there was to say.

But Tim turned back. "You've been very brave, Mrs. Pack. I know you're tired, but Odell—"

"Judge McNamara!" the coroner snapped.

Tim's mouth thinned. "Judge McNamara worries that the description of the ring is too vague. You are positive the ring you saw in Theo Pack's safe belonged to your stepson David Harmony? There's no chance you were mistaken?"

"It was David's ring. There isn't a doubt in my mind."

"Will you describe the ring again, please?"

"It was a plain golden band, slightly wider in the front with a plume design. It had once been thick but was worn thin. You could barely make out the plume lines."

Tim beckoned and the bailiff pulled forward a large easel holding a paper sketch pad.

"May I ask you to draw us a picture, Mrs. Pack? So that we can see this unique ring? Make it as large as you can."

Sondra hesitated. "I'm not very good at drawing."

"That's all right. Do the best you can."

For goodness' sake. There isn't another ring in the world like that. I recognize her description perfectly. Why won't they leave her alone?

Sondra obediently stood up as if in a fog.

Oh dear. Sondra looked like she was going to fall over, but her hands moved until a rough likeness emerged of a ring with a swirl of plumes on the front.

Exactly like David's ring.

Her heart ripped open all over again. She pressed her fingers hard into her eyes to stop the tears.

When would little things stop hurting?

Nick put his arm around her shoulder. She leaned against him.

"Thank you, Mrs. Pack," Tim said when Sondra again took her seat. "I'll ask again, you are certain enough to swear in this court that this ring was in your husband's safe approximately a year ago? And that it's no longer there?"

Sondra's handkerchief went to her mouth. Her throat worked.

Megan, like the others, bent forward to catch her words.

"Yes. Sheriff Attaway had people search all our houses after Theo died, but it's gone. I'm sure Theo must have done away with it after he realized I'd found it."

"And that ring was the sole reason you concluded your husband was a murderer?"

"Yes," she whispered, new tears shining.

"And so emphatic was this belief that he was a murderer, so certain were you that he murdered David Harmony and his brother, that you came up with a plan to prove it and carried the plan through with Lawrence Wykerton's help?"

Her head wobbled as if she would deny it. "Yes."

"Thank you, Mrs. Pack. That'll be all. I'm very sorry to put you through this."

As she started out of the witness stand, she stumbled, evoking a gasp from the audience. She clung to the rail enclosing the front and side of the witness section.

Tim and Amos Lovett both jumped to help her back to her seat. Their row reshuffled itself until she was ensconced between Amos and Dungoode, with John by the aisle.

On the other side of Nick, George sat back down from where he'd risen. Wanting to get to Sondra.

Poor George. Sondra might be a widow and available again, but she'd never end up with someone like him.

Like Megan would never end up with Nick.

CHAPTER 39

"When Somebody Loses (Then Somebody Wins)"
As Performed by Bumble Bee Slim (1936)
With Myrtle Jenkins on Piano
And Casey Bill Weldon on Guitar
Music by Bumble Bee Slim
Lyrics by Bumble Bee Slim

LAWRENCE WYKERTON, AGGRAVATED beyond reason at being dragged into this mess but resigned to the inevitable, was next on the stand. After swearing to tell the truth, he checked his bowtie, smoothed his coat lapels, laid his hands on his lap, and tried to relax.

He wished he had never seen Nick Downing.

The scoundrel.

"What did you think when Sondra Pack told you about the ring?" Tim Purley was a competent attorney, but Lawrence still resented being questioned by a boy who'd worked for his firm and who'd dated his daughter in high school.

Get hold of yourself.

The last thing he could afford was to commit perjury.

A representative of the state bar had already called about an appointment regarding his part in this sorry affair. Depending on the results, his petition to remain executor until the Trust got settled was up in the air.

After thinking through Tim's question, he gave a precise answer. "I knew David would never have given his ring to Theo nor did I believe he would willingly have taken it off."

Tim glanced at his watch.

Humph. He must be eager to get done by lunch.

Lowering his wrist, Tim leaned back against his table. "Because of the ring, you drew the same conclusions as Mrs. Pack? That Theo Pack had murdered David?"

Lawrence considered his answer. "When she came to me saying she had seen David's ring, I concluded that. Yes."

"So you researched the background of Nick Downing and went to England to hire him?"

Lawrence mulled it over. "At Mrs. Pack's instigation. Yes. That is correct."

Tim straightened up, raised and lowered himself on the balls of his feet. "Did you coach Mr. Downing so that he could come in and pretend to be David Harmony?"

Lawrence took a lengthy moment to inspect the ceiling. "I did coach him. Yes."

Tim barely waited for his answer. "Then Mr. Downing portrayed himself to Theo Pack and everyone else as David Harmony?"

"Ahem." He chose his words carefully. "We told everyone he was David Harmony. Yes."

Tim rocked from one foot to the other during Lawrence's unhurried response. "So if David Harmony proved to be alive, that meant Theo Pack would lose out on the Harmony estate?"

Lawrence stared into space. "A good portion of it. All the surviving beneficiaries would still receive their original shares. But James's will left everything other than individual bequests to his sons. Or a surviving son, which meant Theo and Sondra would lose the bulk of the estate."

"Can you tell us the value of the Trust?"

What impudence! That was no one's business but his. "It would be difficult. You'd have to allow for the uncertainty of the stock market and then so much is in property, the value of which can only be estimated, and businesses, which vary according—"

"An approximate figure is all we require."

Damn and blast. Odell had put Tim up to this! Well, no way out.

The amount caused astounded murmurs from the spectators.

"Thank you. You're excused."

It was over. He hadn't perjured himself.

He hopped up and hurriedly pushed out the swinging gate separating the witness chair and bench from the courtroom. Before he reached his seat, the next witness was being called.

"Nicholas Simeon Downing."

He waited at the end of the pew while Nick squeezed past Megan.

Once in the aisle, Nick paused and raised both brows as if in question. "Well?"

Lawrence borrowed Nick's half-shrug.

A little late to be asking guidance now. Not that he'd listen anyway. *Damn the man. I wish I'd never seen him.*

He was tired and felt every minute of his age. This whole situation seemed likely to haunt him forever. Sometimes there was no coming out ahead.

"I shall retire," he muttered to Megan as the impertinent rogue took the witness chair.

She swiveled her head to stare at him.

"If and when this is resolved, I shall retire and learn bridge and raise a vegetable garden and have nothing to do with law ever again."

Megan made a skeptical noise. "Does that mean I'll get a raise?"

Odell McNamara silenced them with a stern glance.

****

"The Great Pretender"
As Performed by the Platters (1955)
Music by Buck Ram
Lyrics by Buck Ram

NICK DOWNING HELD up his hand to be sworn in. This was going to be tricky.

Two years ago he would have dared anything. Without a second thought, he would have laughed at the odds and let the devil take care of his own.

Two years ago he'd had nothing to lose.

The District Attorney intoned, "The evidence that you shall give this inquest on behalf of the State of Georgia, concerning the death of Theodore Rhodes Pack, shall be the truth, the whole truth, and nothing but the truth. So help you God."

"So help me God," Nick echoed.

The truth. He actually preferred the truth, but he was adept at bending or breaking it. Still, plunging into deep water with no life preserver was never his style. He was reckless, not suicidal.

From the looks of him, Whitey had abandoned him.

In a few minutes, he was pretty sure Megan would, too.

There was still time to change his mind.

But he wouldn't. He couldn't. Not if he wanted to live without regrets. Not if he wanted any kind of life with her.

"State your name, please."

"My legal name or my stage name?"

"Your legal name, please."

Nick Downing took a deep breath.

There's no way out now, you prat. Will Megan ever forgive me?

Ah, well. In for a penny . . .

"My legal name is David Paine Harmony."

Shocked faces. Stunned silence. Pretty much what he'd expected.

Then comprehension dawned. An excited buzz began and spread as people mumbled to the neighboring seats, to the people in front and back. Even across the aisle.

The district attorney lost his pomposity. "I—you—" He stabbed his finger at Nick. "This courtroom is not a place for frivolity."

"Heaven forbid there should be frivolity."

The yokel coroner leaned over and peered down at him, eyes wide as his mouth. "Young man—"

"I'm not young though I am sometimes frivolous. But right now I've no intention of being frivolous."

Oops. Not the time for jokes. Sincere, that's the ticket.

"I have sworn to tell the truth and I am doing so."

He looked up at the coroner, he looked over at Sondra Harmony, and finally he looked at a puzzled Megan.

Darling Meggie. Would she ever trust him again?

"I am David Paine Harmony."

CHAPTER 40

"Everybody's Somebody's Fool"
As Performed by Connie Francis (1960)
Music by Jack Keller and Howard Greenfield
Lyrics by Jack Keller and Howard Greenfield

NO! NO, NO, NO!

Megan sat frozen. The rest of the courtroom spectators shifted in their seats and whispered furiously, but she couldn't breathe.

What on earth was Nick doing?

Lawrence!

Lawrence was behind this.

He'd petitioned to extend his executorship of the Trust. Had he meant Nick to claim the money all along? Were he and Nick conspirators? Had she been a fool to trust either of them?

Beside her, Lawrence watched the aisle. One hand was clenched.

She tugged at his coat sleeve. "Did you know he was going to do this?"

"I rather hoped he would end up taking the easy way out."

The easy way out? What did that mean?

Megan followed Lawrence's glance toward Sondra Pack.

Sondra's lips, nearly recovered from her beating, had parted in confusion. When Parrish Dungoode, the attorney from Atlanta, spoke to her urgently, she stared at Nick. Even when she shook her head at Dungoode, she couldn't take her eyes off Nick.

The noisy courtroom muffled her words, but Megan could understand enough.

"No. No . . . can't be David . . . an actor, for chrissake . . . hired him to . . ."

Sondra wasn't in on whatever Nick was doing.

On the other side of Sondra, Amos Lovett gaped at Nick, then Sondra, then Nick again.

John Wilkins conferred with Dungoode.

At the far end of the pew, Linda and the unknown attorney looked shell-shocked.

Nick remained perfectly at ease, so much in command of himself that Odell Macnamara opened his mouth but paused to reconsider.

Then he banged his gavel for quiet and leaned over. "Young man,

I may be a coroner but you don't want to mess with me. David Harmony's fingerprints are on record with the sheriff's department. We can have one of his people come in and fingerprint you."

Nick didn't look at Megan nor had he after reasserting his identity. "That would be my own suggestion. It'll have to be done anyway, I'm sure."

Odell's neck stiffened. "Then we'll take a short recess and set things up. I hope you're aware you can be charged with perjury."

"Quite aware. That's why I'm trying to avoid it."

"Humph," said Lawrence beside Megan.

He sounded disgusted, not like he was behind this.

But Nick couldn't be doing this on his own.

Unless she'd been wrong about him. Maybe he'd been after the money all along.

When Nick came through the swinging gate that separated the witness stand from the attorney area, Megan scooted past Lawrence's knees to get out.

Lawrence pulled at her coat. "Megan—"

She jerked away. "This has gone too far, Lawrence."

Then Nick was at the end of the pew.

"What d'you think you're doing? Nick, how could you?"

"Megan, if there had been any other way out, I would have taken it. Believe me, I would have done anything to spare you this. I wanted to tell you, but I was afraid."

"Afraid?" Her voice rose. "With your brass?"

"Megan—"

"Oh, pack it! I should have known better than to believe anything you said. Don't come crying to me after you land in jail. I never want to see you again."

Pushing him aside with both hands, she rushed out.

Forgetting her purse and music box, she couldn't exit the heavy swinging doors fast enough.

****

"I'm Leaving It All Up to You"
As Performed by Dale and Grace (1963)
Music by Don Harris and Dewey Terry, Jr.
Lyrics by Don Harris and Dewey Terry, Jr.

NICK WATCHED HER march out of the courtroom.

That's torn it.

Just as he'd feared.

As the aisle started filling up with people too excited to stay in their seats, he started to follow but Whitey caught his arm. "Stay here,

Nick. I'll speak to her." He rose, calling over his shoulder. "Save our seats, George."

Would she listen to Whitey? "Get her to give me just ten minutes. Five."

"Why should I?"

"Because you owe me. Please."

Whitey sighed. "Oh my. I'll try." He brushed past.

Leaving Nick easy prey for a furious Amos Lovett who grabbed his arm and jerked him around. "I don't know what you're trying to pull, but you won't get away with it. You can't carry on like this when everyone knows who you really are." A finger poked Nick's chest. "I plan to be in the front row when you go to jail for perjury."

Nick stared at the offending finger so hard that Lovett thought better and stepped back.

Good thing, too.

Nick uncurled his fists. "That sure I'm lying, eh?" He snorted. "A smart man would wait for the results from this fingerprint test they're about to administer. It'll corroborate my identity."

"You're a two-bit actor with no sense of decency! I'd like to break your neck."

"Ouch. And here I pride myself on being rather good at my profession. Talk about being put in one's place."

Lovett turned red and stalked away.

Nick took his seat on the hard pew beside George to wait for the fingerprint technician's arrival. George edged away from him, crowding Hal and Danny.

Wondering what's going on. Worried about his reputation, most likely. Afraid he'll be caught up in a scandal with a squalid thief.

Poor weak George would never be the man his father was.

Distress brought color to Sondra's cheeks, making her look less a grieving widow and more the sexy bird she was. Lovely eyes narrowed when she caught Nick staring.

He hummed.

Don't count your chickens yet, honey-chile.

From behind, he could pick out from the excited hum what people were murmuring.

"Do you think this actor's in it by himself?"

"No, Wykerton's hired him."

"Him and the Wykertons are planning to loot the Harmony Trust."

"I don't believe that. I know Lawrence Wykerton and he's as straight as they come!"

"Ha! The Wykertons been stealing it blind all these years. Ever since Harmony died."

"The girl friend isn't in on it, is she?"

"He's fooled her, too."

"Look at the widow."

"Aw, that pore thing. Bet now she wishes she'd shot *him*, too."

"Wasn't him and her having an affair?"

"That woman lawyer and Theo Pack, you mean?"

"No, the actor and Sondra Pack."

"I didn't know that! How'd you find that out?"

"They've all deserted him. There he is, setting by his lonesome."

Ah, the value of scandal! Such interest cheered Nick immeasurably. An actor's livelihood depends on publicity, and he would certainly have lots of that the next few days.

If his agent didn't come up with a juicy movie contract out of this, he'd find a new agent.

Satisfaction faded.

If only things could have been different.

But they weren't. His fault. Everything could have gone as Whitey planned. But that meant a whitewash with his part minimized.

You hound. You wanted all the attention. Admit it.

He had anticipated Megan's reaction—surely she would forgive him once she understood how much this meant to him—but it hurt all the same. So much neater to have announced who he was and let everybody swoon with delight and accept him and welcome him. So much nicer if Megan had been so happy to have her David back she would have forgiven him anything.

Could he stand having three people in this relationship?

A strange woman in secretarial gray touched his sleeve. "Mr. Wykerton wants you."

Real life was never as neat as movies. That's what he loved so much about acting.

He followed the woman to where Whitey stood at a door marked Solicitor's Office.

"Thank you, Wynette," Whitey told the woman. At Nick's querying brow, he said, "The solicitor's secretary. She agreed to step out so you and Megan can speak in private."

"She'll talk to me then? What did you tell her?"

"That I trust you. I've not gone into details." He sniffed. "That's your affair."

"All right. Thanks."

This would decide his future. For good or bad.

Inside the small office, Megan's elbows rested on a tatty secretarial desk while she held a cup of coffee with both hands. Her mouth was stretched thin.

Not a good sign.

She ignored him. That wasn't promising either.

He took a chair across from her. "Megan, I'm sorry."

"Lawrence reminded me the fingerprint evidence can't be faked in court." She concentrated on the coffee cup. "I don't know what either of you is up to but I'm tired."

"I can't blame you."

She set her jaw. "I'm not made for intrigue."

"I know. I'm sorry. But last night you came damned close to telling me you loved me. Me, Nick Downing. Despite what I am. If I had come up today and said my name was John Smith, would that have changed your mind?"

Threatened tears puckered her face, like a painting blurred by grime. She rested her elbows on the desk, put her face in her hands. "I don't know anything anymore. I thought you were David and I was so happy, even if I was angry with you for going away. And then I found out you were Nick and I hated you because you were pretending to be David and I wanted so much to have him back."

She searched one pocket of her coat, didn't find what she sought and tried the other pocket. "Only by then I was already half in love with you. And I understood what you and Lawrence planned because of what Theo did to the boys. But now you say—no, you're swearing!—that you're David and it's starting all over again and I don't know what to believe anymore. Whether Lawrence is after Mr. H's money. Or whether you're trying to get it. Whether you're working together. I don't know, Nick."

He ought to have told her. Was it worth losing her? Too late. "Believe in yourself. Believe in yourself and your own instincts. But please, believe in me just a little longer."

A tear trembled, but she brushed it away impatiently. A lamentable watercolor of a ship interested her immensely.

Anything not to face him.

"Megan, you said a lot of things yesterday. And so did I. I meant everything I said. Perhaps our life won't be what you envisioned, but we'll be together."

He saw a box of tissues on a credenza, got up, and brought it back to her.

She snatched one and blew her nose hard.

The mundane act brought out more protectiveness than tears. He couldn't bear losing her. Even if he didn't deserve her.

"Megan." How best to approach this? "The boy you loved could never have become the man I am. You know that logically, but deep in your heart, do you understand it?"

She frowned, trying to sort out what he was saying. "So you aren't David."

"David Harmony might have been a nice kid. I don't know. I do know that he could never have turned into a man like me."

"Nick," she began.

He leaned over the table and put a finger against her lips to hush her. "Please. Hear me out."

She didn't pull back.

"Listen, Megan." He wanted her with her eyes open, seeing him for what he was. "If life had been what it should have been, you and David would have married, traveled, played, had a good life. He would have gone to work with his father, and you and he would have had three children and a dog and bought a station wagon to cart them around the mainland."

She brushed his hand away from her lips.

But she was listening.

"That didn't happen. Now it can't happen. And I'm not that boy you loved. I've done things your David wouldn't have done. Some I did to survive, but I still did them."

She screwed up her face. "Why are you pretending you're him?"

"I have to do this." He bent over, wanting to take her hand but afraid to. "I'm begging you to believe in me. Just for a little while longer."

"Why should I?"

"I love you." He wished he knew what to say. "I've been alone for a long time. I never knew, never realized, not till Whitey showed me your photograph last year, what I was waiting for. It was you, Meggie. Is it very conceited to think that you've been waiting for me, too?"

She pulled out a fresh tissue, but she didn't turn away.

"I can't be the David you loved. I'll never be him. You have to take me for what I am. And most of it isn't pretty. I've told you some of my past. There's more of the same, I'm afraid."

She wouldn't be diverted. "But why are you still lying? And under oath? Nick, you're committing perjury." She looked down. "I can't deal with this. I just can't."

This was useless.

She was never going to get past that boy.

He pushed his chair back. "I know I've lied to you. I never wanted to. You were supposed to be gone till this thing was over. I wanted to meet you after, get to know you, court you. But life doesn't always follow plans. That's why I don't make them."

Getting up, he paced as much as the small room would allow. "I won't lie to you once this is through. I might be selfish and inconsiderate and overbearing, but I'll never lie to you again. And I'll love you. I'll always love you."

She snuffled, blew her nose. Downcast lashes patterned her cheek.

One more try.

He leaned over the desk. "When this is done, I want you to go away with me. I want us to be together, Megan."

"You're asking too much."

"We could be happy. But only if you take me for what I am and not a replacement for some unformed boy you loved years ago. Think about it. Please."

She shook her head. "My life is here."

"I understand that. But mine isn't. I could never be happy here."

That startled her into looking up. "You enjoyed the last few days."

"With you, yes. But you're tied up in good memories here, Megan. While I . . ." He swallowed. "I'm not. I want more. Please understand that."

She straightened a folder on the desk.

This wasn't going to work.

A concrete block settled on his chest.

He should have known better. A woman like her needed a straight-arrow man, something he'd forgotten how to be.

Maybe he'd never known.

"I'd better get back. Think about what I said, Megan. I may not be your David, but I love you. I want you but you've got to accept me as I am. It's your decision."

He left, closing the door gently.

She didn't call him back.

He'd lost.

His Megan was far too sensible to take up with someone like him.

Probably for the best, too. She deserved better than a temperamental actor who gallivanted from place to place and did whatever took his fancy.

So why did he feel like a piano had dropped on him?

He took his time going back, stopping at the loo and dawdling at the water fountain.

Better get back into his role before being recalled to the stand.

He was halfway down the crowded hall, weaving through the curious people lining the way to the courtroom, when a door behind him opened.

"Nick!"

Her voice. He spun.

Megan, pale but decisive, stood in front of the solicitor's office. "I have a cat."

What was she talking about? "I know."

"I have a cat. I don't need a dog."

Three children and a dog.

"Bring the bloody cat with you."

"All right." She looked scared to death. "I will."

Balloons carried up his heart. Helium balloons. "Then that's all right."

They stood, grinning like fools, fifteen feet apart but in perfect accord, while a stream of people goggled and parted to get around them.

A bailiff came up. "You're needed in the courtroom, Mr. Downing."

"I've got to get back," he told her.

"Of course you do." Her smile was shaky. "You've made me lose whatever sense I had but it doesn't seem to matter."

"I've never had any sense either. So we're a perfect match, aren't we?"

CHAPTER 41

WHILE NICK MET with Megan, Lawrence shared coffee with Odell Macnamara and Tim Purley.

"I blame you for this entire fiasco, Lawrence!" Odell thundered. "If I hadn't let you talk me into this, we wouldn't be in this pickle! Is he or is he not David Harmony?"

As if it was Lawrence's fault. Confound Nick Downing.

"I have no idea."

Tim looked from one to the other. "Then what am I to do?"

"I would suggest you let Wadley's people do their job by taking his fingerprints," Lawrence said, "and then continue with the questioning."

Odell's chin dropped. "Without finding out who this fellow is?"

"Ahem. All you're interested in is what happened when Theo died, isn't it? Who this man is, or is not, has nothing to do with Theo's death. It's practically irrelevant."

"Irrelevant? The man's lying!" Odell ranted. "If you hadn't hired this actor, if you hadn't insisted on a coroner's inquest . . . This is all your doing!"

Tim Purley, too, was anxious. "I've never had anything like this happen in the entire time I've been district attorney. I've never even heard of anything like this happening. What are we going to do? Lawrence, you need to figure out how we're going to come out of this without egg on our faces."

He couldn't blame Tim or Odell for jumping on him. When he finally soothed them down and returned to his seat beside a chipper Nick, he was frazzled. By that time, fingerprints had been duly taken, and two sheriff's analysts in the courtroom pored over the results.

After taking the bench, Odell barked at them: "What did you find?"

Their heads turned in unison. One hemmed. The other hawed.

Lawrence was pretty sure they wouldn't issue a blanket yea or nay. But there was always a chance he was wrong.

He wasn't.

"It's difficult to say right away," said the first analyst.

"They could match, Your Honor," said the second.

"But I'm afraid we'll need more advanced analysis to make absolutely certain."

"And that means the state lab."

Lawrence relaxed. For years, at Rotary meetings, Wadley had railed about his inept fingerprint people always needing the state lab to interpret prints. It appeared his plaints still held true.

"Ode—Your Honor." Tim Purley was still baffled. "This means we may need more time. Can we call a recess for a week or so?"

"It may take longer than that to send this to Atlanta and have 'em check it out," the first analyst said bluntly.

The other snorted. "Even for rushes it can take a month. They stay behind up there."

Odell pondered, cleared his throat, then latched onto the seed Lawrence had planted amid all the breast-beating and finger-pointing during the brief recess in chambers. "The question of who this man is, or is not, is irrelevant to what's going on here today."

Lawrence relaxed. Odell knew how vital the right decision was for his career.

Pompous old fool. At least he had the sense to use my argument. He looks surprised at how knowledgeable he sounds. I most assuredly am.

Gaining confidence, Odell said, "We're simply trying to get at the truth of Theo Pack's death and decide whether to ask the grand jury for an indictment in the matter. For now, we'll hold off on the question of who Nick Downing is and assume he'll tell the truth as to what happened on the night of Theo Pack's death. Resume your questioning."

"Oh come on, Odell!" Tim spread his hands. "You can't—"

The gavel pounded. "That's *Your Honor* to you, and resume the questioning."

As Sondra and her attorneys conferred in frantic whispers, Nick passed through the gate to the witness stand. Tim led him over his acceptance of Lawrence's proposal and the imposture that led up to the night Theo was killed.

"When Sondra insisted I come alone, I knew he'd be waiting. He was. He admitted before he attacked me that he'd done away with the Harmony boys."

Nick shifted in the padded witness chair.

Tim was wary. "He attacked you without provocation?"

"Yes. No warning whatsoever."

"What happened then?"

"I defended myself. Then I heard Sondra call out to Theo."

"She had not been present up until then?"

"I didn't see her."

"What happened after she called out?" Tim, confidence returning, picked up a legal pad.

"Theo stopped hitting me and stepped back. He looked at Sondra. She shot him. The bullet caught him in the vicinity of the heart."

"He went down immediately?"

"It was a Colt .45 Buntline Special. He wasn't going to break into a tap dance."

Lawrence choked. Confound the man. He couldn't be serious if his life depended on it.

"Limit yourself to yes and no, please," Tim snapped. "What happened next?"

"Sondra collapsed. She had blood on her face and gown. I thought she was dead or dying. My bodyguards had followed me from the cottage and came in about that time. They rushed to see about her and I went to Theo."

"Was Pack still alive?"

"For a moment."

"Was he conscious?"

"Yes."

"Did he say anything to you?"

The spectators leaned forward hopefully.

"To me? Not really."

An audible sigh of disappointment floated in the air. The audience sat back.

"Did you say anything to him?"

Ah. Nick's matter-of-fact answers gave Tim the confidence to fire off questions again.

Nick remained cooperative. "He'd previously admitted he'd murdered Robby and, as he believed, me as well. Before he jumped on me. So when he got shot, I asked him why he'd done it. He looked past me to where Sondra was recovering from her faint. He tried to say something. My ears were still ringing from the shot, but I managed to understand it. 'Sondra,' he said, and then he died."

Tim's relief was palpable. "So you corroborate Mrs. Pack's account of the death of her husband? That it was unavoidable as she defended herself and you?"

Nick drew himself up and turned to Odell. "I do not!"

Oh, that man. He'd turned this into a movie melodrama. Why couldn't he behave like a normal person? What a disaster.

But everyone, including Lawrence, held their breath after Nick's ringing denial.

Nick didn't disappoint. "I believe Sondra Pack intentionally murdered her husband in a premeditated fashion as the culmination of a deliberate and elaborate plot that included my posing as David Harmony and her posing as the innocent victim of circumstances."

Once the spectators absorbed the meaning of his words, the courtroom erupted into pandemonium for a second time.

CHAPTER 42

"I Will Follow Him"
As Performed by Little Peggy March (1963)
Music by Franck Pourcel AKA J. W. Stole
and Paul Mauriat AKA Del Roma
English Lyrics by Norman Gimbel
and Arthur Altman

MEGAN, STRANGELY CALM after agreeing to go with Nick, sat quietly during Nick's testimony. Even the stomachache she'd come to expect whenever she'd said *yes* to a man was absent.

She felt as certain of this as anything she'd ever done.

Once she'd refused to run away with David; if she had, he might still be alive. Given another chance with Nick, she would not risk losing him, too.

So she waited patiently as he'd begged, hoping he knew what he was doing.

And then his bombshell.

Sondra? Sondra had deliberately shot Theo?

But Sondra had loved Theo.

"There will be order in this courtroom," Odell Macnamara called, hammering his gavel. No one within earshot, not even the bailiffs, paid him the slightest attention. "THERE WILL BE ORDER! Or I will have this courtroom cleared. Bailiff!"

The noise subsided as if a switch had been pulled.

Settling back after giving the crowd a malevolent stare, Odell turned to the witness. "We are not interested in your opinions, Mr., Mr., uh, Mr. Downing. Please confine yourself strictly to the facts at hand."

"Certainly, Your Honor." Nick, in the padded witness chair, remained oblivious to the astonished eyes glued to him. "I'll be happy to stick to facts. How's this? Sondra Pack shot Theo Pack because he was drinking heavily, and she was terrified he would reveal the truth about the deaths of her first husband and stepsons."

What truth? Mr. H? Had Theo planned Mr. H's death, too? Did Sondra know?

Megan turned to Lawrence.

Lawrence, unblinking, watched Sondra. A thin layer of perspiration lined his upper lip.

The gavel hammered again as clamor in the courtroom intensified.

When order was restored, Odell sourly gave one final warning to the crowd. "Bailiffs, unless these spectators can control themselves, prepare to clear the room." Then to Nick: "And unless you want to be held in contempt of court, sir, answer the questions you are asked and stop speculating. This is no place for theatrics. Stick to facts."

"I'll try to do better, Your Honor." Nick hung his head contritely, hiding the twinkle.

Nick, Nick. What are you doing?

Odell knitted his brows suspiciously, then nodded to Tim. "Go ahead, then."

Bald head sweating, the hapless Tim plodded to the witness chair.

Poor Tim. If he had hair, he'd be yanking it out.

Because of the prominent people involved, he would have researched every detail of this case and studied it with painstaking care. Now a cut-and-dried affair had turned into smoke. First Nick claimed to be David Harmony, and now he was saying Sondra Pack had murdered her husband.

Tim hadn't the slightest idea of who was who or what was what.

Just like me. Only I don't care anymore. She wanted to laugh. *No, I can't give way to hysterics. Just like a woman, they'd say.*

She clamped her teeth together.

Odell's glacial demeanor bespoke a lack of sympathy for Tim or Nick. "Get on with it."

Tim cleared his throat. "I, I . . . . Are you saying Mrs. Pack deliberately shot her husband?"

"As ordered by the court, let's consider the facts." Nick remained composed. "When she first came out, she picked up the gun and called his name. Theo stepped back. Away from me."

As Tim tried to work it out, Nick waited expectantly.

Impatience won out. "Don't you see? If Theo had intended to kill me, he would never have stepped away from me. He would have held on to me, used me as a shield. Or he would have rushed over to take the gun from Sondra. But he didn't do any of those things. He simply stepped off to the side. And that had to be because he was leaving Sondra room for a clear shot."

"Your Honor."

Across the aisle, Atlanta attorney Parrish Dungoode got slowly to his feet and began to earn his fees. "I must object. This testimony, from some person whose identity we can't even prove, is opinion and nothing more. It amounts to slander of my client."

You can't say anything! Megan almost blurted. Neither Tim nor Odell remonstrated against Dungoode's interruption, the twerps.

Didn't they know the law? Odell had an excuse, but Tim Purley was the district attorney. He ought to have read up on it.

Odell considered. "A coroner's inquest is actually just an informal process. The verdict has no binding powers on the grand jury. We'll go into it a little further."

Tim, who had brightened, drooped. He turned back to Nick. "A clear shot," he repeated. "Are you saying Theo Pack knew his wife was going to shoot him and gave her room to do it?"

"Theo wasn't giving her a clear shot at himself."

How very patient Nick is being.

Megan almost giggled. She dug her nails into her palms.

"He was giving her a clear shot at me," Nick said. "Theo thought Sondra was going to shoot me and was shocked when she shot him instead. She betrayed him."

"Conjecture!" Parrish Dungoode popped up again. "Pure conjecture, Your Honor. You can't allow this."

Two seats down from him, between Amos and Linda, Sondra Pack sat perfectly still, back ramrod straight, lips tight. Beneath her net whimsy, her forehead creased.

Nick must be certain to be perjuring himself like this. Was it true? Had Sondra killed Theo deliberately?

Odell hesitated, longer than he had before. His gaze found Lawrence beseechingly.

Lawrence shifted his head so as to aim a stern glare at Dungoode. His indignant chin signaled disapproval, his open mouth disbelief at Dungoode's audacity.

Maybe Odell would take the hint.

Odell looked away. "This isn't a trial," he finally said, "or even a hearing. This is merely an attempt to discover the truth. This man was there on the scene. We'll assume he's giving his honest impressions about what happened. Let him continue."

He pointed his gavel at Dungoode and said in a stronger voice. "And be so good as to pass any objections you have through the district attorney. I won't have you busting out in the courtroom whenever you feel like it."

Good. He'd noticed Lawrence's glare.

Tim paced. "Doesn't it seem strange, Mr., ah, ah. Doesn't it seem strange that Mrs. Pack, who hired you to prove her husband a murderer, should be conspiring with him to kill you?"

"Not if the two of them had plotted and carried out the murders of my father and my brother Robert."

More gasps from the pews. Megan's urge to laugh fled. Cold seeped up her back.

Sondra and Theo?

"And not if Sondra was afraid Theo was drinking so much he might let something slip to the wrong person about what they'd done."

He doffed a nonexistent hat to Sondra, who stared back stonily. Enthusiasm crept in. "It was really an excellent scheme. Theo thought she was working with *him* to kill *me* so they could collect the Harmony fortune. Lawrence Wykerton would swear she was working with *him* to prove *Theo* was a murderer. I would swear that Theo was trying to kill *me* when she shot *him*. Everyone would agree she had acted in self-defense. With Theo in the ground, no one would ever find out about their crimes. And she'd collect most of my father's money."

A secretive smile played on his lips. "Except she didn't know I'm really David Harmony. It's rather sad, isn't it? She went to all this trouble for nothing."

Sondra, between Amos Lovett and Linda, sat stony-faced. What was she thinking?

"Your Honor." Parrish Dungoode stood, hands spread wide in tolerant disbelief. "My client deserves better than to be besmirched by some cheap imposter trying to cash in on the Harmony name and fortune. She has lost a beloved husband—"

Odell walloped his gavel. "Go through the district attorney if you have questions, Mr. Dungoode. You're out of order."

"I can prove Sondra Pack lied." Nick projected his words over Odell's. "On this very witness stand, she lied about an important piece of evidence that her whole story rests on."

Even those people in the very back of the courtroom could hear.

Odell put his gavel down while Dungoode, abandoning his gentlemanly stance, waved his arms. "Your Honor, we'll sue this man for slander if he continues insinuating my client is a perjurer and murderess." He wagged his finger furiously at Odell. "If this court can't control this witness—"

Oh my. Wrong thing to say.

Odell wouldn't like an outsider telling him what to do, especially an arrogant Atlantan.

Odell didn't. "Don't threaten this court. You may be a big man where you're from, Mr. Dungoode, but you're in my courtroom now. I promise I'll have you removed if there's one more outburst." A hand flapped. "It's your call, Tim." He leaned over to examine Nick as if he were a particularly ugly reptile.

"My call?" Tim protested before recollecting his position. "Er, thank you, Your Honor." He smoothed his coat. "All right, we'll continue. Mr., ah, Mr. . . ." He ran a finger under his tie like it was too tight. "You say Sondra Pack lied about an important piece of evidence in this case. What piece of evidence are you speaking of?"

"The ring," Nick said promptly. "Sondra Pack never saw that ring in her husband's safe because it was never there. Theo never had it."

"Never had it? If that's true, then she had no reason for hiring you to prove her husband a murderer." Tim laboriously sorted it out. "Yet she did hire you."

How had Tim ever gotten to be district attorney?

Nick didn't once show irritation "I've given you the reason she hired me. Because she wanted to rid herself of her husband, an accomplice who was becoming a liability."

"All right." Tim ignored Dungoode's furious hand. "All right. Let me ask this: How do you know Mrs. Pack did not see that ring in her husband's possession?"

"Because I'm David Harmony. I know where that ring is. And I know where it's been for the past seventeen years. It was never for one moment in Theo Pack's possession."

A buzz broke out, but Odell's previous reprimands had their effect. The raised gavel scotched the faintest whispers. No one wanted to be thrown out.

The gavel lowered without rapping.

Tim looked from Odell to Nick and back to Odell.

Lawrence murmured, "I'm glad I'm not in Tim's shoes. Thank heavens it's almost over."

Was it? What was going on inside that white head? What had he convinced Nick to do? Nick had asked her to believe in him, and she'd said she would, but dear God, she hoped he wasn't about to do something that would put him in jail.

Not when she'd finally decided he was what she wanted.

Tim waited for Nick, who was smoothing his sleeve. "Can you tell us where the ring is?"

"Certainly. Shouldn't I tell the whole story, though? I mean, beginning with the night my father died?"

"Odell, I, I, I mean, Your Honor?" Tim threw up his hands, looked around, threw them up again. "I've never had a hearing disintegrate like this. What do you want to do?"

Odell didn't hesitate. "This ain't a formal inquiry. It's just an attempt to get at the facts. We'll let Mr., uh, Downing continue under advisement."

"Thank you, Your Honor." Nick took a deep breath. "The night my father died, the phone rang. Theo answered. After the first hello, he didn't say much. I didn't pay attention once I found out the call wasn't for me."

He aimed a mischievous smile toward Odell. "You know how boys are."

Odell scowled.

Duly reprimanded, Nick turned back to the front. "When Theo hung up, he seemed different. Wound up. He said he needed a relaxer. That's what he called his martinis. He asked if I wanted one, too, which was strange."

He straightened a handkerchief in his coat pocket. "He knew Dad wouldn't approve. My father was quite strict about some things. We often argued about how strict he was."

His expression clouded, as if recalling matters better forgotten. "I rather see his side of things now that I'm older."

"So you accepted the martini?"

"At sixteen? Sure. I felt pretty grown-up that Theo offered it. Gin tastes gawdawful, though. Still don't like it. But I nursed that one till he turned his back and I got a chance to get rid of it. At that time, the conservatory and pool area were open to the outside, and there was a palm in a circle of dirt at the pool's edge by where I was sitting. It was pretty easy to dump it."

The palm by the pool. She hadn't thought about that tree in years. It had been removed when the Packs took over and enclosed the inside pool for air conditioning.

Lawrence must have told him about it. No, Lawrence made him watch those home movies Miss Livvy always took. He saw it in them.

Parrish Dungoode did not get to his feet. "Objection. I see no connection—"

"Overruled." Odell pointed his gavel. "And keep quiet. I won't tell you again. Bailiff, stand by Mr. Dungoode's pew and escort him out the next time he so much as opens his mouth."

Odell, settling back in his seat, was as caught up in Nick's story as anyone else.

Nick smiled angelically. "The martini had something in it. I guess if I'd drunk the whole thing I might not be here today. Anyway, whatever it was still put me to sleep."

He absently swiveled his witness chair back and forth, fastening on Sondra as if waiting for her to contradict him. "The last thing I remember was sitting in the conservatory by the pool. The next thing I knew I was lying on the floor in the cabin of the cruiser, hurting all over like crazy. I couldn't figure out why I was there. I woke up enough to get off the boat but still didn't realize Theo had put me there. It was cool and I felt woozy. I curled up in a pile of tarpaulins in the corner and dozed till someone stepped on the ramp. The hinge always squeaked. It woke me up."

The hinge. How did he know that?

He'd seen the tarps when they took the sailboat out.

Did the ramp still squeak? It must. That was the explanation.

"I was burrowed down in the tarps, but I could see."

There was not a sound in the courtroom. Spectators, Sondra and Tim Purley among them, listened raptly.

Odell lay back in his chair; his lids were down but no one believed he dozed.

"I saw Theo carrying something. At the cruiser, he dropped it and I could see . . . It was my brother Robert. I saw him, his face . . ."

His voice broke.

One of the spectators gasped; Odell's eyes flew open.

Nick's color had faded. She could see his hard swallow. No wonder Nick bragged he was an award-winning actor.

Odell interposed. "Do you want to take a break?"

"No," Nick said sharply. "I want this told now."

Across the aisle, Sondra was shaking her head vehemently in answer to something Dungoode was saying.

He picked at his sleeve, but his voice was steady. "I knew Robby was dead. He had this glazed stare like I'd seen on our dog after he died."

He shivered. "I cowered in the tarps till the cruiser started up and pulled out. I waited a few minutes to give him a chance to clear the inlet before I came out. I was so scared, I was wide-awake. I couldn't think of anything but getting to Dad."

"Your father was dead," Tim objected.

"I didn't know that," Nick snapped. "Theo hadn't said anything about Dad. I realize now that's what the phone call was, but at that time I didn't know. May I have some water, please?"

He had turned absolutely white.

Megan knew he was acting, but for a moment, he had her wondering if his story was true.

Strange how calm she was while he perjured himself.

No matter.

She loved him, whoever he was or whatever he was doing. That left no choice but to believe in him, to let him play out whatever final charade he and Lawrence had devised.

Please, please let them know what they're doing. Please don't let them be doing something awful.

Water was duly brought. Nick drained the glass, returned it to the bailiff. "I started up to the house but was terrified that Theo would come back and catch me. And I was scared no one would believe me. I hardly believed it myself. He was like our big brother."

He swiped a hand across his face and went on. "It was a nightmare. I didn't know what to do. When I left the dock, I decided I needed Dad. That was the main thought that kept going through my mind. Get to Dad. Tell him. Let Dad deal with Theo. Dad always knew what to do."

He inhaled deeply. "I figured if I had some money, I could go to the mainland and catch a bus or train to Washington. The Mulrennons were away, but I knew where Megan hid the money she was saving for college. I used the spare key they kept over the door."

Megan held her breath. He'd seen her take the key down after they'd been over to the mainland. But the money. Had she told him David had borrowed money from her?

"She had several hundred dollars. I took two and left her a note promising to pay it back. I never did." He spoke directly to her. "I will, though."

Megan's heart clutched.

He'd admitted he wasn't David, but how had he known about the note? Had she told anyone?

Sondra. She'd mentioned the note to Sondra. Had she told Sondra what it said? She couldn't remember.

And if she had, how would Nick know?

Had he lied to her? Was he telling the truth now? Was he David?

If he wasn't, how did he know?

He couldn't. That would be a miracle and she'd stopped believing in them a long time ago. She had Nick now. He was enough.

And there was an explanation.

The note was in her scrapbook. She'd caught him with her photo album. He must have found her scrapbook, too. She wasn't even angry that he'd gone through her things.

Her hands were sweating and she wiped them on her skirt.

Nick was speaking.

"I took the Mulrennons' old fishing boat to town and hiked to the train station. Caught a train to Washington. In North Carolina, Nick and Rosemarie got on it. She was a nice girl. She saw I was upset, and I told them some of what was going on."

He coughed. "We got off in Richmond to change trains and were crossing the street when a bus ran over us. Nick's pack with his passport and money somehow ended up under me. When I woke up two days later in a hospital, everyone was calling me Nick. Rosemarie had died and so had Nick. I don't think he was ever identified."

"So that's where you, ah, took on his identity?"

"Yes. But that's unimportant. When I took Megan's money, I left something else there, too, as a kind of pledge for the money I took and for . . . other reasons. I left it in a music box I'd given her. Lawrence Wykerton has asked her to bring it today. If I may have it, I'll show you what I left. Once you see it, you'll understand."

Dungoode opened his mouth.

Odell glared.

Dungoode thought better.

At Odell's nod, the small bailiff came to the end of her row and waited while Megan retrieved the music box.

There was nothing inside it. Not when David gave it to her and not now. What were he and Lawrence doing?

What if Nick ended up in jail?

Her hands shook as she took off the towel and handed it over.

I don't care. It doesn't matter. I love him.

Nick took the music box from the bailiff. "This is a special box. Not many of them around. It not only has the cylinder inside that plays music, it also has a tiny compartment in the back for valuables. My father used to buy jewelry for my mother and hide it there. Sometimes it took days before she checked the drawer and found it. When I gave it to Megan, I didn't have time to show it to her."

Holding the box carefully, he fiddled with the intricately carved wooden front.

Nothing happened.

"A little stiff. Give me a moment."

A small drawer popped out. He reached in and pulled out something he briefly held up.

It was too small for her to tell what it was.

He tried to push it on a finger and failed. "I was skinnier when I was sixteen. I guess it'll have to find a new home."

He switched hands, held this one up in triumph.

A few people in front understood and gasped. Odell's threats forgotten, murmurings rose.

He paid them no heed. "This is my ring. Theo Pack never—not once!—had this ring in his possession. It has remained right here in this box where I put it the night my father died."

Above the racket, his voice penetrated the furthest corner. "Sondra Pack could not have possibly seen this ring in her husband's safe because it's been in this box for seventeen years. She lied because she needed a plausible reason for hiring me and killing Theo Pack."

Without knowing how, Megan was standing, gripping the back of the bench in front of her with both hands.

David!

No one could have found that ring but David!

Across the aisle, Sondra jumped to her feet. "This is a monstrous lie! You and Lawrence Wykerton are conspiring, trying to get James's money. Your Honor, can't you see what they're doing? He's lying!"

Megan rushed past Sondra's pew and the attorneys urging the widow to sit down. She flung herself through the swinging gate that separated the attorney area from the audience.

The hubbub and Sondra's screaming were so loud as to be deafening, but she kept going.

The bailiff by the bench tried but failed to stop her as she hiked up her skirt and leaped over the protective railing at the man on the stand. She didn't care that her slip showed or that her garters were exposed or that her hat fell off.

"David oh David oh David!" She threw her arms around him. "I didn't believe it was you! I didn't believe it was really you! Oh, David! I didn't know! I didn't know!"

She felt his embrace, tasted her own tears, refused to let him go.

From somewhere behind her, Sondra Pack had broken loose from her attorneys. "You little bitch! You're in this with him and Lawrence Wykerton! Well, honey, I've got news for you! He can't possibly be David because Theo put both boys in the boat that night! Do you hear me? Both boys went down with the boat! Theo did just what he was supposed to do! He promised me he'd do it and he did! They're dead, I tell you! They're both—"

Sondra's screams stopped abruptly when both her attorneys pulled her down.

"I didn't know," Megan sobbed.

She was pressed back, far enough for the scarred hand to take her chin and the other to smooth back her hair as he said plaintively, "But I told you I'm an award-winning actor."

CHAPTER 43

"Westward Bound"
As Performed by Noble Sissle (1926–28)
Music by Noble Sissle and Harry Revel
Lyrics by Noble Sissle and Harry Revel

EARLY IN NOVEMBER, the grand jury convened for the first time since Sondra Ann Sellin Harmony Pack was charged with the murder of Theodore Rhodes Pack.

Lawrence, accompanied by Megan, Jobeth, and Nick, attended their presentation. Disbarment still loomed, but he felt it a fair return if the grand jury indicted Sondra.

He had initiated the process of exhuming James's body as soon as Nick told him about discovering David's ring and his other suspicions.

The experienced medical examiner hired by the estate found traces of ethylene glycol. The compound could only have come from antifreeze ingestion.

Since the boys' dog had died from antifreeze poisoning right before James became ill with his first bout of flu, since Sondra had blurted out a confession at the inquest, and since she was with James in Washington when he died, the findings pointed directly to her being responsible for his death.

No one was surprised when the grand jury agreed.

Because of the statute of limitations, the jurors couldn't issue indictments against her for conspiracy or for being an accessory before the fact in the murders of David and Robert Harmony. They did issue indictments on two counts for Theo's murder, along with a separate count of perjury.

Authorities in Washington, D.C., where James died, had already started extradition proceedings.

Lawrence and the others were pleased.

As they went down the courthouse steps later, he said, "Nick, why don't you come by the office and pick up your check?"

After the coroner's inquest, he had charged Nick's fee off to expenses and readied it, hoping to hasten his departure. But Nick had been in no hurry to pick it up. Or leave.

Nor was he this day. Hand in hand with Megan, he shook his head.

"Not now, Whitey. I think we just want to hang out with Ma since it's our last day on the island. Megan and I'll be by to pick it up and say goodbye in the morning on our way out of town. Say seven thirty? We want to get an early start. California's a long way off."

"Fine."

Not that it mattered.

Immediately after Megan's mother got home, she and Lawrence had served as the only witnesses when Megan and Nick got married at the courthouse.

In the probate judge's office, he had apologized to JoBeth profusely for letting the affair get so out of hand.

She had flapped her hand. "What on earth are you talking about, Lawrence? I adore Nick. He and Megan are perfect together. I hate they're moving off, but we have to let our children go sometime. I'm flying out there Christmas, and they'll come back here often."

The confounded man had charmed JoBeth Mulrennon the same way he charmed all females. And the silly woman was so thrilled to see Megan finally married, she didn't pause to consider what kind of man her daughter was marrying.

God only knew how it would turn out. He hoped for Megan's sake she could keep Nick under control, but he had his doubts.

The next morning, to his astonishment, George was waiting when he got to the office at seven thirty.

He raised his brows. "You're here early."

"There are still a few things I can't figure out," George said. "And I wanted to say goodbye to Megan. I'm going to miss her."

"Since she does half your work, I daresay you are."

The Downings arrived shortly, Nick casual in jeans and Wemberly shirt, and a glowing Megan in lavender pants and matching top with a yellow scarf holding the curls off her face.

Her hair was cut short, Nick's idea according to JoBeth. The natural style looked nothing like the sprayed pompadours of most women nowadays, but it suited her.

He set out glasses and the decanter kept in his credenza for special occasions. "It's early, but a jot of brandy never hurt anyone. I think Megan and Nick's departure calls for a toast."

He ignored George's astonishment as he handed out glasses. "Sorry, no snifters."

They didn't drink to anything in particular, simply savored the choice Armagnac in silence. An air of anticlimax hung over the office.

"Explain again how it happened," George said to Nick.

Nick swirled the brandy. "Ask your father. He's the one who worked it out."

Lawrence sighed. "That is patently untrue. Nick's the one who found the ring. He's the one who figured out what Sondra had done."

"How did your finding the ring make you think she'd killed James Harmony?" George asked Nick. "I can't follow it."

"Finding the ring didn't," Nick drawled. "Although it did tell me she'd lied. Then I remembered how Lawrence, on hiring me, mentioned that James Harmony died from heart and kidney failure. When Megan told me about the dog drinking antifreeze and its organs failing, it seemed too coincidental. And I'd thought at the time it was odd how Theo just stood there when she pointed the gun at us. It all added up to something other than what I expected."

Lawrence took a sip. "When Nick came to me about finding the ring, he suggested she might have poisoned the dog as practice for poisoning James. I didn't want to believe it, but his explanation made too much sense after everything else that had happened."

"Why didn't you just go to Sheriff Attaway?"

"We had no proof." George could be so dense. "If we confronted her with the ring, she could have brushed it off as a misunderstanding. We had to get her on record as saying she'd seen that ring with her own eyes. So Nick convinced me he could break her."

He shuddered. How on earth he'd agreed . . .

Not that he'd had that much to lose anymore.

George sighed. "I still can't believe it. I would never in my life think Sondra could be a murderess. Theo yes. He was a hunter, a sportsman. But Sondra?"

"Ahem. Yes."

"Why not?" Nick seemed unaffected. But then he came from a criminal milieu. "From Whitey's drills, I knew she was a nurse in the army stationed near the front, so she was used to death. And Theo never served on active duty. She was smarter than Theo, too. I suspect the whole thing was her idea. According to Miss Bessie and Ma, Theo was crazy about her from the start. They might have planned it even before she married James Harmony."

Megan studied her glass. "Do you think she might have helped Miss Livvy die? The doctors thought she'd live at least another year."

Nick lifted one shoulder. "Could be. And I remember from some of Whitey's background sheets that she was once engaged to a captain in a demolition unit. Maybe she learned something about dynamite from him. Though Theo may have thought of it himself. I expect we'll never know."

"Will they convict her?" Megan asked Lawrence.

"Your guess is as good as mine. Juries do strange things and Parrish Dungoode's a clever lawyer. He might get her off."

"She'd better not get off." Megan waved her glass in the air, endangering its contents.

"Careful, love. If you're going to pour this exquisite brandy out, pour it into mine."

"Dream on. I'm not going on the road with you soused."

Some couples enjoyed quarreling. He and his own dear wife had never disagreed.

Well, not much.

They'd exchanged heated words when she bobbed off her beautiful hair after he'd told her not to.

And right after they married, she'd thrown a Coke bottle at him when he commented on her banana pudding being a tad dry.

Then there was the time she drove to Savannah after he had absolutely forbidden it.

On that occasion, he'd had to eat crow before being allowed back in his own bed.

He ran a finger beneath his suddenly too-tight shirt collar.

George kept digging. "Who made up the tale about you swapping places with David in the bus accident?"

Nick stretched like a lazy cat and put a hand over his wife's thigh. "That was me. David could have been on that train. He could have been run over by a bus."

"But you were so convincing," George said.

Megan beamed. "He *is* an actor."

Tsk, tsk. As if she was proud of it.

Nick modestly said, "Award-winning," and patted her hand.

He rested an ankle on the other knee and jiggled a shabby boot. "I put myself in David's place. If Theo had drugged me and put me in the boat, I wouldn't have known what to do if I waked up. Especially if I saw Robby's body. I would've been afraid Theo would kill me, too, so why not run? Whitey had talked about David running away before so it was easy to put together a story. Theo was the only one who'd know exactly what happened, and he was dead."

"David never liked being James Harmony's son," Megan murmured. "Running away would be something he'd do."

Nick's foot stopped jiggling. He pulled a curl of her newly shorn hair. "I suspect all boys resent their fathers."

"We were fortunate you're an actor," Lawrence said dryly.

Nick grinned. "An award-wi—"

Megan snorted. "Oh, please. Stop preening."

He looked hurt.

"You've been very lucky," George said.

"Yes. And the luckiest thing in all this was that Sondra found you to begin with," Lawrence said. "If it hadn't been for that clipping someone sent her, she'd never have thought this up."

"Luckiest?" Nick slanted a smiling glance at Megan. "D'you really think so? What about me coming across that ring in the music box?"

Setting his glass on his desk, Lawrence leaned back in his chair and made a steeple of his hands. "That was lucky, too, but if Sondra hadn't devised this scheme to rid herself of Theo, they would have gotten away with three murders."

Nick yawned. "Maybe. But you don't ever know. You can't predict the future, Whitey."

Megan said, "Everyone knew Theo drank too much. She might have been right to worry about him spilling the beans. I just wish you'd told me what was going on, Lawrence."

"Bad enough I was involved."

No need to mention the legal investigation going on. He'd known the risks from the beginning.

For the moment, he worried only about getting the Trust in order for its eventual disbursement. Theo's portion would go back into the estate, but until Sondra was legally convicted, the individual legacies couldn't be broken out.

If she was convicted, her share would go back in for division. If somehow—God forbid—she was acquitted, she'd inherit her part.

In the meanwhile, he was working to advance the other legatees at least a portion of their inheritance. The disbursement date had passed, so legally he could disburse. If the state allowed him to.

"No," he said to Megan. "There was no need to drag you into it. And if you hadn't gotten sick at the seminar, you wouldn't have been hit on the head and got run over by a boat."

"Doesn't matter now," Megan said without rancor. "I've been up and down so much in the last two months I don't think I can get upset about anything anymore."

"Happy to hear it," Lawrence said.

"Till the next time you yell at me," Nick said.

She dipped her hand, the one with the plain gold band, into her barely tasted glass and flicked brandy on him.

He caught her fingers and put them in his mouth.

Really.

Lawrence averted his gaze.

George was still puzzled. "Did you suspect it from the beginning? That Sondra intended to kill Theo, I mean?"

Nick gave his Gallic shrug. "I didn't suspect Sondra of anything, not till I got here and saw her and Theo together. Then something seemed wrong. She was obviously the dominant one in the relationship. When I finally learned about the ring, I knew she was lying. That's when everything fell into place."

That put Lawrence in mind of something else. "What made you check Megan's music box in the first place?"

Nick chuckled. "Curiosity. I've seen one like it before and wondered about the drawer. When I saw the ring, I knew David must have left it. What better place to hide it?" He exchanged an intimate glance with Megan. "She had a note from him about taking her money, too.

George shook his head. "Megan, you didn't know the ring was there?"

"Nope. No idea there was a hidden drawer in the box, much less that anything was in it."

Nick laughed. "Couldn't you tell? She was as surprised as anyone else."

"That's what did Sondra in," Lawrence opined. "No one in that courtroom doubted that you were David when Megan recognized you. The way she threw herself on you, even I thought you were David for a moment. And I knew better."

"Planned," Nick said airily. "All planned. I knew if I could convince Meggie that I was David, it would push Sondra—"

Megan gasped. "You did it on purpose? You—you louse!"

He wagged a finger. "Now, now, the honeymoon isn't over yet. Wait to berate me at least another month, please."

Indignation fled. She giggled.

Goodness gracious, the woman was totally bewitched.

George sipped at his brandy. "How did you know Theo took a telephone call that night?"

"From Theo's own story. He said Sondra's secretary called to let him know James had died. I imagine that was his signal from Sondra, telling him it was safe to go ahead and do away with the boys. After all, no use to kill them if James wasn't dead."

Megan's mirth died. She shivered.

Nick used his free hand to pat her arm absently. "It's all right, love."

Lawrence said, "James's will stipulated that in the event he outlived his sons by even one minute, the bulk of his estate would go to charity. They had to kill him first so that the boys would inherit and his will would hold. She knew all the details. James asked me to give her a copy after their marriage."

"But that's so cold-blooded," George protested.

George, George.

Lawrence stifled a moan.

Nick took attention away from George's shortcomings. "Sondra is a strong person, much stronger than she seems. And she's efficient."

Megan, glass still full, agreed. "Mom says Sondra knows what she wants and how to get it, that she wore the pants in that marriage."

"Theo wasn't smart, but he must have been shrewd about some things." Nick, ever fidgety, got up to pace. "He would make sure that Sondra's hands were as dirty as his. Otherwise, what was to keep her from turning him in later? She had to have been involved in such a way that he could point a finger at her, too. She killed James Harmony as her part of the deal, then he killed the boys. Afterward, they were bound to each other inextricably."

"Until Sondra wanted out," Lawrence said.

"I think she probably loved him," Nick said. "But she had to think of her own safety."

George's forehead creased. "It's just so unlike her."

"You can never tell about people. A good lesson to be learned, George." Lawrence drank the last of his brandy.

Nick came back to stand in front of Megan and play with his empty glass on the desk.

The man couldn't keep still.

"I hope she gets the death penalty," Megan said. "When I think of Mr. H, of Robby, of . . ." Her voice broke. "I want her to die, too."

Nick made a noise. "Bloodthirsty wench, aren't you? I hope this isn't a taste of things to come."

Megan's face stayed stormy.

He winked at Lawrence. "Oh, I imagine Sondra's fancy attorney will choose susceptible men to sit on a jury and get her off with life. But she'll be in hell without her designer clothes and makeup and servants. Doesn't that please you?"

Megan's mouth set obstinately. "I'm not that generous. Life in prison is too good for her."

George leaned forward. "One more thing. Who ran over Megan's boat and gassed her?"

Nick said, "Sondra was obviously behind both incidents. Once Megan saw I wasn't David Harmony, her plans would have been ruined. She may have fed Theo some cock-and-bull story about the weight Megan's word would carry if she swore I was David, and got him to do the dirty work, but she was certainly behind both attempts."

"She could have hit Megan's boat herself," Lawrence put in. "According to Linda, she met someone on the mainland that night and didn't get in until late. Theo probably did the gas when he realized Megan wasn't going to denounce Nick."

"Quite possible." Nick reached over, splaying his fingers on

Megan's crown to caress the place where she had been hit. "Sondra might tell us one day, but I doubt it."

George sighed. "So after all this, the Trust still can't be settled."

"Maybe not right away," Lawrence said. "But I am retiring as soon as possible. I am so sick of that Trust I can hardly bear to think about it."

"Retiring? Dad!"

"Lawrence!"

"Now, Whitey, it's almost over." Nick twinkled at him. "You've seen it this far, you can go on to the end."

"No. I can't do anything more for James. I'm done. If the firm is allowed to keep the administration of the Trust, I would have assigned it to Megan to straighten out. That would put her on the track for partner. As things are . . ." He sighed heavily.

"A partner?" Megan perked up. "In Wykerton, Perth, and Ross? Do you mean it?"

George's mouth dropped. "A woman partner?"

"No!" Nick slammed his empty glass down on Lawrence's desk. "She's already resigned. She's agreed to handle my affairs. I won't have her slaving away here while I'm on location in this movie my agent's signed me to do. She'll have to slave away in Italy with me."

"A partner," Megan repeated pensively.

"Megan. You told me you would look after my interests. You promised to read my contracts and interpret them for me." Nick shook his finger in her face. "And you said you would follow me wherever I went. That's an oral contract. I'll sue if you try to break it."

"But Nick. All these years of school, and all the time I've spent in dusty old law libraries doing all the boring research. This is something I never thought I could get."

"We have a verbal agreement."

"But I'd be a partner."

Nick shook his head vehemently.

Such squabbling. A rocky start to marriage.

"You can think about it," he said hastily.

Megan laughed. "I don't have to, Lawrence. Thank you, but I'll be going with Nick. He does need someone to take care of his affairs and make sure he doesn't sign on to make any pornographic movies. I'll also manage the money since he has no concept of what to do with it."

"I'm used to living on nothing," Nick defended himself. "I've seldom had money, so naturally I don't know what to do with it. Except spend it."

"My point exactly."

Lawrence intervened. "Speaking of money." He pushed Nick's check across the desk. "This should last you awhile."

The woman did have some sense left, he was happy to see. She snatched the check up and tucked it away in her purse.

"My offer's always open, Megan."

"Thank you, Lawrence, but I won't change my mind." She got up. "I do want my ring back though. Can you can get it for me?"

"Your ring?"

"David's ring. He gave it to me. It's mine."

"It's needed for evidence. Once Sondra's trial here is over, she has to go to Virginia where James died. Then there'll be appeals, and after that I'm not certain what will happen to it."

"I told you not to bother Lawrence." Nick said. "The ring'll get back to you eventually."

Hmmm. How petulant he sounded. Maybe there was a little resentment? After all, she had made quite a spectacle of herself when she thought Nick was David.

She ignored Nick. "I want the ring back. Can you check into it? I don't mind waiting, but I want it returned to me in the end. It's mine."

"Of course." He saw her point, but Sondra's case could take years to resolve. "I'll keep up with it through Tim until it can be released."

"Oh, and Whitey." Nick took her arm. "What about my fingerprints they took?"

"As promised, I made sure they were destroyed with no copies."

No matter what Nick had done, Lawrence wouldn't be the cause of some Mexican policeman—or British one for that matter— arresting him because his fingerprints had matched up with a crime.

"Good man." Nick picked up Megan's glass. "I can't let this go to waste. To the future. And to you, Whitey. You've had to put up with a lot. Too much." He drained the glass.

Good gracious. What was that all about?

As they walked out to the car, Megan asked, "How's Chauncey's daughter working out?"

"Fine. A little scared mouse."

"So was I when you hired me," she said. "She'll get used to you, Lawrence."

That led to talk about the islanders forming a group to receive their shares of the estate.

Lawrence said, "Some of James's bigger legacies went to islanders who worked for him. Older ones are deceased so their portions will go back in to be disbursed with the whole. But I'm working on advancing part to the survivors anyway, including your mother, Megan. I hope to get it done before the end of the year."

"Mom says they plan to pool their shares and buy the island and the house, maybe turn it into a resort or inn or something to help with jobs. She says you're going to be their manager."

"We'll see. The most urgent thing, as I said, is getting their money out of the Trust."

Outside in the bright sunshine, he stopped short.

What the devil?

A new Ford Galaxie convertible, bright red, awaited. The black top was down, revealing clothes and suitcases piled up in the back seat.

George whistled. "Nice wheels, doll!"

Where was her dependable Studebaker?

"So, Megan. You're managing the money?" Lawrence asked acidly.

"My car was nearly seven years old. I doubt it would make it across country, Lawrence," Megan said without apology. "We got a good deal on this."

"But a convertible?" A frippery piece of machinery for playboys.

She patted his arm. "Nick wanted one. We'll be in sunny California, remember?"

Lawrence bit his tongue. Not a dab of sense between them. Confound it, he'd thought better of Megan.

She hugged Lawrence and George, then opened the driver's door.

George's chin dropped. "Are you letting her drive, Nick?"

Nick opened his mouth but Megan answered. "He doesn't have a choice. They use the wrong side of the road in England. Besides, I've seen him drive. I'm not riding with him."

Nick closed his mouth with a hurt expression. "Someone forgot to tell me that saying *I do* also meant saying *yes, my love*, for the rest of my life."

Megan got into the car. "Good thing you're a fast learner."

George guffawed. "Welcome to marriage, bub."

Megan settled in. "Let's get going," she said to Nick, then looked at Lawrence. "You won't forget about my ring?"

"Of course not."

Nick shook George's hand. "Take care of your father. He's one in a million."

Lawrence's eyes misted. The man wasn't so bad. Not considering his background.

Nick turned to him and took his hand, holding it a moment. "Thanks, Whitey. For everything."

"You're the one who made it work."

The engine roared into life.

Nick kept standing there. "No, Whitey. You handled it perfectly."

Then he did a curious thing. He put his arm around Lawrence's shoulder and squeezed. "But I knew you would. You're the only honest attorney I know."

He got in the car, flashing his angel's grin. His David grin. "Personally, that is," he called as Megan reversed.

Lawrence stood stock still, breath knocked out of him.

James.

He put his left hand on his upper arm where Nick had squeezed. The spot where James would clasp him.

Was this a sign that James approved of his underhanded tactics?

The car pulled out. Nick turned and waved with both hands. The gold morning sun glinted on his new wedding band and fair hair.

"The only honest attorney?" George cried, incensed. "There are plenty of us honest attorneys. Like me! And Megan. What the hell's that supposed to mean?"

His story about waking up in the boat . . . Could it be . . . ?

No. Confound it.

Megan would have heard James teasing him; she was around enough growing up. Or JoBeth. One of them had repeated it, and Nick couldn't resist pulling his leg.

A reprehensible sense of humor. Absolutely reprehensible. Maybe Megan would be all right with the scamp. Still . . .

"Dad?" demanded George. "What did he mean by that?"

"I really couldn't say," Lawrence said slowly, watching the red car pull out of sight. "I really couldn't say."

The early sun painted autumnal sweet gums and dogwoods in rich colors, sketching brilliant splashes among the brooding water oaks. The sky had never been so blue; the clouds were paper-white fluffs.

He lingered, though he had a lot to do. Those damnable Trust recalculations, paperwork for the state bar, a call to the assessor about a current appraisal on the island, the preliminary proposal on the sale to the islanders. Too much to think about.

The devil with it.

He turned to George, who was still indignant over Nick's perceived slight.

George had his faults, but he was basically a decent, honorable person. All a man could hope for in a son. "Let's take the day off, George. Let's do something together."

His son stared. "Feeling okay, Pop?"

"I feel fine."

Actually, he felt better than he had in years.

A breeze ruffled his hair, urging him to look up to where an osprey landed on a dead pine limb. It stared at him, an unwavering stare like James had had.

Almost as if it was trying to tell Lawrence something.

Ridiculous.

Just an osprey, even if it did stand so close and still, and aim its piercing gaze right at him.

As he and George went to get their jackets, his step was light, almost as light as his heart.

He looked back.

The osprey spread its wings and circled twice before heading toward the ocean.

EPILOGUE

"House of No Regrets"
As Performed by Katherine Jenkins (2005)
Music by Ennio Morricone
English Lyrics by Mark Niedzwiedz

OCTOBER 21ᵀᴴ, 2013. NEW YORK (AP) — HEADLINE: ACTOR NICK DOWNING DEAD

Authorities yesterday confirmed Oscar-winning actor Nick Downing and his wife died when a sightseeing plane crashed 460 kilometers south of Lima near the Nazca lines, one of Peru's best-known tourist spots. Four other passengers along with the pilot and copilot also perished.

Their son, video game developer R. L. Downing, issued a statement for the family from his Tokyo office: "We're all devastated, but our parents were very close, and we're thankful they went together, doing what they enjoyed."

A private service is planned on Harmony Island off the Georgia coast where Megan Downing grew up and where the family maintains a second home. A daughter, actress/producer Jamie Liv Downing, flew in from Los Angeles and remains in seclusion with a younger brother, attorney Joe Frank Downing. Seven grandchildren and one great-grandchild also survive.

Nick Downing, whose career began in London and spanned half a century, catapulted to America's attention when he impersonated a millionaire's missing son. He won an Oscar for best supporting actor in his first film and went on to claim two more for best actor. Though he received numerous awards, he credited his wife's acumen for his financial and acting success.

In later years, he was best known for two popular TV series praised by critics and fans alike. A memorial service for the public will be held . . .

If you enjoyed this book, please consider leaving a review to help others discover it. Among sites that offer places for reader reviews are:

http://www.amazon.com

and

http://www.goodreads.com

If you do have the time and take the effort to leave a review, please accept my sincere appreciation and thanks.

www.cherylbdale.com
cherylbdale.blogspot.com
cherylbdale@hotmail.com

A playlist of songs in Losing David can be found on Spotify.

www.ingramcontent.com/pod-product-compliance
Lightning Source LLC
Chambersburg PA
CBHW070532120726
47909CB00007B/2106